Swaran Chandan came to England
ever since. *The Volcano* is his firs
from the Library Association, L
London Borough of Hillingdon an
West Midlands and pursues writing as his full time pro...
present he is working on his next novel set in England of 1960s
onwards.

The Volcano is a sweeping novel about the partition of India and the
painful birth of Pakistan, yet it is told from an intensely personal
viewpoint. Friendships, like the Punjab itself, are torn apart as the
population splits into religious factions, driven by the reckless
ambitions of politicians and power seekers.

This is a novel that brings India to life and gives a vivid glimpse of a
way of life in the dying days of the British Empire. Reading it is a
journey of discovery.

Chris Sawyer
Editor

What difference does it make to the dead, the orphans and the homeless, whether the mad destruction is wrought under the name of totalitarianism or the holy name of liberty or democracy?
Gandhi: Non-violence in Peace and War (1942) vol. 1, ch. 142

The Volcano

A Novel

Swaran Chandan

V

Virgo Books Limited

First published in Great Britain in 2004 by
Virgo Books Limited.
28 Malins Road, Wolverhampton,
W. Midlands WV4 6AW

British Library Cataloguing-in-publication Data
A catalogue record for this book is available on
request from the British Library

ISBN 0-9546765-0-5

Typeset by Virgo Books
Printed and bound by Biddles Ltd.
Cover design by ArtCave

www.virgobooks.co.uk
virgobooks2000@yahoo.co.uk

To Aneesh in whose eyes I see an eternal glow of innocence. And, to those who are seriously committed to saving this innocence and maintaining peace in the world.

Prelude

Does it really matter where, why and how you were born? Probably, not. What is important is when you were born, and at what point of time in history. Time is a vast flow of matter in the universe, an enigmatic mass of solid liquid and gaseous things, of power and energy, of unfathomable depths that defy penetration by the human eye or other human senses, even intuition. Man can know only a minute fraction of this matter, an amount so tiny that it is hardly perceptible in its infinity.

How do we define a history of time? Is it a countable number of years of which we have been able to keep an account until now? Or is it something vaster than that? History and time, time and history; they probably flow simultaneously. They've never been known and perhaps they'll never be known. Only they can know themselves. They are inseparable.

Whatever is born is doomed to die one day. What is born is a small chip broken from time, a negligible chip, which, when it dies becomes fossilised as every 'present' turns into the 'past', just like time itself. Time and history are intransigent. Time is reborn in the form of an organism, a child, and then dies away. So, life in the vast universe is just a fraction, a minute particle of sand or dust, or a raindrop in the ocean, which appears and disappears, comes and goes, and becomes fossilised, forever, forever.

Time and tide wait for no one but everyone waits for them. We are only broken fractions of time, and linger on to be re-associated with it in the final conclusion. Time and history have no dates of birth.

But we are mortals. We have to keep account of births and deaths. That is our limit, our destiny and our consequence.

Book One

The Old Banyan Tree and Qila Vasudev

Once upon a time, in the middle of an antiquated village called Qila Vasudev, there was an ancient and vast Banyan tree.

Larger than a village but smaller than a town, Qila Vasudev stood serenely and silently on the western suburbs of the city of Amritsar in the northern Indian province of the Punjab. Qila Vasudev would, at a later time, merge with the city, losing its individual identity and assuming the character of one of the city's many constituents, such as Qila Bhangiyan. But at this point in time and history, Qila Vasudev holds its individuality and character and is full of its own life. But first thing's first: the centre of our attention should be the old Banyan tree.

Look at it carefully and you'll be surprised by its sheer size, its vast expanse, its puzzling appearance and awe-producing mystery. The ground underneath it swells a few feet higher than the surrounding earth that stretches in all four directions. The swelling is intricately interwoven by the big, bloated, partly exposed roots, which are larger and thicker than the trunks of many trees inhabiting its vicinity. It is more than difficult to walk on the stilted swell without risking damage to your feet, accustomed as they are to treading smooth surfaces. The ground goes up and down, down and up and undulates. But if you are skilled enough to walk on a wall two feet wide, the thick, half-exposed roots may provide you with good trekking, if only for the fun of it. The depth to which the roots might have penetrated into the ground is anybody's guess.

Now look at its size. The ground it occupies is more than thirty feet in diameter, slanting as you walk away from the main trunk, declining like a hillock. The trunk approximates to fifteen feet in diameter. It is firm, solid, stout and robust and makes you shudder with fear when you first meet with *him*.

Watch it closely. There are dozens of shoots dropping from the branches and taking root in the ground, hoping to become secondary trunks, three feet or more in diameter. We, the inhabitants, call them the beard of the Banyan tree. We hang by them, clambering up and down by these would-be-trunk shoots. It is the Indian fig tree, *Ficus Indica*.

Discern it more carefully. Its primary branches are thick, heavy and solid enough to stand the weight of a dozen people without a quiver. The secondary ones can easily carry twelve young lads straddled over them; the tertiary ones appear stronger than the trunks of many other trees. And the height: straighten your head to look above at its peaks and you'll get your cap, turban or hat falling off your head. Beautiful thick green leaves with a multitude of palm-lines, are stalk-bound to the branches, wide and thick at first, and getting smaller and thinner as the eye travels further above. The fruit is dish-green and about half-an-inch thick, rather small compared to the size of the tree, meant for the consumption of a variety of birds. But imagine a larger fruit falling from that height and hitting a bare head. That would cause a problem, wouldn't it?

The age of the Banyan tree is not known to anyone in the village. It has always been there, they say. The phrase 'Once upon a time' simply takes into account the years of us mortals. The Banyan tree is immortal, and is a witness to all that happens in the village, the province and the country. Seeing, watching, observing, discerning and looking – all these different words pre-suppose the 'eyes' to which the Banyan tree offers *himself* to be studied. This is no ordinary tree. This is the special one: a living memory of history and time.

The Banyan tree also speaks. *He* speaks in *his* language of colours. You have to listen to him, not through your ears, but through your wise eyes. He has a thousand and one stories to tell you; a long sequence pertaining to different eras of history: good and bad, bloody and bloodless, moral and immoral - the stories of happiness and disaster that he has lived.

Ears do not grasp his conversation for they are accustomed to listening. Only the eyes understand because they can read *his* changing colours - the colours that hide the messages in a coded language that needs careful decoding, analysing and synthesising. Some of the villagers of Qila Vasudev have, to an extent, learnt to translate and interpret the coded language. Krishan, Kabir, Kinner,

Arjun, Bhagat, Jagat, Sikander Ali, Maula Bux, Chiraghdin, Ladha Kharasi and I, Arya Gold, all have this skill, but the best decoder of his revelations is Noordin, *our Rangsaaz* (dyer). But we shall come to that later on.

Now, witness a summer noon, in June. The Banyan tree stands still, bearing the hot, piercing rays of the hell-vomiting sun on its bare body, unshaken and unrelenting. The thick foliage does not let a single scorching rod of sunbeam pass through its leafy network to reach the people sitting underneath the Banyan. There are about a dozen charpoys accommodating dozens of gasping people, who had to stop their work, unable to stand the heat anymore; they relax away the noon hours underneath his thick and comforting shade. The noon is sultry, the environment oppressive and a whiff of air impossible. But the leaves of the Banyan tree have, somehow, stolen a puff of air from somewhere and have fanned it furiously to spread it all around, over the faces of the refuge-takers, letting them breathe it to work their lungs and hearts.

Amongst the refuge-takers are all kinds of people: the cattle grazers, the cultivators, the ploughmen, the fodder choppers, the fruit pickers, the women and the children, the young, the elders, the urchins. Scattered among them are the cattle: bullocks, cows, buffaloes and horses. The elders have occupied the charpoys and the others have taken the bare ground to be their bed. The boys are playing cards, *barah-tehni*; some are gossiping and chatting while others are dozing lethargically. The cattle are chewing their cud. The urchins are fighting and dodging each other over some other game.

The Banyan tree is a home to all. It offers a perfect open lounge for sitting during the melting hours of noon. It is a life-giving retreat when the brick-walls of the houses emit enormous temperatures, the roofs burn overhead and the ground sucks the last drop of blood from the soles of your feet. He, the Banyan tree, is, in fact, a lot more. He is a meeting place where people solve issues and take decisions, social and political. It is here that that they look back into the past and summon forth events that the people once faced and fought, in order to seek guidance to deal with new and imminent challenges.

The old and the young, all join in. Some are specially invited while others come of their own accord, showing real concern over the boiling matters. The elders do the talking and the younger ones listen.

A consensus is then reached and the decision made on the action to be taken. The Banyan tree, the eldest of all the members in the decision-making committee, is witness to all that takes place.

The Banyan is also a source of spiritual light, which dawns upon the wise ones – the ones who have the promise and perseverance to sit and meditate under its vast umbrella. That was what had happened once in Gaya (Bihar). The old Gautam Buddha sat underneath the Banyan tree and meditated for years on end until he discovered the light – the understanding of why people suffered and how they could be redeemed from that endless suffering. He found the answers to all those long-hidden secrets of life, and it would never have been possible to reach those heights of wisdom without the Banyan tree. Since then the Banyan tree and Buddha have been inseparable. Both stand for the light of Asia, or at least the light of India, from whence it spread the world around.

And now, about our Noordin, the dyer or rangsaaz: Noordin has been there in the village of Qila Vasudev for centuries. The skills of dying and discerning the slightest difference in the shades of colours and studying the language the colours speak, have been handed down to him by a succession of his ancestors so that with every passing generation the craft has acquired more and more perfection.

Noordin's house-cum-shop stands to the east of the Banyan tree. It always displays dozens of dupattas and chunnis (the lady's head cloth) drying in the open yard on the left, where they hang on the line, talking to him and to the passers-by in a language that intrigues and fascinates. He does tie-dye colouring like no one else can. Many girls wearing seven-colour chunnis and dupattas at the annual fair of Vaisakhi speak of Noordin's expertise.

'The seven colours of the rainbow are the basic colours,' he says. 'Then there are numerous others forming from their careful mixing. But to mix them in the right order and quantity is no easy task. It takes a lifetime to learn the adroitness, generations of lifetimes to reach dexterity.' As regards the language of colours, Noordin has volumes to say. 'The colour speaks to you the way a person speaks. It expresses its pleasures, its sadness, its doubts, fears, wrath, and issues you with advance warnings of what's in store for you. At no cost should you take warnings lightly because the colours have a sense of premonition of what the immediate future has to offer or take away from you. A little procrastination or dilly-dallying would cause havoc because time and tide wait for no one.'

Just as Noordin had acquired all his skills from his father, Rukandin, and he in his turn from his ancestors (the list goes on), now Noordin's son, Ferozdin, is imbibing every bit of the craft from his own father. Ferozdin, only ten yet, said one day, 'In me lives not my father alone, but all the generations of my clan. All the experiences and the whole knowledge that accumulated in their craft over the years belong to me now. I'm not what I am but a sum-total of what I have been in the form of my ancestors.' And the villagers, particularly the naïve ones, were taken aback at his proclamation. So, such are the skills our Noordin has, and they shall progress further in our Ferozdin in the time to come.

And when our old, sprawling Banyan tree issues advance warnings of incidents waiting at the threshold by his change of colours, the old heads of the village, incapable of decoding all the messages themselves, summon forth Noordin to spell things out for them. It's then that Noordin begins to show his great worth. He comes ebulliently along, sometimes with his son, sometimes alone, letting Ferozdin control the shop. He looks at the changing colours of the Banyan from different angles so as to negate the effect of polluting agencies such as brilliant light, dark shades and reflections etc., then conducts a series of studies in the light of the happenings in the wider world and begins to unfold the secrets, followed by warnings impregnated with multiple meanings.

Arjun is a regular reader of the newspapers - a daily in Urdu being delivered to him at his house. Not only does he read the news himself but also extends it to the whole village by reading aloud under the shade of the Banyan. Astrology, or better call it occultism, cannot work without this knowledge of social and political circumstances. So Arjun has a duty to provide that information – the happenings in the wider world – to let our Noordin the dyer know and work out his prophecy. That's what happened in 1914. In the month of August, England had declared war against Germany, heralding the First World War of history. India, being under the British rule, was already stifling and choking from poverty, degeneration, huge taxes, draughts, deprivation, infertile land, epidemics and a hell of other things. The declaration of war brought insurmountable grief to the already suffering masses. It was amply clear that the onus of the war would have to be borne by the subjugated nations such as India because the feringhee expected that from their slaves anyway.

It was then that the colours reflecting from the leaves of the Banyan had begun to alter for the worse. The stalks of the leaves turned reddish, especially at the apex of the new branches where buds sprouted into new plumes. The change caused a tremendous fear amongst the observers – a fear that shook them from their foundations. Forthwith, Noordin the dyer was summoned to decode the message hidden in the alteration of colours. Noordin, equipped with his unparalleled knowledge, studied the red-hued plumes and proclaimed, 'India will be immediately yoked to the war efforts; a sign that we shall be further impoverished, denuded and morally emasculated. As is obvious, the war needs colossal resources of capital and men: capital to generate more bullets and men to cool down those bullets. So, both the men and the material will have to be provided by us. War, as history proves, never ends without taking a heavy toll of life and wealth from the sufferers. So get ready to be shoved into the fire of hell.'

And every single prophecy of Noordin had turned out to be true. The worst was now over but the stories of streams of blood dying the whole country red still hung in the air. The stories of the country's wild depredations were told and listened to in every nook and corner. The war had taken over four years to come to its final conclusion – the conclusion that England had come out victorious but only to extend the duration of fetters of slavery for India for another twenty-eight years. But we shall return to that at a later stage.

Now the village, Qila Vasudev, awaits its turn to be given its ordained place in the story.

The stories are often told with regard to the origins, or the genesis of Qila Vasudev. Long before the village appeared, the site had two things only: a small fortress on the western side and a Banyan tree on its left. The fortress had an open, walled but roofless, forecourt, which received the first light of the rising sun. The Banyan tree stood at quite a distance so as not to hinder the rising sun from illuminating the forecourt.

Right beside the big door of the forecourt stood a small monument with an inscription engraved on it in a language nobody was able to decipher – some old, obsolete, dead language, perhaps. It was said that the only two words that the experts understood were 'Durg Vasudev'. The rest of the inscription had lost its imprint and had been irretrievably blurred out of sight. The word 'Durg' was later exchanged for its Punjabi equivalent, Qila. As for the fortress itself, the structure had long collapsed and what was left was a pile of rubble. No methodological research or any excavation was carried out to meet the challenge of discovering the history of the place. However, the word went round that the fortress was erected by the Lord Krishna, who lived here for a while after killing two other claimants (Krishna was the third claimant) of the status of Vasudev that meant God – the supreme spirit which controlled the universe. The two claimants, they said, were the two kings of that era, Shringlav and Praundik. The name of Lord Krishna's father was Vsudev, missing the first vowel when compared to Vasudev. Anyway, if one was to believe all those stories the history of the place went back to times immemorial. But we shouldn't let ourselves loose to that extent. It suffices to believe that the place was remote and antiquated and that the reality and myth together made the meaning.

The ground on which the village stands is quite a few feet higher than the adjoining land so that the rain water runs with the speed of a bullet to the two big ponds, one in the east and the other in the north. The ponds, apparently, had taken shape when the earth was dug to build the houses with. But the ground of the village itself is very hard, gravelly, stony and rocky, and difficult to dig easily. It does not absorb rainwater either and puddles remain until the water evaporates. They say that when they were trying to dig foundations for the houses, their spades and pickaxes were blunted at every stroke. But the benefit they enjoyed now was hard-core ground that never yielded to the pressure of the structures built upon it.

The irony now is that Qila Vasudev is without any Qila, or Durg, or fortress. It is only a name by which the village is known, the village that is larger than a village but smaller than a town. And there are hundreds and thousands of other such villages in the length and breadth of the country and with histories as remote and antiquated as that of our own. The most common denominator, however, is that the fate of none of them differs from the other.

Now, coming to its population, you'll find that it is extremely secular in the sense that all have their ordained place in it: the Hindus, the Muslims, the Sikhs and the cattle. But this is not all. The three religious groups all have their hierarchies long-made for them. There are touchable Hindus and untouchable Hindus, touchable Sikhs and untouchable Sikhs. Although Islam doesn't allow such divisions of the caste system (and nor does Sikhism), yet it is not entirely bereft of them. The untouchables from Hinduism, who at some stage embraced Islam, were never accepted as equal to the ones who came from the original Muslim countries. They were never allowed to climb higher on the social ladder and were given new names such as 'marassi' or 'musalli'. Even the converts from the so-called high class Hindus were never treated equally.

The village has a mosque, a Sikh shrine and a Hindu temple. The people of each religion have their houses built in the vicinity of their shrines, probably for easy access in case of emergency.

The location of the habitations (higher or lower land) indicates the social position of the dwellers. The untouchables live in the mud houses built on the low ground around the two ponds where the dirt, filth and foul water of the whole village accumulate. The area is a sanctuary for mosquitoes, flies, diseases and many other evils. Needless to say, the untouchables, or the ostracised ones, are the old Dravidians. The others are Aryans, except for the Muslims who are either past invaders or converts from Hindus.

So, that's the composition of Qila Vasudev - a village typical of many others in the country.

The Scribbler

I honestly don't know what I prefer to be called, for I've a number of names reserved for me. My villagers have set aside nearly a dozen for me and they're at liberty to pick and choose any one, and throw it at me like a flower or a stone. I'm in no position to disappoint them by reacting peevishly because, at heart, they all love me. Maybe that's *their* way of showing love and affection, and at times, hatred too, for I myself don't spare anyone from retribution of their deeds when I hold my pen and paper in my hands. Even my near and dear ones find no favouritism from me. It's quite natural then that they should love and hate me at the same time. And, their way of expressing either or both is the way they call out my name. All names are pretty good in their meaning, the difference lies, however, in the way of handling them. A name that acquires a degree of dignity in a moment of love begins to stink like a pile of shit in the moment of hatred. So, nothing is good or bad but using makes it so.

Let's go back to square one. The names that have been given to me are: Kavi (a poet), Batooni (a talker), Kahanikar (a story teller), Qatib (a scribe), Likhari (a writer), Kissakaar (a narrator), Munshi (a copy maker), Kalam-ghaseet (a pen dragger), Siaahi-master (an ink sprinkler), Bhasha-navees (a language user), Kalam-dawati (a pen-ink user), Likhanhaar (a script writer), Banaoo-dhahoo (a maker-breaker). All these different names endowed upon one person ... just imagine. Who else in the world can command so many names except a scribbler? Perhaps, there's one more person, and an ever-living one, the Lord Krishna, on whom they've showered as many names as the number of leaves on our Banyan tree. I believe it's because of his theory of reincarnation. He's believed to have been born so many times that even a thousand names given to him won't astonish me. But to have thirteen names in one birth like I have must be thought of as a great achievement.

I beg to reiterate that although I've thirteen names to be called by, the moments of love and hatred make them twice as many. So, I command twenty-six names at the moment. What makes all the difference is the way a name is pronounced. For instance, a prefix or suffix alters it substantially. In addition, a simple change in the way a name is spoken or a person is addressed, makes a world of difference. Again for instance, an exclamation before or after, adds new meanings to a name. Bakhtin was absolutely right when he said the real arena where the sign or the language is subjected to multiple meaning is in the utterance of language. It's there that the sign is pulled in opposite directions by the partakers causing a stressful tension for it to generate infinite meanings. So, it's all linguistics, after all. Saussure's closed system of *langue* stands nowhere near it. It's really fascinating to watch language playing magically at the lips or mouths of the speakers. And while each person differs from the other, so must be his utterance. I can bet that no two people speak similarly; rather, even one person speaks differently at different instances. Worse still, a word spoken at one moment alters in its pronunciation at another, although it may be spoken immediately after the first breath. It's all very tricky and deceiving, isn't it?

I've had numerous discussions with my friends, Krishan, Kinner and Kabir on how big a trickster is the thing called language. Kabir, the poet, somewhat agreed with me after our long heated discussions. However, initially, he was disinclined to accept the fact that it was a matter of mood to write a poem, and once that mood was lost the poem too was lost, as was the meaning. But he resisted by saying the mood (whatever) could be reactivated or brought back and the half-written poem could be accomplished without the loss of a single grain. It was after I reminded him of his numerous half-finished poems – which he had never been able to complete afterwards – that he half-agreed with my argument still insisting that one day he'd evoke the then- mood and complete his lyrics.

As for Kinner, he's a painter and a sculptor, and he talks either with his brush or the hammer and chisel – a dangerous business to get involved in. When he writes in the language of paintings with colours as his ink, the brush as his pen and the canvas as his paper, I like him most. But when he switches to the hammer and chisel, I get profoundly frightened. He brandishes the hammer and chisel in the air in such a way as to cause a terrifying panic all around. He's a great wanderer, too. There's no appointed time for his excursions into the forests, wastelands and derelict sites where he can engage himself for hours on end in conversations with shapeless stones of gigantic size, capable of reducing a man to shreds if toppled on to him. I wonder how he manages to bring those voluminous things home without a lorry or a truck. But he gives those stones a distinct personality by the use of chisel stroked by hammer.

One day, when I expressed my fears of dealing with such perilous weapons, Kinner gave me a scornful look and said, 'Eh, Scribbler, be practical and do something concrete and solid. Stop hankering after inanities. Don't orate but create!' I swear by the Lord's head that I hated his rhetoric; a kind of preaching I've always despised. With a sense of rejection, I looked into his red, bulging eyes that seemed as remote as the sun, and left him without discussing anything about my problem – the question of language.

Krishan, however, is different. He has a thousand and one 'qualities' in him. He's both a friend and a foe - a friend if you agree to what he says and a foe if you don't. He often visits me to listen to my stories. If he agrees, he encourages me; if he doesn't he keeps his mouth shut. To my surprise and to many of my villagers' Krishan's black-bluish skin resembles that of Lord Krishna, which leaves us all puzzled to an extent, prompting us to believe some sort of connection existing between the two, although, we all know he's just one of us. What makes us doubtful about our Krishan's rightful place as our soul mate is the way he sometimes talks – like a clergyman – inducing us to suspect that he might be yet another incarnation of the old Krishna. One day, when he came to listen to my half-written story, he said, 'Your Noordin the dyer can't decode the knotty language of colours.'

'Of course he can, given the generations of experience he has in him,' I countered at once.

'No, I can't believe that for it's my forte to do such things. Remember how I deciphered the unfolding events from the fading colours on the faces of our enemies?'

Way back, some people from the adjoining village had attacked one of our villagers, accusing him of stealing their crop. Krishan had seen them coming when they happened to pass by him, equipped with clubs and running in the direction of the village. Krishan, sensing trouble, took the shorter route and reached the village long before they did. Then our people rounded them up at the outskirts of the village and walloped them well. He was referring to that incident while I suddenly began to think of the divine Krishna.

'Go, graze your cattle, you archaic soul. What d'you know about the soul of colours?' I shouted at him because his father, Girdharilal, the confectioner, had recently bought some cows and buffaloes so he could be self-sufficient with milk at his shop, and Krishan was often seen grazing them in the fields. 'But I do know about the archaic epics such as Ramayna and Mahabharata.'

'Of course you do, but they're as archaic as you are.'

'Of course, of course!' he murmured and disappeared forthwith like an invisible man. I shook my head as though I was hallucinating.

I must admit that that was my fault. I shouldn't have annoyed Krishan just for the sake of it. He'd been ever so nice with me all these years. He had never blurted out any threatening words to me like Kinner had. Krishan always behaves coolly. It must be something to do with his inner self where a thousand things lay hidden until the right moment comes for them to emerge – a business-like attitude. You can't expect a good businessman to lose his temper, not even when someone who's been wronged by him challenges him outrageously.

However, I must come back to the subject of what I should like to be called, or named. There is a bulk of names to choose from but does that matter really? I don't think it does. Going by our Punjabi way, the rose remains a rose no matter what other names are given to it. But there's also another side of the coin. How does it sound to render a rose the name of thorn, or call a thorn a flower? It doesn't match, does it? And it doesn't make any sense either. So, a name has a lot to say. Shakespeare could say anything he wished because there was no one to challenge his authority. Anyway, I was named Gold by my parents soon after my birth, despite the fact that both of my parents were illiterate. But you don't have to be too educated to know the value of gold, or money, or other valuable things. Even illiterates work hard to earn money to buy gold and turn it into a variety of ornaments. My mother, Parvati, has always been highly fond of ornaments. She still is. But my father has absolutely no craze for such obsessions. Place a heap of gold on one side and a piece of land on the other, and he'll run for the second option, more than immediately. Quite the reverse would happen with my mother despite her age, a mere sixty.

My parents did know that I scribbled stories, and that was what my father didn't like me about. My mother's attitude towards my obsession was fifty-fifty. She didn't mind my pursuing this career if I bought her some golden bangles or whatever with the money that accrued from the pursuit. I discovered that when I spent all I had received from getting one of my stories published to buy her a nose pin. She was so happy to have that small gift from me that she kept looking into the mirror, swapping one pose with another.

'I named you rightly, didn't I?' she said, sparing a quick minute from her ebullience.

'Of course you did, my dear Mother,' I replied. 'Could've been better had you named me Diamond.'

'But I don't like diamonds. They're too big and heavy, and useless. They stand no way near gold, do they?' She offered an obstinate justification, still sticking to the mirror like a little fairy.

She was really a fairy, I tell you. Short, slim and trim, fair faced, full of zeal and ambition. She reminded me of a fairy that came down on wings, softly kissed the small sleeping princes on their brows and then floated away leaving numerous precious gifts for them to discover in the morning. She always prompted me to continue my scribbling despite my father's perpetual nagging and discouragement. In fact, she was very fond of little stories herself, although she couldn't write them on the paper. She'd tell me scores of them before I went to sleep, especially during the summer nights. My father would return home often late in the evening because of his overwhelming commitments in the fields. My mother and I would wait for his arrival, relaxing in our beds on the terrace, under the night sky studded with myriad stars of varying colours and brilliance. And she, on my insistence, would commence telling a story, and then another one, and then...until my inducing requests were smothered by overpowering sleep. I hardly knew when my father came home, had his dinner and went to sleep. It would be in the first light of the morning when I'd see his face bending over me, kissing and cuddling me while I was still sleeping, and then he would leave again for the whole day.

My father wanted to see me in the clothes of a big lawyer or in some other high-ranking post that would bring him pride and fame, so that people would approach him for favours, to be given by me, of course. He had absolutely no wish for me to work as a farmer, which, according to him, was full of unrelenting sufferings and insufficiencies due to a host of taxes forced by the government without the slightest consideration of the natural calamities that devastated the crops.

He might not have disliked my scribbling escapades if only I had reached a little closer to his expectations of me. But things always went bad with me. I had little or no inclination to end up as a lawyer or some other high-ranking official. I preferred literature to all other subjects at school and, worse still, the teachers were always complaining about me. My father, obviously, finding all his hopes dashing to the ground, began to pick on me for whatever I did.

Despite being uneducated, my father had a sixth sense in him that kept him informed of things happening here and there. He'd cite the examples of Sarab Dayal Sharma, Bar-at-law and secretary of the local Bar Association at Amritsar, of Moti Lal Nehru and Jawahar Lal Nehru, and many others, to inspire me to work towards the goal he had chosen for me. But it all turned on a deaf ear, with the result that he finally gave in and refrained from seeing my face save for an incidental confrontation, in which case he'd either ignore me by slipping away or turn his glance aside, scornfully. 'Marassi, mother fucker,' he said once when my mother endeavoured to normalise the relations between us.

So, that was the fourteenth name added to my credentials. And if you go by the swearing word included as suffix, the total count mounted to fifteen. Permit me to rectify my sums; mathematics was never my forte. If the total number of names is fifteen, then the grand total, including prefixes and suffixes, should come to forty-five.

And how about the *Marassi*? Well, they are in fact the crux of the lively and euphoric culture of the Punjab, sparing no one no matter how special a person might be. They are poets, tale-tellers, comedians, jokers, off-the-cuff commentators, singers, musicians and even match-makers at times. They've the gift of the gab. That's what they are. In short, they are the true inheritors (*waris: Maurussi: Marassi*) of the culture of Punjab. Their art is their livelihood. But because they are ramblers, a kind of nomad with no fixed home and no other profession to follow except to create impromptu satire, sarcasm and laughter, people lost respect for them. The name 'Marassi' was misconstrued to mean an idler or a waster, making it an abusive term. However, they changed their clan's name to Meerzada but were unable to recuperate the lost glory. There could've been some historical reasons, too, for their failure, such as their non-acceptance by Islam despite the fact that they had embraced it.

Qila Vasudev is visited by the *Marassis* at the eve of a marriage party, a birthday or some festival – when there is hope of a heavy gathering so they can make some money from the donations as a reward for their craft. They always enter a village, a town or a city in the form of a small group of perhaps three or four. I'd seen them in our village a year ago, at a marriage. A sample dialogue from one of their skits may not be out of place here.

First Marassi: Oh, Marassi! When were you born?

Second Marassi: Don't you ask me that, my brother; that was terrible.

First: Why, what happened?

Second: No please, ask me something else.

First: But all the great people round here want to know this.

Second: Let them tell me how and when they were born.

First: They can't tell you that.

Second: Why can't they?

First: Because it's their secret.

Second: What secret?

First: You've no business to ask that. Moreover, great men have great secrets, which can't be leaked to small people like you.

Second: Why do they want to know mine then?

First: Because you're a small man with a small secret.

Second: You mean my mother spent less time on me? Was it four and a half months instead of nine?

First: Who knows?

Second: I know because I spent eighteen months in the womb of my mother – double the time that of your great men.

First: Why? Had you gone to sleep there?

Second: No. I did want to come out earlier but there was war going on out here.

First: So?

Second: So what? I didn't want to get myself killed, and so, waited for the war to end.

First: Then why did you come out during the war?

Second: Because the government came to invent the contraceptives for men.

First: What has that to do with your birth?

Second: It has a great deal.

First: What's that?

Second: I had to come out quick, otherwise I would've remained unborn.

...

And there's nothing special about my birth either, like that of a marassi, or to be a little euphemistic, a meerzada. No skies fell apart and no earth erupted. All that was to happen before or after my birth happened because the foundation of everything had long been laid.

My mother told me the story of my birth, thus: 'In the last two months before your birth you gave me a very hard time, son. You'd turn upside down and extract the whole life out of my weak frame. My lips went dry, face turned pale, eyeballs bulged out of my sockets and the limbs quivered like a tenuous branch of a tree. Moreover, you moved too much, banging your legs and arms against the walls of my womb. Very seldom did you let me have a slight relief, whatever the hour of day or night. Disturbed by your restlessness, I decided to go to a fortune-teller.

The man saw through my agony and anxiety, gave me a thorough check with his wise piercing eyes, read the lines on my palm and uttered, "Your child shall remain restless, unsatisfied and mentally upset all his life. For certain, it's going to be a boy but an unusual one. He'll never sit calmly in one place; he will move on and on to different places, from country to country. All his limbs are bound to live in motion. Stillness and stoppage shall be his enemy and movement his friend. He'll feel utterly insecure if tied to one place, and very secure if left free to move on. If you won't let him do what he likes, he'll turn rebellious and relinquish you forever. And as regards his progress in life, he's bound to be overly ambitious and is likely to take his own life if he fails to achieve what he aims for."

I was terribly shaken at the last words of the fortune-teller, my dear son. Promise me right now that you'll never commit such an act. Do whatever you like to do, I won't stop you, but don't you ever think of taking your life,' she finished and commenced crying bitterly.

I took both of my mother's hands in mine and made the promise, 'Never ever, Mother! I swear it on your head.'

The Three Ks

Probably because millions of lives were to be lost in the foreseeable future, nature decided, in its own special way, to make some compensation in the form of the birth of three Ks in our village, exactly a year before the massacre of Amritsar at Jallianwala Bagh.

The Volcano

So on 13 April 1918, Krishan, Kinner and Kabir appeared in this mortal world, absolutely undaunted by what might happen to them in the face of troubles the world was embroiled in.

It was quite understandable that Krishan had chosen to be born at a wrong time. Perhaps because the wrong time was always the right time for him, for he loved corpses, butchered bodies, mangled faces, chopped limbs, gaping skulls and reddened earth – a spectacle he so relished that, in order to justify it, he had chiselled out an attractive theory of the Soul. No one kills anyone, he'd said, because life and death were, only empty illusions. The reality was the *atma* - the Soul, which never died. It always took refuge in another body, dwelling in it until that body died, too. The atma kept on changing its flesh-and-bone residences. The houses fell apart but nothing happened to the atma; it lingered on unhindered and unmitigated, in fulsomeness. He said further: 'No one gets killed because it is again an illusion of the eyes. In fact, the whole world is nothing but an illusion, posing as reality.'

Going by his fascinating theory, I think, the number of souls as constituents of the Main Soul, *the Paramatma* (the God) are fixed forever. If the soul never dies and only the body dies then why do the bodies outnumber the souls, or is it vice-versa? Perhaps he was about to tell us about the total number of souls and bodies roaming the world when he himself got killed by a Dravidian *bheel,* Jarra. We awaited his answer to another question, too, and that was: when millions die all at once, where do their souls go? Surely it would be impossible to find an equal number of soulless bodies for them to take shelter in? And if the souls equal the bodies, what about the deaths of millions of would-be-mothers in the foetal stages in his country, India, where they want only boys and no girls. I'm sure he must've been dealing with those vital questions and would've offered us the right answers if only his own body hadn't deceived him.

Being only a scribbler I admit I can't unravel these esoteric mysteries of life and death, birth and rebirth, the death of the God (Lord Krishna, for instance), but there's no harm in trying it out, is there? And it all boils down to the fact that even the great God is not free from the chains of life and death, provided we agree to Krishna's proclamation that He Himself was God. However, it was much later when Krishan – my friend – discarded the theory and said: 'Only futility grows out of the barren land.' I was honestly shocked to hear him utter such a blasphemy but we were now heading towards a democracy in India, which entitled everyone to speak one's mind. It may very well be that Krishan had turned amnesiac, and had forgotten all about his past births. But worst are the people who don't turn oblivious to anything at all. Rather they remember everything and keep resuscitating the dead things to seek guidance from them too.

Krishan's father, Girdharilal, was a confectioner or a sweetmeat maker, who had a shop in a bazaar behind the Jallianwala Bagh, and commuted daily from the village to his shop and back. His only son was born after five daughters (Sheila, Laxami, Rita, Sita and Gita). He was so happy that he decided to distribute a cartload of sweetmeats to the whole village as a token of his happiness. I was born a year later, for which I never forgave my mother and father who deprived me of those smart, birthday pleasantries. And, many years after, when I made my complaint to Krishan, he apologised to me with grace, instead of inviting me to a fabulous dinner (debt added to the principal amount) thus making amends for the lost years. He rather whined over his empty pocket.

Girdharilal, after all the initial ceremonies, invited an oracle to foretell the future and the proclivities of his son, especially the amount of comforts that his able son would bring him and his family. Hari Ram Sharma, a Brahmin, arrived, equipped with his Sanskrit booklet and clad in an old, worn out *dhoti*. He wore rubber slippers dragged by his scruffy feet. He had a long, thin tuft of hair dangling behind his neck and, horizontal lines of sandalwood paste on his forehead. A rope tightened a pair of glasses on his tiny eyes. He sat down on a m*oodha,* an Indian stool, beside the month-old baby with an incantation of *Harey Om.* Krishan's mother, Rukmani, and his five sisters served the high caste Brahmin with fresh sweetmeats and *lassi,* the butter-milk, before troubling him to plunge deeper into the unknown and make it known. When Panditji had had his fill, all of them sat down cross-legged on the floor around him, making a semicircle, except Girdharilal. He occupied an old, worn out chair. They all watched the wise man examining the boy's forehead, his half-open eyes (the boy was feeling sleepy as an after effect of being fed on cow's milk because his mother's milk had dried up), and the lines on his palms. Then the fortune-teller flicked through the pages of his booklet. The eyes of five of them - father mother and three elder sisters – stared at each other, wondering at the profound actions of the fate-finder (the two younger girls were only able to wipe their noses yet) who, knowingly or unknowingly, made unnecessary delays in pouring out the blissful words. But they persevered and showing the patience of a saint, resisted interference in case the calculations might be polluted.

'To start with,' the oracle opened his mouth at last, 'his name must start with the letter K. However, it's up to you to find out a name of your choice.'

The girls happily watched each other's faces and then those of their parents who smiled back with soft winks, warning them to keep their pouts shut. But they were happy at the first revelation as they'd been calling the boy 'kaka' which means a child, and which almost all Punjabis used as a pre-name until the real name was found and announced.

'All the stars at the time of his birth were travelling in the right direction and showed maximum illumination, indicating all the gods were rejoicing at his birth on this earth. The demons are scared of such light, the brilliance of comets, and the one who's protected by such resplendence fears no one but is feared by the dark forces of the heavens and of the earth. The ultimate victory is grabbed by the illustrious one such as Lord Krishna – I should bow to his powers.' The Brahmin uttered his words in slow motion and bowed his head to the book carrying a black and white picture of Krishna on the title page. He saw the blooming faces of the parents and those of their daughters, and felt prompted to get on with the second stage of his predictions. 'Your son's face shines like the moon and his eyes glint like stars, an indication that he'll be an earnest devotee to you, a devotee like *Shrawna*. Yes, he's like *Shrawna,* the one who sacrificed his life in the service of his blind parents, carrying them on his shoulders in the two pans of the weighing scale. The moon and stars are devotees of the sun and the earth. Your son shall win every battle, and whosoever tries to block his trajectory shall be destroyed. And when I say his name must start with letter K, I mean he has Lord Krishna's hand on his head. A part of the Lord himself lives in him. He's a fraction of the Lord himself – an atma, a fraction, broken from the paramatma, the totality. Even the name Krishna would suit him splendidly, but the choice is yours.'

Panditji revealed what he had to reveal and closed his booklet – a booklet in old incomprehensible *Sanskrit* and with some sketchy illustrations of heavenly bodies and human hands, and many other unfathomable drawings with the swastika sign drawn on each page.

Girdharilal and Rukmani were satisfied. All the sisters were happy and Panditji was comfortable with the five-rupee note in his hand, ready to go and repeat the long-remembered sermons somewhere else. The Brahmin was his family's only breadwinner. The *mantra* kept his hearth burning and the griddle ready to turn out some more chapattis, badly needed by his seven dependants. He knew what he was expected to say to the customer. So he used his mouth to utter the most hypnotic words that pleased the listener. No physical labour would suit his frame unused to hard work of any hue.

A few more days went by, and the family, after long exhausting discussions on the matter, voted for the name suggested by the palmist, Krishna. But it would be an odd name for a Punjabi family to pronounce because of its prolonged vowel at the end, which made a sound like that of a Brahmin from Haridwaar singing a mantra from the scriptures. The Punjabi language, although derived from Sanskrit, has had numerous other influences over the years and has a more abrupt ending in its pronunciation. So, Girdharilal and family, just as other Punjabis would, brought about a slight innovation and began to call the boy Krishan – a fraction of the Lord himself, if we would wish to plant our trust in the fate-finder.

Now the problem is that the family chose a name that complicates my story. Lord Krishna is going to be confused with Krishan, my bosom friend and vice-versa, and I won't know how to deal with one without the other. The old Krishna (sorry for using an adjective for fear of being misunderstood) keeps tumbling about in the story of Krishan like a stumbling block to make me a victim of deviation but the risk has to be taken. I don't want our poor Krishan – the son of a confectioner – to lose my sight for a split second for it's he I'm most concerned with, and not his predecessor. But you could no longer forget the previous abode of the atma if you wanted to shed some light on the present one, who's a fraction of the old one.

The Volcano

Our Panditji, the fortune-teller, forgot to tell us the deeds of the Lord in Gokul and Vindravana, and went on singing the praises of his brilliance and glory and lustre of the later years. But I must give this episode a film-cut here and shoot out some more footage of other scenes.

One day, pretty late in the evening, Krishan came to visit me, as he often did, perhaps to listen to what I had scribbled next in the story. Unfortunately, I was in no mood to engage in a session of stories that evening and moreover, had written nothing new to share with him. In fact, I'd been distracted from my path and had fallen into a small pond unlike the ones in Qila Vasudev.

It was a pond full of murky water, mud and leaches that hurled around in it like snakes. The walls of the pond were covered with green, slippery fungus. I didn't even attempt to emerge out of its depths notwithstanding the leeches sucking my blood and the splashes of muddy water blurring my vision. I'd begun to take pleasure in wallowing in its mire and felt contented that the luck had given a sweet knock on my door which I had to fling wide open before the luck went back, never to return again.

The Second World War hadn't started on the globe yet, but it had already started inside me. That's what always happens with me. Long before the troubles grip the world, they grip me. I'm always the first one to be tracked down sniffing at them and getting gripped. The distress, then, doesn't end, rather it extends far beyond the point at which the world becomes normal again but I continue to suffer.

Let Krishan wait in abeyance and I tell you my story first. One evening, when I was roaming the streets of Amritsar (for no apparent reason except frivolity), I met a friend of my school days – Surinder. We hadn't seen each other for a long time after leaving school because he'd joined his father in his business and busied himself in travelling to other towns and cities, and I'd confined myself to scribbling like a frog in the well. In our school days, we'd shared the same bench and talked about all sorts of things, from teachers, class-fellows and girls, and exchanged lewd jokes too. In short, he was my chum, and we could easily depend on each other for our secrets.

Surinder was witty, rough and tough, cunning and shrewd (quite contrary to me) and I accepted his authority, let him lead my way, and I followed meekly after. But more often than not, we ended up in a horrible cul-de-sac with no way ahead except to run back on our heels, either wounded or withered. He was a wicked troublemaker and would pick frequent fights with other boys, resulting in hitting, thrashing and walloping them, thereby dragging my name, too, into the matter, without my obvious involvement; I carried half the blame simply for being his friend.

Seeing me, Surinder ran across the road towards me and held me tightly in his clasp. He looked taller and sturdier although the style of his clothes had changed dramatically, giving him a businessman's look. The haughty swaggering of the school days was missing; even his language had turned softer, shinier and scrupulous.

'How are you? Where are you? What are you doing these days? Never saw you in the city for a long time? Where've you been, my friend?' And a score of other questions, all at once, without letting me speak a word. And then, at the end of it all, 'Let's go home. It's just round the corner.'

And, as if mesmerised, I resumed my old habit of following him, my feet dragging me after him without demur. The house wasn't too far away; it took us barely five minutes to reach it. It was my first visit to his house. It was the third house on the right-hand-side in a narrow street, similar to many others in the town of Amritsar. The entrance door was big enough to be compared with that of a small citadel. Surinder gave a heavy knock at the door with his healthy fist, turned round and looked at me with a welcoming smile. The door was unbolted from inside by a young, beautiful girl of nearly eighteen. A sweet smile appeared on her face at the sight of Surinder but then faded away when she saw me behind him.

'Meet my sister, Sonia.' He introduced her to me and added, 'And he's Arya, my friend from the school days.' (This was my real name, given to me by my father. Gold was my mother's favourite, but only used within the walls of the house, at least until now.) The girl greeted me with folded hands and I greeted her back with a hello. It all seemed so simple, but no, it wasn't. Inside me somewhere, I shuddered with an intense, unknown shock, as if touched by an electric wire. I was ravaged completely.

Collecting herself, she let us in. Surinder rushed in instantly while I, in the act of following him, was slowed by the fragrance of a thousand roses when I went past her. I had lost myself to her.

The Volcano

It seemed quite an extensive house with a number of bedrooms, a fairly large lounge and many other attachments.

'I'll be back in a second.' Surinder, having seated me in the lounge, left, maybe to issue some instructions to his sister, or something else. I busied myself looking at the photographs hanging on the walls. There were dozens of them showing the faces of the people unknown to me. However, I did find some I was interested in – Sonia's - in different moods and costumes. In one picture, I saw her in a beautiful saree. She looked gorgeous in all her poses.

The rhythm was broken by the entry of Surinder followed by his sister with a tray in her hands. Sonia served us with tea and some salty Indian mixtures and sweets. But all the while, she kept her glance glued to the floor, abiding by the Indian ways in the presence of an outsider. That day I stayed with them for about an hour or so, and then left with a promise to pop in again. But what a promise! I went to see *them* almost every other day, incapable of resisting the desire to see her standing in front of me, even if only for a minute. I went for Sonia but asked for Surinder as a veneer, and found his mother or his father. Twice or thrice I found Sonia, too, but never alone - my solitary wish. However, one day, by sheer luck, I found an opportunity to confront her when she was alone in the house. She grew hesitant, nervous and frightened, and reluctant to talk to me although I knew from that one chance smile of the first day, that she liked me as much as I did her. We stood face to face behind the closed main gate, while her ears suddenly developed into some kind of device capable of hearing every single stir in the air, however lifeless. It all reflected her terrifying fears of being caught flirting, forbidden by the obsolete norms of that society. I was as scared as she was but I knew it had to be now or never. I gathered all my courage to spin the words.

'Sonia! I've come to tell you that I like you very much, in fact I love you and want to marry you… And if your family agrees would you…?' 'I don't know… you'd better ask my brother and father,' she said in a very weak voice.

'I'll surely do that but I want your assent first.'

'What shall I say…?' she said and blushed crimson. And I knew the answer.

It was this mire I was wallowing in, with no intention of emerging and getting on with my scribbling escapade.

Krishan was truly in a state of trance, sitting in the chair with his eyes shut, perhaps probing his inner soul.

'Krishan!' I woke him from his delirium. 'Have you found your love yet?' I asked, recollecting his old conversation when he'd said that no girl bothered to look at him, let alone love him.

'Love? Are you crazy or something? A commodity such as love's always for the lucky ones, not for people like myself,' he replied with a stern voice and looked at me with the eyes ready to devour me. After a prolonged minute, he smiled bitterly as though mourning my misunderstanding of life's complexities. There wasn't any reason to believe that we were in the middle of some fun of teasing each other, yet my sense of seriousness turned deviant.

'But your namesake had plenty of it,' I pouted, without penitence.

'Hell with him,' he said curtly and outrageously and got up to go. I did want to stop him but just couldn't. So he went away.

Krishan, my friend, went away, and Krishna came back to me, nudging me in my sides, tickling and laughing his heart out. I could watch him play the flute in a crowd of colourful cows and surrounded by *gopies* – three hundred and sixty or more, in Gokul – performing *kathakali or bhartnatayam,* the classical dances exhibiting half naked, silky bodies in the open. I thought of Sonia, awfully frightened in the twentieth century, of meeting a love-seeking man, hiding in the darkened layers of extreme modesty, feeling shame. Were the olden times better than the modern ones? Or was it all gossip, fiction rather than fact, or only the forbidden dreams coming afloat under the guise of epics?

I began to watch Krishna with a renewed fervour. The picture looked pretty glorious. Krishna hid the clothes of the ravishing young beauties, which dipped, chirping like sparrows, in the waters of Ganges, watched by him, voyeuristically, from a hideout. Then, having noticed their clothes were missing from where they had placed them, they began to search for the thief and eventually found the voyeur's eyes engaged in the act of consuming their nakedness. When the *gopies* asked him to return their clothes, the voyeur put forth his stipulation that he'd like to see them come out naked before he gave them their clothes back.

But our poor Krishan seemed to have been left with no luck by his predecessor. The poor guy must be wondering, and even cursing the so-called new era, which had totally denied him a chance of even meeting his basic needs. He was twenty-one and still only longed for, yes only longed for, a *gopi* to come out from somewhere, (not necessarily from the waters of Ganges) albeit completely covered in clothes, except for the face. But what confronted him every morning was a herd of cows and buffaloes, waiting to be unchained and taken to the field full of green grass.

On Vaisakhi day last year, Krishan even bought a flute. It was made from a bamboo branch with seven small holes in it to generate tunes and a larger one to blow into. He made assiduous efforts to play it but the matter didn't progress farther than an odd blow. He began to search for a teacher but couldn't find one. And, instead of encouraging him, Girdharilal began to reprimand him, the sisters sniggered at him and the mother mocked him, saying: 'So, you're going to become another *Ranjha* to renounce everything, cross the river *chenab*, woo the daughter of *Syals* and bring her home to get married to!'

Here-Ranjha is the greatest legend of the Punjabis, just as Romeo-Juliet is that of the English. The legend went thus:

Ranjha would play on the flute and produce such melodious tunes that the whole life on earth began to dance ecstatically, including humans, animals and the crops. He would keep sitting amongst his friends till late (playing the flute for them, obviously) and go home at odd hours, much to the anger of his brothers and their wives, who would have to wait for dinner till late. One day, they all decided to bring him to book. They hauled him over the coals the very next evening. Ranjha, whose father, Mauju Chaudhuri, and his mother had died some time ago, was now at the mercy of his brothers and their wives. He was infuriated by the insult and left home for good. He crossed the river Chenab to land on the other side of the territory belonging to Chaudhari Chuchak, whose daughter Heer was the most beautiful in the area. One day, Heer saw him and heard him playing the flute, turning out heart-rending tunes. She fell in love with him and his flute. The tunes he created made her dance like an intoxicated snake. Heer had him employed by her father to graze their cattle – a pretext to keep him near her and give their love a good cover up. But her lame uncle, Kaidon - a bachelor and drunkard, who was jealous of other people's love, reflecting his own psyche of not being able to find anything of the sort – caught them red handed and got them reprimanded by his elder brother and Heer's father. Then, prompted by Kaidon's inducements, they married Heer off to the son of another landlord in a far off place. But Ranjha followed the shadows of Heer and found her. He won her back through an appeal to a small king of real justice who respected human emotions. Kaidon, playing yet another stratagem apologised to both of them for his misdeeds and vowed an oath to help them get married. He asked Ranjha to go home and come back with a proper marriage party, and take his bride home amid glory. But Ranjha returned only to find Heer poisoned to death by the villain, Kaidon. Then, sensing the remaining poisoned sweetmeat in the dead girls fist, Ranjha took hold of it, gulped it down and died too."

'More likely a Kaidon, instead of a Ranjha,' remarked Girdharilal from beside his wife and burst out laughing. Krishan was so exasperated by his father's comments that the very next day he threw the flute into the thick bushes on the side of one of the ponds to make it irretrievable forever.

Among five brothers and one sister, Kinner was the youngest. Radhika, a year older than Kinner, occupied the fifth place. The four elder brothers were Nag, Bhil, Nishad and Ahir. Had Kinner's father, Bharat Chand, lived, he would have laboured hard to bring up the children and given his wife a little easy life. But he lost his own life in the massacre at the Jallianwalla Bagh - the rendering of Sir Michael O'Dwyer, the Lt.-Governor of the Punjab and R.E.H. Dyer, the Brigadier General. It happened exactly a month after the birth of Kinner.

Reshma, Kinner's mother, had to grind herself in the mill of harrowing labour to look after her large family. The eldest, Nag, was ten at the time, and he worked with a small landlord in the village rearing his cattle, chopping his fodder and helping with the ploughing, sowing and harvesting. The remuneration was a wage of five rupees a month, starvation and a good beating if he failed to turn up on time or forgot to do something he was asked to do. Bhil, barely eight at the time, had a still worse life. He worked at a confectioner's shop, scrubbing big pans with his tiny hands while squatting in a dingy hole under the staircase, engulfed in the dark smoke rising from the furnace and the hot steam flying from the cauldrons full of milk, simmering like him. When, after day's squatting, he tried to stand straight, his rickety legs trembled under his tiny weight and his head went round and round making everything obscure to the eyes. When he finally emerged from the dark hole, he appeared like a little ghost – dirty and scruffy, with a web of withered hair, overgrown and tangled and unkempt. The *Halwai* - confectioner – gave him one *anna* a day, making the total amount of less than two rupees a month. He was no better off than his brother Nag in the way the confectioner treated him when he delayed doing something, came late or forgot to do a job. Both felt orphaned despite their living mother. A living father would have made some difference, but only just.

Reshma, which meant silk, had to leave Ahir behind her to look after Radhika and Kinner before she went to work at several places, accompanied and protected by the male strength of six-year-old Nishad. The work involved cleaning the cattle yards of six different farmers; the same task had to be repeated at each yard. She always commenced her work from the yard that was furthest from her mud walled and thatched hut on the brink of the village pond. By the time she finished her work at the yard closest to her hut, the sun was preparing to pack up its day's journey and drown at the far end of the pond. In each yard she collected all the dung excreted by almost a dozen cattle with the help of a large broom made of a plank fixed with a sturdy upright handle, and deposited it all in one corner. All the while, she would be cautioning herself and Nishad against slipping on the muddy and dripping floor, stinking with animal urine. Then she poured the looser dung into the big baskets made of bamboo, loaded them on her head and delivered them to a marked place outside the village, followed by her son bearing a smaller load. Throwing all the dung away involved six or more journeys. Then the yard had to be washed clean with numerous buckets of water, all to be fetched from the house if there was no arrangement of water at the yard in the outhouse. Ahir helped her to do all this but his tiny hands, legs and body would soon yield. Then came the turn of the firmer dung, to be rolled into round cakes weighing a pound or so and exposed to the sun to dry. Having finished, she would go to the ladies at the house, asking for something to eat and drink. They would, of course, give them something but would throw it in their hands like a bare bone in front of a dog. And, in return for this magnanimous favour, they would strangulate them with yet another job such as cleaning their forecourt or sorting stones out of a bag of wheat. So, by the time she and Ahir had finished their work at the six cattle yards and had met all the pestering demands of the ladies, the time left would be just as much as it took for the sun to plunge into the pond and die. It would be the time to cook, eat and sleep.

Reshma had done that for years at a stretch. She had ground herself in the mill of back breaking labour without much remuneration or any break, but now things had begun to turn for the better, and the credit went to our Kinner. His birth was as hopeless as of any one of them. Twenty-one years had passed by and all these years were petrified on his face, his body and his soul. Half starved, half naked, half human, maltreated, used and abused, beaten and rebuked, insulted and denigrated, Kinner had ended up as a wanderer, a loner, crying in his own lap for comfort and hearing his own bitter sobs. All his brothers had succumbed to *karma* (a retribution for past sins, fed on the indoctrination of the astute Brahmin), but Kinner and Radhika hadn't.

Kinner had the third eye in his head, and he, as a loner and wanderer, began to talk to the stones. The stones talked back and Kinner knew what they said. He'd begun to shape out the inner souls of the stones at the age of ten. All he needed was a chisel and a hammer to make those inner souls come out alive and talk to the eyes of the beholder. He knew what lay dormant in their swaddles, what hid itself from the eye that looked but didn't notice, glanced but didn't fathom below the coarseness. When he chiselled away the coarseness, there emerged a hidden indivisibility of a character, expressing all the emotions capable of grasping the soul of the watcher. Radhika was the first one to identify and appreciate the great artist living in Kinner.

However, it was long time after that that Kinner began to paint pictures of characters that haunted him day and night. He had started with a pencil and paper, sketching outlines and line-work at first. He didn't have the power to buy colours, brushes and canvases, but used charcoal, chalk and household colours mixed with water, and made his own brushes from straws. Then, when he sold his first sculpture he had the money to buy these things. He had made it, and he was making it, and he would continue to make it for years to come. He could read and write Hindi and Punjabi now, and a little bit of English. I'd introduced him only to the alphabet of each language, but all the rest was his own diligence. Once he'd begun he never looked back. In the past seven or so years, he'd really astonished me. He didn't like fiction at all. He liked reading some poetry but most of all he liked history and mythology. When he finished a new book, he'd come and discuss its contents with me at length. He borrowed my books too, and returned them after reading. His awareness of life and its mysteries was increasing by the day. He'd discuss everything in minute detail. But his attitude at discussion would be as harsh as ever, blunt and unforgiving. Probably, he was returning what he'd been given by the world around him – harshness, bluntness and callousness.

One day, when he'd finished a book concerned with Krishna's death caused by a Dravidian Bheel, called Jarra, he came straight to me and asked a bizarre question: 'Do you know me?'

I was embarrassed by his question for I knew him more than well; he had been a friend ever since he was born. We'd lived together, played together, laughed and wept together, and had shared each other's concerns and pains together. But now he was asking me who he was. It was a weird question for me to expect of him.

Then, finding me totally bewildered, he'd said, 'I'm the reincarnation of Jarra, the Bheel, just as he was the reincarnation of Bali who was assassinated by Rama. Bali was reborn in the body of Jarra who killed Krishna and took his revenge.'

'And why is Jarra reborn in your body when the revenge has already been taken?' I asked as if to kill him by his own argument.

'Because the matter hasn't ended yet. They butchered millions of us in the forests including the *Khandav,* where Jarra finally killed Krishna. Do you think one life taken is enough of a revenge for so many?' he explained and posed such a question at the end that I found myself dumbfounded, knowing not what to say.

I thought and thought and discovered a way out of the puzzle. 'Do you believe the theory of rebirth?'

Now he was sunk. It was his turn to think and ask his inner self to show the route out. He looked hither and thither, bit his lips, wrinkled his nose, and narrowed his eyes. 'I suppose I do but in another way,' he said and looked into my eyes with a cutting edge in his.

'In what way?' I asked, pleased that I'd managed to evade the question of revenge and counter-revenge.

Kinner sank once again into the abyss of his inner ocean. 'Listen, I don't believe the reincarnation crap the way it's been going on for ages, but only in the form of rebirth. And furthermore, it is not the rebirth of the body but of history because history repeats itself. This repetition of history is the rebirth of it. And we are but minute components of history. You are not what you are but a collective rebirth of all your ancestors, past generations, a kind of rebirth of a consolidated consciousness. Although your ancestors are physically dead, spiritually they are still living through you. The history they lived was passed on to their next generation and then to the one after, and so on. So, in that way you're the reincarnation of past history - a collective consciousness, a soul, a continuity that never ends. What dies is the body, not what your ancestors handed down to you in the form of good or bad experiences. This is precisely why no new generation forgets the excesses perpetrated on the previous generation, or the one before and before and... The chain goes on to join with the remotest. If there were no rebirths the way I mean, there would be no civilisation, no culture, no civil society, and every individual would have to start history from scratch and finish it when he died. It's this rebirth I believe in, or reincarnation if you prefer. .' Kinner spoke at length and analytically. I was really impressed.

His understanding of history, individuals, generations, and physicality and spirituality astonished me. I could guess how hard he must have been working to stand things logically on their legs rather than on their heads like the old Brahmins. I was absolutely convinced.

'I totally agree with you on that,' I said, adding, 'but I don't find the argument of revenge and counter-revenge very amusing.'

'It's because you don't capture my point,' he said and paused. 'What history passes on to you is either bitterness due to the past excesses, or satisfaction due to an equal treatment, or over-satisfaction due to excessive favours. Moreover, people have a habit of forgetting even the worst excesses if things improve, but they also have a habit of bringing all the old memories back. I know how my mother and brothers suffered at the hands of the mighty ones. I myself suffered terribly. The worst brought all the past worst back to us, thereby igniting the sense of revenge. Then who is to blame? Me, us, us all, or someone else?'

Kinner was perfectly right in his studies. He understood the questions to their extreme depths. I had no answer to offer except to show my helplessness. I was no political puppeteer and held no strings. I felt a sense of guilt in me for the doings of others. 'I do seize your point now, Kinner, but I've to be you to really feel it, perceive the depth of it,' I said, and shuddered, perhaps, under the pressure of guilt passed on to me by the rebirth of history.

Although there was no more conversation after that and Kinner quietly left, it seemed that he'd left an anguish behind him, which still loomed around me. The echoes of revenge and counter-revenge were still audible in the air and frightened me for the life of Krishan, who had virtually nothing to do with the old Krishna. Lord Krishna, who had set the forests on fire, feigning to clear them of snakes and serpents and make the land cultivable but profoundly, to kill the inhabitants – the ancestors of Kinner, whom the Aryans called demons and devils and evil forces.

One day, quite a few weeks later, when Kinner didn't come to see me for some reason, I went to see him. Kinner wasn't home, but his sister and mother were. Reshma seemed to have grown very old and weak and short of eyesight, too. Her emaciated body was a bundle of bones, her cheeks appallingly drawn in, her hair sparse, and her face hands arms awesomely wrinkled. She was lying flat on her cot, unable to swat a fly off her face. The sight of her made me sad.

Radhika understood how I felt. She whispered to me, 'Mother won't live for long now,' having said so she let out a long breath.

'She isn't very old but has suffered too much,' I whispered back, as if from within a well.

37

'Only sixty-two... But the kind of life she's lived can turn anyone to that state,' she said again, dolefully.

She was right. Many other women in the village were far older but hadn't aged the way she had. But these women belonged to the privileged classes, unlike Reshma, who had the privilege of living in captivity and dying in freedom. I could, now, understand the wrath of Kinner.

'Where's Kinner?' I asked Radhika, standing by the side of the cot on which her mother lay, perhaps a little deaf as well.

'He's gone to town and will come back late in the evening. Take a seat,' she said and pointed her finger to the other bare cot near the kitchen. She sat down on a small wooden stool at the entrance of the kitchen and began to play with the half-done dough. I took my seat as she'd invited.

'How're *you* anyway? Reading anything new? Kinner told me you too are a voracious reader,' I asked, looking at her dusky shiny face fitted with bright eyes, medium nose and sharply chiselled eyelashes. A thick growth of black-brown hair tied into a knot at the back of her neck gave her the appearance of a girl well in control of her life and affairs.

'Not much really,' she said and sighed deeply, trying to curb some inner sentiment from surfacing. 'Don't get enough time now to follow this hobby.'

'Why? Have you found some job somewhere?'

'Sort of,' she said and smiled lightly, showing her glittering teeth, which looked like an arch of jasmine flowers.

'Don't you want to tell?' I also smiled.

'It's not that... It's just a small time job as an office bearer with a paper, called 'Who's Harijan'.'

'I see,' I said and wondered that such a paper was being published without my knowledge.

The word 'Harijan' had been devised by the Mahatma for the downtrodden people and he also ran a paper with that name for their uplift. The uplift of the ones who had been razed to the ground by the so-called high class Hindus and who called them *Achhoot* or Untouchables. It was like having mercy on them and putting some odd coins in their begging bowls because the word meant 'sons of God' as though the ones responsible for their plight were sons of

Satan. I could hear the bells ringing behind 'Who's Harijan' (*Harijan Kaun?*) – a movement against the intentions of toying with words rather than doing something really concrete and revolutionary for their uplift and equality.

'I'm glad that such a paper's out but I haven't seen it yet. Have you got a copy?'

'Yes, I have. You can borrow it if you wish,' she said. Elated by my opinion, she went in and came out with the paper. It was in Hindi, showing the title in bold *Devanagri* script.

'Thanks. I'll give it back to you soon after I've read it,' I said and got up.

'Don't worry, give it back when you can,' she assured me. And I left, thinking about Kinner again. He must've gone to town due to some connection with the paper.

My friend Kabir, unlike the old Kabir, the poet of the *Bhagti Movement* – the movement of spiritual reawakening – was the revolution reborn. Unlike the old Kabir – yes, the old Kabir of the middle ages who was born of a Muslim father and a Hindu (Brahmin) mother, our Kabir happened to swap the order: a Hindu father and a Muslim mother. Kundanlal Premi – a Ghadarite from Canada – sometime before the collapse of the *Ghadar Movement* married a Muslim widow from Jalandhar, Razia, whose husband had fallen victim to the widespread influenza and died. Premi was an Urdu poet and wrote *ghazlas* that appeared in a number of papers. In the later years, he wrote memoirs of his life and times and died at the age of sixty-five without having the book published. The manuscript, written in a beautiful calligraphic hand, was now in possession of his son, Kabir. But we shall have a look at that later on.

Razia was fifty-seven now, but was in good health. Premi had left her enough but only just enough, so that she and her son didn't have to worry too much. She was a pious woman and she observed her religious duties of five prayers a day, fasting in the month of Ramzan and giving out alms regularly. Kabir had found a job in the city as a proof-reader with a paper, which offered him the facility of seeing his revolutionary poems consistently published, widely read and appreciated. K.L. Premi had rubbed himself on his son, and had initiated him into writing poetry when he was barely twelve.

The paper *Nizaam* (Administration) boldly criticised the way the Raj was run, unfolding its tyrannies, coercion and depredation, and preached Hindu-Sikh-Muslim unity to its readers, if they wished to get emancipation from the yoke of slavery and subjugation. Kabir's poetry was well suited to the paper's policy. The chief editor, Barkattullah, was very pleased with Kabir and assured him of the position of assistant editor if he continued working assiduously. A salary of thirty rupees per month couldn't be treated as bad pay in that day and age.

K.L. Premi worked for a milder paper, *Mazdoor*, (The Labourer), and was one of its many editors before he died. The paper ceased publication after his death; not because of his demise but because of other reasons, chief amongst which was lack of finance. The paper was partly funded by the communists who, with the collapse of the *Ghadar Movement,* followed by the October Revolution in Russia, the Rowlatt Act, the massacre at Amritsar, the beginning of the World War Two, and imprisonment of the communists, had now been banned. The offices of the paper were locked and its assets confiscated.

The old Kabir condemned the caste system that had bedevilled the Indian society and had doomed it to sharp splits, thereby opening all the frontiers to the foreign invaders who entered the country unchallenged, ransacking its length and breadth for gold, money, crops and women. He had sharply disparaged the Brahmin, the split-maker who, for his parochial interests, had divided a nation into factions, fed the minds on *karma* – the prizes and punishments of the doings of the past births. The Brahmin had invented this false theory of *karma*, the destiny, and was responsible for the plight of the downtrodden, the captivated original inhabitants of India, to let his exploitation continue unhindered. He created it all and blamed it on the past births, thereby fooling the common sense that had grown too naïve and gullible to challenge the concoctions. The old Kabir defied the Brahmin in a verse, thus:

"O Brahmin! If you are so special,

Why weren't you born through another hole?"

But the Kabir of now had a different target to meet, that of the freedom of the country from a more sophisticated hand, which had not only invaded and pillaged, but had seized it forever and dispossessed its people of everything they had. Kabir wanted a revolution, and the reins of the country to be taken over by the poorest of the poor, the workers and peasants, the ordinary masses who, until now had remained passive players in the game, observing and suffering. The voice of Premi, the *ghadarite*, now spoke through him, reverberated in the air, echoed and re-echoed in the weekly *Nizaam*. It invoked a red alert in the eyes of the administration about imminent treason, subversion and disruption. But the administration of *Nizaam*, although revolutionary in theory, couldn't go that far in practice unless it wanted the paper confiscated and its accounts frozen like many others.

'It's too much, Kabir, it's just too much. I don't want to see the paper closed and each one of us incarcerated. We all want independence, even sooner than you do, but not by violence which will breed more violence and kill more people. We want to follow the policy of non-violence and non-co-operation, the one being preached by the Mahatama,' the chief editor warned him.

But Kabir couldn't write in a milder style. The fire that had been ignited in him by his father had grown to double its volume and could no longer be extinguished. Unless all the holes providing it with oxygen were blocked, it would only continue to increase. He didn't change his tone but simply stopped getting the verses published in the paper, minding his business of proof reading only.

It was May 1939, and Kabir had acquired another month of maturity added to his lot of twenty-one years, like two other K's. Razia was looking for a suitable girl to become her daughter-in-law, whereas Kabir had no intention of getting restricted to a married life at this age. He was tall, slim and handsome with a mix of attributes from both his father and mother. He'd acquired the fairness of skin, almond-shaped bright eyes and luscious lips from his mother and his body-parts from his father – the best of both worlds. No girl with a sensible head could turn him down for her life partner. He was already atop the list of a few, it was said. But he was terribly infected with the disease of reading; and it was no ordinary read that could be relegated to one side when a greater fascination came to have a rendezvous with him. He was under the infectious spell of the Russian Revolution and quite incapable of detaching himself from the writings of Lenin translated into Urdu. 'What is to be done?' and

'State and Revolution' occupied the front row on the makeshift bookshelf beside his bed. The row didn't have any gap to be filled in by a book of flesh and bones, at least not as yet. It would be some time before the gravity of the infection would become less serious and recovery possible, enabling him to think about other things.

Razia – unlike the old Razia, daughter of Iltutmish of the Slave Dynasty that ruled India in the thirteenth century, who proved herself to be wiser than all her brothers and inherited the throne, despite being a woman, only to be killed after a brief interval of rule – was a simple woman. She knew only a smattering of what went on around her in the world and much less about what contaminated the brain of her only son. Having married a Hindu gentleman, she had to face a lot of humiliation at the hands of her family and bear the brunt of their wrath for many years. She knew well enough that she wouldn't find a Muslim girl from a well-to-do family for her son because everyone from her old acquaintances had turned their faces away, including her three sisters of whom she was always very proud. A similar fate had confronted Premi when he married Razia against the consent of his family and siblings. But he was a man and made of a different mould. He'd managed to do without any of them. Even the house in which they now lived had been bought with the money he'd brought with him from Canada.

Razia now faced the problem of her son's marriage. There were many Muslim girls around who'd have loved to marry handsome Kabir. Some of them might already be having his dreams but the final decision lay only with the parents who'd think a dozen times before saying yes. A mixture, or a hybrid, has its own virtues but difficulties, too. Razia, too, was caught up in such a fate. At last, she turned to the poor Muslim families in that area. It was from them that her prospective daughter-in-law would finally emerge – a beautiful one but with no dowry whatsoever. She'd quite a few in mind, but only if the contaminated brain valued her ambitions.

'Think of my age and then talk,' she said, countering Kabir's argument of 'enough time for that'.'

'Why, what's wrong with your age, Ammi? You're perfectly healthy, ain't you?' he replied, shoving his head into his book rather than facing her.

'Your father was healthy looking, too. Then what happened to him? Don't you remember?'

'He smoked, that's why. You don't.'

'Shall I start, if that brings you closer to my mind?'

'Come on, Ammi, don't think of negative things all the while.'

'Are you thinking the right ones?'

'Probably, I am, Amma. I want my country to be free first to allow me the best of a marriage,' he uttered, as if from within a dream.

'It'll be best even otherwise. I've saved everything for it – clothes, money, gold, everything. You don't need to worry a bit about that,' she said joyfully, missing the point he was making. Kabir knew none of his arguments would buy her back from where she was. He got up, put the *revolution* back in its gap and began to get ready to go, leaving Razia in a state of pensiveness.

Despite my repeated humble requests, Kabir didn't budge. He (and I don't know why) refrained from lending me his father's manuscript of memoirs. He might've thought that I'd mess about with it or do some forgery. But there was no need for me to do that. All I wanted was to find out some information about the times when I wasn't yet born. But he wouldn't trust me. In the end, I tried the same old tested method of adulation for him and his father; and he, still a little too scrupulous, agreed to lend me the manuscript but only for a day. So I must hurry up without wasting a single second.

Memoirs of Kundanlal Premi
(Some excerpts)

K.L. Premi's memoirs were quite a lengthy account of his life and times. He started from when he was five, slowly progressing to his youth, his vow of celibacy, political inclinations, reading and writing Urdu poetry, his years in Canada and then back home. His marriage with Razia and the birth of Kabir followed by the memoirs reaching their end a year before he died. I shuffled through the whole pack of neatly written leaves but couldn't read even a quarter of the manuscript. How could I? And Kabir didn't trust me to have it for a longer period. A day of eight to ten hours couldn't do the trick. So I began to scribble what I could – some odd paragraphs quite randomly. And then returned the manuscript to its owner. I hoped my sense of time-keeping would impress Kabir, and if I later asked him to lend me the precious work for a longer time, he might not refuse. But for the moment, see what I gleaned.

"I reached the western coast of Canada in May 1909 when I'd just turned forty. Vancouver, in British Columbia, was to become my home where I stayed until the end of 1916. No ships went direct from India to Canada or America in those days. You were required to go to Hong Kong or Singapore first and from thence to the Pacific Ocean. I wondered why was it so? However, the answer wasn't too difficult to find. India was a slave country and nobody gave a damn about its people enjoying the facility of a direct route.

"I'd begun to feel during my excursion in the ship that the whites extremely hated us Indians. Their faces turned sullen and cat-like eyes squeezed in abomination at the sight of us. Throughout my journey I'd discovered that all the whites sat and moved together, distancing themselves from the blacks, yellows and browns. These were the symptoms that would agglomerate in time to come, in that land of dreams come true.

"In 1907, two years before my arrival there, many Indians living in Singapore, Hong Kong and Shanghai had moved to Canada. They'd later tell us that they had come to know about Canada from the Chinese who had shifted there before them. Most of these Indians had worked as gatekeepers, security-men, or as constables in the British police while living in the Far East. The ones who came to try their luck in Canada were quite healthy and worked very hard in the timber mills or other places. Later on, quite a few of them went further south to California.

"With the help of my Punjabi friends, I too found a job in the Dominion Timber Mill, in Vancouver where many Punjabis already worked, most of them Sikhs. But, as always, my political proclivities absorbed me more than the urge to earn more and more money. I'd work only a few months in succession and then, offering some kind of pretence, take a long leave and embark upon a new journey to meet different people in different towns and cities. That was precisely why I had come back to India not loaded with money, but only enough to buy a house and survive peacefully together with my family.

"The presence of our people in large numbers in BC, looking and behaving differently to the local population due to our own distinct culture, caused strange reactions – a mixture of animosity and institutionalised racism – resulting in opprobrious slogans such as: 'British Columbia For Whites Only'. Behind such flagrant manifestations of contempt lurked the politicians, who had their own axes to grind. The malevolent leaders went to the extent of putting the Federal Government in Ottawa under extreme pressure to ban the further inflow of Indians to Canada.

"The Canadian Press contributed a lot towards worsening the situation from the very outset. They published depreciating and belittling stories about Indians on a regular basis. Ostensibly, the papers wanted to make their readership laugh by downgrading others in a vicious manner. The obduracy of the Canadian Press and the callousness of their leaders afflicted our souls in such a ruthless fashion that we sometimes felt ashamed to be Indians. In every town and city where Indians got together – in gurdwaras, mosques or mandirs – they expressed their deepest anguish at these ravaging stories because most of them were imaginative and fictional rather than factual. There were exaggerated and over-inflated accounts of news items, shaped by malicious intent. The motive was to caricature, mock and desecrate, and produce as much hatred against us as they could. There was nothing covert about that. You didn't have to dig deeper into the text to find out who it was aimed at. It was all overtly clear. The negative undertones not only exceeded the positive ones but the total percentage *was* negative.

The newspaper editorials were all full of derogatory remarks about Indian life, culture and civilisation. A small dispute in some remote village, for instance, would be snowballed into a tremendous communal riot to render the impression that India was embroiled in a war of belligerent factions. The editorial would then end in contemptuous derision: 'They're all … idiots'. In one news-story accompanied by a cartoon, Gandhi was caricatured as a naked clown; his non-violence as a dead man's pretence to be living, and his non-co-operation as an infantile effort to get the parents to buy the toy he most fancied, called 'self-rule'.

"They fabricated their own fictitious stories about blind beliefs, superstitions, fetishes, a myriad of animal gods, inane and defunct rites and customs, the caste system, child marriage, self mortification, widow burning and countless other things. The worst thing was the corroboration of all those make-believe stories by funny editorials. These editorial notes saw nothing positive in India, Indian people or their culture. Many people offered vilifying and traducing justifications to the British rule, writing that India was lucky to have the British to rule them, teach them civilisation, bring them out of the dark ages into the modern era and from the forests to the towns. They added that the British were doing their job properly and dutifully and Indians should express their deepest gratitude to them.

"A politician, Miss K, based in Seattle, made a speech quite indiscriminately showering gruesome aspersions on Indians. She asserted that Hindu customs were so horribly hideous in their content and form that they allowed aged men to marry minor girls because they liked eating raw and unripe fruit. They produced little in the fields but excelled every country or nation in the production of a crop of children. Their over engagement in sex at a young age made them old and impotent at twenty-nine. The Indians must be ashamed of themselves, she had concluded.

"Her speech had a sharp and serious backlash from Punjabis in general and Sikhs in particular. In the Dominion Timber Mill, my Sikh co-workers reacted to the last bit quite uproariously.

"'How does the virgin miss know we grow old and impotent at the age of twenty-nine?' asked sixty-year-old Jat Sikh, who worked faster than all his mates. 'Ask her to come and try me one day.'

'She might've dealt with some silly rice eater thus far,' answered the other man.

'I hadn't even seen the naked legs of a lady until after I was twenty-nine,' remarked another one laughingly.

'Has anyone seen what she looks like? Is she like a desert-swept goat or a well-bred fresh pony?' was the reaction of yet another one.

'Does the news carry her picture?'

'What do you want to do with her picture, man? Isn't it enough that she's unmarried and virgin?' remarked another man naughtily.

'Usually the bearings of such sluts are already rattling like spent up rollers, cluttering long before they're even touched,' the last one concluded, utilising the language of the mill."

"All these rotten statements by the feeble minded politicians, mockery by the newspapers, provocation by the law-makers, added fuel to the fire of hatred against the British rule in India. It all worked to mould the opinion of the Indians that they would need to fight for India's freedom if they wanted to live a life of respect and dignity. Their resolve was further strengthened by the nationalist struggles of the Irish, the Chinese and the Egyptians.

"In the beginning of 1913, the Indians living on the Pacific coast assembled in Stockton and laid the foundation of an organisation, called 'Hindustan Workers of the Pacific Coast' with the renowned Sohan Singh Bhakna as its President and Lala Hardyal as its Secretary. Shortly after that, a weekly paper 'Ghadar' was launched by the organisation, with scholarly Hardyal as its editor. Soon the headquarters, Yugantar Ashram, 436 Hill Street, San Francisco, began to be illuminated by bubbling activity, not only by the ones holding responsible chairs but also the ones committed to the cause. I spent nearly two years there and watched closely the force and speed with which the movement strode ahead.

"The first issue of Ghadar, published on 1st November 1913, carried the first of Hardyal's brilliant editorials: 'The time will soon come when rifles and blood will take the place of pen and ink.' The paper advocated the policy of armed revolution against the British to liberate the country from their rule. It preached mutiny and violence as opposed to Ghandi's non-violence. The paper's name Ghadar (Mutiny) gave the movement the name Ghadar Movement. It advised Indians living in Canada and America to go to India and fight for the cause. And all those who were involved, in one way or another, came to be known as *Ghadarites* in the later years.

"In one of his stirring speeches, Lala Hardyal said, 'You must get rid of such leaders that behave like peons, running around in the foggy streets of London, armed with infantile petitions, begging the freedom of India from their white masters in an importunate manner. You must also get rid of the fawning bureaucrats who dare sell your birthright, the freedom of India, to their British masters for a modicum of financial gains. And do also get rid of the Rajas and

Maharajas of the so-called princely states who live debauched lives and dance like whores in front of their white owners... Cast aside your thoughts of slavery and break asunder your begging bowls, because freedom is never begged, it is snatched. Take courage and control your weaknesses, and fight like brave men for only the valiant men win the wars... The scourge of British machine guns has generated shoe-licking leaders, agents of the peace of graveyards and as impotent as eunuchs... Violence is preferable to peace if it creates revolutionaries like Guru Gobind Singh and Shiva ji Marhatta...'

"The Federal Government, under enormous pressure from the anti-Indian elements, eventually instituted some new laws which overtly violated the rights of Indians as British subjects. The conditions they forced on newcomers to Canada were:

1. The new entrant from India must prove his/her economic capability to be able to survive in Canada.
2. The new entrant must be highly skilled.
3. The new entrant must come direct from India without breaking the journey in between.

While the first two conditions were a flagrant infringement of the existing laws, the last one was deliberately added because no ships came direct from India to Canada. They had never done it in the past, they didn't do it now, and there seemed no possibility of doing so in the near future. These new laws not only laughed at the new entrants from India but also mocked the ones already living in Canada, reminding them of their worth as slaves. The Ghadar Party – as the 'Hindustani Workers of Pacific Coast' had now come to be popularly known – took these laws as a serious challenge and began to incite their countrymen to defy them. The party, after long thoughts and discussions, reached a conclusion that the defiance should be solid and shattering. And they found the right man to detonate the bomb in Gurdit Singh – a business tycoon from Singapore.

"Gurdit Singh chartered a Japanese vessel, *Kamagata Maru* in Hong Kong and voyaged to India to get the passengers, already waiting, on board. The vessel made its way to Canada via Shanghai, Moji and Yokohama. As the vessel with 376 passengers on board cruised to the Pacific Ocean, the news spread like wild fire from one corner to the other. The Canadian Press, determined not to miss the golden opportunity, proclaimed the cruise as 'an Oriental Attack on Canada'. The vessel reached the Canadian shore in Vancouver, on the morning of 23 May 1914 and was seized by the waiting vigilante group. The authorities allowed only a few passengers, who satisfied their requirements, to land, these were mostly from the Far East; the rest were ordered to go back. The situation turned tense and the passengers, mostly Punjabis, began to panic. The newspapers of the next day gave grisly scoops to generate as much racial hatred as they could. This state of affairs began to worsen by the hour, especially among those whose relatives and friends were in the cordoned off vessel. They were prepared to make all the sacrifices to get them off the ship.

"The Ghadar Party took up the cause and immediately sent telegrams to the Governor General of Canada, to the British Crown, to the Viceroy of India, to Indian leaders in India and England to intervene and get justice done. But nothing at all happened. Then a *shore committee* was formed by the diligent efforts of Indians living in Vancouver. The shore committee succeeded in taking the case to the Court of Appeal of British Columbia only to hear the verdict that they had no right of interference with the work of the Immigration Department. Days and weeks passed by, but the authorities refused to yield to any request. Meanwhile, the Indians in Vancouver, despite their melancholy, did their best to keep the passengers alive by the provision of food and drinks for as long as they were there. The passengers then took control of the ship from the Japanese crew and refused to leave until one day when the Canadian cruisers surrounded the *Kamagata Maru* and issued the warning that they would fire at them if they didn't leave. So, after waiting for exactly two months in Canadian waters, the vessel finally sailed back to the Pacific Ocean.

"Later, the Indian workers in the Dominion Timber Mill, feeling depressed and deluded, conversed desperately with each other: 'We did whatever we could but there was nothing in our control. We organised protests, collected funds, made appeals and took the case to the court of appeal but to no avail.'

'All others from anywhere in Europe are permitted to come here but not our Indian brothers.'

'When, on 23d July, after two month's waiting, the ship went back, we lost our trust in the British. That trust drowned into the waters of the ocean at that very moment.'

"Having witnessed the whole scenario myself, I had grown so unhappy that I had no wish to stay in Canada any longer. But the senior members of the Ghadar Party such as Sohan Singh Bhakna, Lala Hardyal, Jawala Singh, Santokh Singh and Bhagwan Singh Barkattullah thought differently. The way the passengers of the Kamagata Maru, on their way back, had raised ebullient slogans and displayed the courage to fight until the last drop of blood, had left the impression that people were ready for the revolution and all that they needed was weapons, leadership and a solid manifesto. Moreover, the vessel carrying Gurdit Singh and three hundred and fifty or so men must have been in the middle of their journey when the First World War broke out. It encouraged the Ghadarites to gather momentum and stir up an unprecedented rebellion against the British, and set India free. They immediately held a great mass meeting and took some solid resolves: collect funds, send thousands of volunteers to India, launch the revolution and get in touch with all the Indian revolutionaries in India, Germany, Japan and Britain. While funds were being raised and necessary contacts for the supply of arms were being explored, the Ghadarites, after several consecutive sittings, produced a written manifesto. It was also a kind of strategy to be used to find inroads into the army network and awaken them to the mutiny.

"On the Ghadar Party's widespread appeal for Indians in Canada and America to go to India and fight for India's independence, hundreds of them rose to the occasion and offered themselves to the cause. Effervescent with enthusiasm, they spoke about patriotism, freedom and future of their country. They told others that it would have to be now or never. On their way home, they sold the idea to thousands of others in Hong Kong, Singapore and Rangoon, explaining to them how the whites had treated the passengers of the *Kamagata Maru* in Vancouver.

"We learnt later, in the middle of 1915, that over 8000 men had gone to India to stir up the rebellion. They were to commence their struggle in Kashmir, and having liberated it, to go ahead and do the same in the North West Frontier, then Punjab, then Uttar Pradesh and then the rest of India – all in stages.

The secret news came to us that the Ghadarites had distributed thousands of copies of a handout named *Ailan-e-Jang* – or Declaration of War. They had also installed some bomb-making factories in Punjab under the auspices of an expert, Mr Kohli. More news soon touched our ears; special envoys had already left for a number of army centres in India to incite Indian troops, for instance in Mian Mir, Ferozpur, Jacobabad, Jalaldhar, Bannu, Naushehra, Peshawar, Hoti, Mardan, Jehlam, Rawalpindi, Kapurthala, Meerut, Agra, Allahbad and Benares. This exhilarating message made us believe that at long last an opportunity for reprisal had arrived, and that we had nearly done it. Those were the happiest days of my life. But sooner than expected, the news of a very different scenario began to filter through. Quite contrary to what our Ghadar leaders had dreamed, the conditions for a revolution were far from conducive. The attempts of the Ghadarites to achieve some groundwork amongst the peasants had failed miserably. The same fate confronted them in their struggle to incite the army troops to rebellion, notwithstanding the presence of a capable leader, Ras Behari Bose, among them. We were soon apprised of the imprisonment of most of the prominent Ghadarites, with Ras Bihari Bose having left Punjab in utter disgust.

"The Kamagata Maru, on the other hand, on arrival at the *Budge Budge Ghat* harbour, lost eighteen lives to police fire when all the passengers marched out in a procession, chanting angry slogans against the British. Over two hundred marchers were captured and imprisoned while Gurdit Singh managed to escape with twenty-eight men. However, the positive factor was that none of the captured ones offered any apology to avoid incarceration and let down the Ghadarites. Gurdit Singh and his comrades spread throughout the country to disseminate the seed of rebellion in Indian soil.

As for Hardyal, he'd been busy propagating the programme of mutiny amongst the patriot Indians based in Germany, organising the acquisition of funds from the adversaries of the British and the procurement of armament for exportation to India for the Ghadarites to achieve their goal. In the spring of 1914, we were told, he'd met the Berlin-Indian Committee and, through it, the German Foreign Minister Zimmerman. The man not only agreed to provide handsome funds but also issued instructions to his consul-generals in San Francisco, Shanghai and Bangkok to help the Indian revolutionaries in every possible way. The news of such progress made the eyes of the leaders glitter, indicating the way to success. But the first attempt to smuggle arms from America to India failed when, the chartered ship Henry-s, loaded with five thousand revolvers, was captured by the British navy. H.L. Gupta, the man behind the deal, managed to escape and reached Japan to buy arms but the secret somehow leaked out to the British Intelligence, who alerted the Japanese Government. Gupta had to go underground to save his life.

A second attempt to smuggle arms from America to India was made in March 1915. A ship called Annie Larson, stocked with a variety of war-material, was to be met by a tanker, Maverick, carrying some Ghadarites, and transfer the armament from the former to the latter. The latter was, then, to deliver it to the Ghadarites in Sundarbans in East Bengal. But the meeting never took place. The Maverick was captured by British and American warships, and the Annie Larson by the US authorities.

These failures were, not only disheartening but also backbreaking because they led to the mass hunting down and imprisonment of the Ghadarites throughout India. Lifelong jail sentences and brutal murdering of Ghadarites became the order, and the movement failed tragically. But this wasn't a singular movement; Indian revolutionaries were busy on other fronts, too. The Pan-Islamic Movement, the Silk Letter Conspiracy and the Indian Independence Committee (the German Group) formed by Chempa Karaman Pillay in Zurich, were threatening the British with a lot more to come.

"The reason why the Ghadar movement came to meet its end so soon can be traced to two things: over enthusiasm and idealism. Most of the people behind the movement were politically inexperienced and lacked the techniques to fight a war. The ordinary people, who'd gone to Canada and America with the solitary aim of earning money and come back to India to help the cause, were bubbling with zeal but were bereft of any training to fight such wars. To fight an imperial power equipped with the latest weaponry and strategy needed much more than hollow idealism and skin-deep experience.

"However, only a year later, the British Government in India uncovered yet another rebellion 'The Silk Letter Conspiracy' which was meant to overthrow the Raj at least in the northwestern region of

India. This conspiracy owed its birth to the Pan-Islamic Movement. This movement was, perhaps, the direct result of the encroachment by Christianity on the Islamic world and their cultures back in 1950s, whereupon, the movement felt it vital to arouse the Muslims against such usurpation. The Sultan of Turkey, because of his control over an extensive empire and his being the Khalifa or Caliph – the religious head of the Muslim world – was also the leader of the Pan-Islamic Movement. Although the British knew about the developing relations between the Indian Muslims and the Turks, they took them lightly because the Sultan existed only due to them. So, the British treated the movement as a newly found fashion, meant to save Indian Muslims from falling into the trap of Hinduism.

The British saw the potential threat looming large, only after the Turkish Revolution in 1908. The Young Turk Party who now had assumed the leadership of the movement, turned out to be not only radical but also anti-British. The TPW had an encompassing influence over the Muslim youth all over the world, Indian Muslims being no exception. In fact, the British themselves were responsible for many things: their neutral attitude in the Turko-Italian and Balkan Wars of 1911-13, and the anti-Turk and anti-Muslim speech of Prime Minister Asquith in November 1912. While the anti-British stance of the Young Turk Party and the Pan-Islamic Movement began to rankle the British, the inclination of Indian Muslims towards them further pestered their souls, resulting in the evolution of Indian Red Crescent Societies – a guise for the Pan-Islamic workers.

On different occasions, Dr Ansari, Zafar Ali and Mohammed Ali took their delegations to Turkey to further strengthen their bonds. They publicised the Pan-Islamic ideology through the *Zamindar* of Lahore and the Comrade of Delhi. The situation worsened when the Turkish Consul General in India thanked Indian Muslims (in the form of a bequest of a royal carpet to the Badshahi Mosque in Lahore) for their handsome contribution towards the Turkish Red Crescent Fund.

"The worst happened when Turkey entered the War on behalf of the Germans in October 1914. This was coupled with the Sultan's call to the Muslims to commence *Jihaad* – a crusade, against the British, which was misinterpreted by the Muslims as overthrowing British rule in India.

The key members of the Pan-Islamic Movement in India were Dr Ansari, Zafar Ali, Ali Brothers, Maulana Azad, Obeidullah and Mohammed Hassan of *Deoband Madrassa*. They made a plan to attack the northwestern region of India, aided by Turko-German forces. They also designed a plan to appeal to the religious sentiments of the Indian Muslim soldiers in the British army and rouse them against the British. Dr Ansari went to Turkey to meet Ghalib Pasha, the Turkish General, and brought back his *Ghalibnama* – an anti-British order. They made Kabul their strategic base with the Turko-German mission already there, hoping to persuade the Amir of Afghanistan to join hands with them. The great Indian revolutionaries like Mahendra Pratap and Barkattullah were also already in Kabul, helping various elements in the materialisation of their revolutionary plans. The Pan-Islamists had large quantities of anti-British literature in Turkish and German, smuggled into Afghanistan for distribution to Indians. They decided to invade India from the northwest. They made an 'Army of God' with three Patrons, twelve Field Marshals and quite a few Colonels. Madina was to be the headquarters of the divine army with lesser commands at Constantinople, Tehran and Kabul. They had their own spies and emissaries who took their letters to their Indian counterparts. The letters were written in elaborate ciphers and a cryptic script. In August 1916, some of these *silk* letters fell into the hands of the Punjab government, and the conspiracy was exposed.

Gleaning all the bits of information hitherto available and piecing them together, the British came to the conclusion that the three movements were not isolated incidents but the divergence of a single movement, masterminded by a group of experienced people based in Germany. And they weren't wrong. The revolutionaries in Germany had been in close contact with Lahore, Delhi and Calcutta through their Bengali comrades, with the Ghadarites in America through Hardyal, and with the Far East through Barkattullah. Then, in September 1914, C.K. Pillay obtained permission from the German Consul in Zurich to publish anti-British literature. Having produced some documents he gained authority to work through the German Foreign Office. In 1915, he formed a committee of Indian revolutionaries called the Indian Independence Committee, composed of intellectuals of the stature of Hardyal, Lehri, Dutta, Dass,

Barkattullah, Chakabarh, Chattopadhyaya, Mahendra Pratap, and Gupta.

The Committee devised a general master plan for Indian revolutionaries all over the world and some sub-plans for various territories. By one plan, they sent some men and huge amounts of funds to India to be backed by the supply of arms by Germany. The Committee spread its members as far wide as Japan, China, the Phillipines, Siam and Java to ascertain distribution of arms and funds among the revolutionaries. Another plan devised a way for Germans in Siam, accompanied by Indians, to attack Moulin and the Germans in China; dividing into two groups one would join the party in Siam and the other attack Burma, led by the exiled king of Burma. A third plan involved three ships stockpiled with arms, being boarded by German officers and soldiers, and then proceeding to India. Out of those, one ship would carry 500 German officers and 100 soldiers to the Andamans, where they would release all the political prisoners and then head towards Calcutta. The second and third ships would head towards the western coast of India. The timing was such that just as Burma was to be attacked, the revolutionaries in India would attack Punjab and Bengal, and the Pan-Islamists would invade Afghanistan and Baluchistan."

"The plans of the Berlin Group (C.I.R.) didn't succeed. In fact, by now the British Government in India had become very watchful and allowed no screw to be undone in order to crack down on these plans. An armed struggle in India tragically failed to materialise, maybe because the Indian masses were too weary of the ongoing turmoil and were more inclined to find some other alternative instead of an armed revolution."

"Shortly after my marriage with Razia, the 'Home Rule League' of Bal Gangadhar Tilak and his colleague, Mrs Besant – an Irish lady fighting for Home Rule – became a momentous movement, seeking the solution by peaceful means and winning strong support from the Indian masses. The war was still on, and the British, already sick of the three previous movements, didn't tolerate any action, however peaceful. As a consequence, they issued strict instructions to all the provincial governments to take stern measures to curb the mounting political aspirations of Indians. The Madras government took the first initiative and suppressed the peaceful movement by confiscating the

Home Rule League's press, and subjecting Mrs Besant to harsh internment. The action caused a fury and disgruntlement throughout India, and the leaders began to think in terms of a passive resistance movement.

"America had joined the war by this time and the allied forces were trying to please President Wilson by widely publicising his stand for 'the right of self-determination for all the nationalities' as their aim for the war. The subsequent Imperial War Conference in London, appreciated India's support to the British Empire. However, the Secretary of State, Mr Montague's, indirect denial of the right of self-determination to India offered 'some political and constitutional reforms'. This declaration came as a deadly shock to the Home Rule Movement. It was just an empty promise to step up fund raising and recruitment for the war."

O God! What a boring stuff is all this! It's absolutely humdrum, dry-as-dust and monotonous. There's no story, no fascination, no grip and nothing to intrigue you to go on and find what awaits the characters. I'd better leave it, never to recommence or re-undertake such an adventure. All that wheedling and blandishing were mere wastage. But I'm no oracle to have predicted what the huge volume contained. But never mind, we all learn from our mistakes. The time given to me is fast running out. So, I must hurry up and return Kabir's property before he brings some court orders against me for breaching the unwritten contract.

Men and Money

Arjun the fugitive came to Qila Vasudev in the last quarter of 1917. He became as respected a member of the village as anyone else, but at the time of his arrival he was treated with some suspicion. The people of the village took him as an outsider and displayed a sense of distrust towards him and his wife, Drupti; some called him a refugee, others a fugitive and still others, an absconder. No one believed his story then and they simply jeered at him. But it wasn't too long before all that had happened to Arjun came to confront the villagers of Qila Vasudev too, and compelled them to put some trust in him. Even then, all three suffixes kept chasing his name, not so seriously now and only to differentiate him from the other Arjun – Arjun *akhbarwallah* or Puran Singh wallah whose great-great grandfathers had come from Rajasthan in times immemorial.

It was always the case in almost all the villages of the Punjab that, in the case of more than one person with the same name in the village, the people invented some kind of identification mark for each and supper-glued it to his name, making it inseparable even after death. Arjun, the fugitive, knew it and he didn't mind; people only *called* him fugitive or absconder, they didn't treat him like one. And as for the other Arjun, they called him Akhbarwallah or Puran Singh wallah. That sorted everything out.

'Which Arjun are you talking about?' someone would ask.

'Puran Singh wallah,' the other would clarify.

He was also Arjun Akhbarwallah – the one who had a daily paper in Urdu delivered to him and who informed his fellow villagers about the latest happenings in the world, and by dint of whose information, Noordin the dyer, decoded the warnings hidden in the change of colours of the Banyan tree.

Qila Vasudev being on the border of the city of Amritsar and, therefore, somewhat already a part of it, came under the threats facing far-off villages much later than them. A lamp illuminates all the surrounding area except its own bottom because light travels only in straight lines. Qila Vasudev was as much a bottom on which the lamp of money and men stood as was the city itself. The *light* went to the far-off places, one of which was the village of Arjun the fugitive.

Arjun had to take to his heels under cover of darkness to avoid detection and capture by the *zimindar, inaamdar and lambardar.* The story he told the villagers while sitting under the umbrella of the Banyan tree, appeared strange and weird, but was true. Arjun, Puran Singh wallah, filled in the gaps left by Arjun the fugitive to make the story more fulsome and comprehensible. And the story was told and retold so many times by the people that us children got it crammed into our heads word by word.

By the middle of 1917, the war situation had turned very serious for the British. They immediately needed millions of men and colossal funds if they were to win the war. Now there was no question of recruitment of men only by their choice. Rather it was of using whatever force necessary to recruit them, or conscript them. This led to the formation of the Central and Provincial Recruiting Boards. District officers were constrained to excel each other in the recruitment of men and accumulation of funds. A quota system for the supply of men and money at divisional, district, tehsil and village level had been introduced by the civil authorities and any failure to complete the quota within the specified time-limit was severely punished.

The holders of privileged positions in the government, the would-be Khan Bahadurs and Rai Sahibs, and the existing heads and revenue collectors of the villages were all seriously warned to complete the quota assigned to them sooner than later. And it meant the use of force by them to achieve the results because they themselves were being coerced to meet the demands of the government. The leading loyalists, instead of volunteering their own sons and relatives, began to enlist men from lower strata by deception, force and the fake assurance that their families would be looked after in their absence. Hoping to achieve more benefits in future from the British, the toadies surpassed each other in their use of heinous methods to raise funds and recruit men.

The officials, let loose to use any method, began to raid defaulting villages and families with police parties accompanying them. They whisked away men to the recruiting centres, and insulted and humiliated the women for failing to give clues to the whereabouts of their husbands and sons. The force used to get more men and more money was so brutal that the people began to inform on each other. It was moral depravation.

It was during one of these nocturnal raids on Arjun's village that he made a run for it, leaving behind his mother and wife. His father had died a long time ago and he was the only male member in the house to look after his old mother and a newly wedded wife. But the village *labardara*, when he failed to buy Arjun for recruitment despite his hideous traps, asked the officials to catch him while sleeping. And if it were not for a small back door in the end wall of the house, he would've been caught, and conscripted to die in some unknown land in the war. The second factor that helped his rescue was his mother's insomnia, aided by her sharp power of hearing. Seeing through the tricks played by the *lambardar,* she had had the foreboding sense of losing her only son, making her twice as alert as otherwise. When she heard the footsteps of men thumping heavily in the far distance being howled at by some stray dogs, she knew what was coming. Without wasting a second she crawled to her son's bed, woke him up, rolled the bedding away and forced him out of the back door. Arjun's wife, luckily in a separate bed that night, was left dumbfounded by the pace at which things happened. Only a few minutes after Arjun had left in his three items of clothing, a heart-rending bang on their door almost frightened the life out of their bodies.

Arjun's mother, feigning to be deeply asleep, waited for the second, and the third bang before answering. (Arjun was to know later what'd happened after he left).

'Who's it?' she said, warning Drupti to silence and asking her to disappear from sight.

'It's the government, you old crone! Open the door quick!'

'What you want from us at this time of the night?' she said again in her age- beaten and fury-battered voice.

'Don't ask questions you old slut. Open the door or we'll smash it!' roared another piercing voice.

'Wait... Wait.'

She got up, fumbled for her walking stick, found it, rose to her feet and began to drag her scuffing feet towards the door. No sooner did she draw the bolt off the door than six men (three in police uniform and three in civilian clothes) rampaged in, ransacking the whole house, sniffing at every nook and corner, trying to abduct a male called Arjun. And when they couldn't find him, the three constables rounded up Drupti and began to grope her private parts while the three civilians halted the old lady pulling at her scanty hair and hitting her in the face.

'Tell us where you've sent the bastard otherwise we'll kill you here and now,' one of them roared.

'I've sent him nowhere! Maybe the *lambardar* has already got him recruited because we haven't seen him for a week now,' cried the old lady, unable to turn to anyone for help.

'You'll tell! You'll tell,' yelled the other man twisting her arm to her back. The poor lady began to wail her eyes out when the third man caught her by the breasts and wrung them hard, making her scream loudly.

The constables tore apart all the clothes on Drupti's body and began to play ruthlessly, and amid savage laughter, with her naked breasts, squeezing and yanking them harshly. She was trying to cover her genitals only by her tightened legs.

'She won't tell like this. Let me take her in for a ride,' the sturdier looking man said and dragged her into the room. A few moments later, a terrible scream erupted from her mouth and sank, letting only the sobs float in the air, dampened by her tears. The first constable having raised his share of the war-fund gave a turn to the second to raise his quota and he to the third.

By the time they had all finished and left, the first light of the new day was shedding its illumination on the terrible scene. Drupti, gang-raped and torn apart, never retreated within herself and never recovered. Arjun's mother had only a few more moments to live.

As for Arjun, just as he jumped out of the door he saw torchlight coming towards his house from the west, slicing the darkness of the street into shreds. A sudden shock gripped him and, for a moment, he crouched behind a bush to wait for the invisible men behind the torches to turn at the bend of the street that led to their house. Then, just as they took the turn, Arjun sprinted through the fields towards the opposite end of the village, until he reached the highway. Then something appalling flashed in his mind, like sudden lightning, and he stopped. He thought of what they might do to his wife and mother and turned around, determined to reach home before they did. He went a few steps and then stopped again, thinking about what to do. Ambiguity took hold of him. Go home. Run. Run for life. Then his mother spoke to him in his mind, repeating what she had said a few moments earlier, at the instant of forcing him out.

'If you live, we'll live. If you die, we'll die, too. Life's more important than all else. Run, my son, run!'

He turned back and began to run, through the fields, towards the city, now fast, now slow, gasping, out of breath and shattered. When some vehicle passed by on the highway, a quarter of a furlong on his left, he shuddered like mercury. It seemed to him as if each vehicle carried the feringhee or their stooges, informers, toadies and sycophants. Arjun ran for twelve miles at a stretch until he reached a canal. But the bridge that joined the two banks was part of the highway, a quarter of a mile on his left. Crossing the canal by that bridge would be to run the risk of getting caught and punished and conscripted, to be killed in the war by an enemy bullet.

He waited for his breath to become normal, but it didn't. He was tired in the head, heart and limbs. He felt far from normal. Where would he go? The surrounding area was dark and smelled dreary and dangerous. The occasional sound of a bat's batting, the nocturnal live's breathing or a frog yelling sent shivers making him reel to his spine. He'd been out in the dark a thousand times before but had never known such a fear. In fact, nocturnal wanderings had always fascinated him, if only for the fun of them. But tonight was no ordinary night. It had no fun in it. He could hear guns exploding in every direction, even from within his heart. He looked above at the stars, and found them grimly wounded, ready to leave the battlefield and throw themselves in their beds. He saw the crescent moon hanging by the branch of a grave looking tree, ready to drop into the canal anytime. He saw the daybreak marching fast on its way. He must hide himself before that first light. He must, he thought, and began to take his clothes off to swim across the canal. He wound all his clothes round his head and jumped into the water. It felt cold but not cruel and was moving fast but not with the speed of a bullet. Having reached the other bank, he put his three items of clothing back on. Where to go now was the question. And he headed towards Qila Vasudev. He knew just two people there: Bhagat and Kirti.

A war fund of one hundred million pounds was the target for India to meet in whatever way it could. The means employed to meet the target didn't bother either the government or the ones sponsored by it. Extortion, looting, plundering and grabbing raised taxes from 25% to 50%. Door to door campaigns, over-assessment of incomes, taking away the given favours from the privileged and wealthy, withholding the wages of the employees, prosecution and imprisonment in the case of non-payment, severe punishment for hesitation to pay - even if unable - were all quite in order. Everything was fair because it was wartime. Who knew about love?

History repeated itself; it has always done, again and again. Arjuna the Pandva had to flee the wrath of Aheer Dravidian in the city of Dwarka. This city was founded by Krishna who himself had fled the wrath of Jarasandha and Kalyawana who invaded Mathura constantly. Mathura was where Krishna had come to settle from Gokul and Vindravana, killed his maternal uncle, Kans, and reinstated his grandfather, Ughrasen, to the throne. From there, Krishna shifted to Kush-sthali in Swarashtra, an empty land, and founded the city of Dwarka. It was here that Krishna, the God, was finally put to the sword. It was from here that, before dying, he sent a message to Arjuna, living in Hastinapur, to come and save his remaining people from death (most of them had already died fighting among themselves). And when Arjuna was going back, followed by the remaining men and women, he was attacked by the Aheer Dravidians and was robbed off all the women folk of Aryan blood, who then became their wives. Arjuna had to run for his own life, like Arjun the fugitive in our story, leaving behind his mother to be beaten to death and his wife to be gang-raped.

It was the break of dawn when Arjun the fugitive reached Qila Vasudev. He gave a frightened knock at the door of Bhagat Singh and waited for it to open. Bhagat Singh, bewildered at who might be knocking on his door at that hour, and in times when police were rampant in the villages like bandits, hounding the people for money and men, got out of the bed and asked: 'Who's it?'

'It's me, Arjun from Taragarh,' a jittery voice responded.

Bhagat Singh unbolted the door and got him in.

'Who's it?' asked Kirti, his wife, from inside the room.

'It's Arjun from your village,' Bhagat Singh replied.

The next minute, Kirti came out to greet the guest from her parents' village. All three sat down at the wooden *takhtposh*, facing each other, letting Arjun tell what befell him and his family. The other two listened to in an aggrieved silence.

'Let a few days pass by and then I'll go to your village to find out about your mother and wife,' said Bhagat Singh having listened to his worrying story.

'No, you don't have to. I'll go, for I'm a woman and have less risk than you have in the present circumstances,' Kirti said to the amazement of her husband. Women didn't dare travel on their own, even in good health and certainly not while pregnant with only three months to go before parturition.

'How can you with the state you're in?' Bhagat Singh quizzed quite resolutely.

'I'll manage, don't worry. But I must go to the rescue of the two women in trouble,' she insisted.

Kirti feared the prospective forced recruitment of her own husband who was thirty-one, and didn't want to take the risk. Bhagat Singh feared miscarriage, like it had happened last time. At last they reached a decision. Kirti could go accompanied by Chanddi – Bhagat Singh's elder brother, Jagat Singh's wife.

They went the very next morning and came back in the evening with Drupti in a state of terrible shock. The old woman had died the same night because of a strong blow on her face, which had sent her banging against the manger where her head had hit the pole meant to tether cattle. A gaping wound in her skull had taken her life before midnight. Her body had been cremated yesterday when Arjun was telling his story to Bhagat Singh and Kirti. Arjun would know tonight what his wife had been through.

The morning that followed brought with it a gruesome anguish, a dreadful rankling in Arjun's heart and an angry storm capable of causing a horrifying destruction. The episode of heinous cruelty filled Arjun's eyes with burning coal, ready to set everything ablaze – yes, everything, from culture to nature, from lifeless to living, from administration to the administered and from ground to the skies. When Drupti told the story of her brutal rape by the three constables, using three different holes, including her mouth, simultaneously, she wept, sobbed, cried, whined, whinged and wailed in a manner that could rend the rocks asunder. Arjun listened and couldn't breathe, for the air became too thick and heavy. He wondered how Drupti had survived the hideous crime perpetrated by those who had been let loose by the so-called protectors of people. All through the night the husband (21) and wife (19) cried their hearts out through tightened lips, not letting the sounds escape, grinding their teeth, cutting their tongues and pinching their nails into the palms of their hands in locked fists.

We children were to know some years later that there were thousands of Arjuns and thousands of Druptis in the country in those days. And there was no shortage of constables to dance on the fingers of their masters. And what followed was bound to happen too. History was repeating itself because its readers had forgotten its lessons from the past. Everything seemed to be reborn and reincarnated the way Kinner had said.

A Desolate Land

A few years later, Arjun the newspaper-wallah, would make us (Kabir, Kinner, Krishan and me) sit beside him under the Banyan tree and tell us stories of horror that frightened us and brought before our eyes the scenes of half-naked and half-starved men roaming forlornly in the wilderness.

'Although malaria, cholera and plague,' he would begin saying, 'had ravaged thousands of lives in our God-forsaken land during the war years, the epidemic called influenza surpassed all previous maladies in its havoc and all previous proportions in its toll of human life. The monsoon having failed in 1918, the land dried up and fissures grew wider and wider, enough to swallow men and animals alike. The drought gave rise to famine, and famine, in turn, to grave influenza. Human life succumbed to the epidemic to the extent of over 125 millions of which over fifteen millions died in that year. Thousands of villages became bereft of human life and whatever was left of the crops could not be harvested. They were doomed to decay and degenerate in the fields. The medical services were preoccupied by the ongoing war, leaving the civilians to die like cats and dogs. The worst sufferers were the peasants and the poor people living in the cities, unable to pay the private practitioners. The authorities couldn't care or less. Their chief aim was to win the war, which they did in the end. But their indifference and callousness towards us pierced our hearts. They'd collected millions of rupees from us and had forced us to hand over our young men to lay down their lives for them in the war, but they paid no heed to our plight and abandoned us completely to the mercy of fate. We were as desolate as our land. Half-starved and half-naked men and women wandering about in the lanes and by-lanes of towns and cities offered the sight of hell. When the war ended in 1918 and the feringhee came out victorious, we heaved a sigh of relief in the hope that the authorities would now pay some attention to our tribulations. Yes, they did, but in the form of doubling the prices of atta, ghee, dal, spices, vegetables, oils, milk, cloth, sugar and everything else. The only price that fell was that of the human life. It sank to half, quarter, one-eighth and nil. The middlemen, speculators, withholders of stocks, bankers and wheelers and dealers became more prosperous as people like us became more and more wretched. All our hopes were dashed to the ground and we lost whatever spark was left to us after the harrowing war. We grieved in mortification while the feringhee rejoiced in the delirium of their victory. We were afflicted and they sprinkled salt on our running wounds by establishing the Rowlatt Committee to report on why we opened our mouths when we were beaten. The report appeared in papers saying that India's freedom movement was a sum total of banditry, robbery, arson and murder, and that the freedom fighters were anarchists and as much a danger to society as to law and order. The report recommended the strengthening of the executive permanently with the powers it had had during the war under the Defence of India Act' Uncle Arjun stopped and looked above at the sky.

'But why did the feringhee do all that, Uncle?' I asked. 'Because the victory had infected their brains. They had grown arrogant and revengeful. They were dictating their own terms to the vanquished ones in Europe and practised the same thing on us.'

It's only now that I'm able to think that Uncle Arjun was the real Arjun meaning the Victor – one who vanquishes. He spoke with such command on political affairs that we children would brim with appreciation for him. We would exaggerate his skills in his absence, saying, 'Uncle Arjun remembers all the Sanskrit books by heart. Ask him a word and he'll pour out the whole book.'

While Kabir, Krishan and I listened to Uncle Arjun's stories for hours on end, Kinner sneaked away furtively behind the big trunk of the Banyan tree and then vanished never to return later. He did the same today. We thought he had gone for wee-wee and would come back soon but then, after a good fifteen minutes, we realised his usual trickery. However, we never told uncle Arjun when and where he went. Kinner always sat behind uncle Arjun, to keep his options open. Even uncle Arjun didn't seem to bother much about him. Maybe because he was an untouchable. However, uncle never said so. And once Kinner was gone, only I knew where he would be: wandering about in wastelands and talking to the stones.

'Uncle, tell us more?' Kabir the revolutionary said.

'Right…' Uncle would recommence. 'The Rowlatt Committee's report hurt our pride tremendously. The report showed clearly what the government intended to do. It imposed on us criminal investigation agencies, both at central and provincial levels. These were the kind of reforms they'd had in mind and were now undertaking. The feringhee didn't want to grant us any political power at all. The report was followed by the Criminal Law Bill, which would soon became an act with all the emergency powers incorporated in it. The seeds of the Jallianwallah Bagh massacre sprouted from within this. By the power of this bill, all the Indian revolutionaries were to be subjected to expeditious trials by the court of law without any right to appeal. The bill aimed to crush the spirit of Indian nationalism irredeemably. This bill looked down upon us as savages, robbers and bandits, although they too, had a right of appeal over the judgement of the lower court. But our freedom fighters had none. The feringhee themselves were the complainant, witness and the judge. So there would be no appeal and no *daleel* – argument. The Indian dailies and weeklies protested vehemently against this bill and warned the government of dire consequences, but they didn't care.

So, the indignation swelled and swelled till it reached the point of explosion. The whole of India got embroiled in protests, mass-meetings, resolutions and a commotion of other political activities. The idea was to stop the bill from being enacted as law, but nothing happened. In the end, this Emergency Powers Bill was passed and became the Rowlatt Act on 18 March 1919,' Uncle Arjun said, exhaling a long sigh. He looked into our eyes with a bitter smile, as if saying – you see!

'And then what happened next?' asked Kabir with a frown, stroking his fist on his folded knee.

'I've got to go now. We'll talk about that some other time,' he said and stood up to go.

'Rascals!' exclaimed Krishan after uncle Arjun had left.

'Who do you mean?' Kabir blurted out.

'The feringhee!' he replied to appease Kabir who had misconstrued it.

It was the year 1929, ten years on from when all the above happened. I, Arya Gold, was youngest of them all, although younger by one year only. But we had a solid company together, Kabir, Krishan and I. Kinner, although a part of our clique didn't join us when we went to stroll about in the city. When uncle Arjun had left, the three of us felt a little cheated for it was only just past noon, and we were off from school due to the summer holidays. We wished uncle had told us more about the grim episode. The half-left story annoyed us more than the half completed pleased us. It was like having been half-fed or better still, half-starved. Our minds were not at rest and we wanted more, in whatever form, even if it meant some trouble. Then, suddenly, an idea began to float on the surface of my mind, and I caught it by the neck.

'Listen, both of you. Shall we go to the Golden Temple?' I said spiritedly, waiting for them to give their consent.

'That's a great idea, man,' jumped up Kabir. 'What do you think, Krishan?'

'I'd better ask my mother first, or sister Gita.' Krishan displayed reluctance.

'We won't be long. And you're no more a child, man; you're eleven years old. Look at me; I'm only ten,' I said, braving him.

'And if you went home to ask they might not let you,' warned Kabir.

'See, Kabir's right,' I corroborated.

But it wasn't unusual with Krishan, and the reason wasn't too difficult to understand. He had been born after five sisters; had come after a long wait, and that too, after repeated obsequies to thousand and one gods. The family didn't want anything going wrong with him, much less for him to be lost in a crowd or to be run over in a stampede in the throng of the city. Last time he had gone with us, he had done so without permission and, for some reason, we had turned up late. By the time we had reached our homes, the whole village knew Krishan had gone to the city with us. His mother and sisters had been rummaging for him in every corner, enquiring at all known homes, and had been crying in worried sobs. His father, Girdharilal, having learnt of his son's escapades, had tweaked his ears with his hard thumb and the forefinger, so that Krishan had cried for many days afterwards.

'Alright then, you go and ask your mother,' I said. 'We'll wait for you for fifteen minutes, and if you don't turn up we'll leave by ourselves.'

And off he went, walking dubiously. We knew he won't come back, and he didn't.

We headed east, towards the city of Amritsar – a city that was founded by the 4th Guru of the Sikhs in 1577. The foundation of the Golden Temple was also the beginning of the city. The city had developed slowly and steadily over the years, seeing its climax in the hands of Maharaja Ranjit Singh who, by covering its outer tombs with golden sheets, made it the Golden temple. Previously it was called *Darbar sahib* – the Court of the Sublime, the God. Ranjit Singh had the city fortified by a high wall running around the whole city to eschew enemy invasions, leaving twelve gates by which to enter into or go out of the city. Running around the high wall, on its outside, was a deep, water-filled trench to further repel invaders. Everything stands intact even today as it did then. The gate we were heading towards was *Hakimanwalla*. The road from then on would take us straight to the Golden Temple standing in the centre of the city.

Just as we entered through the big gate, as high and wide as that of a big fort, we met a strange bustle of people, unseen in villages. The shops of sweetmeats, groceries, textiles, hardware and many other things, exhibited their stuff very elegantly to attract more and more customers. Hawkers and itinerants ran after you, cosseting and pestering you to buy, reducing the price each time you nodded in unwillingness. On our right hand side, a horseman was calmly letting his horse drink water from within a cemented trough. Right beside the trough a stray cow was standing, ruminating calmly. We looked at pans full of sweetmeats and many other milk products at the confectioner's shop and felt irresistibly hungry. Kabir nudged me in the side of my stomach and wiped his lips with his tongue. But we didn't have much in our pockets. We continued walking through the crowd, stumbling against the ones coming from the opposite direction. We took the right turn at the fork that would take us to the centre of the city. Further ahead there were houses on both sides of the road, intercepted occasionally by a flourmill, cattle-fodder shop or timber yard. The crowd, too, became thinner and thinner as we progressed. Then we saw three horsemen coming towards us from a distance.

'Feringhee!' exclaimed Kabir loudly, as though that was what he was looking for. But to Kabir's disappointment, and to mine, they turned out to be Indian policemen, although looking as sullen as feringhee would. When they went past us, we looked back at them from behind.

'They seem to work for the feringhee, don't they?' Kabir commented.

'Why? Do you want them to work for them?' I retorted immediately. At that remark, we both burst out laughing to tears.

We went past a street on our right, which I knew was called *Naveen Hawelli* because my father and mother had taken me there once to join in a marriage party. The worst happened when my father drank too much and wouldn't go to bed. My mother and I felt very bad that evening. My mother must've felt more than me because I'd gone to sleep soon after, despite all the sounds.

When I told this incident to Kabir, he said, 'Drinking's bad, very bad. It is completely forbidden for a Muslim, and…'

'But your father's a Hindu, isn't he? I interrupted.

'He is, but my mother isn't. She's a staunch Muslim, you know,' he asserted.

'Then why did she marry a Hindu?'

'Because her first husband had died of influenza.'

'Couldn't she find another Muslim husband afterwards?'

'She might have had she tried. But how do I know?' He looked puzzled.

We reached the *Chowk Chirra,* which was again a fork-like square. The road coming from the other side split into two - one on which we were going and the other one to the other side. They both met in the end at Gate Hakiman. We past this bazaar, past Chowk Katra Karam Singh and entered the *Timber Bazaar.* Now we were in the city but not in the centre yet. This bazaar was much busier than the ones we'd left behind. There was a sequence of shops on both sides; half of the bazaar sold predominantly timber and the other half sold half almost everything under the sun. The crowds of buyers and sellers, wheelers, dealers and middlemen thickened as we went further ahead into another square, called *Salt Market Square.* The square itself was pretty narrow but the road widened as we walked further along the straight road leading to the temple. I, Arya Gold, had no idea at the time that when the volcano would erupt and let loose its lava – red-red-red lava boiling at an enormous temperature, it would flow unhindered from Qila Vasudev to here and reduce every palpable thing to ashes, never to turn to life again.

Anyway, in 1929, Kabir and I had entered the city, a city that was now *developing* against the backdrop of tragic happenings of 1919. For a further one-third of a furlong, the wide bazaar thronged with life, equally shared by Hindus, Sikhs and Muslims. As we, elated by everything around, went further ahead, the bazaar narrowed again reducing to a mere quarter of what it was, perhaps even less than that. But the life bubbled as usual, just as in the wide stretch. But it was so narrow that we kept on impinging on and colliding with other people coming from the opposite direction, like goats on a narrow bridge.

'How do they manage in such narrow streets?' Kabir said, as though to himself. It was more of wonderment than a question.

'They seem to like tight things,' I quipped, quite unaware of my words. He looked sharply into my eyes and giggled, and so did I.

'You're *mayeen* cheeky,' he pouted soon after the giggle, using an *Amritsari* swear word which hid more than expressed – a weird abbreviation for mother-fucker.

The narrowness of the bazaar limited our speed to half but we were in no hurry. We continued straight ahead, watching shops of different hues on both sides of the terrain until we reached another square. The bazaar on the right was again wide enough but the one on the left was still narrower and full of shops selling bamboo. We were in the close vicinity of the Golden Temple now and stood in the centre of the city. The bazaar going straight was wider than its counterpart we'd left behind, and was full of sprawling textile shops all the way. My book of preliminary history explained how in the times of Ranjit Singh, experts in various trades, professions and crafts, were invited and encouraged to settle down in the city to make it the commercial home of Punjab. Experts as wide apart as cooks, chefs, embroiders, weavers, carpenters, blacksmiths, goldsmiths, kite-makers, kite-thread makers, dyers, sculptors, horse-shoe makers and fitters, furniture-makers, upholstery-makers and a thousand other types now prevailed upon the city's life.

We entered the Golden Temple from the south side after depositing our shoes at the shoe storage. The next obligation was to rinse clean our feet at the reservoir standing in front of us. Having done that, we entered the main entrance, climbed down the marbled steps and landed on the *parkarma* – the peripheral path going all around the temple that stood in the centre of the pool (*sar*) of water (*amrit or nectar*) giving the city its name. The reflection of the golden building in the pool swayed back and forth, right and left, as the stillness of water succumbed to the wind-aroused waves. We turned left on the peripheral path and continued until we reached the end of this line of the square to discover a fresh water *chhabeel* – a free service provided by the devotees. On the chhabeel, quite a few ladies were serving water in wide pans, which were also being scrubbed clean by another group of devout ladies; the free drinking water service continued unimpeded.

'Let's drink some water,' Kabir whispered to me and took his place in the queue followed faithfully by me. We drank a pan-full each, placed the pans in the belt that carried those brass things to the scrubbing ladies and left.

'We ought to do some service to the community like them, shouldn't we?' I said to Kabir.

'Why do you want to be a copycat? Do it some other way,' Kabir said and looked at me quite satirically.

'What other way?' I asked.

'Like turning the feringhee out of the country,' he replied forthwith.

71

Perhaps, he was right. That would be more than any other service. I wondered how he learned all those things so quickly, more quickly than I did. But it soon flashed into my mind that he was the son of a Ghadarite who wrote ghazals, wrote articles for papers, and was now writing his memoirs. It made me feel envious of him, of Kabir who had such an intelligent father. It was granted that he learnt all those good things from his father – Kundan lal Premi.

As we approached *akaal takht* we saw a white man, or feringhee, talking to a group of young boys much older than us two. He was wearing a hat on his head and his shirt had round collars, which seemed to be tightening his neck to the point of strangulating it. As we approached, we saw a silver cross hanging round his neck, suspended by a cotton thread.

'Who's he?' I whispered into Kabir's ear.

'Looks like a Christian missionary,' Kabir replied.

'How do you know?'

'I know,' Kabir said proudly, '"cos I saw a photograph of one of them in my father's file'. Instantly, I thought of my father: a simple farmer, with no education, yet wanting me to be a lawyer, like one of those whose names he had heard but whose faces he had never seen. We couldn't catch a word of what the missionary was saying to those big lads. Even the lads seemed to be impervious to his sermons for all they said was yes-yes or no-no. I'd begun the study of English language only a year ago and hadn't moved farther than the alphabet yet.

'Do you understand what he says,' I asked Kabir. 'He's barking, that's all I know,' Kabir said and grimaced. He caught me by the arm and dragged me towards the gate leading to the temple itself. It took us almost ten minutes to go in and come out after paying homage to the scriptures consecrating the inner ambience of the temple. Having come out, we took the right turn at the temple gate towards the clock tower.

'We'd better leave the other half of the *parkarma* to come back and cover later, when we come to collect our shoes. Let's go and have a glimpse of the Jallianwallah Bagh now,' I said when we reached the clock tower.

'That's an idea,' Kabir said and smiled. 'Why didn't it come to my mind?' His words gave me some respite, thinking I wasn't completely an idiot after all. And astonishingly, the thought lessened my jealousy for Kabir.

I knew the place quite well because I'd been there twice before: once with the school trip and once with my mother who, like today, having seen the Golden temple had led me to it with my hand tucked into hers.

From the post office, adjacent to the clock tower, we took the road that went straight ahead. After a T-junction we ended up in Jallianwalla Road. We went further ahead and found another 'T' junction where the road going to the left was called Queens Road. This Queens Road had a statue of Queen Victoria in its centre half way down it. On our right hand lay the small street leading into the Jallianwalla Bagh. We wanted to go there but we saw quite a few people gathered on one corner of this junction. It generated in us some curiosity to know what was going on. To our amusement, it was a *tamasha* (a show of jugglery) by a juggler and his assistant, the *jamoora*. The juggler made his jamoora lie flat on the ground, asked him to shut his eyes and put a sheet of cloth over him. Then he turned to the gathering beating a small handheld drum with thread-knots dangling on both sides. He gave it a good beat and began to speak unhindered in a strange rhythmical language.

'Right! My dear appreciators and depreciators, consecrators and desecrators, lovers and haters, world creators, greater than greaters, earlier than laters, confiscators; watchers and waiters, articulators! You've come from far and wide, on waves and tide, to see my superb magic, a luxuriant tactic! My jamoora knows all about you, about each one of you; about what you do and what you don't; about where you live and where you don't; about what you keep and what you don't; about where you sleep and where you don't; about your inner and about your outer, only because my jamoora is a shouter.' He paused and beat the dugdugi (small drum) again and went round in a circle to come back where he was. He began to say again, 'If you want to see the magic crack, go one step back.' The people moved a step back as he commanded them to do.

'Now! Gentlemen; tell me when; you're ready, still and steady? Take some money out of your pockets, some precious lockets, some golden bangles, a rupee that dangles. I'm not being rude – jamoora and me need food!'

73

When he stopped, the gathering burst out laughing, giggling and grinning and more ready to watch what might happen next. Some of them began to fumble in their pockets for change to hand over to the juggler after the show finished. Kabir and I, almost mesmerised, listened to his rhymes and waited anxiously for the next move he would make. Soon the juggler turned towards his jamoora and said, 'Yes jamoora!' The jamoora answered back from under the sheet, his lips moving along with the sheet, 'Yes master!' Then the synchronisation was followed by a sequence of new dialogues.

Juggler: O Jamoora! Do you know?
      Everyone in this crowd though?

Jamoora: Yes master, I know each and every head,
      I know even those who are now dead.

Juggler: If you don't, look at them all,
      Once more take a circle of the stall.

Jamoora: Master! Believe, I know them in and out,
      And know, too, why they are about.

Juggler: Then tell me what this man has in mind?
      (He places his hand on the shoulder of a man)
Jamoora: He wants medicine for his boil in behind.

At that, the whole crowd cracked up, the laughter swelling ceaselessly by the second. We too, laughed our eyeballs out, coughing and snivelling unstoppably. Letting the commotion subside, the juggler recommenced his show.

Juggler: Jamoore! Turn round and see again,
      Numerous faces aren't here in vain.

Jamoora: Nothing to worry about, Master, 'cause I,
      Was made by the feringhee the best of spy.

Juggler: Then tell us where is this man's wife?

The Volcano

(The juggler strokes his finger on another man's shoulder)
Jamoora: With her boyfriend she's enjoying her life.

They all cracked up again like a balloon in the mid-air. And the man who'd become the target became invisible in a matter of seconds. Then the juggler beat his *dugdugi* again and declared, 'That's all for today. God will give you what you'll pay. All the gurus and saints said, do good always and forget.' The jamoora was up on his feet by now and they both circled around to get the *inaam* (awards) being dropped into their wide spread, hand held bags. People put in what they had or what they could afford. Kabir and I made our way to the Jallianwallah Bagh amidst hearty laughter.

We entered the bagh through a very narrow lane, wide enough to let one person pass if another was coming out. An exposed gutter, flowing in its middle, divided the lane in two equal halves. The lane was made of brickwork and had on its sides huge walls, stretching as high as 40-50 feet, all made of solid brick. At the apex of the lane was a patch of high ground extending a few feet and then dropping down into the ground strewn with stones, pebbles, bricks and some stray logs of wood. There was no grass to be seen like there would be in a proper bagh or garden. It was rather a bare ground undulating at different places and resembling a desolate patch of wilderness wasteland.

There were half-a-dozen other people roaming around and looking at things while an equal number were lying supine on the bare ground. We stood at the high ground and cast a scrutinising glance all around the bagh and at the walls that surrounded it. To the bare eye, the bagh looked approximately 160 yards deep and about 115 yards wide with an abnormal, asymmetrical shape. The left side was specially so. At the far end, a few feet removed from the centre, stood a *samadhi* (a small make-shift mausoleum) with four small trees on its left. On the far left, a few feet this way from the central line stood three small trees and a well with a round wall almost three feet high. The very high wall right opposite to where we stood, carried scores of holes, dug into the brickwork. We were stunned and rushed to stand at the bottom of the wall, looking up at the deep diggings. They were orifices notched by bullets, as big as three to four inches each. The perforated wall told the story of days gone past.

These holes, apparently, were dug by the bullet-shots, which failed to find humans as their targets. Astray as they were, they had found their marks in the brick-wall rather than in bare breasts, stomachs, legs, arms and heads. The sight provoked fear and anger, consternation and vexation. We stood there watching each gape for over an hour, maintaining a dim and dreary conversation between us, crying quietly over the fate that had dawned upon the innocent people on 19th April 1919.

Girdharilal, Krishan's father, had witnessed the whole scenario from above this wall. He had been telling the story for many years now. The story floated in the village air and got stuck at the Banyan tree, like a stray kite. On another day someone brought it down to let it float again in the heavy air under the Banyan, thickened by the listeners, crying their hearts out. We, the village children, had heard the story a dozen times.

After having sliced the air beside the high wall into shreds by our grieving sobs, we turned to our right to approach the long wall about six feet high, that ran the whole depth of the bagh. This wall didn't have too many marks of bullet shots on it, obviously because the shots had found their human targets as they tried to clamber up the wall and jump to the other side, but in vain. The bullets found their targets creeping up, standing on the wall ready to jump to the Jallianwallah Road, half hanging on this side and half on the other, merely waiting their turn to climb, or pulling others down in a vague effort to save themselves from the jaws of death. The stories we were told kept coming back to us while we stood nonplussed watching the wall. The whole scene flashed and re-flashed in our minds' eyes like watching a film being played and re-played.

After that, we turned back and went straight to the opposite end to see the well. Leaning over its circular, raised wall, we peeped into the depth of it. The sight was dark and eerie. We shuddered with apprehension, thinking how many scores of people including men, women and children might have dared to jump into this mysterious well to be choked to death. But perhaps the fear of the bullet was more overwhelming than that of the well. Uncle Girdharilal told us that the people even climbed on the trees, only to be shot and drop dead on the ground.

The wall behind the trees on the other side of which ran Lakkar Mandi Bazaar leading to Sultanwind Gate, had another alley, narrower than the one we had entered through, called *Neevin Gali*, the Lower Street. This wall too, had scores of bullet marks gaping like open wounds, imploring for justice, a commodity always denied to the dominated ones. Kabir and I touched everything, the walls, the trees and the well, and felt their pain and anger in our souls while we trembled with disgust, abhorrence and nausea.

The sun was striding fast to jump into its grave at the far horizon. And before the ghosts of thousands of men, women and children came to laugh their contorted laugh at us we thought it better to run away from here for all other people had left long ago. The Jallianwallah Bagh had begun to haunt me and it would do so for years to come.

Mahatma's Call

The stories, as I said earlier, were hung in the air, and on the Banyan tree and across the rivers and canals in the length and breath of the country. You had to go nowhere in search of them, rather they came to you and displayed themselves in front of you in stark nakedness. If you had an eye to see them, you did; if you didn't you were unfortunate. There was no need to pluck the stories from the village air or off the Banyan tree like its fruit. They were so ripe that they fell down for you to catch and start reading, like a leaf from a book. Every leaf of the Banyan tree had a significant story to tell and the leaves always fell chronologically– the older ones first. The leaf that plummeted into my lap one day had the following story to tell.

When all the efforts of Indians failed to soften the obduracy and insolence of the government to withdraw the Rowlatt Bills, a decrepit ascetic came out in the open, proclaiming that the soul-force was mightier than the physical and the material one. Of course, it was a laughable thing. This tiny man with a loincloth around the area of his groin, had already won many victories experimenting with truth, ingenuity and benignity. Soon after his emergence in the political arena, people derided him, saying: 'The name of helplessness is Mahatma Gandhi.' And they were perfectly right because every satire has a grain of bitter truth hidden in it. Mahatma asserted that if violence was used as a means to wrest power from the British, the latter would use the tremendous military might of the whole empire to crush the effort, leaving the Indians demoralised and prolonging their subjugation for many more generations to come.

'The means employed are more important than the ends,' he said one day. 'We should pay more attention to our means, keep them pure and above board, whatever the result. It is not the achievement of the goal that counts so much as the means applied to achieve that goal or objective.'

After countless sleepless nights, Mahatma chalked out a strange plan, which he named *satyagraha*. It was meant not only to oppose the Rowlatt Bills but, more than that, was a plan to fight the hitherto mightiest ruler without the loss of men and means, so as to continue the struggle until the mightiest was ousted. Soul-power was at the root of this movement: no bloodshed, no violence and no more obedience. And the way of working: no diplomacy, no untruth and no concealment. 'I do not believe in working for a public cause from behind the veil of secrecy,' he proclaimed.

Despite Mahatma's letter written to the Secretary to the Viceroy on 20 February 1919, the government divulged no interest. They remained as intransigent as ever. Then on 23 February, Mahatma declared the launch of satyagraha on 1st March 1919. A long letter and a pledge about the movement appeared in all the newspapers. Uncle Arjun saved a copy of the letter and the pledge, which was sent to the government by the Mahatma. I borrowed the copy from uncle Arjun, and I suppose I should let you see it.

"I enclose herewith the Satyagraha Pledge regarding the Rowlatt Bills. The step taken is probably the most momentous in the history of India. I give my assurance that it has not been hastily taken. Personally, I have passed many a sleepless night over it. I have weighed the consequences of the act. I have endeavoured duly to appreciate the government's position. But I have been unable to find any justification for extraordinary bills. I have read the Rowlatt

Committee's report. I have gone through its narrative with admiration. Its reading has driven me to the conclusions just the opposite of the Committee's. I should conclude from the report that secret violence is confined to isolated and very small parts of India, and to a microscopic body of people. The existence of such men is truly a danger to the society. But the passing of the bills, designed to affect whole of India and its people, arms the Government with powers out of all proportion to the situation sought to be dealt with, is a greater danger and the committee utterly ignores the historical fact that the millions in India are by nature the gentlest on earth.

"Now look at the setting of the bills. Their introduction is accompanied by certain assurances given by the Viceroy regarding the Civil Service and the British commercial interests. Many of us are filled with the greatest misgivings about the viceregal utterance. I frankly confess I do not understand its full scope and intention.

"If it means that the Civil Service and the British commercial interests are to be held superior to those of India and its political and commercial requirements, no Indian can accept the doctrine. It can but end in a fratricidal struggle within the Empire. Reforms may or may not come. The need of the moment is a proper and just understanding upon this vital issue. No tinkering with it will produce real satisfaction. Let the great Civil Service Corporation understand that it can remain in India only as its trustee and servant, not in name but in deed, and let the British commercial houses understand that they can remain in India only to supplement her requirements and not to destroy indigenous art, trade and manufacture, and you have two measures to replace the Rowlatt Bills. They, I promise, will successfully deal with any conspiracy against the State. Sir George Lawndes simply added fuel to the fire when he flouted public opinion. He has forgotten his Indian history or he would have known that the Government he represents has before now surrendered its own considered opinion to the force of the public opinion.

"It will be now easy to see why I consider the bills to be an unmistakable symptom of a deep seated disease in the governing body. It needs, therefore, to be drastically treated. Subterranean violence will be the remedy applied by the impetuous, hot-headed youths, who will have grown impatient of the spirit underlying the bills and the circumstances attending their introduction. The bills must intensify the hatred and ill will against the State of which the deeds of violence are undoubtedly on evidence. The Indian covenanters, by their determination to undergo every form of suffering, make an irresistible appeal for justice to the Government towards which they bear no ill will. They provide the believers in the efficacy of violence as a means of securing redress of grievances, with an infallible remedy; a remedy that blesses those that use it and also those against whom it is used. The covenanters know the use of this remedy; I fear no ill from them. I have no business to doubt their ability. They must ascertain whether the disease is sufficiently great to justify the strong remedy, or whether all milder ones have been tried. They have convinced themselves that the disease is serious enough and that the milder measures have utterly failed. The rest lies in the lap of the gods."

The Satyagraha Pledge submitted reads as follows:

"Being conscientiously of the opinion that the bills, known as the Indian Criminal Law (Amendment) Bill No. 1 of 1919 and the Criminal Law (Emergency Powers) Bill No. 2 of 1919, are unjust, subversive of the principles of liberty and justice, and destructive of elementary rights of an individual on which the safety of India as a whole and the state itself is based, we solemnly affirm that in the event of these bills becoming the law and until they are withdrawn, we shall refuse civilly to obey these laws and such other laws as the committee to be hereafter appointed may think fit, and we further affirm that in the struggle, we will faithfully follow truth and refrain from violence to life, person or property."

But the authorities refused to cast their belief in the gospel of satyagraha and passed the Criminal Law (Emergency Powers) Bill on 18th March 1919 with the assent of the Viceroy and against the strong opposition of the people. Then, on 24th March, the Mahatma pronounced to the world: '... When a nation feels that any particular legislation is a national degradation, they have a clear duty to discharge. In the countries of the west, when the governors did a wrong, there ensued bloodshed. In India, on the other hand, the people instinctively abhor the doctrine of violence. In such circumstances, by what other means can they impose their will on the government? The answer is satyagraha – the force of truth, the force of soul.'

The mythological tale of Prahlad was powerful enough to perpetuate the zeal and bravery of the people; this was the tale they had been brought up on. Prahlad's father, Hirnakush, had acquired all the godly powers and was bestowed with a boon that he would never die: neither in the day nor at night; neither at dawn nor at dusk, neither inside nor outside; neither in light nor in dark. Thus he proclaimed himself to be mightier than the mightiest – the God. Everyone in his empire acknowledged him as Supreme God except his own son, Prahlad. At this, Hirnakush sentenced his son to be killed by embracing a red-hot pole. And when Prahlad was asked to embrace the hot, glowing pole, he saw an ant creeping up it and understood the might of God. He promptly put his arms around the beam without the slightest scathe. Hirnakush grew wild at that and conspired another plan to kill him. Hirnakush's sister, Holkan, also had the boon of never to be killed by whatever calamity, not even by fire. So he ordered Prahlad to be placed in her lap and set the two on fire. Again the miracle happened: Hirnakush's sister was reduced to ashes, but Prahlad emerged unscathed. In the end of the tale, Hirnakush was killed by a mightier one in the threshold of his palace (neither inside nor outside), at the time when it was neither day nor night, neither morning nor evening but between the two. So, Prahlad won all the battles without irreverence or ill will or disaffection for his father. All he did was disobey the commands of his perverted father and to stick to non-violence; he came out victorious. He defeated all his wicked moves by the force of truth, or by the force of his soul.

Prahlad was perhaps now reborn in the frame of the Mahatma. How could I prove my old friend Kinner wrong? The feringhee was reincarnated as the avatar of Hirnakush (full name: Hiranaya Kashapu), considering *himself* mightier than the mightest and the Mahatma was his non-believing son; the former was mendacious and the latter ingenuous. And the battle was to be fought between the two forces; one was to show *his* might and the other his tolerance – war between bad and good as usual. The means to be applied by *the good* were to be peaceful, non-violent and non-co-operative or disobedient,

81

while the ones to be applied by *the bad* were to be warlike, violent, and punishment for the disobedience.

I thought of seeing Kinner at this point of my story who, I knew, wouldn't be found at his home for it was already past evening. I knew where he would be found – most certainly at the office of 'Who's Harijan?' in the city. So, I tidied up all the papers I had scribbled thus far and locked them up in a steel trunk as I always did after my day's work. Probably I'd grown too tired of scribbling and was also sick of the hot heavy air inside the house and wanted to fill my lungs with fresh oxygen from the breeze I hoped was blowing outside. I had thought that a frolic of this kind would do a lot good to my health and enable me to get away from home and the back-breaking work; an enviable rendezvous with nature and its free gifts. It would make me meet Kinner to assess his progress with his anti-thesis of Prahlad – I mean the Mahatma. Last but not least, it would grant me a good round of the city. And just as the image of our city took shape in my mind, *my* sweet-sweet Sonia came to occupy the front seat in the scene. I tell you what, this summer of 1939 was very embarrassing for me. My mind sprinted faster than my legs, my heart throbbed more heavily than the thump of my feet and my lungs craved more for oxygen due to the sultry summer than did my body for blood.

When I finally left for the city, I felt more oppressed by the perspiration that drenched my armpits and my groin area. My underwear grew sweaty and sticky and I began to think of buying a loincloth like that of the Mahatma. The doctrine working behind the philosophy of a loincloth was to wear something tight, instead of loose underwear through which the sweat dripped freely, to tickle you while you walked. A loincloth, tight as it could be, was capable of suffocating all your sweat-generating pores, making them unable to weep. Though the idea was superb, it lacked practicality in my case because I had, as yet, no intention of being associated with ascetics and *sadhus,* who were doomed to renounce the world after enjoying everything profusely. On the other hand, I wanted to get married, explore that part of life and have children before I emasculated myself with the strangulating outfit.

Fortunately, I found Kinner at his seat with his head swooped upon a sheet of paper on which his right hand - sturdy stout and heavy like a rock - scrawled on and on.

'So, there you are, caught in the campaign of abnegating Mahatma's invention of Harijan,' I pinched his nerve. Kinner seemed to have been disturbed and distracted, for when he looked up at me his forehead frowned, eyes grimaced and the wide nose snorted like that of his brother's donkey.

'Why are you determined to chase me to the hell-hole?' he blurted out peevishly, and without as much courtesy as to show even a borrowed smile on his face, let alone offering me a seat.

'It's a sheer disgrace to me to be treated like shit. What worth is your sculpture and your painting and this business of dying the innocent white sheets of paper with ink if you can't even show some hospitality to an old friend?' I felt compelled to vomit all the venom out on him that his untoward words had generated in me.

'Friend? My foot! I'm seeing you today after you met Radhika that evening when she gave you a copy of our paper. Do *you* call it friendship? You're a slur on the name of friendship, man. I'd guessed you'd see me the very next day, but you wouldn't come, would you? And yet, you call yourself a friend and a *storyteller*? What kind of a story is this?' He belched his venom back on me.

'Why couldn't *you* come to see me if I didn't? Are you suffering from some bloody superiority complex of being a better artist than I am? Or an inferiority complex that you can't face me for some reason?' I spat some more poison.

'Shut up you idiot, and sit down!' Kinner said and spurned my advances.

'Thank you for the warm welcome!' I said satirically and took the chair.

'Now, shut your pout and keep quiet for two minutes and let me finish the last sentence. The article has to be published tonight,' he said and leaned back on the sheet of paper with his elephant-hand holding the pen and scribbling. I felt utter pity for the pen that seemed to be gasping in the tight grip of his thick thumb and two fingers.

While he was engaged in completing his sentence I busied myself turning the pages of the recent issue of 'Who's Harjan?' – *'Harjan Kaun?'* The headline on the top of the first page read: 'The

Second World War looms large on the horizon'. I didn't care to read the details. The second news on the same page went thus: 'The plural society rejects minority decisions.' The headline constrained me to go through the text. It said that the plural society consisted of the downtrodden, the real heirs of the country and the minority of Aryans had no business dictating their terms on them or behaving as their masters. They, the Dravidians, were deprived of their rights as equal owners of the country and were yoked to serve the Aryans like animals. The Harijans were 'Jans' and not 'Harjans' as Mahatma put it. They wouldn't fight the feringhee, just as they hadn't fought the Muslim invaders in the past, because what they were expected to fight for didn't belong to them in the first place. The Aryans had taken the country away from them by force. They had been left with no motivating force or will to fight. Let only those fight to whom the country belonged. The story further emphasised that the plural society should be allowed an equal share in land and power and their exploitation by the so-called upper class Hindus should be stopped forthwith.

'How far have you reached with your story?' Kinner asked me, collecting his pack of finished papers together.

'To Mahatma's satyagraha after the Rowlatt Act.'

'I tell you what ... ' he left the sentence uncompleted and stood up to hand the papers to the typist in the other room. I tried to guess what he might say. But before my guess even took off, he was back.

'I tell you what, you're far behind the times. We're passing through 1939, not 1919. Deal with the problems we're facing today and not with the ghost of the past. The past is dead and done with, the future is uncertain; the only reality is the present.' He delivered a small speech while tidying up his desk.

'I don't work with a newspaper conditioning me to concentrate on the present only. And if the past is completely useless then what's the use of running a paper? Every issue gets thrown into the dustbin of yesterday, doesn't it?' I offered a counter-argument posing some questions.

'No. An immediate past is as good as the present, even more relevant than the present. The present can't be shaped without information about the past of yesterday. But you're wallowing in the far past, which is quite irrelevant for our purpose now.'

'Just as the history of antiquity, which you claim always repeats itself, is irrelevant. Is that what you want to say?' I mocked at him.

'Why do you have such a thick brain, *yaar*? Every present is rebirth of the past; that's what I've always said. The present represents the past, or the past manifests itself through the present. I treat the past as a graveyard of the dead, the souls of whom have now come to live in the present. Deal with the living souls and not with the dead bodies. That's what I urge you to do. Do you understand, you thick head?' he reprimanded me.

I knew he would be boiling over with his own philosophy when I met him. He was always like that: one-track mind. It seemed that the history of generations of his ancestors' sufferings at the hands of Brahmins and high-caste Hindus had made him an angry man. His insolence had its own authentic reasons, which could not be refuted. I had absolutely no intention of provoking his ill feelings for me any more than they had appeared thus far. My idea in seeing him this evening was to ask him for his opinion about the gospel of satyagraha. I thought it better to come to that point.

'Of course, I have a thick head unlike yours, which is full of cow-dung passed on to you by the generations. But tell me something about Mahatma's satyagraha. I mean how did the authorities take that challenge in 1919?'

'What satyagraha are you talking about?' He flared up again, as though the smouldering fire in him waited only for the touch of a burning matchstick.

'The one he commenced shortly before the massacre of Jallianwallah Bagh,' I reminded him.

'I *know* that but what do *you* want to know about it?' he stressed the words 'know' and 'you'.

'I mean, did this movement trigger off the later troubles?'

'Look! One who vanquishes in a World War is under no obligation to take dictates from the vanquished ones. Although we're not the ones who were defeated, our position was worse than the defeated ones because of our slavery. Did the Aryans take any dictates from Dravidians? Or did the Brahmin show any mercy towards the *Sudras*? And who made *Sudras* of the erstwhile noble citizens of the country? Only the wearer knows where the shoe pinches. None of you can know the pain and suffering that was inflicted upon us. And this Mahatma of yours calls us *Harijans*. Doesn't this word, this discriminatory word, cause yet more afflictions on already rankling souls? Sons of fucking God, my foot! Are they themselves bastards? Or are they the sons of the devil? They must be if we're the sons of God.' Kinner was out of breath and began to gasp.

'Thank you for your long and eloquent speech and your strictures on the Aryans, the Brahmin and the high caste Hindus, but perhaps I asked you something else,' I said a little satirically. He saw through it.

'You asked me fuck all, to which I offer no answer. Will you now shut your gab and leave me alone to get on with my work?' Kinner declared his wish and bounced up and out of the chair as if ready to bounce me out of the window. I was flustered for a brief moment but then recomposed myself and tried to cool him down.

'Easy man, easy! Shall I sprinkle some cold water on your seething head or buy you a plate of ice cream to soothe your burning intestines? I have the money,' I said mischievously and showed him some odd coins, spreading them on my palm. 'Stop this sarcasm, will you?' he said morosely and began to look at something else.

'I'm not being sarcastic, *yaar*. I honestly mean it. Let's go downstairs and into the bazaar,' I assured him. Then at once, I stood up, held his hand warmly and began to pull him softly towards the staircase. Kinner complied meekly, his face a little less sullen than a moment ago.

The floor of the bazaar was still emitting the sweltering heat that it had absorbed from the sun during the day. Kinner's office was between the Jallianwallah Bagh and the Golden Temple, almost equidistant from both. 'Shall we go to Guru Ramdas *saraan* (inn)?' I asked him, ingratiatingly.

'I don't mind,' he replied briefly. But he appeared more poised now. And quite suddenly, a thought flashed in my mind that the dream of ice cream had worked long before its actual taste. The thought made me laugh but only inwardly. I didn't have the nerve to offend him any more by sharing it.

The time was quarter to eight in the evening and the shops were in the process of closing down but hadn't really done so yet. The hustle and bustle on the roads had increased due to eleventh hour shopping, especially for things you couldn't wait overnight. We went under a bridge and persisted straight along that road. The bazaar on our right hand had a chain of shoe shops on both sides. They sold Punjabi shoes – *juttian*: plain ones, embroidered, hard leathered and soft leathered and limitless other varieties. In the bazaar, through which we were going, there were shops and offices of various Punjabi magazines, weeklies and monthlies. We turned left at the apex and then right a little after. This was bazaar Guru Ramdas *Saraan*. There were restaurants on the right hand side while the *saraan* or the inn stood on the left. The inn, as it was said, was very commodious and had hundreds of rooms and a spacious hall in the centre – all to accommodate pilgrims to the Golden Temple who would pop in, in thousands, from far and wide on two special occasions: Dewali and Vaisakhi. In addition to the inn, the Golden Temple itself had hundreds of rooms for the same purpose, on its three sides, called *boongas*.

There were quite a few hawkers with mobile shops, selling a variety of food and drinks. We soon caught sight of the one selling *faloodawalli kulfi* or ice cream garnished with syrup made from vermilion, in clay pots. We felt irresistibly thirsty and hungry at the sight of the goody. Quite a few men, women and children were already eating the stuff with their faces evincing extreme delight as an aftermath of each morsel.

'How about that, Kinner?' I asked him pointing my finger to the mobile shop.

'Go on then!' he goaded me.

I ordered two *kasoras* (clay pots) of *faloodawalli* ice cream and waited, along with Kinner, on one side. The hawker and his two assistants were really working fast. People came, ordered, got the dishes, ate and went, giving their space to the newcomers. Our order was soon supplied to us. Even the smell was so gorgeous that it filled our nostrils with fragrance. The taste was superb, too, especially in the heat of the dusk that scorched and shrivelled you. We enjoyed every bit of the stuff and felt our parched insides cooled down. No sooner had we finished eating and placing the empty clay pots in their marked place than I saw Surinder and his sister Sonia coming towards us from the side of the Golden Temple's main entrance opposite to that of the inn. Something inside me got churned up and a frisson ran deep into my heart and soul. I found myself caught in a state of ambivalence whether to meet them or ignore them. Sonia looked charming in her greyish *salwaar kameez* and *chunni* and the sight of her tempted me to ogle her glamorous figure for a prolonged while. But the presence of Surinder with her and Kinner restrained me. As a result, I turned my gaze away feigning interest in something in the shop behind us to let them both go unnoticed. However, I watched obliquely, making sure they went past unaware. But I wasn't lucky enough that evening. Surinder noticed me and suddenly placed his hand on my shoulder from behind, sending me reeling. Sonia went past us and waited at a distance, rooted in front of a shop of textile goods.

'What's up, man? Why are you staring at me with such a puzzled gaze?' Surinder asked, grinning at me and stroking my shoulder twice with a hard hand.

'Oh, Surinder! How are you? I'm pleased to see you, man,' I immediately put on a new face and pretended to be so happy to have seen him. Kinner kept reading me all the while.

'I'm fine and in one piece, my boy. How are you?' He gave another strong stroke on my shoulder, as if to a stout horse after day's work.

'I'm not too bad. Meet my friend, Kinner, from my village. And he's Surinder, from my school days, Kinner.' I introduced them to each other.

They shook hands, smiled and engaged themselves in desultory talk while I furtively endeavoured to catch a glimpse of the distant beauty who now seemed to be flouncing with impatience for her brother to hurry up. Had I been alone, Surinder might have extended me an invitation to go home with them but at this moment he only said, 'Come home sometime, yaar!' The sentence meant that he had to go now, and I myself wanted him to leave because the longer he stayed, the more restless would Sonia grow in waiting.

'I will, sometime,' I replied with another fabricated smile and waved my hand when he took the first step away. Just about then, Sonia happened to look at me but just when my eyes met hers she stole her gaze away scornfully, leaving me staggered. Would I call that my unrequited love? I had no idea. Perhaps it was.

'Shall we go back to the office or have you something else to attend to?' Kinner woke me up from my somnolence, from my delirium of gloomy sadness.

'Let's go!' I replied and followed him, a few feet behind, obsequiously.

We took all those turns back again and reached the staircase of his office mounting direct from the road. I had lost my composure and didn't want to get engaged in any conversation subsequent to what had happened.

'Kinner, I'll see you some other time. Maybe at your home,' I said mournfully and advanced my hand to him for a shake.

'What's happened to you all of a sudden, man?' Kinner asked, directing his big eyes at me, which I managed to avoid by looking down at the road.

'Nothing particular, *yaar*. It's just...' I could say no further. In fact, I'd never shared such secrets with him. He was a different type of man, a kind of missionary. I wanted to evade his company for the duration of this emotional stir, just in case I yielded to his wheedling, which he might have done had I stayed longer.

'There *is* something my boy. It's a different thing if you don't want to trust me.' He threw the bait but I refused to take it.

'Nothing at all, *yaar*! Right, I'll see you then,' I said the last words, waved my hand and took to the road instantly.

A few days later, when I'd recovered my lost equanimity, I went to see uncle Arjun to return his copy of Mahatma's published letter and the pledge of satyagraha. He was at home but a little sad and run down.

'Why, what's wrong, Uncle?' I asked, sitting by his side on the bare cot, and without even greeting him properly.

'No, nothing. Only a slight fever. Don't worry, it's nothing unusual. How are you, anyway?' Uncle spoke in an enervated tone, not matching his usual zeal.

'I'm quite fine,' I said and handed him an envelope containing his belongings. He held the envelope in his hand for a second, looking at it in surprise, wondering what it might be. Then suddenly he had his memory back.

'Oh, that letter and pledge!' He muttered and put the thing on the cot. 'So how's your scribbling going on?'

'Still struggling,' I said, and smiled faintly and added, 'I want to know a few things, Uncle, if you…'

'Yes, yes, ask me. I'll tell you if I know it.' And I could see that his vivacity was returning, if only partly.

'In fact, Uncle, you've told us about it a few times before but at the time we were only children and forgot all the facts, retaining only the vague impressions,' I offered a justification for pestering him again. He knew what I meant by 'us'.

'How are all your friends, Krishan, Kinner and Kabir?' he asked while his eyes, focused on the wall opposite, trying to grasp something, perhaps the traces of the days gone past.

'They're all fine, Uncle, all grown up.'

'That's the trouble. As children, you were quite manageable, and I could make you sit and fill your heads with wider concerns but now … now you're all grown up and busy in your own ways. But then, that's how it happens with all of us, generation after generation. I don't need to complain. Maybe old age makes you a child again, to have tantrums,' he said and began to laugh. I only smiled back in reverence. Then, all at once, he sounded recomposed.

'Ask me what you want to ask.'

I began to search for words for the exact question to save him the trouble of going into too many details. 'Well, what were the findings of the Disorder Inquiry Committee in 1920?' I finally asked.

Uncle Arjun thought for a few consecutive moments, rubbing his forehead with the fingers of his right hand and then began to speak. What he explained to me in a sitting of almost three hours can be epitomised in a few words.

The Government had pleaded before the Disorders Inquiry Committee that the British Empire in India was facing a grave danger, both from outside and inside and, therefore, the action at Jallianwallah Bagh was absolutely justified. According to them, there was danger from Russia where a revolution had taken place in October 1917; the country had fallen into the hands of Bolsheviks who wanted to destroy the British Empire. Thus, their sole aim was to crush all opposition of whatever hue, and maintain and prolong the Empire. Perhaps, they also wanted to settle scores with the militant revolutionaries who had triggered off the political awakening amongst the Indian masses. To win world opinion in their favour, they also levelled allegations against the peaceful movement of satyagraha, saying that the Mahatma was deriving support from Afghans, Bolsheviks, Germans, Japanese and Turks, backed by the remainder of the Ghadarites. As rulers, they were determined to unleash terror on one pretext or the other. Michael O'Dwyer, the Lt. Governor of Punjab, was perhaps the keenest among all the bureaucrats to stage a showdown as soon as possible.

The Government also fabricated a story that the Japanese and Bolsheviks had made Amritsar their headquarters, were being supported by the Independent Labour Party of England, and together they were planning to exterminate the British Empire in India. And the first opportunity to stage a severe showdown was taken in Amritsar at Jallianwallah Bagh, when a peaceful meeting of 20,000 people was randomly fired at with 1650 rounds by 50 soldiers, killing over 2000 at the spot and leaving thousands injured, mutilated and doomed to die in the aftermath. Yes, aftermath: trampled over and suffocated under the heaps of the dead.

The Story Board

Kinner's father, Bharat Chand, had died in the Jallianwallah Bagh, killed by a shot through his chest. He was forty-two at the time. Reshma had brought his body home with the help of two villagers and had cremated it amid raucous wails, thumping her breasts and cheeks with both her hands. Kinner was then one year old, like Krishan and Kabir, and I was only just born. Bhagat Singh and Jagat Singh too, were there listening to the *jalsa* – meeting. They still wonder how, by sheer luck, they survived the carnage. They have told the story of the macabre terror that had been unleashed and that of their survival scores of times in the last twenty years. Girdharilal, Krishan's father, witnessed the catastrophe from the roof of his shop, reclining slightly against the high wall, protecting himself against a stray shot. It was the same high wall that Kabir and I had seen a few days ago, and which carried dozens of gaping holes dug into the brickwork by bullets unable to find their targets in flesh and bones. The story he told was a heart-rending and horrifying one. Let us listen to Girdharilal first.

Swaran Chandan

Girdharilal's Story

Because it was *hartaal* (strike) all through the city, no shops
were opened at all. I and some of my assistants had locked the shop
from inside and were busy preparing *laddoos, burfi, khoya, vesan* and
other sweetmeats in the hope that the shops might be allowed to open
the next day i.e. 14 April 1919. It was the first *Vaisakhi,* harvest
festival, in my lifetime when there was, in fact, no festival, no
merrymaking and no get-togethers in the city. Normally the *Vaisakhi*
festival was observed with a lot of enthusiasm and this would be the
only day of the year when we earned enough to last for the whole
year. But this *Vaisakhi* was gravely different from all the by-gone
ones.

The city had been in turmoil for the last four days. Every day
there had been be a peaceful protest in the form of a long, crowded
procession against the Rowlatt Act and in favour of Mahatma's
satyagraha of non-violent disobedience. But always it was met with
more and more force by the government, utilising police, the military,
guns and bullets. In the last four or so days, a number of people had
died and many had been seriously wounded. The young blood of the
city was seething with the sentiment of nationalism. They were not
ready to take the terror of might lying down, but the prominent
congress leaders of the city such as Dr Kitchlew and Dr Satyapal had
managed to keep them and their defiant behaviour under control. But
these two leaders had been arrested on the morning of 10th April, and
transported to Dharamsala under strict military surveillance. Despite
their absence, the marchers didn't resort to violent means. Instead,
they remained cool and composed despite the authorities' provocation
through the use of bullets.

But today, Sunday the 13th April, was the climax of it all. The
jalsa was to take place at 4 pm in the Jallianwallah Bagh. There was
also another rumour that the meeting had been cancelled due to the
leaders' arrest. However, we soon learnt from the young people
roaming the streets that the rumour had been cast into the air by the
authorities themselves. Although it was very hot, people keen to
listen to the leaders had begun to gather together as early as 2pm. I
sent one of my workers on to the roof to find out what was going on.

Having learnt that they were busy making a makeshift stage and mounting loudspeakers, I engaged myself in my work.

I went up on the roof at nearly 4.30pm, when they were already making their speeches. The stage was adorned with Dr Kitchlew's portrait presiding over the function, while others made brief speeches. With a cursory glance thrown down over the crowd, I estimated the number of people present to be over twenty thousands. Not even an inch of space was left unoccupied. In fact, many people were sitting on the left-side wall that separated the area from the Jallianwallah Road. Some had even mounted the trees. Many were watching and listening from the roofs of their shops and houses, like myself. Being the day of *Vaisakhi*, I thought, many of them might have come to bow their heads to *Darbaar Sahib*, and having learnt of the meeting from there, had then come down here.

The roof on which I stood was made of brickwork and it emitted enormous heat, piercing through the soles of my shoes and rising up into my legs and the rest of my body. In just about half-an-hour I succumbed to the sweltering demon and I decided to go downstairs. But just then I heard some alarming sounds, crying: *'aa gaye, aa gaye'* – they've come, they've come.' The very next moment, I saw some riflemen coming out of the narrow alley into the bagh, one after the other, led by their officer who, I learnt later, was General Dyer. The officer and his troops waited on the higher strip of land immediately after the entrance for a few moments while the officer, a tall, slim, uniformed man with a number of medals hanging by his chest, assessed the situation. He seemed determined and completely nonchalant. Then he whispered something to his Captain, who I learnt later to be Captain Briggs. Then, almost instantly, he deployed his troops in line - half the gunmen on his one side and half on the other.

Then, without issuing any warning at all, he ordered the troops to get ready, followed by the order – shoot. I was stunned to see it all happening and began to tremble with fear as never before. However, I hid myself behind the raised wall so as not be seen. The gunmen fired furiously and profusely under his directions: to left, to right, straight and into the trees. The crowd began to run hither and thither, trampling over the fallen bodies of men, women and children. As the whole bagh was full of people without even an inch of ground to run on, people were crushed and smothered in the flurry of the stampede. There were wails, cries, screams, clamours and shouts all around. As the bullets left the rifles in quick succession the people ran, staggered and fell, one on top of the other, making heaps of dead bodies near the walls while the hitherto unscathed used the heaps as ladders to climb up and cross the wall on my left, but they too were shot dead, making the heap still higher.

The young lads perching on the branches of trees were, on stern orders from the General, aimed at and dropped dead with a dull thud on the ground or on bodies. Dozens of men and women ran towards the well and jumped in, only to die from suffocation. The shots were being fired, the bullet-belts moving fast and the bodies falling like rocks broken asunder by the eruption of lava.

The worst thing was that the bagh was completely surrounded by the barrier of house walls. Local people who knew the small exits ran towards them, followed by the tidal waves of others, but were shot dead by the screaming bullets obeying the fresh orders of the General to direct the ammunition at them.

The firing went on until they ran out of ammunition, which could be detected from the emptiness of the shots at the end. Having done their deed, they left victoriously, marching out the way they had come. The time must have been round half-five. They didn't stay longer than twenty-five minutes or so. But those twenty-five minutes cost the people over two thousand lives in one go.

The aftermath of the carnage was even more lacerating and terrifying. Thousands lay dead and wounded. Many of the survivors lay buried under the heaps of dead and were screaming to be taken out. The wounded were beseeching importunately for water but there was no one to supply a drop. And then, suddenly, thousands of kites and vultures appeared in the sky from nowhere, hovering over the dead bodies, blood and wounds in the hope of a sumptuous frolic. The injured survivors couldn't cross the dead bodies to get out. They fell, stumbling against the mountainous heaps, crying with pain and thirst. Even the narrow gullies were full of dead bodies. The injured ones who managed to cross the allies fell down in the bazaars.

I was so frightened, confounded and spiritless that I didn't have the energy to go to the bagh and help the wounded survivors. And then, what could I have done to help them? There were thousands of

94

them there, more dead than wounded. The sounds of horror filled the whole surrounding area - screaming, screeching, bellowing and howling. The sun had set and the dark had begun to engulf everything in its swathe. I came down on trembling legs and found that all my workers had already disappeared, closing the shop-door behind them. It must have been out of dread and shock. The curfew was still on. People were scared to go out just in case they were shot dead because those were the orders: anyone found on the road after 8 pm would be fired at.

I opened the door of my shop and found two men standing in front of it, whispering half-wittedly. Hearing the rattle they turned round and looked at me, then came closer and began to speak as if out of hallucination.

'Thousands have died, *Lalaji*. What shall we do now?'

'The bagh is full of corpses and mutilated bodies.'

'It's all streams of blood and mountains of bodies.'

'The bastards have ravaged us.'

'Shall we go and help the surviving ones?'

'What can three of us do? We need the full force of the community to dispose off the bodies,' I reacted back.

'Shall we only wait and watch while they die?' one of them asked.

'I don't know. I'm grossly puzzled myself,' I replied, yearning to weep my dread and trauma out.

Then I got them into my shop and we sat down, making plans to eschew the curfew order and help the survivors someway. But there was nothing we could do. However, at about 9 pm, when we entered the bagh, we found it smelling like hell and the people there still lamenting and sobbing in pain. There was no light; it was stark dark all around. And there were so many deathly sounds that we could not discern which corner they came from. We saw three or four shadows holding lanterns, moving about and looking for their loved ones. A woman was sitting by the side of her husband. When we approached her, she implored us to get her a charpoy to transport the body to her village. She wouldn't leave the body in case she lost it again, for she'd only found it after two hours of turning over each face to find the one that belonged to her. Where would we get the bed? There was none in the shop. And my village, Qila Vasudev, was far away. I didn't come home that night and my wife and children had assumed me dead as well. I've never found my strength dribbled down the way I found it that night.

Bhagat Singh or Bhaga's Story

My elder brother, Jagga, and I had gone to the Golden Temple as we had been doing every Sunday over the years, to bow our heads to our scriptures.

That particular Sunday, being the *Vaisakhi* day too, we hoped to reap two benefits simultaneously: to register our presence in front of our *Guru Ramdas Ji* and enjoy the festival at the same time. It was only there that we learnt that a *jalsa* had been held in the Jallianwallah Bagh to be addressed by important leaders of the city who followed the non-violent path of Mahatma Gandhi. Normally we would go to the Golden Temple in the morning and return home long before noon. But that year we had sown a variety of wheat that ripened earlier than the traditional variety. So, we began to harvest it a week earlier than *Vaisakhi*. That kept us both very busy throughout that week and nearly half of that Sunday. So, we started off for the Golden Temple at about 3 pm and reached there at 3:30 pm. We spent about an hour or so sitting and listening to the *paath* (reading of scriptures) inside the precinct. After that we left for the Jallianwallah Bagh, to listen to the leaders. We reached there at 4:45 pm approximately.

To our surprise the bagh was overflowing with people and you could hardly get in. In fact, most of the people had arrived far earlier and had occupied whatever small space they were able to get. We went in from the alleyway right opposite the Rani Bazaar (Queen Bazaar bearing Victoria's statue in the centre of the square) but finding no space even to stand, we came out, went round to the left and then left again and climbed up the wall of the bagh and perched on it.

We had hardly attended to a couple of brief lectures when we saw the military coming into the bagh, ready with guns. Their officer stood silent, cast a circumspect look in all directions of the bagh, shouted orders for his men to take positions and then commanded them to fire. There were quite a few other people also sitting on the wall like us two. At the start of firing they exclaimed derisively: '*phokiaan – phokiaan* (only empty shots)'. At that everyone cracked up and so did we. But our illusion winged away soon enough when we saw the shots taking their toll of human lives.

The crowd bounced up frantically and began to run towards the exits, jostling, clambering, elbowing and trampling over each other. People screamed and ran, and were crushed by the ones coming after with a greater momentum. Frightened, we jumped down from the wall into the bazaar, before the frenzied crowds from within the bagh pulled us down in trying to climb up to save their own lives. I saw some people, who'd succeeded in getting up the wall but were pulled down by the ones fighting for a turn behind them. And soon the shots began to be directed at our side, killing everyone on the other side of the wall, in the bagh, amid screams and wails.

From there we went to the shop opposite and climbed upstairs, despite the owner shouting at us and forbidding us. There were already a few people watching the brutal, heartless killings. *They* stayed there for twenty minutes or so and kept on firing on all sides till they ran out of bullets. We saw people falling down like chopped trees with bullet-shots to their legs, in their backs, in their chests and in their heads. They were running hysterically, and like headless chickens, falling down, getting up and then falling down again. Many had already jumped into the solitary well in frenzy. *They* shot the ones who had clambered up on trees, making them fall like wounded mangoes. After the military left, all we could see was a panic-stricken mass of people stumbling against the heaps of dead, against each other, wounded and mangled, falling and groaning painfully for water and help, saying: *bachaao, bachaao* – save me, save me.

The roads and streets sounded and resounded with the thumps of footsteps of the running crowds, all confused and bewildered and awe-struck. We didn't know what might happen next. So we, thrown off balance, climbed down the stairs and began to run towards the Golden Temple. Once we were near the *Guru Ramdas Saraan*, we felt safe, but still scared and perplexed. It seemed that the whole life of our city was now in disarray and would remain so forever. We wanted to reach our village before the curfew started but were also fearful to leave that safe haven, the Golden Temple. And, when we were running back to our village, we found every single road and

97

street bereft of any sign of human life, as though a man-eating monster had entered the city and had left it after devouring it completely. All that we could hear were the sounds of crying, wailing, sobbing and groaning that instilled the air with yet more dread of the known and the unknown.

Reshma's Story

The news of the massacre at Jallianwallah Bagh had spread like the wild forest-fire by about 7 pm. I was cooking *daal* – pulse, when I heard some tumult outside my thatched hut. I immediately went out and found a crowd of men, women and children standing in the open, some crying and others simply awe-struck. I knew my husband had gone to the city to do some shopping for me in the afternoon. He hadn't returned home yet. Sometimes he would be delayed but never stayed away later than 9 pm. On hearing the sinister news, something inside me got stirred up and revealed to me that the worst might have happened to him too, if he had gone to that bagh. What partly confirmed my premonition was his liking for poetry. Whenever he heard of a poetry reading taking place somewhere, he would make every effort to reach it. Although this was a different kind of *jalsa*, even then, I thought, he must have gone to attend it because on such political *jalsas* the poets read their poems first, before the political leaders made their speeches. Although, I couldn't say anything for certain, my fear and anxiety grew and began to overpower me. The fear of the unknown further engulfed me when I looked at the innocent faces of my small children. Kinner was the youngest and had completed one year that day. Radhika was a year older than him. My four other sons weren't that old either. What would I do if something happened to their father? The very thought sucked the whole blood out of me. But there was no way out. I had only to wait and see.

But waiting was the worst thing that could have happened to a wife and a mother of six. Time didn't move, as though it was fettered. There was no sound of his knocking the door by eight, by nine and by ten. My fear began to turn into a malaise and I thought either he was dead or too wounded to walk back home. I went out a number of times to look for signs, to sniff the air of his presence and to listen for his gait. I knew he walked in a scuffing manner, dragging his feet rather than picking the foot higher to take the next stride. I had nagged at him many times but he didn't care. He would only laugh it away, saying: 'Who can turn a Musalman at this old age?'

At 10.30 pm I lost my equilibrium. But what to do, was the question. I thought of going to the city and to the bagh to find him. He might be alive and needing immediate care. The news that had spread throughout the village gave no assurance of anyone being alive in the bagh but my intuition didn't agree to it. Many times I put my slippers on and many times I took them off. To go to the city and find the bagh of which I knew nothing, not even its whereabouts except that it was somewhere near *Darbar Sahib* (the Golden Temple), was no small task for a woman and that, too, at midnight. Helpless, I began to sob with pursed lips, my eyes streaming like flooded lakes. The children had gone to sleep, except the eldest, Nag, who'd wipe my tears off with his tiny fingers. Very soon he also surrendered to the force of sleep. I spent the whole night schizophrenically, and just as the cock cried in the early morning, I got up to go. Then it occurred to me to wonder how would I manage if... I began to knock at some of the known doors in our part of the village. Seeing to my plight, two men got ready to accompany me and help me.

By the time we reached the bagh, the day had begun to break. But the dogs were howling at the passers-by. Roora and Bagga led me into a narrow lane, which abounded with dead bodies lying disorderly in heaps. Trampling over those bodies, I felt ashamed of myself as a human being. One of them could have been my dead husband. This thought sent me shuddering with disgrace. But I was helpless and destined to follow the two helpers.

The smell that rose out of those heaps of bodies and of the coagulated blood that stuck to the floor and walls, and the faint groans of those who lay dumped half-alive under the heaps, shattered my heart and soul into shreds. As we reached the end of the lane and into the actual bagh I found the horror magnifying a thousand fold, enough to make me vomit and cry, and pluck my hair out of my skull. As the day dawned, light increased, more people began to flow in, overwhelmed with shock and awe, to look for their loved ones. Everyone seemed to be feeling ravaged and torn apart, unable to cope with the sudden tragedy that they'd been caught in absolutely unawares. A woman, like myself, was sitting by the side of a dead body at the far end, near the high wall and was imploring importunately for help from ones in no less trouble than her, to take the dead body of her husband home for her. She said she had been in that graveyard all through the night. She was still sobbing and crying bitterly. Her red and bloated eyes, her scruffy hair, her deflated cheeks and her sombre lips told what she must have been through in the land of the dead. The dogs were hurling around with their tongues out and waggling, sniffing at the coagulated blood and dead bodies, whimpering and whining over others who dared to encroach upon their territory. The vultures were approaching fast and were circling above the bagh, waiting to capture a moment of attack and their share of the revelry.

Roora and Bagga had started their search for the familiar face from one corner, turning each dead body over and, when it didn't match the one they were looking for, moving further and further into the bagh. I was doing the same, with my eyes blurred, my face petrified and the corner of my *chunni* tucked against my mouth and nose, unable to stand the hot, deathly smell. It was difficult to see the faces of those who lay at the bottom of the heap but Roora and Bagga moved the bodies aside to have a quick look at the face buried under the piled heaps. The crowd of explorers thickened by the minute, shuffling and reshuffling the dead bodies to find the one they wanted. There were quite a few women and children among the dead. One woman had died with her year-old baby, stuck dead to her abdomen under her. She must have tried to save the baby by bending on top of it but she was crushed under such a weight that her spine gave in, and she was pressed down and down until the baby was crushed. She had a bullet shot in the side of her stomach.

At about 10 am, Roora and Bagga shouted at me, saying they had found the body of my husband, under the heap near the stage. I immediately ran towards them but fell down, stumbling against a dead man's straddled legs. My mouth hit against another dead body's back and was saved from getting bruised, losing teeth or breaking my nose. I saw the face of my man. It had turned as yellow as turmeric. He had been hit in the chest and the blood had oozed out profusely to dye his white shirt red all over. At the sight, I began to wail, beat my breasts, cheeks and thighs almost unwittingly and collapsed on the ground. Roora and Bagga stroked my head and shoulders to calm me down. I soon realised the disaster hadn't befallen me alone but thousands of others. So I stopped crying but not without repercussion. The tragedy solidified itself in my heart, making me dumbfounded until the funeral.

How Bagga and Roora found a bare cot to put the body on and take it home remained a mystery for me. All I knew was that they had left me by the dead body and had gone briefly. When they returned they had the charpoy with them. They picked up the charpoy loaded with the body and carried it all the way home. I just followed them without a word, as though I had lost the gift of expression forever.

Qila Vasudev had lost a few more lives to this man-imposed catastrophe. Sikander Ali Sheikh, who owned the biggest house in the centre of the Muslim territory of the village, with a large iron gate looked after by two rampant lions made of concrete one on either side, and whose capacious roof was fortified by a parapet all around, had lost his younger son Shamus-Ud-din in the disaster. Shamus had a great respect for Dr Kitchlew, his Kashmiri ancestory and his reputed credentials. He wanted to listen to his opinions and reactions about the Rowlatt Act. Despite Dr Kitchlew's arrest the rumour spread that he would address the meeting one way or the other. Shamus, a product of an Islamic school, took along a friend from the city and went to attend the *jalsa*. The duo never came back home alive. He was twenty-four at the time. His elder brother, Abdul Khaliq, though not as educated as Shamus, had other qualities. He helped his father in controlling the land that they cultivated with the help of half a dozen servants. Sikander Ali was quite a wealthy landlord in the Muslim part of the village and commanded a good deal of respect amongst his community. Abdul Khliq had sired three children; his son, Noor Mohammed was my age and his two sisters, Sabiha and Samina were respectively eighteen and sixteen. His wife, Shaista Begam, maintained a kind of relationship with Kabir's mother Razia, but because of latter's marriage with a Hindu, she always kept a distance from her.

Chiraghdin, an *arayin*, who rented out an acre or two from big landlords like Sikander Ali and followed an intensive style of farming, had two sons and a daughter. He had married off his daughter, Mehndi, a long time ago and she now lived in Lahore with her husband Fazal and two small children. Chiraghdin's elder son, Waris Ali, was one of the 381 people whose bodies were recovered from the Jallianwallah Bagh. Waris Ali's younger brother, Farid, was still living in the village and helped his father in his intensive farming. Waris Ali's daughter, Saira (14), helped her mother, Rabbo, in the home, and his son, Hassan (12), went to school in the city.

Maula Bux, *lohaar* (blacksmith) had lost one son, Imam, in the massacre while the other son, Khairu, still lived with his wife and two young daughters, Feroza and Sharifa. Khairu Lohaar was the crux of the whole village as far as the tools of cultivation and harvesting were concerned. Maula Bux had grown quite old and helped his son in doing smaller jobs like sharpening the tools or blowing up the furnace to turn raw iron into solid steel.

Jumma *Dhobi* (a washerman) and his two sons, Ghulam Mustafa and Ghulam Rasul, together with their wives, Nimmo, Balo and Kali were engaged in the age-old profession of washing and ironing the clothes for the village folk. They wouldn't get paid in cash but in kind at the time of harvest.

Laddha *Kharaasi* had a *Kharaas* (a mill worked by bullocks) in the centre of the village. He and his son, Mirajdin, served the whole village by milling wheat, grams, corn, barley and other grains into flour. They took part of the grain as their remuneration and survived. The village had its own clans of barbers, weavers, cobblers, carpenters, itinerants and many more skilled families, all contributing towards the self-sufficiency of the village, like any other in the Punjab.

The people of Qila Vasudev were inter-dependent, inter-related and inter-affected in all events, whether it was pleasure or pain. And when the above deaths occurred, everyone felt severely afflicted. They all joined in to mourn the deaths and carry out the last religious rites, according to the faith of the deceased or their families.

Lakshmi's Wedding

The Volcano

The month of October, in 1922, had just commenced. The spring season, the searing heat and the blooming of flowers had vanished long ago to give way to autumn's mild chill and the withering of vegetation. The season of torpor had set in to prevail for a few months before it would relent again to the spring. Nature went on working in its own special way and in accordance with its own ineluctable laws to demonstrate to the human beings their extreme limitations. But the humans paid no heed to all those manifestations and were always victims of the illusion that they were strong and invulnerable. The day of death cheated their blurred vision and engaged them in all sorts of wars of attrition as if to live forever, longer than nature itself. But nature watched and laughed behind the thunderheads, which could only be interpreted as rain coming.

Plenty of rain came in September, in the form of plague and epidemic that and denuded many parts of the country of every sign of life. Hindu and Sikh moneylenders in Multan and Rawalpindi Divisions had drowned the rural Muslim population in deep debts. The total debt that Punjab owed was nineteen times its land revenue, of which half was owed by the rural Muslims alone. And when the fear of epidemic compelled the usurers to run away for their lives albeit temporarily, the Muslim population depredated their granaries and set the storage spaces and account books on fire, unleashing communal hatred, the impact of which would be realised for years to come.

But pleasures and pains always huddled together, as they did in Qila Vasudev. The wedding of Krishan's second eldest sister, Lakshmi, was fixed for the third Sunday of the month and was now only two and a half weeks away. When Krishan's eldest sister Sheila was married off two years ago he was barely two and remembered nothing of the marriage except that something had happened in the household; a kind of nebulous vision like wandering about in somnolence. Gita, the youngest, who was four at the time, could tell some half-hazy stories that she glimpsed but only to make Krishan curse his late arrival in the world. Sita had enjoyed more because of being seven years old. But Rita and Lakshmi had to work extremely hard. They helped their mother prepare the dowry for Sheila and carried out many other responsible duties with regard to food for the guests, arrangement for their stay for one night, and meeting all the trivial demands made by the friends and relatives of the bridegroom. After the wedding was over and their sister, Sheila had left for her parents-in-laws' along with her husband, Shanti Dev, whom they called *jeeja ji,* they both fell ill due to fatigue of overwork, sleeplessness and a lot of dancing. But they reclaimed their normalcy in just one week when Sheila came to see them for a brief interval. It was then that they had pestered Sheila with irritating questions about her first night with her husband. And when, out of shame and coyness, Sheila wouldn't tell anything, they pinched her skin and tickled her body to encourage her to share her hidden secrets with them. Poor Sheila had grown sick and tired of their young obstinacy.

'Will you shut up, you trollops? Enough is enough. You'll find out everything when your turn comes, okay?' Sheila had finally bellowed at them and had sprinted away to her mother in a burst of resonating laughter, leaving the two to crack up wildly behind her.

Girdharilal and Rukmani had accomplished all the necessary preparations starting from the reception of *baraat* – the marriage party, through to the sumptuous meals, the stay of guests for one night, the *phere*; seven rounds round the fire, the departure of the *doli* or palanquin, and the dowry. Rita and Sita had been assigned various duties befitting their ages and temperaments. Only Krishan was free to do anything he desired. In fact, he was the centre of attention for everyone in the house as though he were the same old sombre Krishna who would be castigated for nothing whether he stole *makhan* or butter, or broke the earthen pots of the village girls gone to fetch water from the Ganges. Many people from within the closer relationships had already begun to gather in the house. They would hold up, kiss and cuddle the four-year-old Krishan with such predilection that the youngest sister, Gita, began to feel jealous of her brother, for nobody picked her up the way they did her brother Krishan.

The whitewashing was going on in the household, and the workers engaged for doing so made their own small demands. They asked for another spare bucket, a larger ladder, a stool, something to eat and drink or some advance to purchase some flour for tonight – all to add to the existing onus on the family. And the existing onus was no less stringent and demanding. The preparation of the dowry for Lakshmi was a colossal task in itself. Most of the women and girls who'd arrived already had been invited earlier on purpose, because of the dowry. They were all busy sewing, embroidering, knitting, ironing and folding suits, *dopattas, chunnis* and piling them up in the suitcases, amidst the crooning of wedding songs meant to pray for the long and happy married life for the shortly-to-be wife. They were to be served well, in time and with dignity if more and more work was to be extracted out of them. The whole household echoed and reverberated with the exuberance of exhilaration. Not only did the women and girls turn out mounds of good work but also made the place rowdier, noisier and more throbbing with life. If only you could listen to those lewd jokes that they told each other amid explosions of raucous laughter and exchange of suggestive glances you would be constrained to admit to the female strength. We children would know and understand those jokes later from the bigger boys who had happened to listen to them from within their clandestine hiding places in one corner or the other.

One day, when all the women and teenage girls were in their high mood, one of the women said that she wanted to go home (she lived in the village) to serve food to her husband. She said that he was due back from his work for the lunch hour and that she would return soon after feeding him. Forthwith, she stood up to go. Just then another woman looked salaciously into her eyes, smiled and said, 'How *long* will you take?' The other one understood the context, blushed and replied, 'Six inches!'

Girdharilal was bound to be at his shop no matter what went on inside the wedding house. He would manoeuvre everything, make all the arrangements for whatever was to be done by sitting at his seat in the confectionery. He would say, 'Marrying a girl off isn't an easy task. Look at the price of gold, silver, food, clothes and you would know!' And he was right. Indian families in general, and Hindu in particular, had to make enormous sacrifices to see their daughters happily married off. The economic burden wasn't so much on the boy-side as it was on the girl-side. And the boy's parents always expected a heavy dowry, even if that meant bankruptcy for the girl's parents. Without the agreed amount of dowry the girl was always in danger of being thrown out after marriage, although the dowry itself stood no guarantee for the happy married life either; the greed for more never diminished. The boys' parents treated their boys as investments, which must bring in more and more interest. The investment must double itself, also threefold and fourfold if possible. Girdharilal had been blessed with not one or two but five daughters. The youngest, Gita, was, as yet, unable to understand why everyone that came in picked up Krishan and not her to shower their love on.

As the day of the wedding approached, the hustle and bustle increased. Everyone in Qila Vasudev knew that they had a wedding going on in the village. Everyone was invited to come and bless the girl and her shortly to-be husband. The marriage was more a social thing than a commitment between the two families, more a union of the two families than a solitary promise between the boy and the girl and more an involvement of the whole society than just the relevant families. It was more an arrangement than spontaneity and more of enforcement than of liberality. The soul-power spoken of so boisterously existed nowhere. In case of a girl being relinquished by her husband and parent-in-laws for no fault of hers except the small dowry she brought with her, or in case of the girl refusing to accept the undue pressures and punishments, the society in front of which she was married off would be summoned back to sort out the matter. If there were any soul-power existing then the matter would be sorted out by the husband and wife themselves or within their family without any extraneous interference. They craved what they lacked or didn't have in the first place. Mutual trust, reciprocal confidence and reliable conscience was nowhere to be found in the land. I, Arya Gold doubt if it ever existed at all.

It was an obligation for each one in the village to pay a courtesy visit to the wedding house, however brief it might be. The daughter of one home was deemed to be the daughter of the whole village, if only in theory, because the love tangles between boys and girls of the same village were always taking place though under strict camouflage. Convinced fully that the lovers would never be allowed to get united (more likely killed for the non-existent sin) they would elope, never to return. But it wasn't so among the Muslims. The son of one brother could marry the daughter of the other brother to evince another terrible extremity. The restriction applied only to Hindus and Sikhs, perhaps for the better, to avoid inbreeding. Yet, it seemed the restriction had extended itself to the point of suffocation because two families ascending from two different clans with different family names were also forbidden from taking such a step in the name of the *same* village.

It was more than three years now since the Jallianwallah Bagh massacre had taken place and Qila Vasudev had lost four lives in its wake – a fair number given the size and population of the village. However, the people had now come to terms with the hand of fate, as they had done many times in the past centuries. The remaining life must go on, they had thought, and had made every effort to build new dreams on the ashes of the devastated ones. They had succeeded too, though not without deep scars on their souls.

The Hindus and Sikhs of the village continued to pop in to the Girdharilal household asking for and offering any help they needed until the marriage could be happily concluded. The Muslims too, came and paid a brief visit, congratulated them on the occasion, contributed something befitting their own capacity, asked for any service they were capable of discharging and walked off with a smiling face, retaining inside any grudge or tension. The Hindus and Sikhs of the village did exactly the same when such an occasion took place in Muslim households.

A few days before the wedding ceremony, Sikander Ali came to pay a brief visit to Girdharilal's house, accompanied by his son, Abdul Khaliq. Due to the rush of people going and coming the door was already open, yet Sikander Ali gave a soft knock to alert the home-dwellers. Ghirdharilal was, at the time, instructing his workers about where to fit the ovens, what to do and what not to do. He heard the knock and gazed at the door.

'Oh, Sikander Ali *Sahib*! Come in, come in please,' he said cheerfully and went forward to receive the guests with a broad smile sticking to his face.

'*Mubarqaan hon, Lalaji.* Congratulations,' Sikander Ali said, shaking hands with Girdharilal. Girdharilal offered two hands to accept his one and then immediately stroked the shoulder of Abdul Khaliq and ushered them both in amid mutterings of welcome.

There were quite a few charpoys already waiting in abeyance for the guests due to the circumstances. Girdharilal invited them to take seats, which they did, and he sat down on the opposite charpoy, facing them and smiling.

'I'm so glad you've come, Ali *sahib*. First of all, tell me what would you eat or drink?' he asked very affectionately.

'No, no, nothing at all, *Lalaji*. It's our daughter's wedding and we're always on the giving end. Here's a small blessing for our *Beti*,' Sikander Ali said and handed over an envelope to Girdharilal.

'Why do you take such trouble? Your visit was enough for a blessing!' Girdharilal said for the sake of it. He knew that was how it had been going on for years.

'But that's our duty, *Lalaji*. And do tell us if there's any other help you need. Send a message and we'll be right here,' Sikander Ali said smilingly and reassuringly and got up to go, followed by his son.

'Hold on, Ali *sahib*, just a minute,' Girdharilal snapped, went inside and came out in a second with a box of *laddoos*, sweetmeats, in his hands. That was the custom. People coming to the house to impart their blessing to the girl or boy would be given a pack of sweetmeats as a token of their gratitude, and this was understood by both parties.

'You've permitted me no chance to serve you with anything at all. Please take this! And thank you very much for putting your foot in my home,' he said in gratitude and handed over the box which Sikander Ali acknowledged without any demur. Girdharilal escorted them up to the door.

Only one week was left before the wedding, and this one week would be glowing with yet more jubilation, more hustle and bustle and with more wedding songs. Girls from all over the village huddled together in the house of wedding in the evening and sang songs of a brilliant future for Lakshmi and her husband. Sheila had come to live with her parents and siblings a month ago, together with her year-old daughter. She and Rita had gone to invite all their friends from the village to come and join in the singing festivity, which was to start this evening and would continue until the evening before the wedding.

The singing and dancing carousal began at 9 pm after everyone in the house had taken their dinner. The girls from the village had started pouring in at 8.30 pm. Although all the girls had already eaten dinner at home, Rukmani, Sheila and Rita compelled them to eat something or the other, and they all complied with the request. After the dinner, the girls admonished all the men-folk and big boys to disappear from the courtyard where they were to perform their art. However, they didn't worry much about young male children like Krishan, Kabir, Kinner or myself. I was only three and my mother was one of the invitees to the gathering. I remember going to sleep in the lap of my mother after the singing and dancing had started. But my mother told me in later years how they had sung and danced all through the night. And still later, when we boys witnessed such performances for other marriages in the village, we knew what they actually did.

They always began with sober songs and, as the time progressed and they got heated up, they deviated and turned towards lewd ones with lots of sexual innuendoes. By midnight, all the men would be fast asleep and the ladies (women and girls alike), as though completely unbridled, would sing and laugh and make fun of each other. The female minds, badly subjugated by male dominance over the years and cloaked under the sheaths of shame and humility, erupted like volcanoes to lay bare the lava of wanton desires and whims. Opportunities such as this provided a catharsis for their dreams buried under a thousand layers of fear of mortification. Female self-denial in Indian society touched its peak in those days.

There were about a dozen women and girls in that gathering in addition to Krishan's mother and sisters. The older ladies took charge of the small two-sided drum (*dholki*) with one of them stroking the outer wooden wall of the drum with a spoon, keeping with the beat set by another woman playing with both hands. One girl began to sing and three or four others took to dancing. It was a mild song, describing the bride waiting for a decent union with the bridegroom and expecting sincerity from him throughout life. The second song was a little sharper and explained the aftermath of the union, resulting in the change of taste to sour and sweet pickles, and lemons to eat. The third song depicted how the bride's private parts narrowed when she went back to her mother's home and didn't have any intercourse with her husband for a week or so. The girls who danced on the floor made all the promiscuous gestures to dramatise the whole content of the song at which everyone laughed their hearts out, blushed and choked. Some of them went to the toilet time and again. When, at four in the morning, they had finished their singing and dancing,

Rukmani gave them a box of sweets each to take home. This *giddha and bhangra* continued for a full week, until one night before the wedding, always replacing the old songs with the new ones. One wondered where did all those folksongs come from? The women and girls remembered each one of them by heart.

On the day of wedding, the whole village seemed to have gathered at Girdharilal's place. The close relatives had arrived with full families while the ones not so close had sent one or two members to represent them and register their presence at the wedding, as they had always done in the past. The idea was to show their unity as a village to the people coming from another village to attend the marriage party with the family of the bridegroom. The party was to stay in the village for one night for which almost every family in Qila Vasudev had contributed charpoys and bedding. The young men coming with the marriage party would be winking lasciviously and hunting for young girls of their choice. The girls too would be sending mixed messages and signals amid laughing and teasing, and the villagers would tolerate all the rowdiness and lewdness for that one night. This night would generate new relationships to form new chances for new marriages, though most would culminate in ephemeral sex scandals. The young men in the marriage party would take it as their birthright to chase, hook and trap the agreeing girls, though quite furtively. Some such confrontations might end up in terrible scuffles between the village youths and the overnight guests. But the young girls of the village always eagerly anticipated and waited such an unbridled opportunity. The boys of the village would do the same when they went with such a marriage party to another village.

On the wedding day, everyone in the household, including the long arrived relatives, woke up much earlier than usual. Lakshmi, who had been given a good massage from the paste made from turmeric, to make her body supple and luxuriant, was given a thorough bath amidst thrilling songs sung by the womenfolk. They surrounded and protected her from being seen by male eyes using a *phulkari*, a red sheet embroidered with a variety of flowers. The songs wished her a long and happy married life. Then came the time to adorn her, making a superb hair-do, fitting her in red clothes (sign of wedding bliss) with heavy embroidery and fringed with gold and silver wires. While Lakshmi's friends and sisters were busy in her embellishment, the children of the village came gasping and apprised them that the marriage party had arrived at the outskirts of the village. Soon, they themselves heard the band being played far away and left everything, and ran towards the far end of the village. The band was leading the party, which was being heralded by a well-decorated horse carrying the bridegroom, followed by a crowd of people. The party was coming with a slow and elegant pace. They ran again to be closer to the party and catch a glimpse of the bridegroom's face so they could tell Lakshmi what her husband looked like. No one had seen Prem Nath yet except Girdharilal and Rukmani. From Lakshmi's point of view, it was like playing a gamble, which more likely than not would turn out to be a defeat of her dreams and hopes, though she would still have to put up with whatever her fate brought to her. That was the irony of every Indian girl in that day and age. Lakshmi wouldn't see him until after the marriage later today. Her only knowledge about her soon-to-be husband would be what her friends and sisters could now bring.

Now, at that precise moment, Lakshmi was all by herself in her room, her heart throbbing with dull thuds, scared of the unknown. If the gamble turned out in her favour, she would be lucky. And if not, even then she would be married and would have to be content with whatever her parents imposed on her without complaint. This fear of the unknown made her feel sick and squeamish. She wished her friends and sisters would come back soon and tell her if he was handsome or if he matched her imagined prince. And even if he didn't match the prince of her dreams she wanted them to tell lies to her that he did, if only to prolong her illusions for some more hours.

But when her sisters came back they were half-lost themselves, for they had not been able to catch a full glimpse of the face of the man who was disguised by thick layers of garlands hanging from his forehead down to his midriff.

'I was able to look at the sides of his face and it seemed fair-coloured to me,' said Sheila.

'I saw him from the left when he pushed away his garlands to listen to his brother and his face looked handsome to me,' Rita emphasised.

111

'Didn't you see his brother? He was quite a handsome man, and so must be our *Jeeja*,' Sheila stressed.

Then soon her friends came back, too, having spent more time in their fact-finding campaign and declared elatedly that the groom was quite handsome, sending Lakshmi swaying in mirth.

The marriage-party was met and greeted in the middle of the village by Girdharilal, accompanied by some close relatives and friends. On the entrance gate to the village they had already displayed a large placard made of silk, saying: 'Welcome to Qila Vasudev'. Now it was like giving a real personal touch to the reception. It was a cordial meeting, extending a warm welcome amidst the exchange of embraces and a formal reception, after which the party was led to the nearby purpose-built hall called *janjghar*. They allowed the guests a couple of hours to rest and relax before the first meal.

The hall thronged with men, women and children and echoed with a loud din of all hues. Some of the guests simply washed their faces while others thought it better to have a full bath and put new clothes on because the ones they had left their place with were now begrimed. Bags of clothes were opened and scores of pairs of shoes, mirrors, perfumery and make up materials were seen everywhere, making the spacious hall look too small and stewed.

The lunch had numerous vegetarian dishes together with *poorian*, oil-fried chapattis. The rice pilao smelled gorgeous and so did *halwa* made from coarse wheat flour, fried in purified butter and mixed with an equal amount of sugar. There were seven dishes of vegetables smelling superb and increasing the appetite at their sight. It was now that the bridegroom took his load of garlands off his head to show his face clearly to the onlookers. And the details of his singular features, fair skin, medium build and enthralling smile travelled to Lakshmi like a supersonic rocket through her confidants, making her feel above the moon and flying high enough to compete with the fastest birds. The gamble had turned out in her favour though only physically yet, for her husband's immanent nature and temperament would only be discovered later, after they had lived together for some weeks or months.

While the marriage party revelled in dainty and piquant dishes in the hall, the girls occupied the corridor above, running on all the four sides, watching them eat. They made incisive jokes and sang sarcastic songs, mocking the groom, his family and friends and other relatives. The songs suggested that they devoured food as though they had never had enough all their lives, and that if they fell sick from overeating where would Qila Vasudev bring a doctor to heal them? They said that the groom's mother (for no females went with the marriage party in those days,) had sent him all hungry and unmannerly to get married to their brilliant sister, Lakshmi. They compared the groom, his father and brothers with different filthy animals, making joke after joke in singing, which nobody took seriously because they were never meant be. Then, one of the small girls, as advised by the bigger lot, stole away the shoes of the groom and handed them over to the girls. They hid the shoes and wouldn't return them until boy's father gave them good amount of money, much more than the shoes had cost.

In fact, everyone enjoyed these different perks. Young and adolescent eyes met each other's, winking licentiously, inviting wantonly and exchanging salacious hints, and asking for merry-making trouble all the way. The elderly took it all quite lightly, too, for that had been their culture for centuries.

The evening meal was served very late, after the seven rounds around the fire had taken place, perpetuated by incantations of Sanskrit verses from the scriptures. Everything was handled by the *Panditji* in a manner quite incomprehensible to the ordinary folk. All they could understand was the word *swaaha* that meant ashes when some *ghee* (purified melted butter) was poured over the flames rising from the small brick-made portable *hawan kund*, a square hearth. The flames swelled to many folds when fed on purified melted butter, met equally strongly by the chanting of *mantras* by the *panditji*. Lakshmi and Prem Nath were made to sit side by side and they obeyed whatever *panditji* asked them to do. In the first four rounds the groom led the bride bound by a knot between her shoulder-cloth to that of the groom, while in the later three rounds the roles of leading and following were swapped over. Once the *phere* were completed, the bride and groom were asked to put *jaimala*, garlands round the neck of each other, so proclaiming the wedlock securely accomplished. At completion, both families congratulated each other while the girl's parents gave costly gifts to the members of the boy's family, yet apologising with seemingly grim faces and wounded conscience that they were sorry for not being able to do more. This importunate begging of pardons was pathetic and even ridiculous. The more the girl's parents bowed down and knelt low, the harsher became the attitude of the boy's parents, for no apparent reason except to make an ostentation of their status as boy's parents, to make their counterparts feel inferior. Perhaps, when Krishan's marriage took place, Girdharilal and his family would assume the opposite role, making their status felt by the would-be bride's parents. How ludicrous!

The next day the whole village observed the departure of *doli*, the palanquin carrying Lakshmi to her husband's village. She went amidst a lot of crying, wailing and snivelling, accentuated by the heart-rending songs of departure that expressed only one emotion: that even kings and emperors had to say goodbye to their daughters because their real home was that of their husbands' while the parental home was only a temporary abode for them. When, at 4 pm, Lakshmi was escorted into the palanquin by her father, he too began to cry, as if he would never meet her again. Her sisters, mother and Krishan cried even more bitterly and loudly, making the rest of the people follow the act. They must have done the same at Sheila's marriage two years ago, and, probably, would do the same until the youngest, Gita, was married off.

In fact, what lay at the root of such emotional outbursts was the feeling of insecurity on the part of the girl and was perceived equally by the whole family. Yes, the feeling of insecurity regarding the inner nature, habits and temperament of the unseen, undealt-with and unlived-with husband and his family who might turn out to be greedy, cruel, enslaving and domineering enough to make hell of the girl's life. Yet the girl wouldn't be permitted to pick a boy of her own choice through love and nearness, for that would be a blistering challenge to the parental authority. So, an Indian girl was transferred from under one dominating authority to another where the former, as parents, might have been a little softer if she adhered to the strict order of traditions, but the latter could be entirely annihilating whether she adhered to the traditional role or not.

Communal Violence

Jagat Singh, more popularly known as Jagga in Qila Vasudev, was to go to see his elder sister, (elder both to Jagat and Bhagat) Isher Kaur or Isho, in response to her letter. The letter said her husband, Piara Singh, had had an attack of pneumonia a few weeks ago and was quite seriously ill. Bhagat, or Bhaga, also wanted to accompany him but it would have been difficult for both to go due to the cattle, which needed to be fed and looked after regularly. Arjun the fugitive had assured them of his services after they were both gone, but Jagga didn't agree despite Bhaga's wish to go. He loved his only sister, Isho, very much and it was now a long time since he had seen her last, almost two years ago, at a family marriage in the city.

Love apart, now her husband had fallen ill and both brothers had a duty to stand by their sister in this hard time. They discussed everything in detail in the household and concluded that only one of them could go at a time. Furthermore, Bhaga's wife Kirti had lost her only son at the age of five due to influenza and was emotionally very upset. She had suffered a miscarriage in the past with her first conception, and now her first born had slipped away from her hands like sand from within the fist. She was left worn out and desolate. She, too, needed to be taken care of. Chanddi, Jagga's wife, wanted her husband to stay with her and let Bhaga go to the rescue of his sister, but was afraid to say so. Even had she said it, Jagga wouldn't have accepted her suggestion. He knew in his heart that if his younger brother, Bhaga went, Chanddi would give Kirti a terrible time because she hated Kirti. Her contempt and hostility towards her had been generated by the heavier dowry that Chanddi had brought with her at the time of marriage, in contrast to what Kirti had brought. This hatred was further fuelled by the fact that Kirti was physically half the size and strength of Chanddi who would begin to give Kirti a severe thrashing whenever she reacted to her inimical attacks of words. Niranjan Singh or Ninja, father of Jagga and Bhaga, had stopped the warfare between the two many times by his timely interference, but he wouldn't be at home all the time.

'Your wife, Chandi isn't Chandi but Chanddi, I tell you,' Niranjan Singh had told Jagga once. Her parental name was Chandi with only one 'd' but it was her father-in-law, Niranjan Singh, who had added another 'd' to make it Chanddi. Chanddi was the belligerent goddess from Hindu mythology, known to be more bellicose than any other warmongering goddess. Guru Gobind Singh, the 10th Guru of Sikhs, had declared Chanddi to be his sword against the tyrannies of the Mughals perpetrated on Hindus taken as infidels or non-believers in Islam. Bhaga and Kirti called her Chanddi, too. Bhaga had threatened his elder sister-in-law many times with death, showing her a large knife he had specially bought for the purpose, the blade of which opened out with a slashing shine at the pressing of a button but the goddess never cared. Although the female warfare had resulted in friction between the two bothers many times, when Bhaga drank on purpose and rebuked Chanddi savagely. But the relations were soon smoothed owing to the past affection, and mediated by their father, who blamed Chanddi for everything. At that, Chanddi would be severely reprimanded by Jagga. And then, Chanddi would deny him the sexual pleasure for days and weeks, which would be hard for Jagga to bear in the face of Chanddi's beauty and virility.

Furthermore, Chanddi had born Jagga two sons, who were seven and ten and would soon be able to help their father with agricultural work. So Jagga's anger would soon be diffused and he would apologise to Chanddi for whatever he had said in the heat of the moment. Then there would be an interval of cold war between the two females until, one day, some new trouble erupted again to end up in the repetition of the old abrasion and friction.

However, in all finality, it was decided that Jagga would go alone to Isho, living at a far off place, called Jehlam, near the North West Frontier Province. It was the beginning of September, in 1924. No sooner did Jagga arrive at his destination than he discovered that gruesome episodes were taking place and gripping the whole area in terror and panic. Small troubles between Hindus and Sikhs on one side and the Muslims on the other had been shaking the area all through 1923, and since the commencement of 1924, but now, so it seemed, the communal tension was aiming to rise to its peak. At the far end of the Northwest, the district of Attock, named after its furious river of the same name, had been caught in horrendous communal turmoil, sending the minority communities of Hindus and Sikhs reeling to their spines.

The Volcano

Attock had a Muslim population of 91 per cent, who threatened the very existence of the non-Muslim minority. Either they embraced Islam or they would be erased from the face of the earth. The position of Jehlam, and the adjoining areas such as Mianwali, Muzaffargarh and Dera Ghazi Khan, was perilous for the same reason. The Muslims didn't want to see a single Kafir or infidel in *their* area. They despised them for idol worshipping and believing in thousands of gods and goddesses and deifying cows to the extent of drinking their urine. Although Sikhs didn't do any of these things, they were deemed to be an offshoot of Hinduism and hence as much to be despised as the Hindus.

A strange kind of communal or religious re-awakening had started with the Muslim population in the west being granted the special right of representation in the legislative assembly in 1909. That right was extended to other communities in 1919. While such special rights were reserved only for minority communities in the rest of India, the communal problem of Punjab was dealt with in quite the opposite manner. Taken as a whole, the Muslim population in Punjab amounted to 55% (decreasing as you travelled eastwards) and thus was a majority. The tension mounted when similar rights were acceded to the non-Muslims while prior to that nothing substantial in the way of communal tension had appeared.

When Jagga climbed down from the train at Jehlam, he quickly realised that there was turbulence and fear looming everywhere. The Muslim population, especially the *Pathans*, roamed the bazaars and streets with ferocious faces, looking at the non-Muslims with obvious contempt. Although Jagga was six feet tall, wide and sturdy, the scene made his heart run in leaps, as though ready to fall out on the bare ground and be trampled over by a multitude of men. He picked up his steel trunk and headed towards the tonga (a horse driven cart) stand. He asked a number of tonga wallahs to take him to his destination but they just looked blankly at his bearded face and then into the far emptiness, turning their gaze away as though unable to make out what he had asked for. He had heard the news of sporadic fights and quarrels taking place in this part of the world from Arjun, the newspaper wallah, but had absolutely no idea of the magnitude of the problem. He resented being required to come to see his sister and brother-in-law in such circumstances. For a quick second he remembered Bhaga insisting on accompanying him. 'Two would've been better than one,' he admitted to himself mutely.

At that moment he saw another tonga-wallah coming towards him. Immediately, he leapt forward and waved his arm horizontally to stop the man. The tonga-wallah halted the tonga right beside him.

'Where'd you like to go *sardar ji*?' the driver asked.

If it were not for the long beard, large moustache and turban on head, Jagga would have taken him for a *Pathan,* for he was dressed like one. He wore a long loose *kurta* (shirt) with a coloured silky half jacket, and a *salwaar* (pair of trousers). But when he spoke in Punjabi, Jagga felt elated and astonished at the same time. So, the man was a Sikh. He felt relieved. Another subtle thought flashed through his brain: there was no hiding for a Sikh, for that was what Guru wanted; to make no bones about being a Sikh and fight until death if faced with the enemy. Jagga shook his head and began telling the man where he was supposed to go. The man got him in the tonga and whipped the horse. The sharp tuck-tuck of the animal's hooves began to rend asunder the sinister silence that engulfed the roads that morning.

'What's wrong here, *bhaaji*?' asked Jagga, feeling securer and in equilibrium. He realised that the tonga-wallah sardarji was older that him and deserved respect; hence he said *bhaaji,* like speaking to an elder brother.

'Same old religious tension, now rising and then ebbing. Where do you come from?'

'From Amritsar. I'm here to see my sister and *Jeeja,* who's a bit down on his health. They said pneumonia, maybe!' replied Jagga.

'May the guru grant him good health. Pray to him and he'll put everything in order,' said the man.

'Yes, guru's the only saviour,' retorted Jagga, looking at the sky overhead and bowing to it with folded hands.

Then there was silence again, save for the horse's hooves striking the road surface.

'Are there many Sikhs in Jehlam, *bhaaji*?' asked Jagga.

'Not many; no more than a pinch of salt in a huge pan of flour. Hindus and Sikhs together make only a few thousands. We always live in fear of being attacked, but what can we do? This is where we were born, and we have to live here no matter what. In fact, ordinary

Muslims aren't bad people at all. It's the fresh inoculation administered to them by the mullahs that turns them against us – a continuous indoctrination of Islam. In normal times we are like brothers, standing by each other. Actually, more is happening in Attock, but the impact comes here, too. We *are* scared but we've to work and earn to live, otherwise my family, my horse – we'll starve to death. Riots or no riots, we have to work. What do you do for living?' the tonga-wallah asked in the end.

'We're farmers. That's what we've been doing for ages. Know no other business except ploughing, sowing, tending, irrigating and harvesting,' Jagga said and laughed.

'That's the best business. No other business can compete with it. They say "Farming's sublime; all other businesses are mediocre but the worst is the service of someone". Do you own a lot of land?'

'Not awful lot. Only just enough to keep us going,' replied Jagga in a humble way.

'Better than digging a new well every day to drink water, like people of my kind,' the tonga-wallah said rather painfully.

'No life's easy, *Bhaaji*. We too, work like oxen before we're able to see a sack of grains. Working all through the ice-cold nights, half-dipped in water that can freeze you to death, and during sweltering summers when even crows get blinded by the melting shaft of sunrays from the molten sky and forget to squawk. No, nothing's easier. The shoes of others appear comfortable but they're not,' went on Jagga as though under some magic spell.

'Probably you're quite right,' concluded the man with a deep sigh. 'I think we've arrived.'

The tonga parked beside a narrow street and Jagga jumped out, making a resounding thump on the road. He paid the man with a little extra flair under the circumstances, got hold of his trunk, bade the man *sat siri akaal,* and made his way into the street. And as though out of some profound intuition or just prompted by the raucous thump audible as far as inside the home, Isho was already standing at the threshold with a faint welcoming smile on her face. The brother and sister clasped each other amidst tears of joy. The latter felt a subtle pain in her heart that emanated from the constant affliction of being so far away from her parental blood relations.

'How is *jeeja* now?' asked Jagga after they had finished greeting each other.

'A little better than before. This present *hakeem* is quite good, but then everything takes its course. Come in *veera* (brother),' she said and led him in, and straight into the room where her husband was laying in the bed. Her only son, about five, was playing with tiny conch shells, cowries.

Jagga placed the steel trunk in the corner, picked up Balwant, kissed his forehead, cuddled him and said, 'Such a big boy and playing with *kaudian*! That's a shame. Go and buy something to eat, some *khoya* or *barfi* or *laddoo*.' Saying this he dropped him on the floor and handed him a rupee coin. The boy hesitated, looking obliquely at his mother who winked to corroborate the acceptance.

He took the coin and was about to run to the shops when Isho stopped him, 'Don't go just yet. It's too much for you to handle. I'll go later on with you.' The boy stopped there and then, returned and hid himself behind his mother.

Jagga went ahead to meet his jeeja (brother-in-law), wrapped in a heavy quilt with his eyes and face as pale as the paste of turmeric. Jagga sat down by his side on the bed, with his legs and feet hanging down to touch the floor. Piara Singh tried to sit up but couldn't. Decrepitude had taken good toll of him. He was only thirty-five but looked fifty. His arms, neck and cheeks were too debilitated, and Jagga couldn't find the man he had seen two years ago at a marriage ceremony in Amritsar.

'Keep lying, keep lying! Don't bother to sit up if you can't,' said Jagga and felt a sharp pain in his chest at the fate of his sister, praying mutely for her husband's good health and long life.

'What does the *hakeem* say now?' he asked with grief and consternation rubbed on his face.

'He's quite hopeful, *veera*! Your jeeja is much improved now, but had you seen him two or three weeks ago you would've... God knows what!' she ran short of words and courage to speak more. Her eyes flooded with tears.

'How's ... everyone ... on ... your ... end?' asked Piara Singh in a feeble voice.

'Everybody's quite okay. They all wish you very well. Bhaga also wanted to come with me but I'd to stop him because of work,' replied Jagga, scratching his forehead with his right hand.

'*Achha veera* (Right, my brother), I'll go and cook *roti* for you. You must be hungry after this long journey,' Isho said and made her way to the kitchen. Jagga followed her and once they were out of sight of Piara Singh, he handed over one hundred rupees to his sister. 'Ask for more if you want; we won't let you down,' Jagga said with streaming eyes and then immediately wiped off his tears with the sleeve of his shirt.

Balwant was circling round Isho, impatiently waiting for her permission to go out to the shops and buy something.

'Bibi! Shall I go?' he whined.

'Alright, give that rupee back to me, take this one anna and go,' she swapped the money and let him go.

On 10th September, the riots spread to Kohat in the Northwest Frontier Province. These riots were much more intense and savage compared to all others, that had previously occurred. Muslim mobs from the surrounding villages banded together and began to butcher the Hindu population quite indiscriminately, looting their houses, setting them ablaze, raping the women and girls and putting to the sword their men-folk, right in front of their eyes. The rioting was so ferocious that even the police and army felt helpless in protecting the non-Muslims, who had to be evacuated and escorted to Rawalpindi, in the north of Jehlam. The news of the riots spread like wild fire in Jehlam and the adjoining places like Shahpur, Gujarat and Mianwali. All these areas were predominantly Muslim territories where Hindus and Sikhs were already living in fear. Although a curfew was instantly imposed on these areas, the mobs still roamed the streets, glittering weapons in their hands and a conflagration lit by Islamic Mullahs in their eyes. For them, killing and butchering non-Muslims was an act of religious duty, or *swaab,* that granted them an assured right to be with Allah and his prophet after death. They were made to believe that, in the process of kafir-killing, even if they lost their lives they would be recognised as sublime martyrs to be counted amongst the chosen few who died in the name of great Islam. If they survived, then a place in heaven would already be reserved for them to go and occupy. So, this kafir-killing was in itself a great act which, instead of being discouraged by the religious leaders was promoted as the way to claim the love of Allah and his prophet, and probably the archangel Gabriel, too. The more kafirs you killed, the more you were applauded and admired. You would be awarded the status not only of a *moman,* but also of a *ghazi.* Whereas *moman* stood for a good Muslim performing five prayers a day and observing the fast in the month of *ramzaan, ghazi* stood for the one who was the leader, fighting continuous warfare to convert kafirs or put them to the sword of Islam.

Hindus and Sikhs became so scared that they locked themselves in their houses and pretended they were already dead. No voices were heard, no kafirs were seen; it was as though they had long vanished.

The city of Jehlam was no different to those in the adjoining areas; the whole landscape was rife with this Muslim reawakening. The accretion of ghazis had taken place like earthworms in the middle of the monsoon season and they roamed the streets of Jehlam, smelling and sniffing out kafir blood.

Forcibly incarcerated in the house, Jagga, who had a habit of going out to the fields early in the morning to look at the growing crops and deciding which field needed immediate watering, weeding or hoeing, felt terribly constricted.

On his first morning, when he tried to step outside, Isho halted him instantly: '*Veera,* no! You can't go out in these circumstances. Let the storm come to a standstill and then do whatever you like to do. You don't know this area but I've known it for many years now. I've seen the ferocity and savageness that reign in the eyes and blood of these Pathans in times like these. Incited by their religious preachers they can do anything. You're not in the central Punjab now, but in the far away land. Given a few more days the blizzard may recede. But now is the time of high tide. So wait. Wait like a good brother.'

Jagga stopped and followed his sister meekly back inside the house.

'Is there enough medicine for Piara Singh to last until this storm is over?' Jagga asked his sister, restoring himself to the seat he had relinquished only a few minutes ago.

'Enough for a month, in fact. Don't you worry about that,' Isho replied, looking at Balwant who was still asleep and looking like a small angel.

'Is this *hakeem* a Muslim?' asked Jagga.

'He is, but very much dissimilar to others of his religion. He's also a poet of Punjabi, a Sufi poet like Shah Hussain and Bulleh Shah. Sometimes he reads out his *kaafian* to your jeeja to console him. He's a very down to earth man,' she explained with a soft smile on her face as though praying for Hakeem's long life.

The explanation comforted Jagga's soul. He knew there were good and bad people in each community, but had little or no idea of the plight of the minority in a far off place like this. The central Punjab was different. No one community dominated the other by sheer numbers, and likewise there were less troubles of this kind. He had been to Lahore and Lyallpur too, and knew the Muslim population had predominance there, but even there, the troubles never touched this kind of proportion. Amritsar was completely different. He had never seen such savagery there. Even in Jallianwallah Bagh, people from all religions had died, suffering the same fate at the hands of someone else.

'Do you live in continuous fear of being done to death, here?' he asked abruptly.

'Yes, we do in days like these, but not when this madness is over. There are two Sikh families living in this street while all others are Muslims. But we meet each other very warmly and cordially in our ordinary life, especially the womenfolk. But the men-folk go berserk when religion comes into play...'

'And how long do you think it'll take to see things returning to normal?' Jagga interrupted her.

'Can't say. Maybe two weeks or even two months,' she replied vaguely, putting the thread into the needle to stitch a broken button on her son's shirt.

'That's ridiculous! Who can survive for two months without going out? Have you got enough food to last for that duration? I think you people had better move to Amritsar after the recovery of Piara Singh. We'll do our best to settle you there,' he said and got up and began to walk back and forth in the small roofless courtyard.

By the time the government, police and army bridled the rampant barbarism in the area, the month had already reached its end. The damage done to life and property was yet to be calculated; the assessment would continue for months to come.

Jagga had taken the first available train to his home city. By the time he reached his village, a lot was echoing and re-echoing in the political arena. Although he was no politician or pedant, his story of forced internment was disseminated in and around Qila Vasudev, like the way the male pollen from flowers is spread by the wind to impregnate female ovaries far and wide. Arjun, newspaper wallah, had read all about the happenings and was worried in case the wild fire came to gorge his side of the world. Bhaga and family had grown tense and were tormented by the news that the newspapers were promulgating. It was the first time that Chanddi, the warmongering goddess, had felt sad and dissipated. Sikander Ali and other Muslims contacted the non-Muslims of the village to express their sorrows and had asked for a helping hand to keep the village air calm and collective. Noordin the dyer made no more prophecies and buried himself far within himself. The Banyan tree kept on changing colours with no one to decode the mysteries.

The month of October had already begun to send cold waves, heralding an early winter. But the surrounding area beyond Qila Vasudev was hot and simmering; the political pundits were busy designing new contours for the country so that everyone, irrespective of their religious proclivities, could live in safety.

According to Lala Lajpat Rai, the Kohat tragedy was a unique tragedy of its own kind. He wrote a series of articles in the papers trying to point out the gravity of the communal problem and its possible ramifications in the rest of the country. A few weeks later he suggested a concrete way to guarantee the stoppage of such communal insurrection and brutality that had shaken Kohat and the adjoining areas. He recommended that Punjab should be divided into two: East Punjab and West Punjab because the eastern part was predominantly non-Muslim and the western part was predominantly Muslim. He argued that if democracy was to work successfully and effectively under the system of communal electorates, the partition of Punjab was essential. But he did not mean there should be a sovereign state for Muslims. The idea was to let no religious majority dominate the minority and make their life hell , which had been the case hitherto. But the idea was misconstrued by many and would result in a permanent partition in 1947 with a division of not only Punjab but of the whole of India.

Uncle Arjun understood exactly what Lala had meant by the partition of Punjab. He, therefore, summoned a meeting of the village elders at the beginning of the next year i.e. 1925. It was the end of January and they, instead of sitting under the Banyan tree, had drifted away from its shade that froze you to ice, and sat under the sun with its warm rays lulling them to ecstatic tranquillity. Having listened once again to Jagga who had had the first hand experience of the gigantic monster of communal upbringing, running wild and aggressive in Kohat and Jehlam, Uncle Arjun tried to tackle the question from the perspective of Lala Lajpat Rai as well as from his own.

"Our Punjab is a mixture of many cultures and civilisations in the sense that no single culture can boast of its purity and dominance. If any Punjabi dwells in such an illusion then he must be dismissed as ignorant and trite and lacking any understanding of the country. Punjab is on the fringes of India and in its very nature an entrance gate for foreigners to the soils of India. Being next to the river Sindh and the mountains of the Khyber Pass and Hindu Kush, it has always been trodden by the feet of countless invaders, starting with Alexander the Great and followed by many others. But that is again our erstwhile history that stretches far beyond, to the time when Aryans came through the same passages, not to depredate and return, but to settle here. They uprooted and destroyed the Dravidians in the land, pushed some of them to the south and enslaved the others. It would be absurd to think the Aryans remained untouched by the life of Dravidians. The clash of two distinct cultures gave rise to something new that was neither completely Aryan not Dravidian, rather a fine mixture of the two.

I am not going to justify the rights and wrongs of that antiquity here. All I want to emphasise is that when two cultures clash they both lose and gain, they intermix, interact and produce a new culture that inherits all the healthy aspects of the clashing cultures and abandons the non-healthy and incompatible features. And centuries after the Aryans established themselves along with Dravidians, subsequent invaders came to plunder and return. Some of them came with the idea of making the whole world subservient to themselves, but the task wasn't easy, and hence they went back to where they had come from or perished in the process. Then came the Mughals preceded by many more dynasties of Mongols and Turks. Invaders, like Mahmood of Ghazni, came with the sole aim of looting and went back, repeating the act seventeen times. But the Mughals came and settled here and the interaction between cultures generated more new things. Conversions took place and many former Aryans and Dravidians and their hybrid heirs embraced Islam. Nothing was pure or foul and nothing remained so. Amalgamation of cultures, blood and histories is at the root of all forms of life. Just as the Aryans ousted Dravidians from Sindh and the old Punjab, the new entrants did the same to Aryans and the rest. They occupied the hilly tracts of the North West Frontier, Khyber Pass and Hindu Kush and the rest of the Punjab, converting millions by force or by guile into Islam. The fate of fringes always plays tricks on them. Now, we're here in the centre of Punjab and are mixed in such a way that no group or community takes preponderance over the other. This kind of diversity has nothing to be afraid of. But the state of West Punjab is different; it's diverse in another way, in the way that the Muslim community has preponderance over all others. A fine balance between different communities prevents them from doing damage to each other while the imbalance goes in favour of the majority community to do what they desire, leaving the minority at their mercy.

In ordinary life, the centre exerts its enormous pressure on the periphery and moulds it to its aims and objectives by itself being influenced by the periphery. But in the case of different religious communities, particularly in the North West, the periphery takes preponderance over the centre and exerts enormous pressure on it, especially on the communal relations of the centre. In these circumstances, the solution offered by Lalaji is genuine and plausible. Punjab should be politically, yes politically, divided into East and West Punjab, shifting the population if need be. The Muslims will feel more secure and less threatened in the west and Hindus and Sikhs in the east. There seems no better solution to the communal tension and we should welcome it one voice."

The Volcano

No sooner did Uncle Arjun finish his speech than Sikander Ali came up with some serious objections about the plan.

'Brothers, I've certain remonstrations to make if you may permit me to speak?' he said, standing up calmly.

'Sure, sure, by all means Ali Sahib,' said different voices.

Sikander Ali cleared his throat by coughing and began. 'First of all, I'd like to draw your attention to what Sardar Arjun Singh has just said about conversions. Islam doesn't believe in coercion or use of force to bring people into its embrace. Not only that, in fact nobody is allowed to become a Muslim if he or she is not fully convinced that the Islamic way of life is most suitable and satisfying to him. So I object to the use of the phrase *by force*. People who embraced Islam from within India did it out of their own sweet will or volition, and not out of coercion. The second thing that I want to point out is this shifting of population if Punjab is politically divided into East and West. Shifting all the Muslims to one side and the Hindus and Sikhs to the other side would close all doors for the cultural exchange or cross-cultural experiences that are vital for people to form a nation. I'm not against this political division but I am against the shifting of population by force of law or otherwise. However, if someone wants to shift of his own free will there ought to be no objection to that. Thank you.' Sikander Ali carried his point successfully and sat down, ingratiatingly eyeing the audience.

Uncle Arjun stood up again and invited more questions or suggestions, but there came none. He finally dismissed the meeting saying, 'Thank you Ali Sahib for your precious suggestions. Your valued opinions will be forwarded to Lalaji. Thank you everyone!'

Dalitism

When I saw the latest issue of *Harjan Kaun*, I was really amazed. Kinner and his staff had brought about huge changes in the paper. For one, he had taken over the paper himself with his brothers, Nag, Bhil, Nishad and Ahir as its managerial staff, and his sister Radhika as its Assistant Editor. Kinner himself was the Editor-in-Chief. The second biggest change was that all six of them had adopted their village's name as their second name, so Kinner was now Kinner Vasudev. The third biggest change was that the next issue of the paper would be called 'Dalit Samachar', the Dalit News. The fourth and the biggest change was that Kinner had expounded the philosophy of Dalitism, an absolutely new way of looking at Indian history. This was a totally new angle of seeing the objective world and a milestone in the history of philosophy.

I began to read Kinner's article, for I couldn't resist any longer. He had used the word 'Dalit' in the sense of the downtrodden or exploited ones. The word stood for one person as well as for the whole generation of exploited people – exploited economically, morally, socially, culturally, psychologically, physically, mentally and spiritually. The exploiter was not Brahmin, but Brahminism in particular and the Aryans in general. The exploited ones were the Dravidians and other poor people from both traditions. Indian women in general were also counted as dalits. Words like *Achhoot* (untouchable), *Harijan* (sons of God), *Sudras* (lowest of the low), *Chandaals* (menials) etc had been rejected as mendacious, misguiding, dishonest and hypocritical. The nearest equivalent he offered for Dalit was the pulverised one.

He went on to trace history, wherein the original inhabitants of India were called *Dasyu, Dalu* and *Nishaads* and were followed by the Dravidians. However, Brahminism regarded them all as non-Aryan and treated them as such. The Aryans used two methods to vanquish and subjugate the non-Aryans: use of arms to conquer them and use of ideology to enslave them. The Rig Vedas (1500 – 1200BC) described non-Aryans as non-human, untouchable, barbarians, outcast, wretched and equal to animals. Kinner referred to some later historical research into the people who were defeated both by Aryans and some of the upper strata of non-Aryans. These people were reduced to the level of *Sudras;* the victors took them as their common property and made them do the dirtiest jobs. Despite being reduced to the level of subservience, Sudras still had some rights, such as religious ones, because they had originally descended from the non-Aryans. That state of affairs continued until the Vedic society persisted. But later when caste-ism clutched the whole society in its cruel grip (600BC) the Sudras were brutally treated, with all their economic, political, legal, social and religious rights taken away.

Manu Smriti (700AD) was at the root of this Brahminical stringency. Manu Smriti went as far as to disallow even the sixth position to the Sudras in the order of caste-ism. It was at this stage that the *Chandaals or Sudras* were ostracised to the outskirts of the community, and society. They were even forbidden to keep utensils and were only permitted to keep dogs and donkeys, could only wear the clothes of dead bodies and ornaments made of iron.

Kinner went on to expose the cunning and cruelty of Brahminism in accordance with the Manu Smriti. If a Brahmin child was ten years old and a Kshatrya's a hundred years, the latter was expected to treat the former as equal to his father. If a king discovered a hidden treasure he was required to let the Brahmin have half of it and let the other half go to the treasury. A *Sudra* was to marry only in his own caste, a *Vaishya* could marry a Vaishya woman or a Sudra woman, a Kshatrya could marry only in his own caste whereas a Brahmin could marry in any caste. If a Sudra tried to preach religion to a Brahmin, the king was required to issue orders to drop boiling oil into his mouth and ears. If a Sudra raised his hand to hit a Brahmin or if he raised his leg, even in provocation, to kick at a Brahmin, the limb was chopped off.

Having taken a few crucial references from history, Kinner went on to define Dalitism. He wrote: ' A person or persons, a people or a nation who has/have been pulverised physically and spiritually, economically and politically, culturally and socially owing to his/their birth can be defined as Dait/Dalits. Dalitism is a movement determined to subvert Brahminism of all shades and hues and establish Dalits as equal partners in India, in its assets (natural or man-made), its life and its running. This movement has a logical and scientific philosophy called Dalitology and its methodology to achieve its aims and objectives is called Dalitlectics (Dalit + Dialectics)'.

Having defined his conceptual terminology, Kinner went on to deal with Dalitology and Dalitlectics. First of all, he differentiated between the natural and the social sciences in that the natural sciences such as physics and chemistry were discoveries of the existing laws of nature. Because the laws of nature were precise, so were the discoveries made by the natural sciences. They obeyed the exactness of $2+2 = 4$. On the contrary, the social sciences were man-made and whatever laws they expounded were inventions rather than discoveries, and were bound to go wrong or get replaced by new inventions or laws. The man-made laws of social sciences or inventions were never precise and never obeyed the $2+2 = 4$ rule. Although they tried to be exact and precise, they were only probable.

From then on, Kinner refers to various social sciences and casts a double doubt on their precision. He treats history as a social science, too. Then he refers to the motivating or inspiring force of history and rejects Marx's theory of class struggle, which is supposed to drive history forward with the inference that caste, race, class or other antagonist struggles, only tend to destroy history instead of thrusting it forward. In the ensuing columns he proves that no invented laws of social sciences are eternal like the discovered laws of nature by the natural sciences. Then, referring to the persistent slavery of India in the last two thousand years, he says that 75% of the people (Dalits) of India were ostracised from life's real arena and were convinced in all finality that they didn't belong to India, that or India wasn't their country. So they withdrew themselves from the central stage of struggle against the invaders and began to move to the fringes of life, bereft of dreams and destinations. And the remaining 25% were already divided into Kshatryas (fighters), Brahmins (worshippers and advisers) and Vaishyas (workers). So, only the Kshatryas were left to fight the invaders. These 8% could in no way fight and protect the country from the foreign invaders, and were usurped, humiliated, looted and ruled by the foreigners for centuries. The victorious Aryans remained slaves forever in history and they still were under the British.

Kinner poses a question here, 'Why and for what should Dalits fight? Should they fight because they are slaves of slaves, or for the country that doesn't belong to them?'

From there, Kinner again takes a leap forward towards the driving or motivating force of history. He says that the driving force of history is internal and not external, intrinsic and not extrinsic, in the human sub-conscious and not the conscious. Dalits were tortured and tormented, and degraded to the extent of being reduced to nothingness. Their Sub-conscious became so wounded and mutilated over the centuries that they developed a sense of unwantedness and futility. This is the state of self-hatred and self-denial. Until this state is reversed and becomes self-respect and self-love, the history of India will not be driven forward rather it will swing further backward as it has done in the past.

So, Dalitology as a philosophy and ideology is meant to generate that self-respect and self-love in the deepest sub-conscious of the forgotten and forlorn children of the land through equal partnership in every walk of life and by whatever means. The driving force of history, that is intrinsic and not extrinsic (unlike Marx's class struggle), will have to be revived with the help of positive discrimination.

This positive discrimination was deemed by him as the vital part of Dalitlectics where internal contradictions between Brahminism and Dalitism were to be revolutionised in favour of the latter by free education, to the highest level, for all Dalits. This would put them on a par with the hitherto hegemonic possessors of knowledge, who denied Dalits their right of education. Kinner had rejected the concept of class in favour of the concept of caste and had given new dimensions to the Hegel's Dilectics.

I was stunned by his new way of thinking and I wanted to see him as soon as possible, but then I decided to see Kabir, who had been busy with 'State and Revolution'.

Kabir had already read Kinner's article. When I asked him how he felt about it, he reacted furiously.

'How on earth can Kinner reduce a class ideology to caste alone?' he shouted with a dull thump of hand on his book.

'Because India's not gripped with classes but castes,' I argued.

'That's absolute rubbish. There's no society in the world that is free from classes; the exploiter and the exploited; dominator and dominated. The lower castes are part of the exploited and dominated class, and they've to join hands with this class if they want to see themselves emancipated from the grip of the exploiter. And...'

'Who's the exploiter at this very moment?' I interrupted.

'Seemingly the feringhee but our black feringhee are no less dangerous. Look at those princely states; their kings and princes are devouring the soul of India. Then the congress leaders; they don't come from the wretched families. They're equally dangerous because they come from the bourgeoisie. And if you start talking about castes or Dalits, you'll be playing into the hands of the capitalists and the bourgeois. You'd be creating divisions in the working class that would weaken it further.' Kabir went on and on, giving an outlet to his freshly acquired knowledge.

'But the class-divisions already exist. There are divisions within the same class and these are defined by their interests. Do you think all capitalists and imperialists are united? They're not; that is the very reason behind the wars. There are factions in each of the two classes and that'll remain so forever because each faction has its own interests. And if Dalits have their interests then what's wrong with that? Why to make a mountain out of the mole hill?' I countered Kabir's arguments to infuriate him further.

'You're a nutcase! You don't understand philosophy. Our interest as exploited people lies in making use of the existing divisions among the capitalists and the imperialists, which we can do only by keeping ourselves united. If we divide ourselves on the basis of caste we'll be playing in the hands of the rulers, enabling them to rule us for another century or two, or maybe forever,' he said, mocking my limited knowledge.

'Yes, but Dalits are 75% of the population, or even more, and are the major force in the country for overthrowing foreign rule. And it was because of their non-involvement over the centuries that the country has been enslaved by different powers. They're now looking for due recognition by the society, which was and still is denied to them. I think Kinner's thesis is superb. We've seen the active involvement of the 25%; now comes the time to see the involvement of the larger number.'

'Well, I do agree with Kinner that Dalits are a force large enough to be reckoned with but I don't agree with the idea of splitting the class into fractions and replacing the concept of class by caste or castes.'

'I think you're making the mistake of studying the individual only as an economic unit or at best a politico-economic one. The driving force of history, as Kinner portrays it, lies within the individual and not outside of him, as Marxism understands it. Gandhi's talking about the soul-power and, I think, this power is the crucial power with which to drive history forward. India has to revive the soul of the Dalits, re-ignite the power of self-respect, which Brahminism extinguished. The question is not only of *swaraj* alone but also of maintaining it in the long run. Self-rule and self-respect are inseparable. ' I made some vital points, which Kabir heard carefully and relegated the 'State and Revolution' to one side. Kabir kept on musing for a few seconds and then came up with another concern, certainly from the book he most cherished and still held in his mind.

'It's all very well to play with words and theories, to swap philosophies, but the real thing is to actually change the world for the better, to unite theory and practice together; theory without practice is barren and practice without theory is blind. Kinner's sitting in his newly found office refuting and re-framing the laws of philosophy like another Marx or Lenin, and that makes me laugh,' Kabir said and burst out laughing in an effort to humiliate Kinner.

'Look, Kabir, philosophy is a means of understanding the world and society we live in. The world would still be running as usual if there were no philosophy. All that philosophy does is to bring forth some laws or generalisations of the way in which the world runs. To assign philosophy a role to change the world for the better or worse is no more than dreaming for Utopia, reverie and nothing else. Nature didn't start by pre-fixing a philosophy on which to base the world, rather the laws of nature are inseparable from matter, which is as much in flux as nature itself. In short, philosophy is not interchangeable with nature or its laws. Why then should philosophy, a way of comprehending, assign itself the role of changing the world? And as social science is man-made, no philosophy is final, and cannot be the last word,' I said and got up to go. But just as I was about to step outside, Auntie Razia stepped in.

'How're you *bete* (son)? It's nice to see you after a long time. Where've you been? Come, sit with us for a few more moments,' she said so affectionately that I couldn't say 'no' to her. I followed her back into the room where I had been sitting with Kabir.

'Hello Amma!' said Kabir and began to make space for the two of us.

'Auntie, have you found any girl for Kabir yet?' I asked when she was comfortably seated.

'So many girls, *bete*, one better than the other,' she replied gleefully.

'How many times do you want to marry your son off,' I said satirically and laughed.

'Why, only once, of course. What I mean is that there are quite a few girls around to pick one from, if only this friend of yours agrees to get married. You should tell him that this is the right age for marriage.' she paused and looked at Kabir. 'Amma has nothing else to think about except my marriage, as though I'm already on the borderline of my age,' Kabir pouted grimly and looked obliquely at me.

'She's right, *yaar*. You've already crossed twenty-one and are no more a teenager, are you?' I pulled his leg.

'Shut up, will you?' he retorted angrily. 'How old are you, my boy?'

'Much younger than you; almost a kid compared to you!' I snapped, smiling with sarcasm.

'Dramebaaz!' he retorted, declaring me an actor, and twisted his eyes and lips in derision.

Then suddenly, mischief stirred in my brain, making me crack up before I said, 'Auntie, show me all the girls you've seen for him and leave it on me to pick one up for him. I'm pretty sure he won't mind. And if he doesn't marry the one I choose for him, then I will marry the girl myself. Is that fair? 'You're trying to be naughty with your Auntie. How can you marry a Muslim girl? And moreover, your parents won't agree to that either,' Auntie Razia grew serious.

'Don't you worry about that, Auntie. I'll bring them round, so that they allow it. There's only one problem, and that's Kabir. He'll have to go without marriage if the one I pick for myself is liked by him, too,' I said and smiled naughtily.

'You are both the same, taking nothing seriously except your books,' Auntie said and drooped. 'But I do want Kabir to get married as soon as possible. If his father were alive, I wouldn't worry so much but now I do. I wish to see him settled before I die.'

'Come on, Amma, I'm settled already. And you won't die for at least twenty more years yet. If you don't believe me then take a look at yourself in the mirror. The mirror will tell you the truth.' Kabir tried to soothe her.

'Yes, the mirror will read my face, but not my heart. And you too, are a mirror, for you see my face only and not my heart, do you?'

Razia grew a little restless, perhaps with some hidden grief and anguish. She began to cry.

'Oh my dear, dear Amma!' Kabir said, leaping up and wrapping his arms around her. Then he began to wipe her eyes with the fringe of her *chunni*.

'See! How much trouble and discomfort you give Auntie. That's bad. That's very bad thing to do,' I acted again. 'Auntie! I say yes on his behalf. You fix his marriage as soon as possible and I shall see how he dares to refuse. I'll get the whole village to start a movement of non-co-operation and civil disobedience against him. We'll go on hunger strike and stick to it until he yields to your decision,' I said to make her laugh, and she did.

'You're a right *nautankibaaz*!' Kabir grinned.

Seeing the mood was altered, I stood up and said before leaving, 'Now, Kabir boy, behave yourself if you don't want to be boycotted by the surging masses. Now is the time for you to put all your crammed up theories into practice, okay?' I said, *'Achha Auntie'* and left, leaving Kabir looking at me, slightly provoked.

The Related Agonies

Although Drupti had physically recovered from her worst nightmare long ago, her agony still persisted. The night when Arjun had had to turn fugitive, leaving her at the mercy of brutal policemen, had devastated her irredeemably. The three policemen had used and abused her body in such a manner that her womb had lost its fertility forever; she had not been able to conceive ever after. If it were not for the company of Kirti, Drupti would have found herself long dead. The afflictions of her mind, her soul, her psyche and her total personality were so gigantic and festering that she would begin to tremor with fear at the smallest stir of something unusual. The incident had left an indelible impression on her that would last as long as she lived.

Arjun the fugitive had found a job in the city; he would leave at 7 am and come back at 8 pm. Although he had a world of sympathy for his wife's condition, Arjun was able to do only a little in the way of compensating her for her losses. Had she been given proper medical treatment she might have regained her capacity to become a mother, but Arjun could do no more than feed her with what he earned as a daily wage earner. So, his sympathies, although emerging from the depth of his heart, did little or nothing to bring back the lost glory and dreams of a woman. What being a mother amounted to was far different from being a father. To be a father was, perhaps, a feeling of virility, or the satisfied ego of manhood, whereas to be a mother was a feeling of being capable of creating a new life. A lone stretch of barren land capable of growing nothing would be the worst possibility for a woman to visualise. Fecundity, on the other hand, even if it produced only small and stunted grass, brought self-pride and satisfaction, and built hopefulness for future. Whenever Drupti witnessed an alkaline stretch of land in the village, she would begin to sob and shed tears.

Kirti understood her pains, her sobs and her tears. At such junctures, Kirti would clasp Drupti's head in her arms, kiss her forehead softly, wipe her tears away, stroke her back and would, in the process, begin to shed tears herself, frequented by deep sighs and sobs. A moment of truth would fill both with intelligible emotions wafting from one side to the other. Then the roles would be swapped over and Drupti would do what Kirti had done for her a minute ago, despite the fact that Kirti looked like a mother and Drupti like a daughter. No words would be spoken; no utterances were necessary. Unbroken silence would speak its own language and was understood quite impeccably.

Bhaga and Kirti had allocated a small separate portion of the house to them by partitioning it temporarily from the main house. The skilful Drupti had devised a small kitchen, a reasonable bathroom and a room for the two of them to sleep in. No rent was charged from them; it was free accommodation. The house was actually owned by Niranjan Singh, Bhaga's father. He had divided it into two equal halves and had given one portion to each of his two sons. He himself had the freedom to live with Bhaga or Jagga, as he pleased. So, he spent some weeks with one and some weeks with the other, but he always felt more comfortable living with Bhaga and Kirti than with Jagga and Chanddi - Chanddi, whom he had declared to be a warmongering goddess. The only benefit of staying in Jagga's part of the house was in getting the children, Amar and Mukhtar, to do odd jobs, like fetching him a packet of cigarettes or *bidis,* or smouldering his hookah for him. He was a Sikh and yet he smoked and that was quite unusual for a Sikh. But he didn't care. Family and friends had grown accustomed to it and no longer bothered. Bhaga and Jagga had grown up seeing hookah or bidis in their father's hand, accepting it all like the first rays of the sun when their eyes opened or they learned to see and their consciousness imbibed the first impression of things around them. When they were still children they had tried to emulate their father by doing *gurgur* into the hookah but the damn thing didn't work for them. One day, Bhaga, instead of exhaling his breath into the pipe of the hookah, made the mistake of inhaling it. He had received a mouth full of water, choking him and giving him an eye-bulging cough. That was the last time he had tried the contraption.

Chanddi the warmongering goddess had her full thirty-two teeth in her mouth, yet her tongue was hardly scared of being hacked to pieces. When she spoke or made full use of her tongue, it hewed and slashed everything in front of it into shreds. Quicker than that of the she-snake, sharper than shards of glass and more poisonous than the venom of the cobra, her tongue left lasting impressions on the soul of her victim. No woman from the village enjoyed confronting her when her tongue came into play. And play it would, no matter when, where or what time. They all talked about her but only at her back and terribly feared her seething anger.

Kirti remembered a day shortly after her miscarriage when Chanddi was seated beside her. Kirti was still lying in the bed, groaning with pain. All that she had said was that the life of a woman was full of troubles, from birth till death. She had, in no way, offended Chanddi, but the goddess flared up: 'Lives of women like *you* are full of trouble because your parents never fed you properly, never gave you enough, never bore you decently. You're the product of weak-bodied parents, midgets, rickety and shrimp-sized. I've no trouble in my life. I'm blessed with two handsome sons and with more to come, and still I'm able bodied and fit to run mile after mile.' she had gone on and on, despite hearing no reaction from Kirti, who had turned on her side and was gazing away from her. Her indifference had further fuelled the fire in Chanddi, and she had begun to rain all the curses of the world upon her, imprecating barrenness, desolation, death and God knew what else, to her and Bhaga.

Kirti also remembered the day when she, accompanied by Chanddi, had gone to her parental village to rescue Drupti, just a day after her husband had to turn a fugitive for fear of forceful conscription. Kirti was pregnant with only a few weeks left to parturition and couldn't walk fast enough, while Chanddi was running like a trollop. At Kirti's request to walk slowly, she had started her tirade and had continued barking at her unstoppably until they had reached the village. Even Drupti's grisly tragedy had failed to stir up any human emotions in Chanddi, who had kept on grumbling reproofs of malevolence upon Kirti and Drupti alike on the homeward journey.

But now, the presence of Drupti in the household gave Kirti some sense of respite from the wickedness of Chanddi – a kind of sentimental support. Despite being the wife of Arjun, Kirti's far off cousin from her parents' village, Drupti had an abstruse relationship with Kirti and vice versa – a relationship of ill-fates, which had brought them closer and closer to each other over the years. Although Kirti was pregnant once again, the loss of her five-year-old son, Nindi, had had traumatic effects on her. A sudden illness had overtaken the boy. He had suffered for a good week and then suddenly died one night, leaving Kirti and Bhaga lamenting and wailing their hearts and souls out. The way Drupti, the other victim of ill fate, comforted Kirti, helped her and dedicated herself to her, was beyond the capacity of words to express.

Long after, both of them had been sitting at the spinning wheel in the courtyard at noon, when Drupti suddenly began to sob bitterly. Terribly shaken, Kirti held her hand in hers, and asked compassionately what had happened, though she knew the answer well enough.

'Shall I never become a mother?' Drupti had groaned with utmost pain. Kirti had no verbal answer to offer and it was not the first time she had asked the question. Probably Kirti's present state of pregnancy had prompted Drupti to look at herself again, and in the fresh light of all improbabilities. 'You keep the one I'm going to bear now. Maybe, he or she will live longer with you,' Kirti said and sighed deeply, linking her ill fate with Drupti's.

'But, shall I never have one of my own?' Drupti asked, amidst heart-rending lamentations. Kirti patted her on her back and said, 'We'll play Devki and Yashodha. I'll bear and you'll rear.'

The story belonged to Krishna, who was born by Devki and was brought up by Yashodha. Drupti looked into Kirti's eyes to find the offer of partnership and shared lives.

Whenever Kirti saw Chanddi's two small, sharp eyes, she compared them with two small streams of lava flowing and incinerating everything that came their way, however precious. The supercilious gaze roared with hatred and anger, with fire and acrimony. Her sizeable, wide face glowed with the inferno of hell, and the way she snorted through her nostrils made Kirti tremble to her spine. Chanddis's lips never quivered. They always remained curly, stiff and shocking, and heinous. Her other sister, Lachhi, whom Kirti had seen a few times when she had come to stay for a day or two due to a shopping spree in the city, was very different – almost diametrically opposite to what Chanddi was. Lachhi spoke so sweetly and so calmly that Kirti couldn't believe she was Chanddi's elder sister. Lachhi was tall and slim with a familiar kind of face as though there must be more of them in the world, reminding you of an eternity of ingenuity and goodness. Kirti wondered how, both having been born to the same parents, there was this difference between the sisters - one belonging to the North Pole and the other to the south.

Kirti still remembered the afternoon when Lachhi had come to the village without informing anyone in advance. Having discovered that her sister had gone to attend to a funeral and was not due back until the evening she knocked at Kirti's door. When Kirti went to the door, she found Lachhi standing in before her smiling gracefully. She smiled back welcoming her, invited her in and offered to sit on the multicoloured *peehri* belonging to the days of her marriage. Despite Chanddi's terrible nature, her bellicosity and the rankling wounds she had inflicted on Kirti's soul, Kirti held no malice against her sister Lachhi. Lachhi seemed quite a gem of a person, slightly reserved, scrupulous and kind-hearted. When Lachhi had settled comfortably, Kirti asked, 'How's life treating you? How's your family and farming and everything else?'

'Everyone's fine … no complaints … I'm thankful to God for everything,' she replied briefly and at intervals.

'I think *bhainji* has gone to some funeral in another village along with *bhaaji*,' Kirti said with self-restraint.

'Yes, I learnt that from the children and then knocked your door,' Lachhi said and smiled faintly.

'*Jee aayan nun* – Most welcome! Treat this like your own home and tell me what would you like to eat or drink?'

'Only a glass of water for now,' she said.

'That'll be supplied duly, but what else?' asked Kirti with a faint smile.

'Nothing more at the moment. Let some time pass and then I'll see whether…' she replied apologetically.

Having gulped down half-a-glass of cold water, Lachhi felt more settled and began to tell the story of her sudden trip.

'My eldest son is due to be engaged to a suitable girl we've found for him. The guests are expected anytime next week. So, I thought of doing some necessary shopping. In fact, I wanted my husband to come with me but he was too busy with work and so were all the boys. So, I entrusted my young daughter to my youngest son and ventured on an unplanned journey. And in the middle of my journey I began to think how would I carry the whole load home on my two shoulders?' She began to laugh. 'Then the idea occurred to me that instead of going straight to the city, I should come here first and take my sister along to help me. And when I arrived here I found that she has gone to attend to some funeral. So, nothing's going to happen today. I'll have to wait until tomorrow,' she finished her little speech and gazed at Kirti's face.

'Can I be of any help?' Kirti asked.

'Of course you can, but let's forget about shopping and talk about our lives. The business of the world will carry on regardless. Happiest are the moments you get to spend with some loveable one. And I find you very much so,' she said warmly.

Kirti was amazed by Lachhi's opinion of herself. She was further surprised to discover that Lachhi, whom she had always found shy and reticent, was actually quite garrulous, though still sensible. In fact, whenever they had met in the past, the ghost shadow of Chanddi had always hovered around and obfuscated the real side of her sister's character. She would hang around, constantly watching, discouraging them from getting to know each other better. So, the relationship never went farther than a 'hello' and 'how are you'. Today was the first time ever that they had sat face to face and at ease with each other.

'Where's your son?' asked Lachhi looking around vaguely.

'He was bored, so I asked Drupti to take him on a village tour,' Kirti answered with a light laugh.

'How old is he now?' Lachhi asked, a blissful look discernible on her face.

'Two!' Kirti replied briefly.

'May God bless him with a long and happy life!' Lachhi wished.

And Kirti felt blessed by the soothing words and wondered again at the difference between the two sisters. Chanddi would have her tongue cut out rather than say such a thing in favour of her son. 'Sister, please don't mind my asking, though ask I must... Why is there a world of difference between you and your sister? You're so nice and sweet and caring, and...' Kirti hesitated and left the next sentence unsaid.

'You're not the first person to ask me that question, Kirti, and perhaps you won't be the last person either. My husband has asked me the same thing quite a few times,' she said. She mused quietly for a few seconds and then added, 'She's been like that from day one, ever since she was a child. Probably she took after my father while I took after my mother. My mother was very docile, meek and submissive while my father is dominating and excessively possessed by false pride in himself. He always loved and adored her more than me. But, I think, she isn't bad at heart, just like my father. The only thing is that she wants full submission from you. You can get her to do anything by wheedling her, but she becomes increasingly repugnant when she's opposed. Although she's younger to me I always treat her as older than that and that's what she wants, a little coaxing,' Lachhi replied in detail and explained the whole matter with a smile.

And, now it was Kirti's turn to muse mutely and digest the disclosures. Why should a person rebuke and swear at others? Why should she imprecate evil upon us? Why is her face always sullen and grim, and menacing? Why is the distortion of her features the very hallmark that she must stamp on everything and every person? No, Lachhi's her sister after all, and she must stand in her favour, she concluded, but only to herself and dismissed the matter without protracting it any further. And the woman, who had appealed to her as most benign only some time ago, now began to irritate her. But she didn't want to show that she held contradictory views so she wore an impenetrable smile and said, 'You must be right, *bhainji*. Now tell me, what would you like to eat?'

Just then there was a knock on the door and she thought it must be Drupti and Nindi. But when she opened the door she saw Amar, Chanddi's elder son who said, '*Chachi* (Auntie), my mother's come back so send my *massi* home.'

Having heard and recognised the voice, Lachhi got up and asked for Kirti's permission to go, promising her another visit, some other time.

No sooner did she step out than Kirti saw Drupti and Nindi coming towards her. She stood there in the doorway and watched them coming, trying to wash away a number of blemishes that had settled down unduly on her erstwhile impeccable mind.

Convolutions

The Banyan tree had been changing its colours since the riots in Kohat had taken place. Many Hindus and Sikhs had lost their lives and their properties were set ablaze by the frantic demagogues. Fear of still worse to happen loomed large everywhere now that the Hindu Mahasabha, diametrically opposed to the Muslim League, had also come into play, spewing religious venom at people. They had no shortage of demagogues either. The Muslim League was equally adamant and it appealed to the extremity of savageness embedded in ape-turned-man in no smaller way than its opponent. The Banyan tree had begun to show signs of change; change for worse to happen. Aurjun, the newspaper wallah noticed the sudden alteration in colours and was alarmed. Sikander Ali and other Muslims of Qila Vasudev witnessed the transmutation and were terrified. Jagga and Bhaga and their father Niranjan Singh were appalled by the vicissitude. And the news soon spread to every member of the village, to the dwellers in the city, to the whole of Punjab and then across the country.

The change needed to be decoded and understood before it was too late. So they summoned forth Noordin the dyer, the common link between them, like the Banyan tree himself, like Qila Vasudev and like the long history they had lived together over the centuries.

The month of March in 1925 had half gone, welcoming the Spring season, the revival of vegetation, the re-blooming of perennial shrubs, trees and hedges and replacing the torpor with full-fledged life. And now, when they anticipated the harvest only a month ahead, the Banyan tree had come up with strange and abstruse warnings, encroaching upon all their pleasures. They had no idea of the lava that had been accumulating for so long under the crust of the land and, which was now ready to break asunder and erupt in profusion, turning everything into dust and ash. It was this lava that had percolated through the swollen roots of the Banyan to rise as high as its peaks transforming all the existing colours to something different. Noordin the dyer arrived equipped with all his age-old skills, with the stethoscope of his vivid eyes and ears and with his prophetic sixth sense.

Noordin commenced his studies while others watched. He began his study by watching the bloated and undulating roots bulging out of the ground showing a colour that was an intermix of green and orange and brown. He carefully hopped over the protruding roots so as to avoid the imprint of his feet on them for fear of contamination. When he noted down the colour in his diary, the onlookers saw his face turn grim and serious. Jerking his head to the tune of yes, he made a full circle of the jutting roots once again, looked at the marks on the bark and found scarlet freckles. He scribbled another note in his diary. Then came the turn of shoots dropped by the branches, which had taken root in the ground and had become secondary trunks, one, two or even three feet in diameter – known locally as the beard of the Banyan tree - straggling on all the sides. Some shoots came straight down like a thick rod while others made a variety of knotty or gnarled shapes. Noordin studied them closely, drawing his eyes closer and closer, touching those gnarls with his fingers, dusting them with the fringes of his white turban to ensure that no fingerprints were left on their solid torsos. He noticed that the skin had grown harder, more rough and merciless, perhaps burnt by something arising from within. The appearance was brownish, bluish and yellowish, which Noordin noted down in his diary accompanied by a special note at the end: 'The appearance must reflect the essence or the essence must be revealing itself through the appearance.'

There were over three dozens of those shoots, some of which had established their roots in the ground while others were still in the process of doing so but were, as yet, hanging precariously, like young children swinging in the village compound. Noordin looked at each one of them very carefully and, having finished with one side of the Banyan, turned to the other. Immediately, his well-trained eye caught sight of some new buds sprouting, and reflecting the essence in crimson. He jotted that down in his diary, too, and began to look at other shoots from as close as an inch to find the signs that authenticated the previous findings. And soon enough he discovered a multitude of such signs in corroboration of his previous research. Then he noted down three words consecutively: crimson, scarlet and vermilion.

The next step was to study the main trunk. It was fifteen feet in diameter endowed with thick, hard bark, capable of seriously bruising your forehead if you hit your head against it. The skin looked cracked and streaky and would peel away the epidermis of your hand if you touched it inadvertently. Noordin, the veteran dyer, knew how to approach his adversary. He took out a solid pair of rubber gloves from within his bag, put them on to his hands and went towards the challenging trunk like a cavalier to the battlefield. He stroked a tiny part of the trunk with his right hand and when he pulled it back the skin of the trunk had punched small holes into the sole of the glove. Soon our Noordin realised that stroking the ruffian was to invite the trouble, for it was absolutely unrelenting. However, he travelled around the trunk a few times, simply making use of his piercing eyes and abstaining from touching the trunk. To his extreme chagrin, the trunk supplied no clues of what was boiling over in its covered cauldron of a monstrous stomach. So, realising his limitations against the demon, Noordin took control of his vexation and noted down the apparent colours of the skin: brownish, greenish and orange.

By the time Noordin had finished dealing with the primary trunk of the Banyan tree he was exhausted and wanted to take some rest before mounting the second attack. It was also time for lunch and the villagers were already preparing to take a break of an hour to deal with the food they had brought with them. They laid out some charpoys under the shade of the Banyan and offered the first one to Noordin, the hero of today's drama. Each household had sent some food for the occasion and it was all vegetarian to avoid any religious conflict as Muslims would not eat Jhatka (meat of quickly killed animals) and Hindus and Sikhs would not eat Halal (meat of animals killed slowly with incantations from the Koran). Moreover, Muslims hated pork and the Hindus worshipped the cow. So to be and remain a vegetarian was to reap the benefits of both the worlds, wide apart from each other yet destined to live together.

Sikander Ali's son Abdul Khaliq had brought a cauldron of *pilao*; rice cooked with vegetables and herbs, smelling gorgeous and tasting delicious though a little piquant. Girdharilal had sent a big basket full of sweetmeats (*pere and barfi*). Chiraghdin had brought two big pans of well-cooked spicy *sabzian* or vegetables: one made from cauliflower and potatoes and the other from the leaves of mustard mixed with spinach and other tropical herbs. Ladha Kharasi had brought a load of chapattis softened with butter, while Jagga and Bhaga had brought pickles and chutneys and loads of salad made from radish, carrots, cabbage and onions. Everything was dainty, scrumptious and yummy and everyone ate it to their fill amidst talking, joking and appreciating each other's dishes.

The aftermath of eating began to show itself through yawning, sleepy eyes, lethargic conversation and finally they all decided to have a small siesta. Some lay down on the cots or charpoys and others on the floor, snoring and making other alarming sounds through their nostrils and throats. People swatted the flies that landed on their lips and noses where the smell of food emerged, attracting the tiny creatures. The sun was right over the head of the Banyan tree, vertically mounted in a sky that seemed confusedly dazed and dazzled. The shade of the Banyan tree contracted to a bare minimum with many sleepers now exposed to the direct sun. The awakened ones began to grumble at the heat and awoke others who were resting under the shrinking shade.

It was nearly 3 pm when they all woke up and began to sprinkle water on their eyes to get freshened up before embarking upon the second bout of unravelling the mystery of the changing colours. Noordin asked one of the young men to bring a ladder and slant it against the trunk to enable him to conduct his research on the branches, leaves, buds and the apex of the Banyan tree. And as the ladder was laid against the trunk, people gathered in a semicircle to watch the veteran dyer decode the inscrutable enigmas hidden in the Banyan.

Noordin took off his soft-soled shoes and put on hard-soled ones, together with a boiler suit on top of his clothes. Then he climbed up the ladder like a mountaineer about to conquer the Everest. People applauded his courage and watched Noordin's moves with restrained breath. He went up and settled himself on a flat space on the trunk, from where primary branches diverged in different directions. Then he began to look closely at one of the primary branches and then the secondary branches that emanated from it. Moving on to the tertiary ones he noted down every discovery he made. Having spent nearly half-an-hour there he went further up and then further up and then still further, treading over the branches quite sedately, keeping his equilibrium intact, until he was nearly at the apex. Everybody watched and witnessed the determination and courage that he showed and the circumspection with which he worked and the assiduity that he employed, thereby setting a trend for later researchers to follow. Everyone wished that his son Ferozdin had been here to watch his father's expertise but he was required at the shop where he would be dying girls' *chunnis* in a variety of colours by tying and dying to make them appear like a rainbow. If only he had seen his father at work he would have learned a million moves of the trade. But alas; if only things could happen the way we wished!

Noordin spent a good three hours combating the war with the giant of a tree, the big, big Banyan and then came down victoriously, taking each downward step discreetly and carefully.

When he had finally landed, the villagers began to call 'Noordin – Zindabad' or 'Long live – Noordin'. The village elders patted his back and said, 'Mothers ought to give birth to many more sons like you.' His equals in age congratulated him and the younger ones touched his feet in reverence.

Then there was a brief intermission when he sat alone and away from the crowd, so he could analyse the results of his discoveries and decode the message so he could put his prophecy forward to the people of Qila Vasudev, a unit that epitomised the whole of the country. He took nearly thirty-five minutes to accomplish his post-research work and then came over to sit on the podium that had been made ready for the purpose during while he was busy with his analytical work. The podium consisted of a wooden plank measuring six by four feet and was showered with the fresh green, fluffy leaves of the Banyan. No microphone was required for such a close gathering. Arjun, the newspaper wallah, acted as compere and Sikander Ali as the president of the convocation.

Uncle Arjun came on the podium and announced, 'Brothers and villagers! There's no need for me to explain the purpose of our gathering here today because it's self-evident. What I want to emphasise is that the Banyan tree and us are inseparable from each other. It's impossible to imagine the Banyan tree without us and us without the Banyan tree, which has been blessed to grow only in India and more so in Punjab. Our roots are common, our trunk is one, and yet, we, as its branches and leaves differ from each other. That's what we call unity in diversity or diversity in unity. Those who make the mistake of treating the Banyan tree as only a tree can't understand us. Just as India belongs to the Indians, so it does to the Banyan tree. Any study of the Banyan tree is, in fact, the study of the Indian people. And any change that appears in the body and soul of the Banyan tree is the change in the body and soul of the people of India. So, make no mistakes in understanding the duo. The land of India belongs to its people and its Banyan and none other. With this brief foreground, I invite Noordin the veteran dyer and decoder to address you and present his results. The last word will be said by our president, Sikander Ali *sahib,* but first of all the results of today's research. Please Noordin *sahib*, come!'

Noordin walked slowly and steadily to face the audience with his diary in his hand, cast a careful glance around, coughed his throat clear and began. 'Brother Vasudevans! Let's first take a look at the Banyan tree under whose vast umbrella we're sitting or standing. As our brother Arjun has said, there is no mistaking the fact that we the villagers and our Banyan are inseparable from one another. So let's look closely at the Banyan tree and ourselves; it would appear to be one and the same thing. Allow me to explain its composition. Its buds are our eyes by which we see new dreams. Without dreams man is only a dead mass. When the dreams die away, man dies away as well. Desolate are those people who have eyes but have no dreams. Unfortunate are those who have eyes but can't see. Then comes the turn of leaves, which are countless. At the beginning of the autumn, the leaves fall off, but at the commencement of the spring season, new leaves begin to take the place of the old ones. A new generation of leaves replaces the older generation, which falls off, withers, etiolates and passes away. These leaves are no others but us, we the people of the land. The branches on which they grow are our communal territories, our religions, our faiths and our beliefs. The Banyan tree lets no branch suffer for its individual existence as a distinct faith, as a distinct religion, and doesn't discriminate against any of them. They all get food from the same trunk and through the same roots, planted in the same land. The trunk of the Banyan is our common history, which we've lived and endured together for centuries. The roots are the common culture through which we draw our life-giving nutrition, for without a common culture we couldn't have lived together for so long. This culture is a mixture of many things starting with our common language, our geographical unity and our common history, climaxing with our common denomination as brothers. And the soil in which the Banyan is planted, in which or we are rooted is India – a common soil, our blood and bones and our very soul. When, because of the overwhelming heat, wrath or anguish, hatred and malice, the leaves (that is us) begin to curl and contort, we know they are hiding secrets, holding grudges and breeding contempt. The leaves or men begin to change colours, looking green outwardly, but turning yellow, black, blue and red inwardly. This is what we call the convoluted thinking. This kind of thinking is at the root of communal riots, tensions and troubles. And once we're convoluted, the demagogue, the religious impostor susses it out and incites us to kill and mutilate other leaves in order to satisfy his own selfish motives. The surface or the visible side of the curled up leaves exposed to sunlight remains green through the process of photosynthesis, but the inside of the curled up leaf, being deprived of sunlight, turns yellow and red and blue, and finally whitish brown. That's when the trouble comes. And, I humbly say that, please, don't take me lightly or for an ordinary dyer, because I am a chemist. I like the chemistry of colours, so I trained to be a chemist. Dying clothes is my hobby and my dying factory's my laboratory where I do my experiments. The chemistry of colours is no ordinary chemistry because colours are of paramount importance. Without colours, the world would be hue-less, odourless and tasteless.

I've closely studied the changed colours from within the convoluted leaves and I find this change is not for the better but for the worse. Following the killings and arsons of the North West Frontier Province, perpetrated by convoluted men, there's terrible tension here now. It seems to me that the next few years will take a heavy toll of human lives, whether those are the lives of Muslims, Hindus or Sikhs. I want to warn you to beware of demagogues of all hues, for they can see through your convolutions like dark forces at work. Once they see in you a dim shade of hatred against other human beings, these dark forces erode you of your humanity and sanity, and stimulate you to kill others, like the leaves of one branch of the Banyan killing the leaves of the other branch. This is all I have discovered from my research and study today. Thank you very much.'

Lastly, Sikander Ali wound up with these words, 'Brothers! You've listened to what our honourable Noordin Sahib had to say. It would be futile to add anything more to what he has already said. My words, even if spoken with full might, may not have the same impact as those of an expert, a specialist in the science of colours. I'm thankful to Noordin Sahib for guiding us on the right path at the right moment. Now my earnest request is that we are leaves of the same tree, our grandest Banyan tree, our India, and we should not convolute and hold secrets and grudges, hatred and malice against each other in our hearts. In the end, I thank you all and to brother Arjun for bestowing on me the honour of presiding at today's function. Thank you all!'

Centre and Periphery

Since the decline of the Ghadar Movement and incarceration of all its prominent leaders, save for those who had fled back to America and Canada, Kundan Lal Premi, Kabir's father, had become a recluse. Disappointment and frustration had overtaken him. His condition had been further exacerbated by his age-old asthma, intensified by his smoking and he found it difficult to breathe properly, particularly at night. He used to smoke twenty cigarettes a day but lately he had reduced the number to ten. Yet, according to his doctor, even that was detrimental to his health. The wheezing sound from within his chest had become noisier and was audible to a person standing or sitting even at some distance. Razia would do anything to stop him from smoking but was helpless before his obstinacy. Kabir was now seven years old and was in the third class of his primary school situated on the outskirts of the city, hardly a mile away from the village.

Too much talking was also injurious to his chest and throat because he had developed a swelling in his lungs. And the throat that once gave out clear and conspicuous sounds had begun to sound hoarse. Lately the sound had begun to turn into gargling noises. So, a once excellent speaker on the stage had now turned mute and muffled. He still wrote ghazals but was not able to read them out to the public on the podium like he used to some years ago. However, his ghazals did appear in papers and were widely read and appreciated by the readers, especially by those who belonged to his generation of revolutionaries. He also wrote a few pages of his memoirs almost every day but he would soon get exhausted. 'I shall have to complete my memoirs before death overtakes me.' He disclosed his intentions to Razia when she asked him to be more cautious about his declining health and stopped him from working. However, he still did his job as one of the editors in the Urdu paper 'Mazdoor'.

The incidents at Kohat had terribly shaken Premi. His anger was now exasperated by what he had heard from Noordin the dyer that day. He hadn't seen the whole programme because he had been at work in the city. He had been walking slowly towards the village after finishing his duty at 6 pm. He was at a distance of a couple of hundred yards when he saw a congregation of men near the Banyan tree, making him walk faster to find out what was going on. When he reached there, Noordin had only just started his analysis - the chemistry of colours. Premi listened and it was a turning point for Kundan Lal Premi. He was shocked to find out that factions of Hindus and Sikhs on one side and the Muslims on the other were bent upon destroying each other the way they had never done before. The Ghadar Movement, of which he was the product, was composed of all of them with no religious demarcations at all, all three working for the one and the same cause – freedom of the country. But what was happening now? And the very thought shook him to the depth of his soul. He thought of himself, Razia and his son, Kabir, and grumbled, 'What religion does my Kabir belong to?' But the answer wasn't easy to find, especially in the tangled scenario of the day, and that made him full of rage and consternation. Later, passing through the process of deep thinking, he made an unshakeable resolution that he wouldn't remain an indolent spectator of events anymore, but would work to influence them in whatever small way he could – a resolution to abdicate the state of recluse and come out into the open. 'It's better to die earlier than to live longer, but away from the *karmabhoomi* or the field of practice,' he muttered to himself as he made the resolve. But unlike Uncle Arjun, he had always been a man of the pen, a pen-soldier, as he called himself. So, he took the oath and threw himself heart and soul into the task of writing a series of articles for the more popular press, which would later become material for his memoirs.

Kabir had agreed to lend me the cuttings of papers containing those articles, which his father had deposited in a safe. At a glance, I could tell that the articles began from 1924 and went to the end of 1929. There were quite a few repetitions here and there, which needed to be edited. Having read all the articles, I made a condensed summary of them all so as to fit into my story organically. In his observation and interpretation of historical events, Uncle Premi seemed closer to the Mahatma than to any other, because his very first article began with *swaraj, swadeshi and satyagraha* etc. In fact, like many other revolutionaries of that day, he too, was Ghandian at heart. All his articles carried different headings in accordance with the month or year witnessed

1925

151

The Montagu-Chelmsford reforms of 1919 seem to be at the root of what has been happening since 1920. The reforms made the provinces an arena of paramount political activity and significance, boiling over with frenzy as never before. Men with political ambitions and inclinations have been running around like headless chickens to wrest power and take control of the resources. They have been dying to wrench political power through legislation, administration and patronage, and through exploiting religion and communal or sectarian emotions. The Kohat tragedy that inundated the NWFP and its adjacent areas is just one of the several manifestations of what these reforms have amounted to. I should not call them reforms but destruction. The grim religious tensions, confrontations and killings that followed 1919, prove the point that Indians are not capable of controlling themselves let alone controlling the country. They have grown accustomed to being whipped in order to be controlled.

Mahatma seems to have been grossly misunderstood by all of us. We interpret *swaraj* only as governing the country ourselves whereas it means governing ourselves. *Swaraj* is self-rule. How can an individual or a nation rule the country if it is incapable of ruling itself? Today, all the provinces in the country furnish an example of lawlessness, manslaughter, brutal killings, rampaging and chaos. Our political subservience is the result of social and moral crisis. Moral degradation is the worst thing that can happen to an individual or a people. This is what we have to tackle first. We shall be in no better state if we replaced the British in the existing seat of government. We shall have to learn to control ourselves before we are able to control the country.

Self-rule or self-control means to control your desires and to live within your means. As Indians our means are limited and so must be our desires that lead to the concept of *swadeshi*. Increasing your desires beyond your means is bound to lead you to become subservient to others.

Self-control and *swadeshi* together will lead to unity among Indians. Unity is disrupted only when desires (economic or political) become uncontrollable. It is then that we begin to rob others, dispossess others in order to possess things ourselves. Strangulating competition and unity are diametrically opposite to each other. You get into this competition and you want to run the race and surpass others culminating in disunity with others.

Dispossessing others to make yourself rich results in inequality. Inequality leads to further social grading and the creation of Untouchables. Every poor person is, in a way, untouchable. For the eradication of untouchability we need a system of equal distribution of resources among men. Equality lies in self-control and not in conflicting competition. The unbridled desires of men can cause havoc in the world.

The concept of provincialism, an attribute of the aforesaid reforms, has already caused enough destruction, and it is still rampant in the Punjab and UP and other provinces, consuming more and more lives every day. Although the Mahatma was released from the prison last year, he seems to have lost heart because of being misunderstood. Now he seems to have taken recourse to social work and spinning.

I think his gospel of *ahimsa* and *satyagraha* has been misconstrued as well. Satyagraha, or soul-power, can be trained to become the mightiest influence, through self-control. Our servility to our desires erodes our soul, leading to loss of self-control, and if there is no soul left from where would soul-power come? Violence, too, destroys the soul but non-violence generates and preserves the soul and its power. Satyagraha cannot exist without non-violence. Once you resort to violence, it breeds more violence and then more violence and the process becomes unstoppable. Satyagraha, non-violence, self-control and tolerance of violence perpetrated by others to a certain specified extent, would lead to eventual *swaraj*.

Where a conflict of opinions and interests occurs, the right response would be the peaceful persuasion of the opponent of the rightness of your cause. But always be ready to compromise, except on vital principles. Action should only be used as a last resort. Action would be satyagraha. Whether it rouses the consciousness of the opponent or not, I have absolutely no idea, but you will definitely have to suffer the consequences. It would be the test of your self-control and hence your integrity. And as long as your commitment to your cause is strong enough you will not be able to bear the consequences or sufferings.

1926

The extension of unlimited political powers to the provinces by the Montague-Chelmsford Reforms has created a kind of provincialism that can be defined as a haven for factionalism, communalism, classism, casteism, Hinduism, Sikhism and Islamism. The national struggle for *swaraj* seems to be over. The All India Hindu Mahasabha, and the Muslim League are at loggerheads with each other. Congress, which once showed the promise of taking the country forward on the path to freedom, seems to have lost its charisma. There was once an alliance between the Muslim League, the Khilafat Committees and Congress but the non-co-operation movement that had its roots in this grand alliance and ran from 1920 to 1922, has finally collapsed. The split sent all the three participants in different directions. 'The political action towards the provinces' – a calculated strategy under the veneer of reforms, has broken apart the fabric of the society into shreds, thereby showing how myopic and parochial we Indians are. The so-called reforms have laid bare the Indian soul, which is full of selfishness, filth and untruth. Perhaps, the rulers knew it already, and that was why they did what they did. It shows what kind of country free India is going be, if ever it comes about.

Communal hatred is ubiquitous, in each town and city and in each village. Until yesterday, the communal strife was confined to the cities but now the villages, far removed from the cities, are the scenes of communal riots. Older people have surrendered to despair and the younger ones are interested only in their own advancement by whatever means and however reprehensible. Congressmen councillors are tumbling over each other to shake hands with officials and are clandestinely attending official functions. Whatever India is to become in future is visible today.

A strange kind of new order is emerging, not according to Gandhi's *swaraj*, not according to the dreams of great gurus, but according to the ethics of brutal killing and plundering, and selfish motives and ends. Unity has vanished, the character has disappeared, the soul has become invisible and the whole body of the country has become paralysed. It is all the more upsetting that the Muslim League held a separate conference two years ago in 1924 and Congress met separately. This formidable division is going to take us nowhere except to a protracted period of slavery. The strategy of the Muslim League portrays a federal structure for India in which the provinces would be largely autonomous and in which the Muslims will continue to have separate electorates. It is very clear that the provinces with majority of one faith would rule the roost and the minorities would be suffering more than ever before.

So, provincialism suits those who are in majority but the danger is that Provincialism would eventually lead to anarchy and to sharp divisions between communities of different denominations. The pattern of adjustment to the new order has resulted in a sharp break between different communities on the basis of religion, factionalism and gruesome ill feelings against each other. The relations between Hindus and Muslims have grown bitter; minorities have been relegated to the fringes and those who want political power have drawn themselves nearer to the rulers. The Indian perception of identity and the right framework for their lives has undergone a tremendous change for the worse. There is an acute divide between the 'no changers' and 'pro-changers': all the territories with Hindu or Muslim majorities are pro-changers while the ones with equal or near-equal numbers of disparate factions are no-changers. The national unity that was forged by the Mahatma a few years ago is now in ruins as a result of provincialism encouraged and augmented by the unsavoury new reforms.

1927

We are reaching the end of the year and it is about time that we had a close look at where we started and where we have finally landed. Starting with a non-violent, non-co-operative movement as a united people we have reached a stage where nothing is united anymore. Disintegration, disunity, communal tensions and factionalism are rife and are devouring the heart and soul of the country. The figures of communal riots that engulfed the country resulting in colossal number of deaths and injuries are to hand now, and they make one tremble with fear of times to come, shedding a lot of light on the dangers and uncertainties of our ways. A series of communal riots occurred in Calcutta last year (1926) and this year, killing 197 people and injuring more than 1600. Similarly, the riots that have taken place in UP in the last 4 or 5 years have left 81 people dead and 2301 injured. Over 40 riots took place in Calcutta and over 88 in UP. Communal antagonism is prevalent everywhere in the country, especially in the Punjab, UP and Calcutta. City streets and village alleys have seen hundreds of dead and thousands of injured according to these reports though we know the official figures always err on the minus side. The reports are silent about the anatomy of these riots, about their flash points, leadership and the way their news spreads to ignite further conflagrations in other towns and villages. But it is not hard to fathom who masterminds them.

The conductors of Hindu Mahasabha and the religious fanatics from within the Muslim League are the ones who do it all. Their motive is to divide Indians on religious and communal lines. When we look at the incidents of cow killing, music outside the mosques, and examples of religious processions turning into occasions of potential riot between local Hindus and Muslims, we cannot shut our eyes to the cause of it all. Firebrand religious leaders and demagogues together indoctrinate the rabbles in such a manner and to such an extent that the killing and injuring of people of the opposite faith becomes a pastime for them. During the last three or four years the pattern of conflict, violence and counter-violence has remained the same. Rumours of actual or suspected violence bred more violence through retaliation. The fears of the minority have increased because the majority can now put the resources of new provincial political structures to immediate use. Muslims majorities in the West of Punjab have resorted to using the power of legislation, administration and patronage in this way, thereby improving their own position and shaking the minorities to their very roots.

The last four or five years have also seen economic dislocations and financial constraints on the governments, thereby further exacerbating the rivalry amongst different factions, who fought to extract the maximum out of limited available resources. The Hindu Mahasabha's reclamation programmes of *shudhi* and *sangathan* and the Muslim League's programmes of *tableegh* and *tanzeem,* and the British missionaries' outreach have further intensified concerns over religious boundaries and the numerical strength of the religious groups – another rendering of the new order of provincialism – leading to tumult and disruption. It has generated a fear of change in the balance of numbers between Hindus and Muslims. All these chaotic situations have been created by the politicians at both provincial and pan-Indian level, and from the actions and propaganda of both communities.

This year has seen Jinnah toying with the idea of trading joint electorates with others to safeguard Muslims where they are in minority. He has been busy playing with the acquisition of one-third of the seats for his minority. The Muslim majority areas like Punjab and Bengal have already seen increasing provincial autonomy that suits them best. However, now there is a split in the Muslim League as well, with one section following Jinnah to a meeting in Calcutta, and the Punjabi Muslims secure in their provincial majority, following MA Shafi to a meeting in Lahore.

In the face of all this, Mahatma seems to have lapsed into despair at the crumbling of the communal unity that he had perceived as one of the pillars of his *swaraj*. Now, he has resorted to prayer and personal friendship as an alternative to the concept of *swaraj*.

1928-29

These two years have been ones of turmoil, both for the British and for the Indians. The British confronted a major challenge to their position as legitimate rulers and the Indians faced the challenge of the emergence of new political alignments. The western models of politics were questioned quite seriously and as an alternative, the British found that Congress, the disparate Muslims groups and the princely order were inadequate as reliable sources of political authority.

As a reaction to the aftermath of communal tensions and dissidence of Indian leaders, the British Government appointed a statutory commission chaired by Sir John Simon under the 1919 Government Act. It's role was to report on the system of government in India and on desirable changes. But Indian opinion was hostile to the appointment of the commission because it was composed of Britons only. It was a negation of the imperial promises of consultation with Indians and their incorporation into all the decision-making procedures. As a result, the commission was boycotted by Indians as a whole, including the Muslim League. Following the resentment over and rejection of the Simon Commission, an all party conference was organised by the Indians, resulting in the formation of a sub-committee consisting of T.B. Sapru and Motilal Nehru. Their task was to draft an Indian constitution as an alternative to the Simon Commission's would-be report.

The Nehru report proposed of an India with the same status as other self-governing dominions within the British Empire. The report had tackled quite a few other questions in the context of relations between the centre and the provinces. It said that the devolution of power to the provinces would not be increased and the residual powers were to remain with the centre. The report had treated the Muslims as Indians with full freedom to abide by their faith and conscience and had agreed to the provision of new Muslim majority provinces, including Sindh and NWFP, but denying them separate electorates. However, in the case of majority in any province, seats were to be reserved for them in addition to the reserved seats in the centre.

But Jinnah's section of Muslim League rejected the report with the criticism that it gave ascendancy to Hindu majority and was thus anti-Muslim. M.A. Jinnah insisted that the residual powers should be vested in the provinces rather than in the centre, as a guarantee of Muslim interests against a Hindu dominated state. Thus the fissure between Hindus and Muslims widened into a chasm and Jinnah made the 'Parting of the ways' proclamation. Motilal Nehru urged Mahatma Gandhi to return to active politics to avoid the split, at least in the ranks of the All India Congress. The Mahatma agreed to do that saying that it was his sacred duty to strengthen the Indian unity for *swaraj*. In spite of that, Congress lost most of its membership, dropping from 500,000 to 50,000 only.

This year has seen the All Parties Muslim Conference under the Agha Khan's presidency to protect the Muslim interests. By the middle of the year, the only Muslims who were left in Congress were the nationalists of the All India National Muslim Party with A.K. Azad, R.A. Kidwai, Syed Mahmud and M.A. Ansari as their leaders. They are important to Congress if it wants to project and maintain its image as a national party.

The Nehru report was received with open discord among the ranks of Congress with a powerful section advocating complete independence for India rather than being a dominion, as was envisaged by the report. But now it seems that they have all agreed to submit the Nehru report to the Government on the understanding that if the report is not accepted by the end of the year, Congress would advocate the case for full freedom.

A close study of 1928-29 boils down to the fact that the Muslims are bent upon making the provinces or the periphery much stronger than the centre, in particular the provinces of Punjab and Bengal and other provinces in the west where they are in very large majority. On the other hand, Congress and non-Muslims want the centre to be stronger than the periphery. The antagonism is not going to end here; it will lead to many more ramifications in the foreseeable future. The divide between Hindus and Muslims has now widened to form a schism, resulting in new and unexpected political alignments never before envisaged.

However, there is also a new generation of would-be leaders coming on the scene from whom we can expect some good sense, leader such as Jawaharlal Nehru, Rajindra Prasad, Valabhbhai Patel and the like.

It is now up to them to stem the tide of communal upsurge, riots and disruptions, to unite the whole nation into a single entity and take it across the tumultuous rivers of lava of mutual hatred.

Special Note: At the end of the last article Kundan Lal Premi had given a note of apology, which I am obliged to give here in italics so that you know why Uncle Premi stopped writing these articles.

Note of Apology: Because of terrible decline in my health I shall not be able to write any more articles for which I apologise to my readers who have always taken the trouble of reading me and writing letters in appreciation of my articles. Thank you all.

Might is Right

It was as though Krishan was waiting only to be twelve; and when he was he became a worshipper of Hanuman, the monkey god, the son of the wind whom people adulated as 'pawanputra Hanuman ki jai' – victory to the son of wind, Hanuman. Krishan's conversion took everyone by surprise, even his mother and father and his two remaining unmarried sisters. But no one mocked him as they would some years later when he bought a flute and began to play it, but in vain, and catapulted the flute into a thicket of bushes on the side of the village pond, where it was forever irretrievable. Now in 1930, not only did he worship the son of wind but he also took the solemn oath to adhere to all those things that went with Hanuman's worshipping.

For instance, he began to consume a good amount of fresh butter and buttermilk, or *Punjabi lassi*. He began to exercise every morning. It was his way of creating a strong body for he knew that a sound body carried a sound brain and a weak body carried a weak brain, which was the reason why he didn't like Gandhi Baba.

There was a joke in the air in those days with regard to Gandhi Baba. One day, nearly a year after the Jallianwalla Bagh massacre, Mahatma Gandhi paid a visit to a village near Amritsar. He was guarded by two well-built Pathans, both over six feet tall. Many people came to see him, the man who was determined to shake the British Empire to its very foundations. Then came a tall, broad chested and sturdy farmer to see the shaker of a man. The farmer saw this small, skeletal and shrimp-like creature amid the crowd of onlookers and felt unable to place his trust in the bare-bodied ascetic. Then he went to the centre where the Mahatma and his body-guards were planted, held the shoulder of one *Pathan* and said to the gathering, 'You should've cast this man as Gandhi, not him; he's too weak to be one.' At that the whole crowd burst out in a choking laugh.

No wonder then that my friend Krishan found himself in the position of that farmer and placed no trust in Gandhi Baba. He did one hundred *baithkaan* or sit-ups, and twenty *dand,* or lie-ups, adding more to the number, gradually. His thighs and arms swelled with power, like the son of the wind and, Krishan felt exhilarated. Of course, he had to rub a lot of mustard oil on his body and massage it well into the pores of the skin before he embarked upon the daily quota of exercise. Having done everything to his satisfaction, he would have a thorough bath with cold water and then eat as much as was placed before him, sometimes asking for more.

But perhaps that was not enough for the pursuit of a sound body. The body had to be put to an arduous labour, too. And for that reason he began to go to a wrestling arena in the middle of the city, called *'akhara Hanuman'* or the arena of Hanuman where only the worshippers of the son of the wind were permitted to put their muscles to fight in traditional Indian wrestling. A non-worshiper or a non-believer in the monkey-god could enter the place only as an observer.

The other thing that went with the worshipping of the monkey-god, or the son of the wind, was the observing of the cult of *jati-sati* or *tyaag,* or abstention from sex. So, my friend Krishan began to observe this abstention from the age of twelve. He didn't look at any girl that came his way, and when he talked to his mother or his sisters he bowed his head down, never crossing his eyes with their eyes lest his pledge should be broken. 'It's vital to be a *jati-sati* like the lord himself if I want to acquire physical power because sex destroys your might, which has to be gleaned bit by bit,' he explained to me one day.

'And what do you do to be a *jati-sati*?' I asked him out of curiosity, for I had no idea of what sex meant in those days, being only eleven, a year younger than the 3 Ks.

'A loincloth, wearing a loincloth before you put on your underwear is the answer to the crisis. Keep you genitals under strict control. Make them all dead and suffocated,' he clarified, lowering the cord of his underwear and showing me the red loincloth underneath.

'Who did you learn all this from?' I asked, bewildered because there was no Hanuman temple in Qila Vasudev and thus no worshippers to learn this from.

'From a friend of mine in my school, whose father is a strong wrestler and a stern worshipper of Hanuman, the son of the wind,' he replied mirthfully and bubbling with delight at having known something we didn't.

'Is his father a *jati-sati* as well?' I asked again.

'Must be, otherwise there's no point in following the path of the *pawanputra* Hanuman,' he concluded.

'How was his son born then?' I enquired. Krishan listened to me and began to think deeply, scratching his head with his finger, and then said, 'You do have a point there, but I don't know the answer.'

But that didn't deter us from talking further about his newly found pursuit.

'Next time when we perform the *Ram-leela* (the drama of Rama's life) I would like to play the Hanuman's role in it,' he said. Ever since we were children, we had seen *Ram-leela* being staged in the village. Later, when we grew up, we had begun to take part in it ourselves. It was an ongoing thing; every year. Some excerpts from the great epic of Ramayana would be chosen and staged. Although the characters and their fates were already well known to the audiences, yet they rejoiced in seeing it played, played and played again. The skill was in the presentation of a particular character and the way dialogues were delivered. There were many such groups in the city and they all presented different episodes in their own particular way. It was a countrywide thing and Qila Vasudev was no exception.

The fun of staging the drama of *Ram-leela* was that you didn't have to have the whole cast ready to perform the full length of the saga. The story was extraordinarily long and could continue for years like a soap opera and yet without coming to the final conclusion. The minimum number of actors needed was two and you could stage just one episode from this classic with the same intensity as with a larger part or the whole drama. Last year, when we did the *Ram-leela* we had only four actors available to us; we made Krishan play the female role of Sita, wife of Rama, Kabir took the role of Rama, Kinner that of Ravana, and I acted for the part of Lakshmna, Rama's younger brother.

All these characters of the epic have been exiled from Ayodhya for a period of fourteen years and are now somewhere in the land of Ravana, the demon-king of Shree Lanka. While the two brothers, Rama and Lakshmna, go to fight a war against the so-called evil forces - apparently Dravidians, of whom Ravana was the King - Lakshmna draws an *agni-rekha* round Sita (a circle beyond which there is evil) and announces, 'As long as thou stay in the bounds of this circle you will be safe but once thou cross this circle you will be unsafe.' But unfortunately, Sita steps across the circular line one day and is abducted by the demon-king, Ravana, resulting in an outbreak of an open war between Ravana and Rama (or Dravidians and Aryans). Here you need lot of extras, which every village abounds with, particularly on the slopes of the village where the *Sudras* live. Their children play as rabbles or the *vansena*. All you need is a kind of tumultuous atmosphere on the stage, as though a lot of real fighting were going on. It is always better if you have more actors. You need someone to play as Ravana's brothers Vibhishna or Kumbhkarna or his sister Shurpanakha, and someone to play as Hanuman the son of the wind, a Brigadier-General of the army and a rabble-rouser – all to fight in favour of Rama and Lakshmna and against Ravana. But if you don't have that many characters it wouldn't matter, for it is easy to take one mask off and put another one on, or to replace one cap with the other, like the Indian political defectors.

As a general rule I would be the writer, director and producer of the epic-play or any part of it, and Krishan's sudden defection to the sect of Hanuman posed some very serious practical problems for me. For one, it took me long time last year to teach Krishan how to walk, talk and behave like Sita. A melodious way of talking, a majestic walking and an air of feminine charisma were not naturally forthcoming in his actions. But then somehow he learned it. And now, if he changed his role to that of the monkey-god I would be in double trouble again, for altering him from femininity to masculinity would be like replacing all his genes. Then there would be the problem of who would play Sita's role. The only possibility would be Krishan's sister, Gita, but who would allow her to expose herself to the audience, especially now, when she was fourteen. So, my business as a writer, producer and director of the play would be seriously jeopardised unless I did something to remedy the situation very soon, before the moment slipped out of my hands.

On another day, I requested Krishan to take me to the *akhara* of Hanuman too; not because I wanted to follow the faith or cult but because I had developed in myself a kind of curiosity and wanted to know more about the worshippers of the son of the wind. One reason among many others for this inquisitiveness was that Krishan, who until last year had been scared of accompanying Kabir and I to the Jallianwalla Bagh and was overly controlled by his mother and sisters, had now turned out to be somewhat brave and courageous. The son of the wind had made him a valiant and had instilled in him a sense of defiance, for until last year he wasn't even allowed to travel to the city along with us, let alone all by himself. But now he went alone and came back alone, too. So, he condescended to my request and took me along the very next day.

First of all we went to the shop of his father, Girdharilal, who served us with a large glass full of milk each, topped with lot of *malai* or milk fat that was thick, creamy and delicious. Then he gave us a plate of *barfi* to share between us. By the time we had finished eating *barfi* and drinking milk I felt heavy with a surfeit of food. It was a nauseating experience for me. But Krishan, it seemed, had grown used to eating and drinking such amounts of fatty food as he showed no sign of such discomfort.

'Now, go to the *akhara* and do some strenuous exercise. Your uncle Motilal will be waiting for you there,' Uncle Girdharilal said and began to serve a newly arrived customer.

The *akhara* Hanuman was not too far away from the shop; it took us barely fifteen minutes to reach it. The *akhara,* or arena, was a part of the Hanuman temple situated at the end of a road called Hanuman Road. It was a cul-de-sac, a no through road. Right at the entrance to the temple, mounted quite high, was a gigantic coloured portrait of Hanuman flying like a giant bird, carrying a small mountain on the palm of his right hand – a mountain with the accretion of a host of plants, trees and shrubs growing in thickets. The muscles of the son of the wind were swollen and twitching to the extent that I was scared enough to shudder involuntarily.

The story went that once upon a time, when Rama's younger brother Lakshmna became faint or went in a coma due to extreme wounds on his body, inflicted by the war between Rama and Ravana's armies, an ascetic told them to go to the Himalayas and bring back the herb called *sanjeevni.* The smell of this herb would break the delirium and bring Lakshmna back to life. When the puzzle of going to the far-off mountains faced Rama and others, Hanuman the son of the wind offered his services to his lord Rama. However, when Hanuman reached the mountain ranges he couldn't discern the right herb from the wrong, because there were thousands of different varieties. Embarrassed and confused, the monkey-brain uprooted a part of the mountain, perched it on his hand and fled back to his lord.

In another portrait on the left hand side, the monkey god had elongated his tail to a hundred times its normal size, had agglomerated it into a high and tapering heap and was perching on it, looking jovial and gay. In the middle of the temple courtyard stood a huge sculpture of the son of the wind in white marble, looking ready to fly to the Himalayas, to the snow-laden peaks of Everest. The walls of the temple had depicted the monkey god in various poses, painted in a variety of colours, some appallingly seditious and others covetously enthralling.

When we reached the rear of the temple, we found a multitude of men and boys engaged in vigorous exercise, engaged in sit-ups and lie-ups, in rubbing mustard oil on their bodies and massaging it deep into their pores. Some were fighting duels in the *akhara*, which was full of soft, protective and oily earth. All of them seemed to be worshippers of the monkey-god, Hanuman. While I occupied a corner near the wall to watch attentively what was going on, Krishan went straight to his uncle, Motilal, who I was to see for the first time ever. Motilal (as I learnt later) was the cousin of Girdharilal, who had charged him with the responsibility of looking after his son and shaping a good bodybuilder and a wrestler out of him. When, Krishan had expressed his ambition to become a worshipper of Hanuman, Girdharilal had immediately summoned his cousin Motilal and was pleased to find this new proclivity developing in his only son.

'Why do you wish to be a bodybuilder and wrestler and a worshipper of Hanuman?' I had asked Krishan on our way to the city.

'Because only Might is Right. A physically weak or enervated person has no life in the world. You ought to be powerful like Hanuman to wield the world around you. To remain *jat-sati* or celibate is also vital for a *bhagat* or worshipper of the Hanuman,' he had explained. And I had wondered how could Uncle Girdharilal divert his only son towards celibacy when he himself had sired six children?

Motilal seemed to be in his late thirties and was one of the important men of the *akhara* Hanuman. He trained new recruits to the sect and the *akhara*. Quite well built and tall, Motilal was wearing a loincloth covered with an underwear in a strong fabric. He was standing in the middle of the *akhara,* teaching the boys disparate tricks of the craft of wrestling. He saw Krishan *arrive* and went ahead to touch his head and stroke his face with affection. Soon after that Krishan began to get ready for the exercise by taking all his clothes off and retaining only the red loincloth.

I could see a small group of men making *shardai* in a large stone trough filled with almonds and seeds of various fruits, grinding the whole thing with a strong, stone spindle and adding milk to it slowly and steadily. Once the strong white liquid was ready, they began to distribute it among the men and boys, glass by glass, until it was finished. They would serve it again, later on. So, that was what this business of bodybuilding, wrestling and worshipping Hanuman, the sturdy son of the wind, was all about. Eat and drink like a pig and digest it like a monster. There was no need for brain; all that you needed was muscles. Mighty muscles meant force, and force meant usurping what you could. Might was right, that was what my friend Krishan had come to believe in, at least for now.

There were about two dozen men and boys in the whole place. When a new duel was started, both the wrestlers blurted out one phrase: Hanuman ki Jai – victory to the Hanuman - and began to fight. The fights were between wrestlers of the same age or strength, boys with boys and men with men. To me, they seemed to have forsaken all their other concerns about the world outside the *akhara* and were limiting their interest to themselves, and to what they were wallowing in. Soon, I began to feel bored, sick and repelled by the monotony of the game, and made up my mind to relinquish the place straightaway. But it was necessary to inform Krishan of my intentions, and as soon as I found him on the brink of the throng I rushed to him, whispered into his ear, 'I must go now, Krishan. I'll see you at the village.' I left without waiting to hear his reaction.

In the world outside the *akhara* Hanuman, there was lot of turbulence about the *purna swaraj* (full freedom), and against the Dominion status. The Mahatma had resurfaced and was about to launch another bout of civil disobedience starting with the salt-march. The concept of Dominion status had proved irrelevant for Gandhi and others, and even the Round Table Conference in London had failed to achieve its objectives.

We, the children of yesterday, were fast growing up, stirred and shaped by the political events taking place around us, and we inherited and imbibed what our elders were doing. It was impossible to shut our eyes to those all-pervasive developments. Conflicts and consultations were going on simultaneously: the civil disobedience was the conflict that united the people to force their way forward, though non-violently, and the Round Table Conferences were the mode of consultation to thrash out a solution that would be acceptable both to the British and the Indians.

The civil disobedience had gathered a lot of momentum and it became a national movement in span, drive and intention. The kind of political awareness and action it generated had never been known before. The range of people involved in it showed how significant it had become. The hard core of participants in processions, meetings and overt law-breaking were townsmen joined by a considerable number of students, although boycotting of government schools and colleges was significantly not a part of the programme. Most participants came from the middle classes and from prosperous and respected backgrounds, and could not be dismissed simply as rustic rabbles.

Peasants, businessmen and workers – all were making monetary contributions to the coffers of Congress in order to support and enhance the movement. Those who could not participate physically acquiesced in the boycott of the foreign cloth. Despite being under economic and social pressure, they hoped to force the British to concede financial control of Indian affairs to Indians. The most exceptional feature of this new wave of civil disobedience movement was the participation of women. It was first time ever that the women had joined actively, taking their place in the local Congress organisations and forming picket lines with Mahatma's particular encouragement. Mahatma knew the non-violent method suited the female temperament and talent. By the end of the year as many as 360 women were in jails for their active parts in the campaign.

Kabir and I often joined the processions in Amritsar, which were always peaceful. It was at this stage that both of us had begun to wear *khadi*. Kabir wore a *khadi topi* or cap and I wore a *khadi* turban, just like other grown up congressmen. A lot was being heard about another Ghandi in the North-West Frontier Province, who had come to be known as 'Frontier Gandhi'. Uncle Arjun and others from Qila Vasudev resented the non-co-operation of Muslims in the central Punjab and explained the reasons in terms of the 'end of khilafat issue' that had once given the movement a formidable cutting edge in the early twenties. In Punjab, mostly Hindus and Sikhs made their contributions to the civil disobedience movement while Muslims held themselves aloof. The newspapers published the news of the total number of imprisonments for the year in the whole country. The figure was over thirty-thousand people, of whom less than two percent were Muslims.

Sweep of Nationalism

Kinner wasn't lucky enough to have had the formal education that the rest of us had had. His mother, Reshma, was old and worn out but still worked as much as she could to keep the family going - but only just. Kinner's brothers found odd jobs here and there and brought some money home to make both ends meet. Radhika had taken over the household duties from her mother when she was barely ten. Life was desolate and precarious for all of them. Nobody paid any heed to the miserable plight in which they lived. They existed on the margin of society, were treated as untouchables, low-caste and wretched ones. A mud-house with a thatched roof standing on the downward slope of the village, at the side of the pond – a sanctuary for mosquitoes and malaria – was what they had in the name of the property, was what made them belong to the village. That was their house, their village, their city, their province and their country and their Hindustan. Was that what Kinner would have been expected to fight for with the British? What kind of nationality and what kind of nationalism would be expected of Kinner and his family and their likes in the length and breadth of the country?

I often found Kinner teetering on the margins of the village, wandering forlorn on the fringes, talking to stones, to trees and to the ruins on the far side of the village. One day, when I was coming back from school with my small satchel slung on my shoulder, I found him sitting on a stone, all in rags, looking into the far distance quite

168

drearily. It was the end of 1928. I stood close to him, trying to see what he was watching in the distance. But there was nothing there except a haze, a flimsy film of smog caused by the dense population of trees and bushes. My presence didn't bother him at all. He kept on looking regardless of my existence. A little intrigued, I began to look at him more seriously. Unkempt hair, smudgy feet, scruffy hands and forearms, and blackened neck with overlapping layers of dust – he seemed strangely outlandish. I began to feel pity for him. It was not the first time that I was seeing him. He had been there in the village ever since I had begun to see things with my own eyes. And I had noted his predicament many times before but hadn't really felt it as deeply as now. His plight filled me with awe and commiseration at the same time. I took my satchel off my shoulder, placed it on the ground and sat down beside him on a smaller stone.

'What're you thinking about, Kinner?' I asked him.

'Nothing,' he replied as though from within an abyss.

He stopped looking into the distant haze and tilted his head down, concentrating on his bare feet, cracking miserably at the heels. His toenails had overgrown and were protruding like tentacles.

'Can I help you in any way?' I asked again, this time holding his scruffy hand in mine.

'I don't know whether you will or will not!' he uttered.

'I promise I will,' I assured him.

But he lapsed again into a well of silence and began to look away into the distance where a couple of cows were grazing in an uncultivated field.

'I promise I will,' I reassured him.

'Can you teach me to read and write?' Kinner asked me, looking sharply into my eyes.

'Yes, I can but only as much as I know,' I said.

'From when?' his eyes began to glitter.

'From when you're ready,' I said.

'From tomorrow?'

'Alright!'

'How about books, copies and pencils etc?'

'I've got my old books still with me, and I'll manage all other things for you,' I replied with certitude.

'Thank you! I'll wait for you here tomorrow. Just this time,' he said and got up. When we were walking towards the village, I found Kinner undergoing a metamorphosis already.

Kinner had an extraordinary knack for reading and writing and for sculpturing and then for painting. He was a born genius with phenomenal talent bestowed upon him by some mysterious force of nature. His capability astonished me every day after I began to teach him. His hunger for more and more knowledge, for more books, for more erudition was insatiable. By the end of 1929 he had learned everything that I had learned in so many years at school. And now we were in nineteen- thirty-one.

Swaraj, swadeshi and civil disobedience had begun to sweep the whole nation directing it towards nationhood; Punjab, like other provinces, was full of frenzied activity. It was unlikely that the tide of nationalism wouldn't take us youngsters in its resolute grip. While all other interests were declining, the interest in India's complete independence was waxing constantly. One day, an extensive but peaceful march and rally was taking place in Amritsar. Kabir and I had decided to go as usual but we wanted to take Kinner and Krishan along too. So first of all we went to ask Krishan, who, at the time was doing his sit-ups and lie-ups and was wearing the same old red loincloth with his body well-massaged and shining with mustard oil like a greased horny bull. I gave a knock on the door and waited for an answer. Soon Krishan's sister Gita unbolted the door from inside and opened it. She had been playing *addi-tappa* in her courtyard and so was breathless. She was fourteen now and the clothes she was wearing seemed too tight for her, especially her shirt, which her well-grown breasts seemed to be tearing apart. The sight sent me reeling and something churned in my heart. The act of *addi-tappa*, a girl's game of hopping up and down on one leg, had made her cheeks glow red.

'Is Krishan in Gita?' I asked, gazing evasively at her cleavage with eyes tilting down every second. She immediately took note of the intention of my gaze, put her arms around her breasts in an effort to camouflage her cleavage, turned round and shouted, 'Krishan! Your friends are looking for you.'

170

The next moment, Krishan was right in front of us like a mini Hanuman.

'Eh Hanuman, we've come to take you to the city to join a procession,' said Kabir, looking at him from head to foot and evincing a suppressed smile.

'All right then. Allow me half an hour to take a bath and get ready,' he said sharply.

'Allowed! Meet us under the Banyan, okay?' Kabir commanded him before we bounced back, turned round and began to walk away.

Then we made our way to Kinner's mud-hut. Radhika was home but not Kinner. She told us that Kinner had gone out in the morning and hadn't yet come back. 'I know where he might be,' I told Kabir and whispered his hiding place to him.

'Why is he always looking for ruins to conceal himself in?' asked Kabir, wondering more about his peculiar habit than posing me a question.

'He's an intellectual, a genius and a mental giant. And I tell you what, one day he's going to become someone very special, a celebrity. The ruins have a lot to offer a person who has the capability of comprehending its secrets. Kinner's a born philosopher, a genius and a brainy man,' I went on speaking, selecting the best words I had learnt so far to reveal his gifts.

'How do you know all this?' he asked, quite sceptically.

'I know because I spend a lot of time with him. Already he knows much more than either of us do, and that's despite the fact that he's never gone to a formal school like us,' I emphasised.

'Yes, but you've been teaching him, haven't you?' Kabir questioned back.

'Only what I know; the rest is all his personal effort and talent,' I reasserted.

Passing by the side of the pond on the northwestern side of the village we went over a small bridge and down towards the highway at the feet of the vast ruins, full of detritus, stones and bricks. As we drew closer we saw someone hiding behind the relics of a demolished wall like a spectre.

'Is that his hiding place?' asked Kabir despicably.

'That's right ... I hope it's him,' I said.

Yes, it was Kinner, squatting in the corner under a collapsing, half-ruined wall, reading something. He looked at us and began to smile.

'What brings you here, boys?' Kinner asked satirically and deposited his book into a small bag.

'We've come to interview you for a paper,' said Kabir.

'Shut up!' said Kinner, prolonging his accent.

We sat down on two separate stones facing him and Kabir began to cast cursory glances at our surroundings

'Do you know the history of these remnants?' asked Kabir, gazing into Kinner's eyes.

'Histories of all the ruins are the same. Every present ruin must once have been a grand habitation of people, bubbling with life until some invaders razed it to the ground,' replied Kinner, looking at the large stones perching farther up the slopes, around which grass had grown to half-swathe them.

'What you mean by invaders?' retorted Kabir as though Kinner had meant some particular invader.

'Anything from men to natural hazards, all are invaders,' he replied.

'But I'm talking about this particular place, and who devastated it,' Kabir insisted.

'There're no particularities in history, generality is always the answer,' Kinner said, musing like a philosopher.

Kabir, a little stunned at Kinner's words and the way he had spoken them, began to look at me as though acceding to what I had said about Kinner some moments ago.

'But for today we've come to you for a particular business,' I said with a dim laughter.

'No business is particular either, it's always a part of the general and larger business. What do you want from me, anyway?'

'We seek your kind company at a rally in the city to which we've decided to go,' I said sarcastically.

'I'm sorry, rallies and demonstrations and marches aren't my forte,' he put a full stop to any further discussion.

'What's you forte then?' asked Kabir furiously.

'I don't know yet. Maybe I shall know it in a few more years,' he replied with a deep sigh and reclined back against the falling wall.

'Let's make it an outing,' I tried to bring him round.

'This is my outing, which I undertake everyday,' he refused to budge.

Kabir seemed to have grown sick of Kinner's obstinacy and rudeness. 'Let's go then. Krishan must be waiting for us,' he said, standing up and beginning to walk away, assuming that I would follow him anyway.

'Kinner, can't you do it for my sake?' I asked using the last trap.

'I can do anything for you except this business of rallies and processions,' he replied curtly and then apologised. 'I'm really very sorry, Arya.'

'Alright then, I'll see you some other time,' I said and followed Kabir, who had travelled quite a distance by now. I had to run to catch him. All the way Kabir was as quiet as a mute stone and I didn't think it worth the effort to engage him in any further conversation, for I knew he was no less stubborn than Kinner.

When we reached the village we saw Krishan waiting for us under the Banyan tree, all in his white *khadi* like a true congressman. We too, had *khadi* on. Together we began to march towards the city.

The procession was overflowing with people of all ages including women. The ebullience with which they all boiled over showed the vivacity that was taking the country across the troubled waters. It seemed as though the whole of Punjab had gathered in the city of Amritsar. The length of the procession was immeasurable; the strength was obvious and the discipline was peerless. They had spinning wheels with them and they were spinning cotton into thread that would, later, be woven into *swadeshi* cloth to cover Indian bodies, replacing the foreign textiles.

They were also selling salt to defy the law: another feature of the civil disobedience. Volunteers were serving water to the thirsty while many were donating free meals for anyone to eat. Self-restraint and control were the hallmarks of the whole crowd who were in *khadi* with seriousness engraved on their faces. The police were roaming about boisterously but were unable to provoke Mahatma's disciples. The humming of the spinning wheels provided the necessary orchestration to the seriousness of the song of self-rule. There were

Hindus and Sikhs in the procession but the general absence of Muslims was miserably felt and deplored. A countable number of Muslim leaders who shared their conviction with Mahatma were on the front lines, while the actual procession declared their stark absence. The communal cleft seemed to be widening by the day, a bad omen for the days to come.

The procession moved slowly, now stopping and then recommencing its march, allowing the spinning wheels to hum out their call of *swadeshi* and the soul-power. The humming would force the authorities to call the Mahatma again to London to sit on another Conference around the Round Table to thrash out solutions. To mobilise such large numbers of men, women and adolescents like us in every town and city and in every province couldn't be an easy task. The credit went to the Mahatma and people sang his praises.

Fascination and captivation went hand in hand. It was fascinating to see it all happen and it was captivating because you felt inclined to join in yourself, to be one of them. The battle was being fought with soul and spinning and not with sword and shield. It was a subtle method of fighting a battle that emerged that day for the first time in the history of the country, and on a monumental scale. We went from one part of the procession to the other and found the same order and discipline being adhered to everywhere. No disruptions, no clamouring, no vilification and no slandering. Unable to resist the temptation of involvement we too, joined the league of volunteers who supplied drinking water to the procession.

It was announced that the whole procession would later reunite in a rally at the Company *bagh* where some prominent leaders would peacefully address the participants. So, the procession began to head towards that spacious garden at a slow pace. And when, at 5 pm, the procession reached its destination, the participants perched on the green grass and began to play on the spinning wheels and listening to the speakers simultaneously. Complete independence was the crux of each speech. The rally lasted for one hour and then the people began to disperse. We went to the *thandi khoohi,* the cold well, known for its provision of chilled water even during the hottest summers. There were dozens of hawkers on the road on the side of which this *thandi khoohi* stood, selling *chhole-bhathure, gole-gappe, poorian, chicken tikka, seviaan, daal-roast* and many other things. We had a plate of *chhole-bhathure* each and drank ice-cold water from the *thandi khoohi* and by the time we finished with all this the time was 8 pm.

'It's about time we left,' said Krishan. We duly accepted his counsel and took the road leading to Qila Vasudev.

Hiatus Widens

1932 was the year of despair and frustration for the Sikhs of the Punjab but a year of buoyancy and exhilaration for the Muslims. The long-awaited Communal Award had treated the Sikhs with bias and discrimination. In spite of their unique position in Punjab, they were not given the same status in the legislature as the Muslim minorities were given in other provinces. The Muslims had 14.8% of the population in UP and were given 30% of the seats in the Provincial Assembly whereas the Sikhs were given 18.8% of the seats in the Punjab Assembly against their population of 13.5%. The position of the Sikhs had been further weakened in the formation of the Provincial Cabinet. In the days of dyarchy they were given 33% seats in the cabinet or at least 25%, but now they were to be given still less.

The progressive deterioration of the position of Sikhs in the Punjab Cabinet was strongly resented by them; the discriminatory treatment meted out to them encroached on their religious and cultural rights as a minority, indicating a waning of their influence on the political and economic life of the country.

The Sikhs were lamenting the betrayal by the British for whom they had contributed eighty-thousand men to fight the Great War, in addition to thirty-two thousand and five hundred already serving. The number of Sikhs in the defence forces exceeded any other community and was out of proportion to their population of six million in India as a whole. Furthermore, they were the erstwhile rulers of the Punjab under the rule of Maharaja Ranjit Singh until 1849 when the British had assumed that rule. The Communal Award was meant to safeguard the interests of a minority in a province but in the case of Punjab the safeguard of the interests of the Majority (Muslims were in majority in Punjab) had been ensured. It was a sheer injustice to the Sikhs and a violation of the basic nature of the award.

Uncle Arjun, newspaper wallah, was extremely sad when I last saw him. He had two houses in the village: one in which his family lived and the other where he stayed all day, reading books and meeting people who came to see him from within the village and from the city. He went to the family house in the evening. I knew where he would be after 7 pm, obviously in his family house. So I went straight there, knocked at his door and waited for it to be opened. The door was unlatched from inside by his eldest son, Udham Singh, a military man of about forty-five, who had probably come home for a short holiday. Uncle Arjun had five sons and two daughters – all his sons were in the British army, recruited on a regular commission and held good positions. The villagers called them five *pandvas*. Resham, Thakur, Balbir and Gurbir were younger than Udham. Both the daughters had been married off long time ago, also to military men. Uncle Arjun's father, Puran Singh, had died when he was ninety years old. Uncle Arjun was now sixty-eight years old.

Among all the families of the village, Uncle Arjun was the richest with almost twice as much land as Sikander Ali. All of his sons were over six feet tall, like Uncle himself. I didn't know how we children came to call him Uncle when all his sons were equal to our fathers in age. They were equally uncles to us, and in that sense Uncle Arjun should have been our Grand Uncle. But never mind, as long as Uncle Arjun didn't object to our addressing him like that.

All five brothers had been married long ago, and we children knew nothing of them. They had their own large families but we saw them very rarely. The families lived with them wherever they were stationed. Ambala, Jalandhar and Meerat cantonements were the commonly spoken names when the elders talked about the brothers and their places of employment. The sudden appearance of Udham Singh from behind the door puzzled me, for I had thought the knock would answered by either Uncle Arjun himself or his wife, Auntie Ghulab Kaur. My immediate reaction to the receptionist was my folded hands and the utterance of *sat sri akal*, the Sikh way of greeting. Udham Singh was in his military uniform with quite a few ribbons hanging on his chest. It looked as though he was ready to launch an attack on the enemy with a pronouncement of *ready...steady...shoot*. I was so nonplussed that I stood there rooted like a small tree in front of the Banyan. Seeing me bewildered, he mustered a smile on his face, caught me softly by the arm and said, 'Come on, my boy, why are you hesitating? Haven't you seen me before?'

Encouraged by his words, I let myself be dragged in. Soon, I saw a beautiful lady in a bluish Punjabi *salwaar kameez,* sitting on a cot with her legs hanging down, talking with Auntie Ghulab Kaur. I bade *sat sri akal* to both of them to which they both responded mirthfully.

'*Bapuji*! Your Arya Gold is here,' Udham Singh made a loud announcement while I stood beside the two ladies answering their question as to how my father and mother were.

Uncle Arjun came straight out and waved his hand to me inviting me in. I could tell from his grave looks that he was disconsolate. I followed him in and perched on his bedside, trying to interpret his mind.

'I'd like you to be a historian when you grow up – a historian of Sikh affairs. That has been our snag; we haven't been able to produce a good Sikh historian, who could write our history. Do you have any interest in writing?' Uncle Arjun asked me. I had just begun to do some odd scribblings, which he didn't know about, in fact no one did, and I hesitated to tell anybody at that stage.

'I'm fond of reading books and magazines and sometimes a newspaper if I get it from somewhere,' I replied.

'That's good. Reading's crucial to becoming a writer. What kind of books do you read,' he asked.

'Nothing selective; whatever comes my way,' I said.

'No, that's not a good thing. Always stick to one subject, no matter what that subject is. Read history if you have some interest in it. Reading history is to know your roots and moreover, history unfolds many secrets in front of you,' he said and paused for a few seconds.

'You must've heard about this communal award,' he recommenced, 'that has just been announced by the government. It shows how unjustly the Sikhs are being treated at every level. But this Baldev Singh and other Sikh leaders seem incapable of presenting the case of Sikhs to the authorities. The Muslims seem to have more efficient and brighter leaders than we have. We're in a

177

very small minority in the Punjab of today because its boundaries have been artificially extended. The Punjab proper used to extend to the bank of Jehlam, excluding Jhang and Multan districts. The trans-Jehlam area was added to it by the conquest of Maharaja Ranjit Singh, and then retained by the British for administrative convenience. This extraneous trans-Jehlam population of Muslims, who came into the province of Punjab only by accident, cannot be allowed to dominate non-Muslims. If that area is taken out of the province and the Punjab proper is kept as it used to be before its inclusion, then Muslims and non-Muslims would be equal in number and neither would be able to dominate the other. That's what it should be like. But in the present state of affairs, we, as a minority, should be allowed the right of representation in the Provincial Assembly in accordance with what Muslims have been allowed in UP as a minority. But our leaders are absolutely hopeless, I tell you. We lack leaders and historians. We can create history but can't record it for posterity. That's why I want you to grow up as a brilliant historian to record the wrongs that have been done to us.' He explained the case in detail and came back to the point of departure again.

'I'm going to ask your father, Shiv, to encourage you to study as much as you want to, for a historian must be a very learned man. I know you're quite clever and intelligent and you can make my dream come true by being a historian. I'll tell Shiv to back you up with a strong hand,' he said his eyes gleaming at me.

'But he wants to see me as an advocate!' I said abruptly as though the position of a historian would be more acceptable to me than that of an advocate. Although, as yet, I wasn't clear in my mind what actually I wanted to be. Scribbling was what I did, if it meant anything to anybody.

'It's the same old trivial stuff. Every Punjabi peasant wants the same; wants to have his son fighting litigation cases for him by being a lawyer or an advocate. It's all so ridiculous. They don't seem to think anything about the nation. All they want is their own petty benefits. That's why they always lag behind others. But no, you must become a historian, a Sikh historian. If Shiv doesn't let you then I'll talk to Parvati. She's much wiser than my stupid nephew Shiv.' Uncle Arjun said the last words quite furiously.

The Volcano

Uncle Arjun and my grandfather were cousins, being from the same clan. We descended from one ancestor some centuries ago. Yet, I wondered how Uncle Arjun's father Puran Singh had gathered so many acres of land when we had comparatively few. Uncle's house was a big *haweli* whereas ours was an ordinary house. I had no answer to that and had never attempted to know it until quite recently. Maybe, I would ask my father or my mother; she would know it, I thought.

I didn't mind Uncle Arjun swearing at my father, calling him stupid because he had done so once even to his face and my father had just laughed it all away. It was like my father calling me stupid, which I wasn't supposed to take badly. These were the ways of all the fathers in the Punjab and he was no exception to this grand rule. Could well be that I would do the same to my son.

Uncle Arjun seemed to have relaxed a little after letting his stress out by talking to me. He knew I was a grand listener and a retainer of things, ideas, opinions, and knowledge in my memory. And he liked me for that.

'Uncle! Don't you like my friend Kinner?' I asked, knowing not why and whence this Kinner had suddenly got in. Probably, somewhere in my subconscious mind I had retained the impression that Uncle Arjun didn't bother whether Kinner sat amongst us or went away when Uncle was talking to us.

'Well, there's no reason for me to dislike him. He's as much a member of Qila Vasudev as anyone else. Moreover, my religion, Sikhism, doesn't permit me to look down upon anyone, as does Hinduism. Hinduism and more especially Brahminism, treat them as Untouchables but not Sikhism. In fact all the Sikh Gurus tried their level best to eradicate *Chhooa-chhaat* (casteism) from society, and that was precisely why the last Guru Gobind Singh had his five loved ones selected from the downtrodden people, baptised them with *Amrit*, life-giving nectar, and got himself baptised by them. There is no place for untouchability in our religion. Even the poets like Kabir, Ravidas and many others from the so-called lower castes have been given an honourable place in our holy scriptures. I'd be deviating from the path of Sikhism if I disliked them or treated them differently from others. But what makes you think that I dislike him?' Uncle explained the tenets of Sikhism and then asked me a question in the end.

'Nothing really, Uncle. It just occurred to me all of a sudden and I asked it,' I replied with a wince.

Soon after that I made up my mind to leave. Uncle didn't stop me. So I left his room, bade farewell to the ladies and Udham Singh and stepped out of the door. It was the end of November and the trees had shed all their leaves to go stark naked. The sight suddenly brought back in my memory the forgotten lines of a poem written by an anonymous poet.

> Cajoled by weathers these credulous trees,
> Now hide behind leaves then go stark naked.

The thought was really marvellous. It was the height of personification in poetry. However, the weather was really gloomy, dismal and saddening. I made my way straight to Kinner's thatched mud-hut and found him home by sheer chance. His moves were always unpredictable. He was like a gust of wind; now here and then there. Restlessness was his whole chemistry. A lover of volcanoes and ruins and lava, he wanted to see everything demolished and then re-made from scratch.

'Kinner, how do you feel about what Dr Ambedkar has achieved?' I asked him when we sat down face to face on string cots in the front yard of his hut.

'What has he achieved?' He cross-questioned me with a grimace across his face.

'One hundred and forty-eight seats for untouchables in the provincial legislatures – double the number that was offered in the Communal Award,' I explained, citing the figures in case he had missed the news.

In fact, the political events had taken a very serious turn in the last year. Although Congress, as a political party, claimed to be representing the whole nation, its claims were often belied. The communal minorities didn't support it fully and the Award was announced by the British, without the Indian agreement. Mahatma had opposed the separate electorates for untouchables, but the All India Muslim Conference held last year in Delhi had claimed separate electorates for Muslims in addition to special representation in provincial and federal legislatures and the creation of some new Muslim provinces, with the provinces retaining the residual powers in the federation. But the nationalist Muslim leaders opposed the separate electorates together with Congress, although they had very little or no influence among Muslims of the provinces. Later on, Ambedkar, with a solid majority of Untouchables behind him, joined the Muslims. The government wanted to appease Muslims in every way to prevent them from joining the anti-Imperial movement started by the Mahatma and his Congress.

The Mahatma had threatened to fast to death if the Communal Award granted the untouchables a separate political identity from other Hindus because he didn't want further social divisions taking place, which he considered as false and damaging to the Indian nationhood. Finally, the matter was resolved by the Poona Pact: separate electorates for untouchables were abandoned but reservation of double the seats for untouchables was agreed upon, together with a sum of money from every provincial budget for free education for untouchables. Then the Mahatma drafted a resolution that was approved by the Bombay Conference under Mr Malavia. It said: 'No Hindu should be regarded as Untouchable because of his birth, and those who had been called Untouchables would have equal access with other Hindus to public wells, roads, schools and other public institutions.'

'It's going to make no difference, no matter what your Mahatma says,' Kinner responded in agitation.

'What should be done then?' I asked.

'Demolish, and reconstruct everything from scratch,' he asserted.

Just about then his sister Radhika entered the house with a couple of packets in her hands. She, it seemed, had done some shopping from the village grocer. She was a year older than Kinner and according to my immediate calculation, would be fifteen then. She was looking gorgeous with her dusky skin and black hair, done in a knot at her back, and her curvaceous, firm breasts covered with her green *chunni* in a way that drove you mad. She was tall and slim, and captivating with her usual suppressed smile running across the sides of her thin-lipped pout. 'The real Radha of Lord Krishna couldn't be more beautiful than her,' I thought to myself and felt enthralled by her charm and personality that had developed so suddenly over a couple of years, despite all the constrains and hardships they faced.

'Shall I make some tea for you people?' she asked in a voice that equalled the singing of bells in some remote, far-off, sacred place.

'Yes, do it,' said Kinner in a cacophonous voice.

'Do you have to speak so rudely to her?' I objected to his rough and discordant style.

'I haven't learned to hide my usual self under the so-called civilised veneers,' he grew rude with me, too.

I didn't feel offended because I had grown used to everything that he said and did. In addition, the centre of my conscious attention was Radhika. He was only the subject of my off-the-cuff remark whereas my whole being was occupied by the smell of nectar that rose from the make-shift kitchen and reached me unhindered, making me imbibe it and get intoxicated, ending in delirium.

Shakespeare
Under the Banyan Tree

Noor Mohammed, the grandson of Sikander Ali, came very rarely to stay in Qila Vasudev, and when he did, it was for a week or two and no more. His young sisters, Sabiha and Samina, though they lived in the village, hardly ever showed their faces to the villagers, let alone strangers. The courtyard of their *haweli* was their only world; it was there that they roamed, played, sang or quarrelled with each other, or did whatever they wished to do. They must have been subjected to strict discipline by their mother, Shaista Begam, their grandfather, Sikander Ali, or their father, Abdul Khaliq. We boys hardly ever saw them out on their own. Even on Eid and other special occasions, Shaista Begam escorted them to the mosque. Such severe restrictions were not imposed on Feroza and Sharifa, daughters of Farid the vegetable grower or *arayin*. They roamed freely in the streets of Qila Vasudev and went where they had to go. The economic and social status of a family had a lot to do with the amount of freedom allowed to the female members of the household; the richer the family, the lesser the freedom, and vice versa.

Noor Mohammed lived mostly in Lahore with his grandfather and grandmother, the parents of Shaista Begam, where he studied in an English medium school. We, the boys of Qila Vasudev, would wonder why he looked like a white *sahib* when he paid a short visit to the village during his holidays from school. He looked like a white *sahib* because he wore English-style clothes unlike us: trousers, a shirt with a tie and a hat on top of his head would be his usual appearance, and it repelled us, for he seemed like a foreigner to us, not one of us. All that we (Krishan, Kabir, Kinner and I) did was to smile to each other when we saw him coming to the village in a motor car or in a bagghi, a high-class horse-driven cart. He would step out of the motorcar or bagghi and go straight into his house. He seemed outlandish to us and we must have been for him. Except for those few days when he stayed in the village, and we talked about him, trying to envision his usual surroundings, the white teachers and the classrooms of his school, he was almost non-existent for us. We sometimes thought that he might take us for uncivilised, rustic beings, lacking sensible ways of dressing, behaving and talking. We were always dressed in our usual Indian clothes and sometimes walked and played barefooted. So, despite being from the same village we belonged to two different worlds; the distance between those two worlds was so enormous that our voices would have been inaudible to each other even if we spoke at the highest pitch. It could well be that we would have failed to comprehend each other's language. It would suffice to say that we flowed in two separate cultures, he in Western and we in the Asian.

But the summer of 1933 surprised us all. Noor Mohammed spent nearly two months in the village and most of this time he was with us. We were further astonished to know that he spoke Punjabi as well as any one of us, Urdu as good Urdu as none of us, and his English – well, it was bound to be excellent, for he studied in an English medium school.

We knew Noor had come home from Lahore and expected him to stay for a week or so and then go away. That was what usually happened. But it didn't happen that way this time. On the second or third day of his stay in the village he came out in the evening, clad in a *Pathani salwaar kameez* like any other Muslim, or like his grandfather Sikander Ali or his father Abdul Khaliq. Suddenly he caught sight of me standing near the Banyan tree, approached from behind and surprised me by saying, 'How're you, Arya Gold?' I turned round immediately and was nonplussed to find Noor talking to me, for almost the first time since we had grown up. He had spoken in Punjabi, and had structured bridges over the rivers of distance that had stretched between us all these years. If he had asked that in English the distance must have stayed as it always had.

'I'm fine, Noor, how are you?' I responded in Punjabi, and with love and affection, and a welcome-gesture written on my face.

'I'm fine too, but I always miss Qila Vasudev and this Banyan tree in Lahore. There must be many of them there but not even one where I live, I mean the school hostel,' he explained with a tinge of pain in his small sharp eyes.

'Why can't you come back and join an English medium school in Amritsar? There must be one or two around?' I suggested.

'I don't know. We never enquired about that,' he said and gave out a light laugh, which was meant to dismiss the matter.

'Will you stay here for some time?' I asked.

'I could if there were something for me to do,' he said.

'What do you mean?'

'I mean, we do lot of extra-curricular activities during our school holidays there in the hostel to keep ourselves busy and away from boredom. Those activities sharpen our existing skills and also add to our experiences. But here…'

'What sort of activities are those if you don't mind telling me?'

'No, not at all. We pick up some play, rehearse it and stage it. It's all very fascinating; and the time sprints by like a bullet too. Two months of summer holidays pass away like two days there. But here, time creeps like an ant. And you can't study books all the day, can you?'

'Of course not,' I said. 'And why can't we do a play here? I mean we do have talent in the village. The only thing is to channel it in the right direction. How about staging a play here, then?' I offered him an idea.

He began to think and look around as if the idea had rung some bells in his brain. After a little more musing and circumspection, he whistled and clapped his hands.

'Yes Arya, we can stage a play here, under the Banyan tree. We'll play 'Merchant of Venice' under the direction of Shakespeare himself. We'll adapt it to our conditions and call it 'Merchant of Amritsar'. I'll prepare the script and play Shakespeare and the merchant, while you and your friends shall play other characters. How about that then?' he said euphorically with his eyes glinting.

'Splendid! You get on with your script and I'll arrange the cast. But mind you, the play has to be in Punjabi as our audiences are Punjabis,' I cautioned him.

'That won't be a problem. I'll write Punjabi in the Persian script, is that right?'

'Yes, that'll be fine,' I said jovially.

'And I suppose we'll stage the play, say a month from now if everything goes well,' he envisaged.

'Fantastic!' I exclaimed.

He shook his hand with me and went away, saying, 'Sooner the better.'

Noor Mohammed took two weeks to finalise the script, which turned out to be an abridgement and adaptation of the Merchant of Venice suited to Indian conditions. As for the names of characters, Antonio became Deewan Shah, Salerio became Somnath, Bassanio was replaced by Basant Kumar, Portia by Paro, Narissa by Nandi, Duke by Nazim, Shylock by Yahoodi and Balthasar by Prem Singh Judge. Many other characters were simply ignored or removed from the adaptation because it was impossible for us to find the actors from within the village. Shakespeare and Deewan Shah were to be played by Noor Mohammed, Somnath by Kabir, Basant Kumar by Krishan, Paro by Radhika, Nandi by one of Radhika's friends, Nandi, Nazim by Kinner, Shylock by me and Prem Singh Judge by Radhika in disguise. Soon after the script had been discussed and finalised, we began to do the rehearsals. Another four weeks went into this arduous preparation and by the time we were ready to stage the play, Noor Mohammed was left with only one more week of his school holidays.

Auntie Razia, Kirti, Drupti and Rukmani designed the costumes for the actors and the stage was set by all of us. The date for the play was fixed for the following Sunday at 2 pm, and we distributed hand-written posters throughout the village. Something absolutely rare was taking place in our village, and everyone was enthusiastic about it. Although we had been very busy all through the project, the last two days were the busiest. The first major problem confronted us because of the undulating surface of the ground under the Banyan tree, owing to its bloated and bulging roots. The actors could easily stumble against those roots and fall, resulting in fractures or strain to their feet and ankles. So we had to run to the local brick kiln to get bricks and had to request the village bricklayer to lay them in such a way that the floor became even, or nearly even. We had been so consumed by the rehearsals that none of us had thought about that problem until we started doing up the stage underneath the Banyan. Kundan Mistry, our village bricklayer, had already committed himself to do someone else's bricklaying job that day. It cost us lot of effort and energy to convince his customer to postpone their job until next day. Now, Kundan had to go without wages for one day, but he didn't mind it. He laid down bricks in between the roots in such a manner that the ground became reasonably even. The whole of Friday was eaten up by this business of bricklaying but we were happy that some progress had been made in the construction of the stage. The next thing was to divide the stage into three or four small compartments, which we did by the use of curtains. The court scene was made ready by the use of two larger tree stumps to serve for desk and chair for the judge, while the smaller ones could be used as benches for other characters. The characters could easily hide behind the big trunk of the Banyan or behind the secondary shoots when their part was over or while they waited for their turn to come. The music was to be provided by the singer-priest from the village's Sikh temple.

By Saturday evening we had sorted out everything but were still nervous as to how the actual performance might go. Noor had suggested that we would have to do two or three rehearsals on the actual stage to gauge the effect. So, on Sunday, we got together under the Banyan tree at 9 am and began our rehearsals. The villagers began to gather in front of the stage at 1pm. They sat on the floor, carpeted with hay that made the floor fluffy and comfortably cushioned. By

1:30 the whole village had gathered and were listening to the songs emerging from the stone-records being played on a gramophone provided by Uncle Arjun, which people called *vaaja*. One of the songs was *akhian milake, jia bharmake, chale nahin jana, ho chale nahin jana* (Don't you go away after meeting your eyes with mine and stealing my heart forever). By 1:45, all the prominent people of the village had assembled and were seated in the front row. These were Uncle Arjun, Sikander Ali, Girdharilal, Niranjan Singh, Abdul Khaliq, Noordin the dyer, Jagga and Bhaga and KL Premi. At exactly 2 pm we started the play – Merchant of Amritsar.

...

(Noor Mohammed appears from behind the big trunk of the Banyan tree)

Noor Mohammed: Brother and sisters, Vasudevans! Today, we are going to stage a play here, a play that has been written, directed and produced by the Great Shakespeare himself. The play is called 'Merchant of Amritsar'. I want to say no more except that I'm going to ask the great writer, director, producer and actor to confront you in person. So, I beg your leave now and hope you like the whole show. *(He disappears behind the trunk and comes out from the other side with Shakespeare's clothes and mask)*

Shakespeare: Hello everybody! I'm Shakespeare, born first on 23 April 1564 in Stratford on Avon in England and now, reborn in the land of Lord Krishna. Lord Krishna said that the soul never dies; what dies is the body, the ephemeral abode of that soul, whereas the soul puts on another body, then another and then another. I'm no ghost standing in front of you. Instead, I'm Shakespeare's soul in another body, a more recent one. So, don't be afraid but co-operate with me. They say 'while in Rome do as the Romans do', but I want to say 'while in India do as the Indians do'. Am I right?'

The audience shouted back, 'You're perfectly right, old man.'

'Right then, listen carefully. I wrote a play in 1595 called 'The Merchant of Venice' which I've now changed to 'The Merchant of Amritsar'. As the writer of the play, I'm omnipresent in every character. I'm everywhere and nowhere. I exist and I don't. I speak and yet I don't speak. And you must've been surprised to hear me speaking in Punjabi. I do speak Punjabi because I learnt it soon after my demise in 1616, under the auspices of East India Company in Shri Rampur College at Calcutta. Now, I shall only start the play but I won't end it, for by the time it ends I would be gone to take birth in some other part of India the land of re-incarnations and rebirths. Plainly speaking, nothing ends in this world because every end leads to a new beginning. Only forms change and nothing else. There's no shortage of Shylocks with inborn malice to take the flesh of others to end their lives in India. So the drama continues. It does not end. Shall I start the play?'

'The audience shouted back, 'Please do, please do.'

'There you are then!' He disappeared behind the big trunk and then came out with new costume and new mask as Deewan Shah, followed by Somnath.

Scene One

Deewan Shah: I don't know why I'm so sad. Where does this sadness come from? Is it that I've yet to know myself?

Somnath: You're sad because your mind is tossing on the ocean where your ships are sailing – ships loaded with merchandise. And there're so many traffickers and pirates around these days.

Deewn Shah: You may be right, Somnath, but my sailing ships aren't the only ventures I'm involved in. My fortune isn't locked in one place but in many. So it can't be the ships' cargoes that are making me sad.

Somnath: Then, let's say that you're sad because you're not happy and that's what keeps you from laughing and leaping. (*Enters Basant Kumar*) Here comes your bosom friend, Basant Kumar, better company for you. I would've stayed till I'd made you happy, but now I must go and leave you two together.

Deewan Shah: I'm sure your own business calls you my dear Somnath. So go if you must. (*To Basant Kumar*) Hello, my friend Basant, how are you?

Basant Kumar: I'm fine, Deewan, but you don't look very well. What ails you my friend?

Deewan Shah: Nothing in particular, Basant, it's just one of those things. Everything has a reason, but some don't. What brings you to me today, anyway?

Basant Kumar: My debts, my heavy debts, if you wish to know, Deewan! It's well known to you that I've crippled my estate. I just want to escape from my great debts. And to you, my friend, I owe the most in money and love, and from that love, I'm sure, you'll unburden me from my debts.

Deewan Shah: You stand aloof in the eye of honour, Basant and for that reason my purse, my person and my extreme means lie unlocked for you.

Basant: I hesitate to speak to a friend and I don't know why.

Deewan: You know me full well, Basant, don't you? Then do tell me what I should do that in your knowledge may be done by me?

Basant: Well, there's a rich heiress in Bombay, called Paro. She's fair and fairer than that word with wonderful virtues. Sometimes, from her eyes, I have received silent messages. The whole wide world knows her worth and, therefore, well-known suitors from all four corners of the world come to beg her hand in marriage. Oh my, Deewn, if only I had the means to rival those suitors I would definitely make her mine in marriage.

Deewan: I understand what you mean, Basant; but as you know, all my fortunes are at sea. I have neither money nor any commodity to raise a sum. But go forth and try what my credit can do in Amritsar. The money-lenders do trust me yet and may lend you enough in my name to enable you to ferry to Bombay, to your fair Paro.

Scene Two

(Enters Paro with Nandi, her maid)

Paro: I don't know why my body is weary of this great world.

Nandi: You would be, my dear madam, if your miseries were in the same abundance as your good fortunes. People with abundance can be as unhappy as the ones who starve for want of bread.

Paro: Good sentences and well pronounced.

Nandi: They would be better still if well followed.

Paro: If it were easier to follow than to say, things would be completely different and better than they are. I can teach twenty people but can't be one of them and follow my own teachings. But this reasoning is not the way to choose me a husband. Oh, how I hate the word *'choose'*. I may neither choose whom I like and nor refuse whom I don't – so is the will of my dead father. Isn't it all very hard, Nandi?

Nandi: Your father was a virtuous man, fair lady. Holy men always leave good inspirations. Your picture can be found only by someone, who opens the right chest out of the three: the gold, the silver and the lead. The one who discovers the secret shall have you as his woman. But how do you feel about the suitors you've already seen?

Paro: All right! You name them one by one and I shall tell you how I feel about them.

Nandi: First of all there's the soldier prince.

Paro: No, he sounds like the son of a blacksmith, for he said that he could shoe his horse himself. He does nothing except talk about his horse all the time.

Nandi: Then there was Mr Sulky.

Paro: He does nothing but sulk. He hears merry tales but frowns. He will prove a weeping philosopher when he grows old, being so sad and sullen in his youth.

Nandi: How about the Frenchman?

Paro: He could pass for a man but he's every man in no man. If I should marry him, I should marry twenty husbands. If he would despise me, I would forgive him, and if he would love me to madness, I shall not be able to requite him.

Nandi: And how about the Englishman?

Paro: He doesn't understand me, nor do I him. He has no Hindi, no Punjabi and no Urdu and you'll bet I don't have a paisa-worth of English. He looks like a proper man but who can converse with a dumb show?

Nandi: And what do you think about the Scottish man?

Paro: He seemed to have borrowed a box of the ear from the Englishman, and would pay him back when he was able to.

Nandi: How about the German?

Paro: Very vile in the morning when he's sober, and most vile in the afternoon when he's drunk. When he is at his best, he's a little worse than a man, and when he's at his worst he's little better than a beast. I shall make shift to go without him.

Nandi: Then how about the Indian – a scholar and soldier – that came in your father's time?

Paro: Yes, yes, it was Basant Kumar – that's what he was called.

Nandi: True, madam. Of all the men my foolish eyes looked upon, he was the best, deserving the fair lady.

Paro: I remember him well. He was worthy of your praise.

Scene Three

(*Enter Basant with Yahoodi*)

Yahoodi: Three thousand rupees. Well.

Basant: And for three months.

Yahoodi: For three months, well.

Basant: For which Deewan Shah shall be bound.

Yahoodi: Deewan Shah shall be bound. Well.

Basant: Will you oblige me? Shall I know the answer?

Yahoodi: Three thousand rupees for three months, and Deewan Shah bound.

Basant: Your answer to that?

Yahoodi: Deewan Shah is a good man.

Basant: Have you heard anything to the contrary?

Yahoodi: Oh no, no, no, no! I mean he's sufficient although his means are in question. His ships are afloat to many lands. He has many ventures abroad. Ships are but boards and sailors but men. There are land rats and water rats, land thieves and water thieves – I mean pirates. Then there's the peril of waters, winds and rocks. But never mind the man is sufficient. Three thousand rupees for three months – I think I may take his bond. May I speak with Deewan Shah?

Basant: If it pleases you to dine with us.

Yahoodi: No, I will not eat with you Hindus. I will buy with you, sell with you, talk with you, walk with you, but I will not eat with you, drink with you nor pray with you. (*Enters Deewan Shah*) Who's he that comes here?

Basant: This is Deewan Shah.

Yahoodi: He looks like a fawning Congressman. I hate him because he's an Aryasamaji; I hate him still more because he lends out interest-free money and brings down the rate of usage in the Punjab. If I catch him once then I will have revenge for the ancient grudge I bear against him. He too, hates our sacred nation of Jews and he rails at me in the presence of merchants who are my clients. He scoffs at my bargains and my well-won thrift, which he calls the interest. My tribe will be cursed if I forgive him.

Deewan Shah: Yahoodi, I never lend or borrow. I neither take nor give to excess. Yet I'll break a custom to supply the ripe wants of my friend. (*To Basant*) How much do you want?

Yahoodi: Three thousand rupees.

Deewan Shah: And for three months.

Yahoodi: Three thousand rupees for three months and your bond. But let me hear you, I think you said you neither lend nor borrow on advantage.

Deewan Shah: Yes, I never do.

Yahoodi: And it's my thrift that keeps me going and not the interest. But my thrift makes money grow faster.

Deewan Shah: The devil can say anything for his purpose. An evil soul looks like a villain with a smiling cheek – a good-looking apple rotten at heart.

Yahoodi: Three thousand rupees. It's a good round sum. And three months from twelve - let me see the rate.

Deewan Shah: Shall we be beholden to you?

Yahoodi: Well, many times you've mocked me for my money and my usury but I've tolerated it with a patient shrug, for suffering is the badge of our tribe. You called me a bastard, a cut-throat and a dog and spat on my beard. And all for use of what is mine. But now you need my help: you who did void your spittle upon my face, you who spurned me with your feet. Tell me, how can a dog have money? You called me a mongrel. Can a mongrel have three thousand rupees? But I shall lend you the monies, nevertheless.

Deewan Shah: I'm likely to call you so again, to spit at you again and spurn you, too. Don't lend me the money as a friend because we never were. Lend it me as your enemy and exact the penalty.

Yahoodi: Look, how you storm! But I would be rather friends with you and lend you monies, forgetting the shames you stained me with, charge you no interest and chase you not for return.

Basant: That would be kindness.

Yahoodi: Yes, I'll show you my kindness. Go with me to a notary. Seal me your single bond there. And if you don't repay me my money on a fixed date, at a fixed place and a fixed sum or sums as expressed in the condition of the loan, then the forfeiture would be a pound of flesh in weight to be taken by me from any part of your body that pleases me.

Deewan Shah: I'll seal to such a bond and say there's much kindness in the Yahoodi.

Basant: You will not seal to such a bond for me, Deewan!

Deewan Shah: Don't you fear anything. I'll not forfeit it because in these two months, that's a month before this bond expires, I expect the return of my fortunes more than three times the value of this bond.

Yahoodi: Oh father Abram! Look at these Hindus, whose own hard dealings teach them to suspect the thoughts of others. (To Basant Kumar) What do I need the flesh for that's neither estimable nor profitable like that of the goat, lamb or chicken? I only extend a hand of friendship if he takes it, and if he doesn't then let him not do me any wrong.

Deewan Shah: Yes, Yahoodi, I'll seal into this bond.

Yahoodi: Then meet me forthwith at the notary's. Get the bond ready; and I'll meet you there with three thousand rupees. (Exits Yahoodi)

Deewan Shah: The Yahoodi will turn into an *Aryasmaji* soon.

Basant: I don't like the villain's mind and his terms.

Deewan Shah: Come on. My ships will come home a month before that day.

Scene Four

(Somnath enters the stage)

Somnath: If what I've come to know is true then that's very bad, indeed. If the ships of Deewan Shah are wrecked on the Arabian seas, a very dangerous and fatal place where the carcasses of many a tall ship lie buried, then that would be the worst thing that happened to Deewn Shah. I feel very sorry for him. (Enters Yahoodi)

Yahoodi: Sorry for whom?

Somnath: Sorry for my friend Deewan Shah.

Yahoodi: Why what happened to him?

Somnath: Don't you know, Yahoodi? His ships have been wrecked in the Arabian seas. Now, if he defaults, you won't take his flesh, will you?

Yahoodi: I will take it. I will take it.

Somnath: What good will it do to you, this pound of human flesh? You are not a cannibal, are you?

Yahoodi: If it will feed nothing else, it will feed my revenge. He disgraced me many times; he laughed at my losses, mocked my gains and scorned my nation. He thwarted my bargains, cooled my friends and heated my enemies. The only reason to do that to me is that I am a Yahoodi, a Jew. But this is no reason. A Jew has eyes, hands, organs, dimensions, senses, affections and passions like the rest of you, like you Hindus. If someone wrongs you then you do revenge him. And if you wrong us, shall we not revenge? If we are like you in every way then we will resemble you in this, too. Revenge is what I want.

Scene Five

(Enter Basant Kumar and Paro on the stage)

Paro: I'm locked in one of these three chests. If you do love me you'll find me out. (Basant opens the leaden casket)

Basant: There you are then, I've found you because I love you. Here's the picture of you that no previous suitor could find. They must've been opening the golden or silver caskets instead of the leaden one. But you were hidden in the leaden one. Thank God, I've found you.

The Volcano

Paro: My lord Basant, I'm lucky to become your wife from now on. Until now I was the lord of this house, master of my servants and queen over myself. But from now, the house, the servants and myself are yours. I give them all to you with this ring, which should you part from it, lose it or give it away, let it presage the ruin of love.

Basant: I'm bereft of all words. But when this ring parts from this finger, my life, too, will part from me. You can then declare Basant Kumar dead.

Paro: I'm sure you will never part with this ring and hence with me.

(Enters Somnath)

Somnath: I have very bad news for you, Basant Kumar, the worst you could hear.

Basant: What is it, Somnath? Tell me quickly. (Somnath hands over a letter to him)

Paro: Who is the letter from, my lord?

Basant: It's from my bosom friend, Deewan Shah, who got me money from a Jew on his personal guarantee – three thousand rupees for three months. Failure to repay on time will lead to forfeiture – a forfeit of a pound of flesh from his body, from where the Jew would like to take it.

Paro: (worried) Read out the letter, Basant.

Basant: (Reads the letter) My dear Basant, all my ships have sunk into the Arabian seas, my creditors have grown cruel, my bond to the Yahoodi is forfeit and in paying the pound of flesh I may not live. All debts between you and me should be deemed cleared if I don't see you before my death.

Paro: Oh love! Dispatch all business and be gone.

Scene Six

(Deewan Shah is behind the bars and the Yahoodi stands outside)

Deewan Shah: Hear me yet, good Yahoodi.

Yahoodi: Don't speak against the bond, for I'll have my bond. I've sworn an oath that I'll have my bond. You called me a dog without any reason and now beware of my fangs. The Nazim shall grant me justice, I'm sure.

Deewan Shah: I pray to you Yahoodi, let me speak.

Yahoodi: I shall hear nothing; I shall have my bond. I won't be made a soft and dull-eyed fool, shake my head, relent, sign and yield to a Hindu.

Deewan Shah: All right Jew, I'll wait for Basant Kumar to come. He shall pay you my debt and I shall be freed.

Scene Seven

(Enter the Nizam, Deewan Shah, Basant Kumar and the Yahoodi)

Nazim: Yahoodi, the world thinks, and I think too, that you have malice against Deewan Shah. You should show mercy and remorse rather than cruelty against a human being. You want a pound of flesh from the merchant's body, leading him to death, whereas you should show human gentleness and love towards him. Given his losses in the form of wrecked ships you should let go even the principal with an eye of pity. You should commiserate with his state rather than showing a heart of flint.

Yahoodi: My lord, by our holy Sabbath, I've sworn to have the due and forfeit of my bond. Why I want his flesh and not three thousand rupees is a question I cannot answer. But say it's my humour. I hate Deewan Shah because he hates me.

Basant: This is no answer, you cruel Yahoodi.

Yahoodi: I'm not here to please you with my answers.

Basant: Do people kill all that they hate?

Yahoodi: What would you do if a serpent stings you?

Deewan Shah: Basant, why do you engage in discussion with a Yahoodi? How can you ask a wolf to stop eating lambs? How can you forbid mountain pines to wag their high tops and make no noise? You can't soften his Jewish heart, so make no more offers.

Basant: No, Deewan, let me make an offer. For your three thousand rupees, here's six thousand, Yahoodi.

Yahoodi: I won't accept it even if you make that offer a hundred times over.

Nazim: How can you hope for mercy if you render none?

Yahoodi: I dread no judgement because I do no wrong. Would you have mercy on your slaves and set them free, instead of using them like asses, dogs and mules? You use them like abject things because you bought them. Your answer would be that those slaves are yours. And likewise, the pound of flesh that I demand from him is dearly mine because I have bought it. I'll have that flesh anyway. And if you deny me my right then I spit upon your law.

(Enters Paro dressed as a man with a turban)

Paro: (Hands over a letter to the Nazim) I'm the doctor and have been appointed by Mota Singh, the senior Judge, to conduct this case which has to be dealt with by a qualified doctor.

Nazim: (Reads the letter) Take your place as the judge, Sir. Are you acquainted with the suit?

Paro: Yes, my lord. I'm informed thoroughly of the case but who's the merchant here and who's the Yahoodi.

Nazim: Deewan Shah and Yahoodi, both stand up. (They both stand up)

Paro: Is your name, Yahoodi?

Yahoodi: I belong to the Yahoodi nation but my name is Shylock.

Paro: I shall call you Yahoodi, nevertheless. Your suit is of a strange nature yet the law of the land can't impugn you. (To Deewan Shah) Do you confess the bond?

Deewan Shah: Yes, I do.

Paro: Then why ought the Yahoodi to be merciful?

Yahoodi: There's no compulsion for me to be so.

Paro: The quality of mercy is not strained. It drops gently as gentle rain from heaven. It blesses the one that gives and the one who takes. Mercy's like a monarch without a crown. Why must you insist upon being cruel to the merchant?

Yahoodi: I'm doing nothing unlawful. All I want is the forfeit of my bond.

Paro: Is he not able to discharge the money?

Basant: Here, I tender him the money in the court, twice the borrowed sum. If that doesn't suffice, I'm ready to pay ten times over on the forfeit of my hands, my head and my heart. If still it's not sufficient then malice seems to bear down truth. Do what you can, fair judge, curb this cruel devil of his malicious will.

Paro: The decree can't be altered by any power in this country lest we run the risk of recording that as a precedent to defame the law.

Yahoodi: Oh wise and young judge, I honour you for your fair comments.

Paro: Shall I have a look at the bond?

Yahoodi: Here it is, most reverend doctor!

Paro: Yahoodi, if they give you three times your money, would you accept?

Yahoodi: I shall lay no perjury on my soul because I'm bound by oath.

Paro: This bond entitles the Yahoodi to have a pound of flesh cut off by him nearest the merchant's heart. (To Yahoodi) Be merciful, take thrice the money and bid me to tear this bond off.

Yahoodi: Proceed to judgement, fair judge. There's no power in the tongue of any man to alter me.

Deewan Shah: I beseech the court to give the judgement.

Paro: You should prepare your bosom for his knife.

Yahoodi: Oh noble judge! Oh excellent young man!

Paro: For the intent and purpose of the law, the penalty is forfeiture according to this bond. Therefore, lay bare your bosom, Deewan Shah.

Yahoodi: 'Nearest his heart' – those are the very words.

Paro: It is so. Are there any balances here to weigh the flesh?

Yahoodi: I have them ready, fair judge.

Paro: Have you got a surgeon to stop his wounds lest he should bleed to death?

Yahoodi: Does it say so in the bond?

Paro: It's not expressed in the bond, so what? Can't you do some charity work?

Yahoodi: I can't find it. It's not in the bond.

Paro: Merchant, do you want to say anything?

Deewan Shah: Only a little. Give me your hand, Basant. Fare you well. Don't grieve that I've fallen to this for you. If fortune wants a wretched man to outlive his wealth, it's better to die. Commend me to your honourable wife. Tell her the process of my death. Don't you resent that your friend didn't repay your debt, for I'll pay it instantly with my life when the Yahoodi cuts deep enough into my heart.

Basant Kumar: Deewan, I'm married to a wife who's as dear to me as my life but I could sacrifice my life, my wife and all the world for you, if only I could save you from this brutal devil.

Paro: Your wife would've given you a little thanks for that if she were here to hear you make the offer.

Yahoodi: Don't waste time, I pray you pursue the sentence.

Paro: A pound of merchant's flesh is yours. The court awards it and the law does give it.

Yahoodi: The most rightful judge!

Paro: And you must cut this flesh from his bosom. The law allows it and the court awards it.

Yahoodi: (To Deewan Shah) A sentence: come, prepare. (Sharpens the knife)

Paro: Wait a second. There's something else. The bond allows you no blood. The words expressly are 'a pound of flesh'. Take then your bond. Take your pound of flesh. But if you shed one drop of blood in cutting, your lands and goods will have to be confiscated by the law of the Punjab.

Yahoodi: Is that the law?

Paro: You can see the act yourself. You want justice and you will have it more than you want.

Yahoodi: I take the other offer. Pay me the bond thrice and let the Hindu go.

Basant: Here is the money.

Paro: Take it easy please; the Yahoodi will have all the justice. No haste please. He shall have nothing but the penalty. Prepare yourself, Yahoodi, to cut off the flesh. Shed no blood, cut neither more nor less but just a pound of flesh. If you waver from what the bond says you will lose your estate and you will be hanged till you breathe your last breath.

Yahoodi: Give me my principal and let me go.

Basant: I have it ready for you.

Paro: No, he has refused it in the open court. He will have only justice and his bond.

Yahoodi: Shall I not have barely my principal?

Paro: You will have nothing but the forfeiture, to be taken at your peril, Yahoodi.

Yahoodi: Why does the devil give him good of it all?

Paro: Wait. The law of Punjab has yet another hold on you. If someone seeks the life of another citizen by direct or indirect attempts, the party against whom he contrives, shall seize one half of his estate and the other half will go to the privy coffer of the province. And now your life – that lies at the mercy of the Nazim only, against all other voices. Beg mercy of the Nazim.

Nazim: I pardon your life even before you ask for a pardon for the half of your wealth, which is now Deewan Shah's. And the other half belongs to the province of the Punjab.

Yahoodi: Take my life and all and do not pardon me. I don't want such a pardon. If you take away all my means what good would it be to live, and what for? Death is better than to live as a beggar (begins to wail loudly and bitterly).

Scene Eight

(Enter Deewan Shah, Basant Kumar and Paro)

Basant: Worthy Judge! How can we remunerate you for the excellent services you've given us?

Deewan Shah: We offer all these six thousand rupees to you with our heartiest thanks.

Paro: (To Basant) Just give me that ring if you insist to pay me for my services.

Basant: This ring. It's nothing in the way of our gratitude to you, worthy Judge. Take the money and buy as many such rings as you want.

Paro: That means you don't want to pay me as I wish.

Basant: Spare only this ring and take whatever else you like, I pray you worthy Judge.

Paro: In that case I'd better go without anything.

Deewan Shah: Basant, give the Judge your ring.

Basant: No, my friend this is my wife's gift to me, a love-gift. And a love-gift has an emotional value. I can't part with this ring in any circumstances.

Paro: Thank you. I'd better be gone.

Deewan Shah: Wait please. Here's the ring (He takes the ring from Basant's finger and hands it over to Paro)

Paro: Thank you very much. I've got the ring but I've lost my love today.

Basant: How do you mean?

Paro: Look at me! (She takes her turban, artificial beard and moustache off)

Basant: (Highly surprised) Paro you? I can't believe it. Oh my love, you are a gem, a real diamond, my Koh-e-noor. (Tries to take her into his arms but she spurns him)

Paro: Touch me not, for you've parted with the ring that contained all my love for you. I can't trust you any more.

Deewan: He didn't part with the ring, Paro, my sweet sister-in-law, rather I took it off from his finger by force and gave it to you. So, the punishment should be given to me, not to my bosom friend and your sincere husband Basant.

Paro: All right then Basant, I let you go this time but make sure you don't lose it again, for if you do you'll lose me forever.

Basant: I promise with my life that I will not lose it again. Can I touch you now?

Paro: Yes, you are allowed.

Basant: Thank you, my dearest Paro. (He holds her and gives her a hug.)

(Enters Somnath)

Somnath: (To Deewan Shah) I have just learnt that all your ships have arrived safely at the port of Bombay.

Deewan Shah: That's splendid. That's really splendid. All is well that ends well.

After the play was finished, the elders gathered round the stage and began to cheer us and rain plaudits on us, embracing us and patting our shoulders. They were then followed by other villagers who smiled and expressed their admiration for all of us. We felt extolled and exalted.

An Adventure in the Jungle

What *Ramleela* couldn't do in so many years Shakespeare did it in a jiffy. The great writer brought us adolescents closer to each other than we previously were. The play had made all the difference and Noor Mohammed too, ought to have been garlanded for that. It was his initiative, although I too, had a small share in it. I had given him the idea of doing a play in the village, but the idea had set his mind in motion.

Ramleela, being a Hindu ideology, did not have the content in it, which could attract everybody equally, irrespective of religion. The religious difference was, in fact, at the root of what we did and what we did not, both at the local and the national level. Kabir, being a Muslim for instance, would be repelled by the idea of doing a Ramleela or *Dushehra* (burning the effigies of ten-headed Ravana together with those of other members of his tribe). Or celebrating Diwali festival, that's celebrating the return of Rama, Lakshmna and Sita to Ayodhya after the completion of their exile of fourteen years, thereby defeating the *demon* king Ravana. He didn't oppose the celebration of Hindu festivals overtly but only tacitly, saying he wasn't interested. His father KL Premi, being a broad-minded communist, didn't do either Hindu things or Islamic things. He didn't bother if others did what they desired to do. Kabir's mother, Razia, followed all those rituals, which Islam demanded of her. The worshipping of idols was not permitted in Islam, was even despised as infidelity and thus could attract no Muslim on earth, whereas the whole soul of Hinduism rested on this.

Krishan, on the other hand, took this idol-worshipping as quite normal and even enjoyed it now that he worshipped Hanuman, the Hindu monkey-god; the son of the wind. Krishan said nothing about Eid and other Islamic customs and fashions but didn't like to take any active part in any of them. And our Kinner was opposed to the very concept of religious beliefs, even religion itself, no matter in what content and form it confronted him. He was a forceful heavy-weight logician, if anything. Kinner was a fervent believer and observer of nature and could indulge in a prolonged dialogue with it, though mutely. He had already begun to show the signs of a good philosopher. He was staunchly devoted to the scientific analysis of the vastness of nature. He believed that there was an unknown that would remain unknown no matter how much humanity tried to find it. He said to me once that the unknown in nature was the ignorance of man, which they called God, and that God would always remain because ignorance would remain.

And, as for myself, I was no longer a teacher of Kinner, rather his follower and was impressed deeply by his conclusions. I never contradicted him; instead I only provoked him so he could say more on these matters. The mode of my provocation was very subtle and spontaneous, adopted only to make him speak more, for if I remained a quiet listener he assumed absolute silence at once. One day when I said to him that he had some mental problem, he came forth with a long tirade on how the minds of intelligent people worked.

'Draw a question mark in front of every cliché,' he began. 'Question every belief, faith and platitude, even the proven things and then you'll begin to know how banal and worthless many ideas are. It's only when you accept everything as it's given to you by the antecedence that your mental disorder begins to show up. Accepting ideas and notions is not what you ought to be doing, but you should challenge them, and not let them pass by you without defiance,' he harangued.

Anyway, we had better come back to our Shakespeare before he takes root somewhere else owing to his newly found convictions of rebirth and reincarnation. The play had proved central to all those who played in it and those who had witnessed its performance. Its subject was common to all the people because of the extortionate Punjabi *banians* looting the farmers with their exorbitant rates of interest, compounding the principal amount manyfold, thereby pushing them to the verge of bankruptcy and poverty. Moreover, usury was an anti-Islamic activity. So how could Shylock or Yahoodi, a moneylender, hold a trustworthy place in the minds of the people of the village? I myself, having played the character of Yahoodi, had seen how the villagers hated me in that role, especially when I was sharpening my knife on a stone and was chuckling to myself in a malicious way. Noor had made me wear a turban like that of the *marwaris* of Rajasthan or Gujarat, which had accentuated the effect many times more. It was only after the play was finished that the audience had come to recognise me as one of them; during the play they might have desired to take my flesh instead of me taking that of Deewan Shah, played by Noor himself.

However, our closeness to each other had developed while we rehearsed together for over four weeks. The common subject, common characters and common problems, central to all the people regardless of anyone's faith or belief, made us all laugh together and become part of each other. A problem faced us only when Kinner had objected to having Radhika play the part of Paro, for no one else could. Kinner's argument was that if no other girl from the village could be permitted to play a role in the play involving so many male characters, then why had we thought Radhika's family would permit her to take part. I really had to work hard on him to convince him that others were constrained by their religious beliefs whereas he was a free-thinking man with no preconceptions of any kind, always ready to question backward ideas and the established way of behaving and believing. He had finally acquiesced; and after this one hurdle we went on doing everything as smoothly as it should have been.

Soon after the performance, Noor Mohammed went back to Lahore and we returned to school. After some months we felt a vacuum in our lives, and so I floated another idea among them all. The idea was to undertake an adventure to the forest that lay at *Hari ke Pattan*, a kind of delta where rivers Beas and Satluj meet and merge together. There were many more forests past Lahore but we knew little about them, and they were so far away that going there involved a journey by train. The forests of Lyalpur, Shaikhupura and Montgomery had long been converted into cultivable land with colossal capacity for agricultural production. The land raised a higher yield of crops than any other soil in India. Decades ago, the people who had uprooted the jungle and cultivated the land, had come from the East Punjab. Irrigation had been possible due to the new canals devised by the British. The land was then divided into villages named after the ones the new settlers had left behind, although in the papers of the irrigation department the names were given in accordance with the number of the water-exit from those canals, called chucks. The various units of the jungle-turned-arable land were also called *baars* by the new settlers, such as *neeli baar, ganji baar, saandal baar* etc. Yet, despite this reclamation effort, there were many more forests that were dense, ferocious and full of dangers; to go there was to ask for terrific trouble if not complete annihilation.

Kinner, I knew well enough, would be thrilled by the idea, which he was, almost jumping out of his clothes.

'I didn't know you had a little bit of nature residing in you,' he said when he had digested the idea.

'You've yet more to discover about me, young man!' I replied with an arrogant air.

'Discover you … my foot,' Kinner said and smirked.

'I don't mind your saying anything to me now, for I know you're a malicious little sod,' I retorted back in a commotion of laughter but he kept smiling.

After that we went to Kabir's home and found him in. But instead of talking to him in the presence of his mother and father, we took him out and went to sit under the Banyan tree. When we broached the topic of an adventure to the jungle he showed no interest; instead he took out an Urdu poem from his pocket and began to read it out to us. The poem was addressed to Indians in general; the message it carried was that they should unite together firmly to throw the *Angrez* out of the country. The reasons he enumerated were hackneyed and platitudinous; that's the *Angrez* ate beef or the meat of cow worshipped by the Hindus; ate pork or the meat of pig hated by the Muslims. The poem reprimanded the Angrez for pilfering Indian wealth, depriving Indians of their sanctity and bemoaned the overall exploitative nature of their rule, equating them with devils and condemning them as an evil force.

'They're not all evil, I suppose. They've done some good things for us Indians, haven't they?' said Kinner when Kabir had finished reading his poem.

'What good have they done for us, tell me?' Kabir quizzed furiously.

'Don't you know? Can't you see for yourself?' Kinner counter-questioned.

'It doesn't matter how benign a devil makes itself look, it remains a devil nevertheless,' Kabir said and squinted his eyes in disgust.

'To start with, there're no devils and no saints on the surface of this earth. And if there are, they're all double-faced monsters. A devil for one can be a saint for the other; and a saint for one can be a devil for the other. The whole bloody history is full of these double-faced devils and saints. I can cite hundreds of examples but there's no point slipping into that kind of metaphysics if we want to concentrate ourselves on the issue of *Angrez* alone at this moment,' said Kinner while I continued to be a silent spectator and listener to the two confabulators.

'Well. Go on then, tell us what they've done for us?' asked Kabir, tauntingly.

'Okay... What was India before the *Angrez* came? An accretion of small, separate and stringent states, fighting each other, depredating each other's subjects, making the general public cry in anguish, their teeth biting their own tongues. There was no concept of country or nation then because it was foreign and unknown to us. It was only brought to us by *the Angrez* because they were at an advanced stage of social and political development. And owing to their general development, they also progressed in science and technology. That was what they brought us, although not out of some gratitude to us but out of their own necessity to run this country the way they ran theirs, although, economic and political exploitation was their ultimate motive. But then who would've done it without any interest of their own? They gave us railways, road networks, communication systems, postal systems, industry, trade unionism, the concept of fortification of the country's borders, modern police, army, navy and a myriad other things, of which we had no knowledge. We were so far behind, still living in the dark ages of history. And because we were far behind them in every way, after the establishment of the East India Company, a trading concern that developed into a mighty empire, they were gradually able to dominate our whole country. I, by no means, say that we shouldn't make efforts to oust them from this country. I want them out as much as you do, but not by saying they made no contribution whatever to the quality of life in here. That is the way illiterate people talk, not educated ones like you.' Kinner's ardent speech was followed by a prolonged, stunned silence between all three of us.

'And what did you want to say about the double faced devils and saints?' Kabir managed to rupture the silence.

'Are you testing me or teasing me?' said Kinner, slightly provoked.

'I'm doing neither. I just want to know what you mean.' Kabir grew callous too.

'Do we have to have all the discussions today, yaar?' I interposed, to prevent them from getting into any trouble.

'Why, what's wrong with it?' said Kabir, mourning my lack of interest in their grating discussion.

'Nothing of course; but tell us if you're willing to accompany us to the forest for an adventure?" I asked him, coming to the point.

'I'm sorry, I've no interest in forestry, wilderness, animal kingdom, or fauna and flora,' he said peevishly and got up to go. He had gone only a few steps when I thought of calling him back but Kinner held my hand and stopped me.

When we approached Krishan, he too, was a little reluctant at first, but it didn't take us long to convince him that the adventure was worth undertaking. The only difficulty was to find an excuse to hoodwink our parents. Kinner was free to do what he desired, for his brothers, mother and sister knew his loitering nature and had accepted it long ago. The difficulty posed itself in case of Krishan and I, but after a lot of strenuous thought, we decided that the pretext would be to go to Lahore to visit the Shalimar gardens for the whole day.

We began our journey on our bikes on the following Sunday, in the last week of April in 1934. We took a good amount of food and three gallons of water with us. If more water was needed, it would have been easy to get it from any well that came our way, and the whole of Punjab was full of such wells, anyway. These were the Persian wells we relied on for irrigating our fields in those remote days, in addition to the canals the supply of which came from the rivers. But when the rivers dried up in April, May and June, or were left with scanty water, the canals would be nothing but sand meant for building works or for young children to play in. This was the time of the year when dozens of wells would get worked up for the supply of water both for irrigation and for domestic need.

Krishan, Kinner and I left the village at 8 am sharp and were sure to reach our destination by 10 am, long before the vertical rays of the sun sent streams of melting lava to burn our heads to madness. The route we had chosen was to the south-east, to *Hari ke Pattan*, a place not too far from *Tarn Taran*, where the two rivers merged.

Up to 1849, the river Satluj worked as a boundary-line between the British occupied Punjab and Maharaja Ranjit Singh's Punjab. Under the treaty of the river Satluj, Ranjit Singh's Punjab, which extended as far as Kabul, was treated as the Punjab of Khalsa or Sikhs. But the British only bided their time until this Khalsa Raj collapsed, which it did after the demise of Ranjit Singh. The British captured it after a bloody war with the Sikhs. And the Sikhs, to this day, were still seen to be sighing for lost glories, nearly eight decades after having lost their hub.

Tarn Taran was a place with a huge Sikh shrine, the same size and stature as the Golden Temple of Amritsar – a memorial to the fifth Guru of the Sikhs, Arjun Dev, who founded the shrine and the city. Hari ke Pattan was approximately twenty-five miles from Qila Vasudev and, at the speed at which we were wheeling on, it would take us two hours to get there, if all went well.

On both sides of the road and as far ahead as the eye could see, the spectacle of golden foliage swaying majestically to the caress of a slight breeze intoxicated us with pleasure. It was the crop of wheat come of age and waiting for the touch of sickle to be reaped and harvested. The peasants had begun the harvest after the Vaisakhi festival; they were progressing fast in taking the grain home. Some late runners were still waiting for more pairs of hands to reap and more cattle to trample the cut crop, to dissociate the shell from the grain, which would then be blown apart manually. This was the time of the year when the peasants were most worried in case some natural hazard like rain or blizzard plummeted on the crop to destroy it and mutilate their hopes of working with full stomachs throughout the year until the next crop came.

Notwithstanding the morning hour, Krishan and I had begun to perspire profusely. Kinner pedalled on so fast and energetically, shouting at us, 'Come on, come on!' that we were unable to keep pace with him. He was leading us, and we were blindly following the direction chosen by him. Krishan came second to him in riding the bike and I was last. Kinner was stronger and sturdier than I, that I knew, but that he was also stronger than the worshipper of Hanuman, the son of the wind, and his yearlong history of sit-ups and lie-ups and wrestling in the *akhara* Hanuman, was incredible. Furthermore, Krishan consumed a rich diet of milk, butter, lassi, pere, barfi and the like, whereas Kinner had always been denied that kind of luxuriant food by some hidden powers of nature which, according to him, worked in its own mysterious designs. Things could have been a little better if his father had been alive but his poor old mother, Reshma, could hardly feed the family with bare minimum. They couldn't dream of eating the kind of food Krishan ate. All they survived on was a couple of chapattis each with some kind of vegetable or dal in the morning or forenoon and a similar food in the evening. The kindness of some village households provided them with some lassi or buttermilk, which they doubled by adding water and shared between the whole family.

As for myself, I was skinny from the outset and had never allowed another layer of flesh mount over any part of my body, no matter how dearly my mother fed me on butter and milk. 'My son's body is inexpressive of any gratitude at all' she had always complained. But it wasn't my fault; I followed her very own physical traits. She too, was slim and trim, except for her mammary glands, which my father liked so much. Yet, none could say that I was weak, for the skinny body carried enough strength to enable me to do anything I liked to do with the solitary exception of the work that our Hanuman did.

We had gone nearly half way when Kinner's tyre got punctured and he had to stop. 'See! That's another mysterious way of nature's working. You wouldn't pedal slowly so nature pedalled you down. This is how nature has listened to our request,' I took the opportunity to screw him a little. Kinner looked at me but said nothing. Rather he began to inspect the tyre. It happened at a place where there wasn't a single shop in sight to repair the tube. It was no proper road either but an unpaved path, deserted path, which meandered through the fields. The three of us stood there, scratching our heads in desperation

'Are you sure you led us on to the right path?' asked Krishan, wiping his sweat from the forehead with the sleeve of his shirt.

'Of course, yaar. It's a short cut to another *pucca* road that leads to *hari ke pattan*,' he replied.

'So, what shall we do now?' I asked.

'Load the bike on Kinner's head and let's go,' said Krishan, laughing.

'Shut up and listen. I'll drive one of your bikes, you hold mine at the handle and sit on the carrier at the back,' he suggested.

'How can you hold a bike and sit at the carrier at the same time?' remarked Krishan.

'Hanuman was thick and so are you. Sit on the carrier of the one I drive and hold on to my bike. Does that enter your thick crust?'

'Oh yes, oh yes,' pouted Krishan and swapped his bike with that of Kinner.

We recommenced our journey but at a snail's pace because Krishan found himself unable to manoeuvre the damaged bike, which slipped from his hand and fell every two minutes. The idea didn't work, at least not with Krishan on the carrier. So, we swapped over again. This time Kinner drove my bike and I sat on the carrier behind him, holding his bike. But the bike soon went out of control and fell. After a few minutes' thought, Kinner conceived another idea, which worked quite satisfactorily. He drove my bike holding the handle with his left hand, kept his right hand on the damaged bike, carried me on the carrier behind him, and succeeded in doing everything cleverly. The difference this method made was to decrease the speed from 10mph to 5mph. The other difference, a good one, was that I was set free from labouring at the pedals. And, once the speed was settled, I began to amuse them by telling a joke.

'Right, boys, listen,' I commanded their attention. 'Once upon a time in a village there lived two very fast friends: one, a farmer and the other, a Brahmin.

One day, soon after the harvest was over, the farmer said to the Brahmin, "We're close friends and have spent so many years of our life together, but we've never travelled together even once. Isn't it a matter of shame for us?"

The Brahmin said, "Of course it is. What do you suggest we should be doing then?"

The farmer said, "We should embark upon a journey that lasts a month or so."

The Brahmin agreed with him and said, "My bosom friend, let's go to *Haridwar* then. It'll do us double good: first, we shall have a long journey together and second, it'll be a pilgrimage to a sacred place, which is known to bless you with a better kind of rebirth after death."

The farmer agreed and they fixed a day of departure. Having done so the Brahmin suggested another idea, saying, "It'll be no good if we both go on walking and exhaust ourselves. The best thing would be that one of us told a tale and the other carried him on his shoulders. Once that tale was finished the other one would begin his tale and get seated on the shoulders of the first tale-teller until his tale was finished, too. That way, we'll each walk only half the miles."

The farmer thought for a while and said, "Alright then. You be the first to tell the tale and perch on my shoulders; I'll take the second turn."

That was what the Brahmin wanted, anyway. So, the journey began on the appointed day with the Brahmin sitting on the farmer's shoulders with his legs dangling on both sides of his chest and the tale pouring from his mouth. The Brahmin began to tell the story of Ramayana. "Once upon a time, the king Dashratha lived and ruled in the land of Ayodhya," the Brahmin began. The main story had a myriad of sub-stories to it and the epic was long and intricate, the characters numerous and the incidents far too many. It was bound to continue unstoppably for miles on end. The farmer kept listening to the story and carrying the Brahmin's load, which to his hard working body didn't matter too much. But he was able to see through the cunning of the Brahmin and said in his mind, "Don't you worry, Brahmin, your story is, after all, a story and it's bound to end one day. And then I'll show you what I'm made of."

So the story continued with the farmer saying, "Yes… then… What happened after that? … I see," and so forth. He was right. The story had to end one day, and so it did, although by that time they had already covered half the journey.

While the Brahmin was advancing towards the end of his story, he was also thinking in his mind that the farmer was at best a farmer and not a storyteller. If he told a story it wouldn't last for more than a mile or two; and when his turn came again he would start telling the story of Mahabharta, twice as long as the Ramayana.

Anyway, his first story was finished and the farmer climbed up his shoulders, perched there comfortably and began to tell his story, "Once upon a time there was a small farmer in a small village. His holding was very small but he was hard working and assiduous."

The Brahmin, reeling under the weight of the farmer's well-built body, thought to himself that though the farmer cultivated the land, he had never cultivated his brain and had thus begun to tell the story of one of his kind, that would end before they had covered another mile.

But the farmer continued, "The farmer ploughed his fields, then re-ploughed them, harrowed them and re-re-ploughed them so many times that in the end the earth became like freshly milled wheat flour."

"What happened then?" asked the gasping voice from the listener's mouth.

"Then he sowed the seed of wheat in them," the farmer replied.

"Then?'

"Then the seed began to germinate and once he was sure the radicles had taken strong root and the plumule had turned into healthy enough shoots he supplied a scarce amount of water to the crop," the farmer said.

"And then?" the panting breath asked.

"Then the crop began to grow higher but slowly and steadily. And after a few more weeks the farmer irrigated the field again, this time a little more prodigally because the crop was strong and high enough to stand the flow of water," he replied.

"Then?"

"Three months went past and the crop came to touch the farmer's knees, then to his waist and then to his midriff," the farmer told.

"Then?" the voice underneath the farmer groaned.

"Well. Then the crop began to change its colour from green to golden with spikes spinning webs of starchy-milky grains and gradually ripening to maturity."

"Then?"

"Then came the Vaisakhi, the harvest season; and the farmer began to reap the gold with the help of a few fellow villagers to whom he had rendered help in their time of need."

"Then?"

"Then the final operation of thrashing was completed; the grains were separated from the straw, the straw was housed in a conical makeshift pyramid and the golden grain dispatched to the village," said the farmer.

"Is the story finished?" asked the Brahmin.

"No, the real story starts now because that was only a prelude," replied the farmer.

The Brahmin had already begun to laugh in his stomach at the *stupid story* that had reached a *banal* conclusion so quickly. He was, in fact, mustering words to start his saga of Mahabharta and sit calmly on the shoulders of the farmer for the rest of the journey but the farmer's words nonplussed him.

"What happened next then?" he asked.

"Well, the farmer had only one room in which he stored all the grain. The room was commodious but the trouble was that it was roofless with only four walls and a door."

"So then?"

"Then… Then there was only one sparrow about, a regular visitor to the store, who would come, pick up one grain and fly away. Once the fresh grains were in she only doubled her visits, coming and taking one grain in the morning and one grain in the evening."

"So?"

"So she came, picked up a grain and went away."

"Then?"

"Then she came again, picked up a grain and went away."

"Then?"

"Look my friend," said the farmer, "there's a spacious store full of grain with only one sparrow to eat the lot, which she won't be able to finish for years to come. Thus, the story will be finished when the grain is finished. So continue the trudge until the grain and the sparrow are there."

"Didn't the farmer eat anything himself?" asked the debilitated voice.

"No, he was on a long journey like I am with you now."

As I concluded the story, Kinner and Krishan began to laugh like mad men. Unable to drive the bikes with rib-breaking laughter they had to stop. Krishan's eyes had swollen up with his pupils floating in salty lakes. Kinner, suffering from the effects of his own loud laughter added to the chest-straining pedalling of one bike while pulling me behind him and dragging the other one along, had begun to cough.

'So you are that same farmer and I am that same Brahmin. Is that what you mean?' asked Kinner, kicking me at my leg.

'No, no, no. It's only coincidence that the story has taken that turn,' I said evasively.

'No, Kinner, he's made it all up knowingly,' Krishan added fuel to the fire.

'Well then, you'll be carrying me to the *Haridwar* now, I mean the forests of *Hari ke Pattan*,' Kinner said and handed me my bike. So, the story began to cost me dearly. For a stretch of five long miles, I drove my bike with Kinner on the carrier behind me, and dragged his bike too, until we found a tube repairer.

And, by the time we reached the place where the river Beas merged with the river Satluj, it was 11 am and, we felt more famished for food than for an adventure into the forest. However, the merger of the two vast rivers into one, offered both an appalling and fascinating sight. It seemed like an enormous mouth gulping billions and trillions of gallons of water and yet without turgidity. For the first few minutes, we kept watching the massive expanse of the merger, almost awe-struck, open-mouthed and wondering at the boundlessness of nature. Then we found a comfortable place on the riverbank, sat down cross-legged and attacked our food, sharing it between us.

'I've never seen such a thing in my life!' mouthed Krishan.

'How could you? Your world extends between Qila Vasudev and akhara Hanuman and the rest is all emptiness,' I only tried to tease him because I myself hadn't seen such a thing before.

'As if you've celebrated all your birthdays here!' retorted Krishan.

'Not me, but Kinner has,' I needled Kinner knowingly.

'Shut up you pigs and eat your food,' Kinner shouted, his voice full of vituperation.

While we were munching our food, a bunch of black, clone-faced rats scurried past us, one after the other. I looked in the direction they had come from, instead of where they had gone.

'Are you expecting some more to come?' asked Kinner.

'No. I thought there might be a lion behind them,' I replied with a cheeky laugh.

'Are you under the influence of some hallucinating drug or something, trying to find lions out of rats?' he said and shook his head in mock despair.

'I thought some lion might be chasing them,' I insisted.

'You've gone mad, Arya,' he pronounced.

'Maybe, but listen to a joke first,' I said. 'A large bunch of rats were running at full speed in the jungle when they met a passer-by, who asked, "Why are you running so fast? What's up?" To that one of the rats replied, "Someone back home molested the wife of the lion and he suspects *us* of doing that."

'You cheeky sod,' said Krishan and they both burst out laughing. A few minutes trickled by and then Krishan, too, came up with a joke.

'A rat and a she-elephant fell in love in a jungle. One day the she-elephant said to the rat, "I'm dying to make love with you, darling." "No problem, sweet heart," replied the rat and began to kiss and cuddle her. "There's no need for foreplay, darling, I'm perfectly ready for the final act," said the she-elephant. So the rat climbed up at her back and began to do his business. But soon he felt a severe need to kiss her face, as without kissing he could not keep his erection. So, he ran all the way to her face, kissed it passionately and scuttled back to carry on the half-left business. But soon the erection died, showing the desperate need to kiss again. So, he ran forward, kissed and came back; scurried fast to the face again and came back, repeating the process quite a few times. Finally, he began to gasp miserably until he fell down on the ground and became half-unconscious. "Is that all?" the she-elephant ridiculed him. "No my dear, if it were not for the long distances to travel, I would've made you beg for my mercy."

And, just as the bout of jokes ended, we stood up amidst throaty laughter and proceeded on our expedition. We hid our bikes in the thicket of bushes and marched ahead like soldiers to the battlefield. Until now we had remained outside the jungle that seemed fascinating and enthralling to the senses but just as we made our entry into it we began to feel the ferocity, savageness and insanity of it pouncing on us. Suddenly we felt we had been reduced to creepers and the high gigantic ghostly sprawling trees began to trample on us like monsters trampling on ants.

'Listen!' said Kinner. 'The jungle seems too dense and uncertain. If you lose your way, take these bamboo trees as your mark to return to.'

'Let's make every effort to stick together,' cried Krishan.

'Don't surrender too much to the phantasma of the jungle,' squeaked I.

Everything seemed different to what it was outside the forest. Outside, the sun was shining and its piercing rays drilled numerous holes in your body seething you to your soul, making you perspire endlessly. But in here, the jungle had its own rules and norms. Melancholic and dreadful, dark and dreary, it allowed only sparse rods of sun to pass through the cloudy cobwebs of leaves to touch the floor. The shafts of light that managed to skim through the leafy network were obstructed midway by primary, secondary and tertiary branches of trees, shrubs and a myriad other plants, bushes and stray foliage. Surprisingly enough the leaves were invariably thick, green and succulent. You couldn't even visualise a day such as this inside the jungle until you entered it. It felt as though the evening had already set in and was heading towards night by the minute. The voices of birds issuing from jungle, coming from far and near, were really frightening. Some voices were like the earth cracking, some similar to the falling of trees, some analogous to creaking of solid wood and many others corresponding to the rumbling of bulls. But they all mingled to form a fearful orchestration, gripping you by the neck like a momentous roaring devil and strangling you to death. None of us had the guts to say that he was not fearful of roaming around freely on his own in the vicious forest.

'They say that you should never sleep at night in a jungle abounding with bamboo trees,' said Kinner, touching a bamboo tree.

'Why?' Krishan and I uttered simultaneously with freckles of dread wreaked on our faces.

'Because the bamboo grows out of the ground so suddenly and rapidly at night that it pierces through the body of the sleeper like a long needle through the flower,' he told us.

'How about during the day?' asked Krishan.

'They only grow during the day but at night they germinate and erupt suddenly from the ground, attaining quite a few feet in just one go.'

We could believe anything Kinner had said because he was a bookworm and as sagacious as Buddha. His revelation developed in Krishan a sudden sense of repulsion for bamboo, and with fearful agility he moved away from where the bamboos were.

As we went further ahead we saw a puddle full of turbid water. We stood at its bank and watched, wondering what was in there that we couldn't see. Kinner broke a piece of stick from a nearby tree and began to stir the water. 'Water snakes!' he shouted as if electrocuted, and bounced back at once. The stir had incensed the slithery creatures and they began to scurry turbulently in all directions. Krishan and I stayed behind our leader, Kinner.

'We made a mistake to come here without any weapon, such as a camping knife or a good club,' Kinner said.

'A club isn't a problem. We can chop one off from a tree,' I suggested.

'With what?' he asked. It was only then that I realised that a camping knife was more important.

Further away, a branch of a small shrub-like tree entwined itself in such a way that it exhibited a sequence of knots like the gnarls on the beard of our Banyan. I went and put my hand on the branch but found it fluffy and slippery to the touch. That was strange. How could the branch of a tree be so silky, smooth and slippery? And just as I looked at it again something began to unravel itself from the branch. It was a greenish-brownish snake. The sight sent me somersaulting to where Krishan and Kinner stood with their backs towards me.

'What happened man?' asked Kinner, fearfully.

'Look,' I said, pointing at the disentangling thing and stood up from where I had fallen. The snake uncurled itself from the branch, slithered quickly down the small trunk and disappeared into some secret hole in a matter of seconds, so fast that the eye couldn't keep track of it. 'We've got to be more careful, boys,' said Kinner and began to look at everything doubtfully.

There wasn't a drop of rain out there but inside this strange, uncertain, wild world the water kept dribbling freakishly from the leaves of some trees as though they were shedding mournful tears over the death of some loved one. Everything, from the ground underneath to the high peaks of trees, seemed so treacherous and so hostile that we began to feel a lump of fear agglomerating inside us; in Krishan and I in particular. Kinner, if fearful, didn't show it much.

We were convinced by now that if we made the mistake of getting separated from each other we might not meet again. So, we stayed together, walking one after the other, with Kinner leading the way.

Kinner suddenly stopped at a spot in front of which there was a large marshy stretch full of slush, morbidly bubbling out steamy air.

'Look. It's a swampland, full of mire, God knows how deep. If someone falls into it, he would never get out. Don't ever go near it, for if you slip in by accident it'll swallow you up in one gulp,' said Kinner, uttering every phrase distinctively and frighteningly.

The croaking of frogs, howling of jackals, moaning of monkeys, twittering of birds, hissing of serpents, roaring of winds, cracking of trees, rumbling of heavy animals, the unceremonious muttering of smaller things, the sudden shrieks of unknown living things, the screams of mammals and the bellowing of bulls – all these different discordant, unceasing voices filled the environment with terror, making us shiver and perspire. The time was 3 pm already and we hadn't seen even a fraction of the forest yet.

'I don't think we should go too far into the jungle without any weapon. All these different voices coming from the middle of the forest are enough of a warning that to go that far may not be devoid of serious dangers from wild animals and many other callous and cruel forces of nature,' said Kinner, rooted a few feet away from the swampland.

'How far should we go then?' asked Krishan.

'Wait!' Kinner said and looked back to where we had entered. 'We're about fifty to sixty feet in and we should appoint this as our boundary line so that we go left or right from here but not further ahead.' And we immediately accepted his proposal.

So we turned left from there and continued till we reached a large pond full of muddy water, in which some buffaloes were dipping their heads in and out. But the ferocity of their eyes, the sight of their curled up horns and the way they began to stare at us, the unsolicited intruders to their private lives, made us shudder with fear and stay at a safe distance.

'That's where beasts drink water,' said Kinner. 'There must be many more of them in the forest.'

While we stood watching the beasts, camouflaged behind the trunks of trees, something fell from the nearby tree, hitting the ground and exploding like a bombshell, spreading a white fluid all over. It was a coconut, unripe and inedible, but the sound it made sent us reeling.

Further away, behind a tapering heap of granular earth, stood something that looked like a wide shining leaf or a spectacularly customised kite flying near the ground. It had small sharp eyes and a variegated face.

'Look at that, yaar. What is it?' I said zealously and pointed my finger at the kite-like thing.

'Fucking hell, man, it's a cobra,' Kinner announced. We began to run away in a horrified stampede. The dread of the cobra and it's venomous sting that could make a human body turn blue, with froth spilling from the mouth, and the man falling into delirium until the soul disappears, went deep into our hearts. The sheer imagination was sufficient to make our feet roll like wheels. To our astonishment we ran so fast that we ended up on the other side of the pond, being constantly watched by the wild buffaloes whose faces and eyes veered round to take the whole semicircle. And then, all of a sudden, two monkeys fell down from nowhere, from out of the blue and began to screech and bare their teeth at us, keeping a tactical distance ready to run if an attack came. Soon they hopped up the trunk of a tree, somersaulted to the other tree and then on to another where they began to raise a terrible hue and cry so that in a matter of minutes many more monkeys came and gathered around us.

'Sons of Hanuman!' I cried and leapt backward in an upsurge of fear, as their screeching and yelling reached a crescendo.

Krishan was scared to his depths and was moving furiously backward, his countenance turning a deeper shade of turmeric with each moment. As the dread possessed us, the courage of the monkeys waxed, and they came forward, slowly and steadily. I counted the number and found there were seven of them, all young and agile with long serpentine tales sweeping the ground. It was all very alarming and I felt awareness cheating me when it was most required. An attack by the beastly creatures was looming in the air. But where was Kinner? I looked behind me and saw Kinner breaking a heavy branch from a tree. He had almost broken it but was trying to wring it apart from its last remaining connection with the bark of the tree. And there he was, coming valiantly and fiercely, equipped with a sturdy weapon, ready to deal a severe blow to the bestial invaders. Conscious of the approaching danger, the monkeys began to scamper hither and thither but refused to disappear altogether. Some climbed up the trees and others made long leaps to hide behind the trunks, yet looking furtively at Kinner, the Tarzan. But they continued screeching and gibbering and hopping up and down the branches, now with one arm and then with two, showing us their circus. Kinner went near one of the trees and hit the trunk hard with his branch, producing an explosive thud almost shaking the tree, resulting in the fall of some dried up leaves. The noise induced the tree-mounted monkeys to jump from one tree to the other in quick succession yet daring to look back and forth in indignation. Only when they had all scattered into the distances, did we come to see ourselves out of imminent danger.

'O Kinner, you're great! I applauded him.

'He's really very quick,' said Krishan admiringly.

'He's our Tarzan!' I remarked.

But soon after the monkeys had vanished, there came a herd of wild cows, ferociously looking at us with their big bulging eyes and shaking their horny heads viciously to inject such fear in us as no other attacker had done. They were still at a good distance when Kinner declared, 'Run!' We began to sprint towards the edge of the jungle, followed by the herd. Probably running was what made them suspect us as trespassers in their territory. Had we stayed there calmly or climbed up the trees, they might have given it all a miss. But now they were running wildly after us. When we reached more open land and stopped to look back, the cows stopped, too. It seemed like a hide and seek game, or run and follow, or stop and watch. But whatever it was, it sucked half the life out of us. Out on that side where we now stood watching the cows glaring at us was a small hill the shape of a pyramid. And because we were not left with enough blood to re-enter the jungle and face new challenges we made our way towards the hill.

'In fact the whole planning was wrong,' said Kinner. 'Partly I also blame myself for this. You shouldn't expect to go on such a wild adventure without proper weaponry. We Punjabis are made up of extemporisation alone. Have you ever heard of an Englishman embarking on such an adventure without preparation? It was absolutely diabolical! To go to a suburban ruin or to a cultivated field or a farm is a different matter because you can't expect such dangers there. The most you can confront there is a snake, a stray dog, a wild cat or rats, but not herds of wild cows, monkeys, cobras, or buffaloes, no. It's a jungle, man, and the jungle has its own rules, the strongest of which is survival of the fittest. A jungle stands in contrast to the civilised world because it's raw and natural. A constant battle of life has to be fought there, and one who survives one battle has to fight another and then another and the process continues. One battle is against other competitors and the other against nature. If dinosaurs won one battle, they lost the other imposed upon them by nature and became extinct forever. Millions of smaller species have become extinct, too. Life in the jungle develops its own survival mechanisms through the process of adaptation to nature by outliving the natural hazards; once it has done so, the next battle confronts it in the form of competition with the mightier life.

The descipline of a civilised life as against a natural one is governed by legal laws and social norms. Anyone disobeying them suffers either at the hands of judiciary or the society in which he lives. But the law of jungle is enforced by nature in an unwritten form, which deals justice in a different way. The cost is mostly paid with life or a heart-rending mutilation, eventually resulting in death. So, either you live or die, there's no other way. The mightiest law of jungle is force and we had entered without it. That was our blunder.' Kinner went on fulminating until we reached the pyramid-like hill.

His criticism was in no way wrong or in vain, for our misadventure could have cost us our lives. If it were not for Kinner the very monkeys could have pecked our eyeballs out, scratched us badly leaving weeping bruises and wounds, or torn us apart with their sharp steely fangs. What Kinner said had a grain of bitterest truth in it.

'What shall we do now? Go home or linger for another hour or so here?' asked Krishan, dismayed and jittery.

'What's the time now?' Kinner asked.

'Five o clock,' he replied. His was the only watch we had.

'Let's rove about for another hour or so and then we'll pack up,' said Kinner. We began to climb the hill. Kinner had his branch-turned-club slung on his shoulder.

The hill was about forty feet high, and was scattered with stones, and some dwarf variety of natural grass. The earth was a little swarthy, hard and unrelenting. It may once have been a small fort, for we glimpsed the signs of sunken vaults. There were quite a few shrubs and bushes, and thorny and succulent plants here and there. The exquisite thing about the hill was that it was flat nowhere. Either you could ascend higher and higher or you could descend lower and lower until you reached the ground.

As we reached its peak we found another bunch of monkeys sitting there, idly, scratching their heads and armpits and looking worryingly at us, more at Kinner and his club. But we were not scared now, for the competition could not be tougher than we had already seen. And as Kinner took the club off his shoulder and put it down on the floor with a dull thud, the monkeys screeched, their teeth bare, and swung into the air. Then they took rapid flight, one after the other, until they disappeared into the gloom of the jungle.

'Force or strength is the law of the jungle,' said Kinner smiling, and looked at us triumphantly.

'How about when the jungle enters the city?' Krishan asked, to my amazement, for I could never imagine Krishan talking something of that stature.

'The worshipper of the monkey-god does have a brain after all. I'd thought he was capable of nothing more than sit-ups and lie-ups,' I remarked sarcastically. 'You, too, can talk now,' commented Kinner, protecting his devoted listener.

Kinner's cupidity for more and more knowledge about anything and everything was his indefatigable obsession. He often sat in seclusion, and mused over and digested that knowledge, making it the blood and bones of his 'self'. He questioned everything he read, rejecting or accepting it. He was more practical than theoretical; more pragmatic than idealistic and more utilitarian than simply academic so that his knowledge gathered many dimensions.

'Mind you, life originated in its primitive form in the jungle,' he began to expound, 'the very home of nature. Civilisation as we know it today took millions of years to reach this level. So, we're basically animals, though somewhat refined ones. We made laws and norms to bind ourselves to some kind of relationship to each other. The animal inside us hasn't completely died but has turned dormant, but can awaken as soon as the laws and norms are slackened, just as a tamed animal can turn wild when there's no scourge to control it. For us the scourge is the order enforced by social norms and legal laws. Withdraw the order and you'll find chaos everywhere. So the jungle enters the city or civilised society, not from outside but from within because it's embedded in us, inherent and inborn. Once the scourge of laws and norms is put aside or the system we've devised is deranged or disrupted, the jungle surfaces. And then, what's left is force: the law of the jungle. We are but tamed animals and nothing else. Maybe, we're excessively tamed, overwrought and well-tempered but once we're loosened from the scourge we're capable of surpassing every beast in this jungle, on the road to perdition.'

As Kinner accomplished his last sentence, I began to clap followed by Krishan the follower of the son of the wind.

'Kinner the Tarzan-cum-philosopher; Kinner the Analyst; Kinner the Sun of our Solar System...' I went on and on.

'Shut up, you worthless rascal, and let's make a move,' he interrupted me in the middle of my accolade to him.

'Where've you learnt all this from, Kinner?' Krishan asked on our way down the hill.

'From the Hanuman temple,' I said, laughing.

'Shut up you, Arya,' grumbled Krishan. It seemed that the satire, though cut lightly, could bring some good results later.

The serrated shadows of trees had lengthened enough to warn us of the approaching dark. If the day of the jungle was so mysterious what could be expected of the night? So, we retrieved our bikes from the thickets of bushes and began our journey back home.

Sins of virility

I, Arya Gold the scribbler must, at this point of time (namely 1935), make some confessions if only to absolve my sins. The age I *was in* and the age I *was passing through* had a lot of bearing on my proclivities now that I was sweet sixteen. But to me, I was a sour sixteen, for a kind of bitterness had begun to overtake me, not because I was incapable of reaping the benefits of my age but because I was a bit too capable. I had developed a crow in my throat and my voice had grown heavy and husky, a mark of puberty which, according to the dictionary, is the period of life at which a person becomes capable of begetting or bearing children; the age at which a plant begins to flower. The age of puberty in boys is deemed to be fourteen and in girls, twelve. If I adhere to this doctrine then my pubescence had gone past two years ago and that of Radhika six years ago, for she was two years older than me. Two years ago, when I was fourteen, I had hardly ever thought about her and six years ago, when she was twelve, she might not have thought about me. I wasn't too sure if she thought about me now or not, but I was pretty certain that I thought about nothing else but her. I imagined her naked in front of me and found her most captivating and sexy. I also imagined myself sleeping with her; face to face, bosom to bosom, my arms around her and hers around me, my lips on hers and hers on mine - both of us stuck together like a pair of copulating buttons. It's all sin, isn't it? Isn't it a moral degradation, a spiritual depravation or an ethical turpitude? That's the confession I wished to make to absolve my sins - the sins of my virility.

In fact, the whole fault lay with Shakespeare or Shakespeare under the Banyan tree. It was then, during that play, that I developed a weakness for Radhika. She, as Paro, had played the character so well and so beautifully that I sold myself to her forever, not for lucre, which she never had, but for her dusky charm. Just imagine her twilight face, dusky devilish skin running all the way down her cheekbones to her sweet sharp singular chin, and the face filled with two small brilliant, lantern-like eyes, provided with an outline of thick brows and fringe-like lashes, smiling to keep pace with the glinting pupils. And just visualise her body: a slim neckline falling on to her thin feminine shoulders, where the contours expand with two mango-like magical works, taut and firm, standing out stubbornly, waiting to see if you have been truly ravaged. The contours then ebbing down to the small waistline to make you utter cries of awe and sigh deeply for not being able to touch it.

You might be remembering that I had played the character of Shylock, a miserable Jew, asking for the forfeiture of a pound of flesh from a human body, averted skilfully by Paro. That was where Shakespeare the bard had wronged me, for who could love a wretched fellow, a usurer, a mean and malicious Jew? No one could, I admit; and so would you. But did Paro or Radhika love or adore or like Krishan, or in this case, Basant Kumar or Bassanio? No, she didn't. And, I'm pretty certain, Krishan the disciple of Hanuman, the son of the wind, didn't like, love or adore Radhika, although he never admitted to it. But I still vividly remember how he had embraced Radhika in the final scene, despite the fact that she was drifting out and away from his voluptuous hold. Even our director Shakespeare, or Noor Mohammed, had told Krishan at the very outset that a play was only a play and it only amounted to the creation of an illusion of reality. But our Krishan, maybe because of some illusion, took the reality for the illusion and held Radhika in his arms until she made a desperate effort to loosen his grip and extricate herself. Fortunately enough, Kinner, as Nazim, was behind the scenes at that time otherwise the tension between illusion and reality could have taken a very serious turn. It wouldn't have mattered if Krishan had embraced her so tightly when she was in the guise of a turbaned judge, performing as a male but it did matter when she had taken her turban, beard and moustache off and was Paro or Radhika again.

And now, because I've made my confessions, I take it that my sins are absolved and I can talk with free and flawless conscience. I do also promise that at some time in the future I will express my extreme love to my Paro and shall refrain from indulging in reveries. The age-difference of two years might pose some problem but there's no harm in trying, for I don't want Paro to go after Basant Kumar or Radhika after Krishan, or Krishna, this time. She needs to marry Aryan blood, and this Krishna was, perhaps, a hybrid.

This should suffice, for the present, to let you know the age I was in. Now comes the other aspect: the age I was passing through. The age I was passing through (and so were others) could be summed up in three words: virtues of sterility. Whereas my virility turned out to be a sin, the sterility of the Mahatma turned out to be a virtue.

Our Gandhi Baba had to yield to the pressure exerted by the Congressmen from mid-1933 onwards to extricate the party from the sterile politics of confrontation and work towards finding an amicable solution to the problem of dissatisfaction with the British. Thus the movement of disobedience had to be abandoned in 1934, although the popularity and reputation of the Mahatma as an all India political figure was now hard to jettison. Although the Gandhi-Irwin pact of 1931 had already paved the way for discussions leading to the Round

Table Conferences in London, the real issue of forming a new constitution to provide India with a durable federal structure was not forthcoming due to confrontations. However, it was now clear and, even the government recognised that no major decisions about India's future could be made without the participation of Congress.

And finally, the 1935 Government of India Act received its royal assent in August 1935 – a kind of conclusion to the process of reforms commenced in 1919 whose provisions were to come into operation a couple of years later. The Act was a major experiment in the devolution of power to the provinces. It confirmed not only the autonomy of each province but also its unique identity and the power of strongly based provincial leadership, which would later lead to a host of other problems.

Mahatma's self-rule or *swaraj* contained the grain of renunciation or abdication. I wondered how a person could renounce sex if he was virile and how he could have sex if he was sterile. Maybe the abdication worked as a camouflage to hide inadequacy or sterility. But if virility turned out to be a matter of shame for me, the sterility forged itself as a matter of pride and fame and envy for the Mahatma. He had gone ahead with his civil disobedience, non-violence and non-co-operation with the idea of attaining self-rule for himself and self-government for India. He ended up with this fabulous Act, on the pretext that the whole thing *might* prove a framework for attaining that same goal.

In fact, my India has been like that from antiquity. Gautma Buddha, the prince of *kaplavastu*, renounced his palaces, his riches, his wife, his son *Rahul* and a luxurious lifestyle to go and sit under the Banyan tree, looking for *nirwana or mukti* or salvation. Had he remained where he was nobody would have bothered about him, and whether he attained *nirwana* or not. But once he abdicated everything including the clothes he was wearing, people began to extol him as infallible and invincible.

The Mahatma's *nirwana* assumed the name of *swaraj* but the approach remained the same. Nobody bothered a penny about him when he had his clothes on but when he took them all off, the rabbles began to follow him like the eyeless follow a single-eyed person. The philosophy of *tyaag* (the English version being renunciation, resignation, abjuration, abdication, relinquishment and a dozen other words offered by the dictionary) is what India is made of. I shouldn't call it a philosophy for it would be an injustice to the lofty word; rather, I should call it an infatuation, a freakish obsession, a craze, an infantile fixation, madness or disease.

Abstain from going near a woman and command as much respect as you want. Take your clothes off and move about naked in Yorkshire and be treated as a saint. Abdicate your wealth, become a street-beggar and you'll be treated as a man of vigour. Relinquish all your kith and kin, end up as a loner in a forest and get yourself venerated as a sadhu, a rishi or a holy man. Wear a loincloth, stay amongst your followers day and night (for if you don't they'll vilify you as a trickster), and be ready to be treated as a man of insurmountable tolerance. However, notwithstanding your facade, do anything you desire but do it all secretly, and get yourself labelled as the apostle of truth and one thousand and one other virtues. Of course, our Mahatma was an exception.

You can cover all your weaknesses under the mask of abstention and abdication. The exposure can mean castigation and the hiding can mean a golden reward. Be double-faced if you can – nay, even three-faced, four-faced, ten, twenty, hundred and a thousand. Your success is offset against the number of masks you can wear. Your failure is your disclosure or frankness, your truthfulness, your confession and your obduracy to reveal, and your wilfulness to conceal nothing.

It's quite timely to tell a tale from folklore. A king had seven daughters. They always have odd numbers in my India, for the even numbers don't find favour with them. An even number reflects an even mind and the odd number... So, seven, five, three, one is the order you must follow lest you'd be labelled as non-Indian or a foreigner. The upward sequence can go to any number of digits: one hundred and one and so forth. That's what we do when we pay tribute to a newly married couple, to a newly born baby or to a religious place. We like to fit odd into the even. We do have even numbers but we devote them to other purposes. They are synonymous with greed, lust, sex and covetousness: three hundred and sixty concubines, sixteen *sringars* or adornments etc. but they reek of impurity, maliciousness, non-sanctity, prostitution and, in short, evil.

So, in accordance with the lawlessness of the land, our king had seven daughters. He loved and adored them all but he loved most the youngest one called Rajni, the queen of the night. All the seven princesses loved their father, too, but the youngest, Rajni, loved him the most. One day the king decided to test their love. He summoned them all into his vast slumber land and sat them in front of him and said, 'My dear daughters, the time has arrived for your test, but I do know in my heart that all of you are going to be successful.'

'Of course, we will, father! Tell us, what's your test?' replied the eldest daughter while Rajni, sitting by the side of her father, kept looking at his profile.

'Well, then tell me how much you love me?'

'Too much,' said the eldest.

'Very much,' pouted the second.

'Very, very, very much,' asserted the third.

'Immeasurably,' replied the fourth one.

'I love you as much as I love the sweetest things,' answered the fifth daughter.

'Father, I love you more than I love the sweets,' responded the sixth daughter.

The seventh, Rajni, was still in the process of musing, yet looking at the profile of her father.

'How about you Rajni, my night princess?' asked the king.

'Well… Father, I love you as much as I love salt,' she said.

The king thought for a while and posed another question.

'Well. Now the final question: do you accept me as the strongest man on this earth?'

To this question all the six elders replied immediately in positive but Rajni remained hesitant until the king asked her himself.

'No, my dear father, God is stronger than you and us all,' she replied with a deep satisfaction showing on her face. But the king didn't want to hear anything to the contrary. So, he felt insulted and disgraced. The king married off all the six elder daughters into royal families but when Rajni's turn came he picked a lame and mutilated leper for her, married her off in private and said, 'I'll see what your God does for you now.'

Rajni, without losing her equanimity, seated the leper in a bamboo basket, lifted it on her head and left. Days and weeks and months trickled by, and then, one day, she reached a place, as a matter of serendipity, where there was a small pond. She put the basket down on the floor near the bank of the pond and made her way to the town to beg as she had done all these weeks and months. But this pond was no ordinary pond, rather a special one, full of life-giving water. The leper saw a crow, a black crow dipping in its water and turning white at once. The magic power of the pond enthralled him. As a result, he began to crawl towards the pond and once he was on its bank he threw himself into its waters. When he came out, he looked as handsome as a prince. In fact, he was a prince. Once, when he had been out on a hunting escapade he was caught by a group of bandits, who robbed him of everything he had and incarcerated him in an underground cell, inaccessible even to the sunlight. It was there that he caught this horrible disease, and when someone freed him, years after, he had become a leper.

When Rajni came back with her begging bowl, she found her husband missing and this handsome young man sitting near the basket, instead.

'Who're you? Where've you thrown my husband? God will never forgive you for this cruelty.' Rajni reprimanded him in full swing.

'Don't panic, Rajni. I'm your husband, the leper. Look there,' he said and pointed his finger at the pond. Rajni saw with her own eyes another black crow dipping in the water and getting out as white as a white pigeon. At that, she looked above to the skies, prayed to God with folded hands and fell into the arms of the prince. Then they went to the place where the prince was the would-be king. They found that his father had just died and the courtiers had been trying to find the prince to take over the throne.

After the coronation was over, they went to see Rajni's father, who was now sick and suffering from diabetes. The royal *hakeem* forbade him from taking both sugar and salt. He didn't find it difficult to eat things without sugar but it was unbearable to eat vegetables without salt. He had grown sick and tired of all this. When Rajni and her husband reached the palace in their royal clothes, all the courtiers were taken aback. When Rajni's father was told of their arrival he called them straight in. He, too, was astonished to see the leper-turned-prince and now a king, like him.

The Volcano

'Hello father, meet my husband, king Anupma Dutt, the one you chose for me. I'm really grateful to you that you picked a prince for me, who's now a king of Dharampur,' said Rajni politely and sat by his side on the bed, looking quietly at his profile.

'I apologise to you, my dear daughter, you were perfectly right. Only I was unable to understand your logic. You can live without sweet things but you can't live without salt. And God is the strongest of all. God bless you, my daughter, I've learnt my lessons the hard way. And, you're the wisest of all my daughters and love me most,' the king said with tears in his eyes and kissed Rajni's forehead.

The tale from folklore ended here and so did Mahatma's salt march. He must have read or heard this folk-tale in order to be able to defy the law. I wonder, however, why didn't he make sugar from the sugarcane? He went straight to the sea and made the salt. But never mind, because he ended everything last year, even the popular civil disobedience, the non-co-operation and the soul-force, for the *Raj* agreed to permit peaceful picketing in pursuit of *swadeshi*, and to allow the inhabitants of salt-producing areas to collect salt for their domestic consumption.

Even Irwin did not want any trouble at this stage because Congress had gained enormously in prestige and respectability in the much publicised and prolonged discussions between its main spokesman, the Mahatma, and the head of the *raj*. The incarceration of Gandhi had already cost the *raj* dearly in the form of lost sympathy for the *raj* among potential Indian collaborators. The 1935 Government of India Act couldn't have been thrashed out had the *raj* not changed it tactics.

But the change didn't occur only in the tactics of the *angrez* it also occurred in our Krishan. He had now stopped worshipping the monkey-god Hanuman, the son of the wind, and going to his temple and the *akhara*, and had begun to read books. I wondered whether it was the influence of the unruly monkeys we met in the jungle last year or the influence of Kinner's erudition. It could be either or both. But as our Deewan Shah said in his last dialogue in the 'Merchant of Amritsar' 'all is well that ends well'. Whatever might have become the medium, monkeys or Kinner, the effect was good. Krishan's red loincloth had vanished and so had his sit-ups and lie-ups. The gallons of mustard oil that he used to massage his body with had to be saved now, keeping to the country's economy, which was crumbling fast. But the whole new order, with which he had replaced the old regime, showed him in yet another extremity: reading books and looking glum or wistful.

He had found a book in Hindi from his school library called 'Prakriti and Darshan' that's 'Nature and Philosophy' and had begun to read it. The terminology was different to what he had read thus far in his school text books, and he came to ask me the meanings of many words. The better person to guide him would have been Kinner, but he was hardly ever available at home. He could be anywhere from the central library in the city to some derelict site, ruin or dilapidated fort. To find me was easier, for I was basically a home lover. So, he didn't bother, at least at this stage, to chase Kinner too much. And, I knew that I wasn't too agnostic, at least for Krishan, who was completely nascent in this new venture.

The book began its study with Matter, which it called *padarth* in Hindi. It defined Matter as anything and everything, which filled this universe, from an atom to the sun, moon, stars, air and clouds: everything observable and unobservable, palpable and non-palpable. Then it explained the mode by which Matter existed in the vast universe, and called it *gati* or motion. It said that everything from an atom to the sun was in a state of motion; the sun wasn't one but many and every solar system had its own sun. And this motion was produced by opposites, which were immanent in matter. This was where Krishan was stuck at the moment - on *virodh* or opposites.

'What does it mean by 'unity of opposites and action'?' he asked.

'Well, before you ask this question you should be ask, "what are the opposites", for without knowing the nature of opposites you can't understand their unity and action,' I said.

'All right. What are the opposites?' he asked as though he were bent upon learning.

'Well, opposites are like negative and positive in electricity or like north and south poles of a magnetic field, like male and female in every human being or like plus and minus in sums. There's nothing in this world that doesn't abide by this law of nature. All life is possible only due to these opposites. You can't walk fast on sand but you can on a hard ground because the hard ground offers your feet an equal and opposite reaction. So, these opposites are destined to live together and yet they work against each other. This opposite reaction leads to *gati* or motion. And, whereas the forward motion becomes progress, the backward motion becomes regress. But the final analysis is always progress. This is what we call "unity of opposites and action". So everything in this vast universe is in continuous motion and this motion is the very mode by which matter tends to exist,' I explained to him.

'You do know quite a bit,' he said and smiled.

'But not as much as Kinner does,' I replied humbly.

'He's a giant genius, anyway. Had he been able to go to a school like we did he would've turned out as something extraordinarily special,' Krishan said with utter confidence.

'It's not necessary, Krishan. He might have turned out daft, for you strive for what you don't have. I may be wrong but still I think that inadequacies and insufficiencies are your driving forces. The dynamics of life work in a weird manner. He turned out brilliant because he has a compelling ambition to acquire and possess what he has been denied by nature or by society. He knows he can survive only by being the fittest and this determination injects lot of blood into his veins – the blood of struggle and victory against all odds,' I elucidated and took the matter to an altogether different direction.

'You may be right, Arya,' he acquiesced.

On another day, when Krishan came to see me, he was droopy and sad.

'Why, what's up now?' I asked.

'My father wants to buy some cows, so as to have his own supply of milk to make the sweetmeats, or to be self-sufficient as he puts it,' he told me.

'And what's wrong with having your own cows?' I questioned.

'Wrong? I'm going to be wronged if anyone at all,' he flared up.

'How?'

'Well. He says I've done my tenth class, and that's enough for the son of a confectioner. No need to study further.'

'But where do the cows come in?'

'He wants me to graze them, look after them instead of going to college for further studies,' he said wistfully.

'Your namesake, Krishna, was doing the same, wasn't he?' I said satirically.

'Will you shut up, Arya! Don't pour salt on my open wounds if you can't help to heal them.'

'I'm sorry, yaar. I was just joking. When does he want to buy those cows?'

'Not just yet but you never know. The brains of these shopkeepers work in a different way. If he's bent upon he might go for them today, and if he's busy and overburdened with work he might let a few more months, or even years, pass by.'

'And how can you overburden him with work?' I asked.

'By sacking some of his assistants at the shop,' Krishan said and cracked up and so did I.

'Well, do that then.'

'How can I do that, yaar?'

'Pick quarrels with them, beat them up, swear at them so they leave,' I suggested laughing.

'Good idea!' he said and began to think of plans to pick quarrels with them secretly.

And in a few weeks' time I got the reports that out of six assistants only three mature and skilled ones were left. The young and hot-blooded ones had packed up and found work elsewhere. The idea had worked well, at least for the time being.

Night of the Crescent Moon

It was a sultry night, close and still, and oppressive. Although I was lying in bed upstairs in the open, the lack of the slightest whiff of breeze was almost enough to send you into delirium. I was perspiring endlessly with the heat the roof exuded from beneath my charpoy. The hand-fan, with which I was trying to conjure up a little bit of air on my face, did little or nothing to produce a cool puff to let me breathe. The air it thrust on me was hot and humid, and choking rather than relieving. My mother and father were sleeping downstairs in the open courtyard, surrounded by ten feet high walls on all sides.

The Volcano

They were both snoring, and I wondered how they managed to have such fast sleep when I was struggling to breathe.

Moonlit nights always seem to lull me to sleep and that night a crescent moon, accompanied by myriad stars, illuminated the night reasonably. It should have sent me into a restful slumber, but it did not. Even a full moon couldn't have sent me to sleep because there was no air to fill my lungs. My mother and father must've been deadly exhausted to be able to sleep immediately after they threw themselves on their beds. That was what always happened in the harvest season; weariness and exhaustion because of too much running around sent you snoring the moment you fell on your bed.

I was a little tired, but not as much as my mother and father must have been. I had spent the whole day in the city, treading melting tarmac roads, bearing the vertical rays of the brutal sun on my head, neck and shoulders. The road beneath my feet sent up steam that seemed to perforate my groin. I had gone to the city to submit some important papers regarding our land to the *tehsildar*. I had my father's clear and elaborate instructions to give the papers to none other but the *tehsildar* himself. To my dismay and prolonged embarrassment, the *tehsildar* had gone out somewhere (the officials wouldn't tell me where) and was not due back until the afternoon. It was this interim period of nearly four hours (from 10 am to 2 pm) that kept me trudging aimlessly on the city's roads. I could have stayed inside the *tehsil* until the officer came but the things were even worse there because of no aeration at all. The best solution to the problem of biding time was to either sit and yawn under some tree on the roadside or loiter about and watch people going about their daily lives, which might lend me some new experience, the very thing on which my scribbling depended.

A city being a city as opposed to a village, had lot to offer no matter what time of the day or night, you entered it. It had been my observation over the years that a city, Amritsar or any other, had a variety of life, ranging from one extreme to the other, from the simplest to the most complex, because it was the point where diverse life-styles converged and formed a panoramic cobweb of chequered patterns. A village, on the other hand, was just one pattern, a single coloured sheath of fabric with unitary form, like an amoeba consisting of a single protoplasmic cell although its shape was continuously changing. That was why people enjoyed having a spree in a town or city.

As I left the *tehsil* and made my way towards the centre of the city, I was intrigued by the sight of different kinds of people, engaged in different kinds of work, speaking in different accents and dialects. They looked different to each other both in style and shape and clothes and the way they behaved. The city seemed like an endless ocean in which swam all kinds of life. There was the wreckage of life, its proliferation and tangles, its accretion of wretched life - a situation that provoked awe in me. For instance, near the station, I saw forlorn beggars swaddled in rags. I observed mangled bodies, simultaneously selling eatables and scratching their weeping wounds. There were emaciated men pulling rickshaws loaded with overgrown, flaccid bodies twice the size of a man, and skeletons pushing *thellas* stuffed with as much weight as only a truck should carry. It wasn't the first time that I'd witnessed this creeping and crawling aspect of life in my city, but it was first time ever that I had consciously noted it, or felt it affecting my soul. Seeing and forgetting in contrast to noting and retaining was what made all the difference today. It was like being estranged or moved from reality and then being brought back for shocking cognition of it. This kind of life had always been there, rotting and decaying, degenerating and decomposing, but the city-dwellers had grown accustomed to it and refused to note it down. It all looked normal and natural to them, like air and water, like moon and stars and like the sun and its rays, as if they had grown situation-blind, incapable of discerning good from bad and vice versa.

I went over the railwaybridge and then entered the Hall Gate. The sight was no different to what I had seen at the station, except that the beggars here, instead of slumping on the roadsides, were walking with their bowls firmly gripped and shoving them into the nose of everyone, begging importunately for alms. Some paid and some didn't but the beggars just went ahead, looking for some other kind heart.

Then suddenly, I saw a procession coming from the opposite side, from the direction of town hall or the Jallianwallah Bagh. Hundreds of men, clad in khaki uniforms, dressed like *Pathans*, with spades slung on their shoulders, were marching towards where I was standing, shouting *chapp-raast* or left-right with army-like discipline.

These were the soldiers of the Khaksaar Movement, popularly known as the Belcha Party or the party of spade-bearers, pioneered by Alama Mashriqui – a misdirected genius.

Born and brought up in the city of Amritsar, Alama Mashriqui had expounded the aims and objectives of his Belcha Party last year. He said, 'To obliterate all kinds of differences among Indians (including caste, colour, creed and religion) by hewing them off with the spade and bringing them all into the one true religion of God – the Islam.'

The members of his Khaksaar Movement (movement of the *down-to-earth* people) usually came from the lower rungs of society such as hawkers, small shopkeepers, or those surviving on the margins of society. They paraded regularly in the parks with their *Pathan-like* look, clad in khaki *salwaar kameez*, shouldering their spades and chanting Islamic slogans. However, this was the first street-parade I had witnessed. It was a well-known fact that Alama Mashriqui disliked Mohammed Ali Jinnah who led a part of the Muslim League. Mashriqui was an expert in Islamic affairs; he had written quite a few books in Arabic and Persian, had paid many visits to Egypt and Turkey and had delivered his famous *khutba* in favour of the Sultan of Turkey, who was also the caliph or the head of the Khilafat. That was past history, yet his influence on the Muslims of India in general and those of Punjab in particular, still lingered. But owing to Mashriqui's past in the context of Turkey, the British viewed him with suspicion and subjected him to strict, secret surveillance. His activities, at a later stage, would disrupt the working of the Provincial Government of the Punjab under Sir Sikander Hayat Khan as the Chief Minister.

It took well over an hour for the procession to pass out of the Hall Gate and turn towards left to move on to areas such as Islamabad, occupied predominantly by Muslims. Islamabad rested on the road that emerged from the Lahori Gate, one of the twelve gates of the city devised by Maharaja Ranjit Singh to keep a close check on the entry to and exit from Amritsar. In fact, all the areas on the outskirts of the city abounded with Muslim population, such as Islamabad in the west, Sharifpura and Maqboolpura in the east and Hussainpura in the east west. The spread and settlement of population of the city corresponded very much to the Punjab as a whole. The city being the miniature form of the province showed the settlements in accordance. The Muslim invaders in the past had settled on the outskirts, especially in the West of Punjab close to the northwest frontier, Sindh and Baluchistan, owing to severe resistance from the non-Muslim habitation in the centre. And the same held true when it came to settling in or around the city.

The Muslim population in the west of the Punjab exceeded all other areas by a very large percentage. Attock, for instance, had 90.9%, Jehlam 89.1%, Dera Ghazi Khan 88.7%, Mianwali 86.9%, Muzaffargarh 86.8%, Gujarat 85.4%, Jhang 83.2%, Rawalpindi 82.8%, Shahpur 82.7%, Multan 80.3%, Gujjaranwalla 70.8%, Montgomery 69.8%, Sheikhupura 64.1%, Sialkot 62.8%, Lyallpur 62.6% and Lahore 59.2%. The percentage of Muslims in the population decreased as you came to the centre of Punjab, indicating the severe resistance that might have been offered to the invaders by the original inhabitants.

The centre of the city, too, had some Muslims living in it, but the proportion stood in sharp contrast to the non-Muslims, the latter exceeding the former like the former did in the west of the Punjab. The focus of political appeals to the Muslims, of whatever hue, would always be the outskirts of the city, or in the immediate vicinity of some of the twelve gates. Even the names of these gates (Gate Hakeeman, Gate Khazana, Gate Lahori and the Gate Sultanwind, etc.) proved their linkage with the predominating community.

Once the procession had passed and Hall Bazaar had begun to breathe easily, I proceeded towards the town hall. The time was 12 noon, and I had yet another two hours to kill. The best way was to stroll the city with a more open heart and wary eye than had been possible in the past. On my left stood the Religious Society's book depot and hall. They dealt in Christian Education and their missionaries were engaged in the gimmick of spreading Christianity in the non-Christian world. In fact, it was the effect of Christianity, which had aroused local religions, including Islam, making them fortify their defences and their hold over the people, many of whom, especially the poor and the deprived ones, were ready to or had already embraced Christianity. To counter this encroachment upon the boundaries of the local religions, local religious societies had also accelerated their pace of reawakening. And the process had not only threatened Christians. The main religions began to suspect each other's intentions and reacted furiously against a supposed or imagined adversary. This rivalry had begun as early as in the last quarter of the 19th century and prevailed till this day, with more intensity. The Singh Sabha Movement of Sikhs, the Hindu Mahasabha and the Muslim League were now the obvious manifestations of what was going on in the interior fabric of the society, with many more overt and covert ramifications on local, provincial and national level. Each religious community thought the other was trying to undermine it by converting their adherents to their own faith to increase their strength. The situation was further worsened by the political opportunists, who would hire men to ignite trouble by placing a slaughtered pig in front of a mosque, the head of a cow at the front gate of a Hindu temple or by throwing a packet of cigarettes into a Sikh shrine. The divide was already there and anyone who widened it through such treacherous means benefited from it in one way or the other. So divide and rule was the best policy serving the parochial motives of all the interested parties.

I went further ahead and reached the Chowk Khansama wallah about a furlong or so away from the Hall Gate – the square of cooks and chefs, it was called. The chowk abounded in *dhabas* and restaurants on all sides. If anyone wanted to hire a chef or a cook, this was where the search would begin. From the hiring of crockery or decorations for tents and marquees, all were available here in the specialist shops in the gullies and bazaars that merged into the square. But all those things were meant for high society people; the lower strata had to eat on palm-leaves or, worse still, on bare hands. The cost of hiring any one item could easily provide a whole village with one meal. I had never seen such an extravagance in Qila Vasudev. It was the prodigality of the cities only.

Further along, on my left, past the Khansama Square, was the National Bank of India, a fabulous feature of the Hall bazaar where the excess money of the well-to-do people lay in the coffers.

After that was Chowk Gas Walla, which was famous for its big gas lamps that people would hire for marriage parties and other events of huge merrymaking. After Chowk Gas Walla and the Chartered Bank came the Town Hall where the bazaar narrowed to half its normal width so that only one *buggi* or *tonga* could pass through it. The Town Hall had the Kotwali, or City Police Station too, in its vast expanse. It was a red-brick building with numerous rooms, offices, lock-ups and all that one could ask for in the name of law, to force people to behave properly and in accordance with the law makers and enforcers if they wished to eschew rigorous punishment. In the days when the Jallianwallah massacre had taken place, this police station and its chief police officer in charge of the city and his assistants were in full rampage. They brandished their swagger sticks in the air and threatened to teach lessons to those who dared shed a tear or utter a cry as an aftermath of tyranny. Ironically enough, this very road led further to Chowk Malka or the square where the statue of Queen Victoria stood, and then to Chowk Jallianwallah Bagh where, if you turned right, the road took you to the entrance gate of the Golden Temple. But the time was 1.30 pm and I was due back to the tehsil. So I re-traced my steps, without letting any unwanted sentiment possess me, as was expected of a good law-abiding citizen.

Having submitted the papers to the tehsildar, I looked at nothing and made my way to the Gate Hakeeman and from there on to my village. Suddenly, I was possessed by the idea that if everyone did what I did, all our troubles could be over. The trouble begins when you begin to look deeply and think about things. Shut your eyes to reality, constrict your senses to all perceptions, to every stimulus, and you'll be freed from all troubles. We do something similar to our bullocks when they are made to take rounds of the well; we blindfold them with leather blinkers so they don't see, don't get scared of anything, don't even see what they are doing. If, when without blinkers, they see a snake ahead they'll refuse to move, but blindfolded they see nothing and move on. If we, as an authority over our oxen, want their obedience and subservience, then so do our authorities from us. And, better still if we shut the eyes of our soul, our mind and our consciousness. Because that's where the feelings and grievances grow, *unwanted* sentiments and emotions take birth and refuse to abide by the law and begin to respond to the external stimulus – the very source of all our troubles.

While I was proceeding on my way to Qila Vasudev, I felt I was turning into yet another Buddha. While Buddha traced the source of all our troubles to infinite wants and desires, I traced it to *seeing* and *thinking*, to consciousness. I thought I had, to my utmost pleasure, discovered the truth and all I had to do now was to sit under the Banyan for an hour or so and declare my revelations to the world. For, at the end of the day, it was the Banyan who would corroborate or confirm my findings. People would not believe me without the active participation of the Banyan in confirming my discoveries. And, if I made my proclamations from under the Banyan tree with his witness intact, people would have no reason to disbelieve that the revelations were passed on to me through some archangel dropping all the way from skies to the peak of the Banyan and then to me.

But when I reached the village and sat under the Banyan, it was so hot and close and still that I had to postpone the idea of sitting there for long enough to become the rightful receiver of those revelations from the archangel. I made up my mind to do it some other time when the weather was better and the heat lessened.

As I said earlier, I wasn't too tired; if I were, I would've gone to sleep forthwith. But now, as I lay sleepless on my bed, I was thinking about what I had seen and musing over it. The crescent moon looked like a scythe, a curved sheet of metal glowing red and hot. It seemed as though a blacksmith had just taken it out of the furnace and had begun to beat it hard with a solid and powerful hammer on the anvil, thereby causing thousands of chipped atoms to scatter around in the shape of equally hot stars. The freckled sky seemed like a black sheet of cloth chequered in spots of red. A complete absence of even the faintest gust of air made me schizophrenic and I began to hallucinate about the after life. What the hell might be like if it did exist at all? Could it be better or worse than tonight? Would it be hot, sultry and still like this night on earth?

And then visions of cauldrons full of boiling and bubbling oil, with mounds of fuel being shoved underneath into the furnace began to rise up before my eyes. Along with that went the clattering and rattling of heavy metal chains holding back the people who waited to be thrown in one by one. And then I began to see sudden fires erupting on all sides of this hell, their red tongues bulging to devour every sign of life. The whole thing looked terribly frightening and quite unlike this world. And then an accretion of vast leafy webs of tangled things suddenly mushroomed up like a crop of vampires. The earth was rent asunder and the demons took shape, their gigantic distorted mouths and protruding teeth slavering incessantly so that the lacuna underneath was filled with the steamy liquid. Even if it was just the wandering of my mind, it was lacerating to my soul. To evade further wandering in the heat of hell I began to think of a different hell: that of cold countries. Their hell must be full of mountains of snow and ice, and frozen rivers and streams with the trapped masses of men and women stuck in them, with only their heads sticking out, crying and clamouring for help. A cold hell of this kind sounded better to me than the one I had imagined a few seconds ago. Perhaps the hot hell might appeal to the dwellers of the cold climate as a heaven. So, the hells and heavens too, differed in context with where you lived on this earth. No inhabitant of a hot country would like to go to a hot heaven; and no one from a cold country would relish a cold heaven.

Surely the people from the scorching deserts, where the sweltering sand-dunes perforated your feet and the hell-vomiting sun poured lava over your head, would find an after-life dwelling in perfumed gardens of heaven watered by running streams quite an attractive bargain. But how about those believers who live in cold climates and are freezing to death already? Surely, they would love to go to a hot heaven instead of a cold one. They would love to sit in front of a nice warm fireplace, glowing with reddened coal instead of sitting by the side of a freezing stream, their teeth chattering with cold. It would be absolute injustice to send them to the frozen lands of northern Russia. But ironically enough, all the believers (regardless of the hot or cold climates they live in) are promised only one heaven with a cold climate and perfumed gardens watered by running streams for their after-life abode as though they would all go from the scorching sands. But then they are believers and you can't stop them from being so.

My hallucinations didn't end here. Once I had begun to wander in my mind, I continued for hours on end. The hell of Hindus and Sikhs was a torrid place. The *yamraj* - dressed as an appalling monster, half-naked and half-covered - came to catch you by the neck. He whipped you ceaselessly and took you away to be tied to a red-hot pole of steel (which he might have imported from the Tata Steel Works of India). He then opened up the book of accounts written by *Dharmraj*, counted all your deeds, both good and bad, in this mundane world, and assessed your situation. If your sins overweighed your virtues then he referred to another book, called the book of hell, which determined the compartment you'd be placed in; if your virtues excelled your sins then he referred to the book of heaven to find you a compartment there. So, 'compartmentalisation' was a better and euphemistic term coined by the archangel to replace this worldly, over-used and hackneyed expression, the Caste System. By his very looks, *Yamraj* seems to belong to a class of wretched ones, for he's so black and fatty and terrorising that you would like to send him to the worst hell if you were the decision maker. But never mind him, because he's an archangel and *Dharmraj's* assistant in the matters of death and punishment, a registrar as well as a penalizer, although our births and deaths in India were never registered until recently. The angrez tried their level best to teach us methods of keeping such accounts but couldn't succeed because they taught us in English and we wanted to learn in our vernaculars. Moreover, we believe in death and not life. Life is ephemeral, temporary and a dream-like situation according to our scriptures; the real life begins only after death. So, be ready to die if you want to live, or be ready to live if you wish to die.

I looked at the crescent moon again, and the scythe brought my senses back. The hallucination stopped and I began to feel suffocated and drenched in perspiration. Insomnia was tenacious and unrelenting; it allowed me no respite. I wasn't aware of the precise time but thought it was past midnight, though only through some sense of intuition. My armpits were sweating badly, my groin was inundated and my forehead was drenched. The bed sheet underneath my body was crumpled owing to my restlessness. It reminded me of one morning when my father had just left for work in the fields and my mother, in a state of hurry, had forgotten to do the bed. And, when I entered that room, the crumpled bed sheet brought pictures to my mind of the scenes that must have been enacted there. It took me some days to forget the signs that told of a story being scribbled between a man and a woman. I was only six at that time.

Insomnia-filled eyes, a dull and vapid body, needles pricking from underneath and an unsettling mind, all due to heat and sweat and the stillness of night, eventually compelled me to pick myself up and wander about on the roof instead of in my mind.

I went to the parapet and began to look at the dreamy village, the houses and the droopy Banyan in the centre. In the half-lit night, everything seemed blurred, camouflaged and melancholy. During the nights of the full moon, I could easily and clearly see Krishan's house, but now it seemed like a brownish outline shadowed against the darkness. But I could never see Kabir's house, for it was in a back street and also dwarfed by the vast *haweli* of Noor Mohammed. Moonlight or no moonlight, sunny day or dull day, Kabir's house always hid itself from my eyes like he did himself. I would have to make some effort at some stage to make him expose his inner self to me.

The scythe moved on, seeming like reaping a handful of wheat crop or fodder at each stroke. Was it earth and I that moved while the scythe stayed still? Or was it that everything moved although all seemed still? Krishan's book of nature and philosophy sided with the second opinion. And, what if someone from over the crescent moon clambered down its bow-like vault and saw me standing here? The thought made me smile despite the weather. Then another thought captured me: how many people in my village would be awake at that time of the gasping night and how many asleep. And then: how many people in the whole wide world would be awake and how many in a deep sleep. And then another thought followed: all the dead in the world would come alive on the day of *qayamat* or doom's day. This thesis came from Christianity and Islam; Hindus and Sikhs didn't believe it. If by 'all the dead' the theory meant literally everyone, how could the dead of non-Christians and non-Muslims be revived or resurrected if they didn't believe the doctrine? And if all the dead were going to be brought back to life, where would they live? The earth was already occupied by teeming millions. Probably, the theory had some other task to perform. Perhaps it was to dispel the fear of death so that people are not afraid of dying, because they will be reborn on the day of *qayamat*. I was going on and on, standing as still as the night, looking vaguely and blankly into the dark shadows made by houses, trees, hedges and shrubs, and the Banyan.

Just then, I saw the outline of a shadow coming out of Krishan's house and walking slowly but steadily towards the Banyan tree. Having reached there, the shadow stood still. But it was difficult to guess whose shadow it might be, at least from where I stood. It could be of Krishan or of one of his sisters. Out of five, one or the other would keep coming to the parental house. Rita, the youngest, had been married off last year.

Now the shadow began to move this way and that as if having a night walk. I became somewhat suspicious, waited for a few more moments, and when the shadow didn't go home, I decided to follow. Very quietly and softly, I stepped down the flight of stairs, opened the outer-door furtively and went out, closing the door behind without the slightest rattle. I soon found myself walking evasively towards the Banyan. I was quite a few yards away from the Banyan and behind the wall of a house when I saw another shadow coming from the side of the pond where Kinner's mud-hut was. I planted myself there and watched the new shadow reaching the old shadow. The old shadow opened up its arms and the new shadow disappeared into its folds. The two shadows mingled into one, silhouetted against the trunk of the Banyan. I went as far as the wall went and stopped. To go further would have exposed me to the consorts. So, I stood rooted there and eavesdropped. But all I heard were the first two phrases, one from each mouth: 'O my Krishan!' and 'O my Radhika!' Every bit of the rest of the conversation was as blank for me as the night.

So, Krishan had made the move already and I was still in the process of thinking, wallowing in yes's and no's, in pros and cons. Shakespeare had wronged me again. Had I played the role of Bassant Kumar or Bassanio then Portia or Paro would have been mine, as would Radhika after she took her guise off. But no, this wasn't my fate. This was the fate of Krishan. Why was Shakespeare so kind to some and unkind to others? My grievances against the great bard will always remain and I won't be able to forgive him for doing all these wrongs to me by the creation of Shylock.

My next move was to retreat, to go back home without letting even a straw know that I was there, that the night of the crescent moon ever existed in my life. As a scribbler I was destined to do other things such as 'seeing' and 'thinking', 'looking' and 'musing' and imagining things, to be imaginative, to take imagination as my fate and as my only fortune. That was what the bard wanted me to do, and that was what he himself had been doing. And that was what I had asked for.

Swaran Chandan

Ends and Beginnings

1937 was the year of the end of many things and the beginning of many others, both at local and national level. While Kundan Lal Premi, Kabir's father, was breathing his last breath in Qila Vasudev, the country was going through the process of constitutional experiment to transmute the 1935 Act into practicality. While the Krishan-Radhika love-tangle was curtailed and ended in fiasco at local level, the rift between Hindus and Muslims culminated in a chasm at national level. While Congress bagged landslide victories in the centre and the Northwest Frontier, the Muslim League lost ground from underneath its feet in Muslim minority areas.

The death of K.L. Premi marked the end of an era begun in 1914 as the Ghadar Movement. He was perhaps the last pillar waiting to be knocked down, although it stood only as reminder of the aborted struggle for freedom that had commenced in America and Canada - a kind of miscalculated venture, more inspired by emotion than objectivity. Uncle Premi was suffering from lung cancer, and was unable to breathe properly. Razia knew he would meet his end soon and, accordingly, she had prepared herself for the worst. And when he breathed his last at midnight, she only sobbed quietly and did not let too many cries out, just as the Ghadar Movement had left no potential mourners behind.

Yet Kabir cried and lamented endlessly. Uncle Premi was not only his father but also his preceptor and mentor. He had taught his son to write Urdu poetry and had lit in him the flame of love for the country, for its freedom and unity. Uncle Premi adored Dr Mohammed Iqbal the famous poet and philosopher of the era, and so did Kabir after him. Kabir remembered dozens of Iqbal's poems by heart and had read them out to us many times. The most famous that stood for the communal unity of India went thus:

"Sare jahan se achha, Hindustan hamara
hum bulbulen hai iski, ye gulistan hamara"
(Grandest is our India in the whole world;
this is our orchard and we are its nightingales.)

Another couplet that he read quite often to us was like this:

"Khudi ko kar buland itna ki har tadbir se pehle,
khuda bande se khud poochhe bataa teri raza kya hai"
(Lift yourself to such heights that God,
before planning anything comes and asks you, 'What do you
want?)

Premi himself treated Iqbal's poetry as sublime verses of heightened sensibility. He would read out a few of his couplets to the wider audience as a prelude to his own ghazals during the days when his throat was musical and his performance enviable. His most favourite couplet was:

"Phool ki patti se kat sakta hai heere ka jigar
mard-e-nadan par kalam-e-normo nazuk be-asar"
(It may be possible to cut the diamond with the petal of a
flower
but it is impossible for an idiot to be inspired by a delicate
piece of poetry.)

Premi, before saying goodbye to this mortal world, handed over all his works of poetry (some hand-written and some in print as cuttings from various Urdu publications) and memoirs to Kabir. Premi hadn't got any anthologies published but the manuscripts were ready in chronological order. He had lost his voice for quite some time, so he handed over a written note to Kabir along with the manuscripts. 'I hand over this treasure to you, my son. Get them all published in my name when you can. Lend them to no one because there is so much plagiarism going on out there. Let not a word from my writings be edited, deleted or replaced. And, do record the reservation of copyright in your mother's and your name. Also disseminate my written word as widely as you can.'

The note was written in Urdu and it showed how much trust and confidence Kabir's father's put in his son. This very thought made Kabir blubber his heart out when Premi breathed his last puff of air of this world.

Premi's funeral and cremation was yet another weird thing that could happen to the people of the village although it wasn't so with his close friends from the city. He had left another elaborate note, which Razia took out from her jewellery box when the pallbearers asked her about Premi's will regarding his last rites. The will read thus: 'Let nobody mourn on my death, for lugubrious songs are meant only for those who haven't lived the way they liked. Read no scriptures on my demise because I was never a religious man. Let my body be wrapped in a simple white sheet and offered to the fire. Don't pour my ashes into the Ganges because it's full of sins of horrible kind. Decant my remains to any canal or river where water flows continuously. I wish you to observe no religious rites whatsoever, rather stay calm and composed but not mournful. Do all your daily chores as you did when I was living amongst you. Serve the people who attend to my funeral just as you served them in my presence. Stay simple and normal at and after my cremation. Any aberration to all above would displease my *atma* or soul.'

When Premi's Will was read out by Kabir to all those who were present, they began to watch each other's faces in astonished bewilderment. Kabir had felt somewhat betrayed by his mother who had not shown him the 'Note of Will' earlier, for otherwise he wouldn't have lamented the death of his ideal father the way he did. He would have stayed calm and composed, no matter how painful it might have been to see his preceptor die. From that moment onwards, he exercised a vehement control over his emotions for the departed soul. People were stunned to see that neither the son, nor his mother cried, rather they pursued every detail of the will with strict compliance. Premi's brothers, disregarding the Will, wanted all the Hindu rites, but Kabir wouldn't let them. If they'd had to deal with Razia alone they would've most certainly taken the reigns of cremation in their hands, but they were unable to persuade or disregard their brother's legitimate son, Kabir. Razia's own sisters and other close relatives hadn't bothered to come to the funeral of a *kafir* or a Hindu infidel, despite the message. But all the villagers did come to pay their last tribute to the departed soul, although some came only briefly. All the ordinary Hindus, Sikhs and Muslims stayed for as long as the cremation demanded while the *zamindars* such as Sikander Ali and Arjun Singh came only to have their presence registered in the eyes of other villagers and went away. However, Premi's friends, those with whom he had spent his good and bad days, shared each other's grief and concerns had stayed with Kabir and Razia until the last moment, and they did it all regardless of their religious affiliations. Krishan, Kinner and I stayed with Kabir all day and felt as though he had suddenly aged in that one day. We were sad because our friend was sad. We were sad because we had seen and lived with uncle Premi in the village ever since we were born, had assumed consciousness and grown to become men. We witnessed Kabir discharging all his duties as a worthy son in the best possible way. It was then that we found out how strict and rigid our Kabir could be when faced with a new set of circumstances, and we admired him for that.

Uncle Premi didn't live to witness the national scene that year, which was wholly occupied by the ballot box. The elections were held under the provisions of the 1935 Government of India Act, so that a western-style federation on the continental level could be hatched and the provinces could be given complete autonomy. It was a franchise to Indians on behalf of the British Government, which, in the centre could make and run the provincial governments without too much interference. By this time, the Muslim League was almost powerless in the Muslim majority areas, and Jinnah's prime focus was Muslim minority areas. His relations with the leaders of the Muslim majority areas such as Punjab, Sind, Bengal and NWF were more or less acrimonious. Congress, too, had no influence in these provinces, barring NWF. When the results were announced, Congress won and made their governments in Bombay, Madras, CP, UP, Bihar, Orissa and NWFP while non-Congress governments were made in Bengal, Assam, Sind and Punjab.

The Punjab ministry was formed from a stable cross-communal coalition, the National Unionist Party led by Sir Sikander Hayat Khan, composed of landed peasantry or *zamindars* regardless of their religion. It represented the broad agrarian interest of the Punjabi agriculturists and reflected the social and communal structure of the province. The most important reason for its smooth working lay in two measures: one was the restriction on the alienation of land to non-agriculturists, and the second was the confinement of the powers of moneylenders, thanks to Shakespeare. Both Sikander Ali and uncle

Arjun supported the Unionist Party with the former having close links with Sir Sikander Hayat Khan the Chief Minister of Punjab and the latter having close ties with Sir Sunder Singh Majithia, head of the Khalsa National Party.

Whereas the National Unionist Party won its victory by the support of all Punjabis, regardless of religion, the Muslim candidates holding Congress tickets were badly defeated except in the NWFP. It was a special case dating back to the co-operation between the Pan Islamic Movement and the civil disobedience. Whatever the outcome of the 1937 elections, the Muslim League proved no match for the Congress at that stage, though it would raise the slogan of Pakistan shortly afterwards.

The masses had a great joke to tell in those days. "A male jackal and a female jackal – husband and wife of course – were passing through the jungle one day when they found an elephant lying flat on the ground. They took him for dead although he was alive and taking sound rest with his eyes shut.

'My dear wife, look; that's our ration for the whole year,' said the he-jackal jubilantly.

'Fantastic!' she-jackal exclaimed. 'But how shall we take it home?'

At that the he-jackal scratched his head and said, 'Easy. You tie my tail to his, and I'll just drag it home without any trouble.'

So, the she-jackal tied his tail with that of the elephant in a tight knot. But just then, the elephant woke and stood up. He began to walk with the he-jackal dangling behind him in reverse. The he-jackal tried his level best to disentangle himself but he couldn't even touch the ground.

The she-jackal watched him floundering for release and said, 'You won't succeed like that.'

'How shall I succeed then?' he asked, almost crying.

'Use some trick of politics,' advised the she-jackal.

'But he doesn't let my politics touch the ground,' whimpered the he-jackal in despair and yielded to his misfortune."

Not only did Congress not let Jinnah's politics touch the ground, even the Muslim majority provinces and their ministries treated him as an alien.

The alienation between Krishan and Radhika happened for other reasons, quite apart from politics.

Soon after the night of the crescent moon, one of Krishan's sisters saw him sneaking away in the middle of the night and began to follow him clandestinely. She was flabbergasted to see him meet Radhika, an untouchable. Having witnessed the malpractice forbidden to a class-Hindu by the Brahminic order, she returned home and immediately told the whole story to her father and mother, who began to boil with rage. When Krishan came back from his *vindravana*, they were waiting for him. 'So you've found a *chamari* (a leatherworker's daughter) for your *raas-leelas* (love-plays), hey?' Girdharilal shouted at him with angry eyes and a roaring voice.

Krishan felt his tongue cut out.

'You're the brother of five sisters, all happily married, loved and respected by their husbands and their families. What would they all think of our family if they got to know your mean deeds?' roared his mother.

'I know an idle brain is a devil's workshop, so I must buy some cows for you to graze and look after. You will milk them, wash them and be so dead tired by the evening that you will be looking for nothing but bed,' came the threat from his father.

'I know these low caste girls; she must've sprinkled something on your head so that by capturing you she captures control of this high-caste Hindu house and all that your father earns,' Rukmani passed the judgement.

'Couldn't you find a high caste Hindu girl to do your *raas-leelas*? Why did you descend so low, on the heap of filth like a wretched crow?' Girdharilal screeched.

'Go and take a bath right now, then sprinkle some *ganga-jal* (water of Ganges) over yourself so that it purifies you from the abominable contact with an *achhoot* girl. Don't enter the kitchen or bedrooms until you've done so,' warned his mother.

'Is there any *ganga-jal* in the house?' Girdharilal asked.

'Yes, there's a bottle full in the kitchen,' answered Rukmani.

Krishan didn't say a word. He showed no reaction and no protest and offered no argument. All his philosophy, if there was any, seemed to have drained away. He was sitting in front of them with his head down and dumped onto his folded knees like a culprit waiting to hear the punishment and carry it out without demur.

'Would you meet that lowly trollop again?' Girdharilal asked fervently and furiously.

'No,' came the whispering answer.

'If she advanced towards you then what would you do?'

'I'll change my track.'

'If she tried to speak with you then what would you do?'

'I'll run away.'

'Good! Now go and take a good bath and then come back here. I'll exorcise you from the grisly sin with *ganga-jal* and with the reading of mantras from the scriptures,' commanded Girdharilal.

In the morning, the news of the love-encounter between Krishan and Radhika and the story of Krishan's chastisement spread out all around the village. Someone from the adjoining house must have eavesdropped on what had happened in Girdharilal's and given the episode its wings.

Reshma heard about the doings of her daughter from a third mouth and was left awe-struck. The good thing was that all her elder sons had left the house early in the morning and would not return until much later in the evening after work. And Kinner, as usual, had disappeared to some remote and derelict place. Only she and Radhika were home when a lady from the neighbourhood called Reshma out and began to whisper, 'I wish it were a white lie, Reshma, but unfortunately it is not. It doesn't take long, you know, for mind and milk to split. A tiny drop of lemon-juice turns the milk foul, and so does the young age to the mind,' the lady began to prepare ground on which to build the edifice of the story.

'I don't know what you're talking about, Channo. Why don't you come straight?' Reshma questioned.

'Well, I don't want to upset you but it's a matter of honour of our tribe, you know. You're my god-sister, so I can't turn my eyes away from the reality because it affects you as much as it affects me. The whole village's full of mouths, you know, which you can't stop from talking. Gone are the days when people kept their tongues under control. It's no more so now...' she lingered on.

'Will you come to the point or I should go?' Reshma issued her ultimatum.

'I'm scared what you might do when you hear it, you know. I'm such a frank woman. You've known me now for decades... Well, the people are talking about some sort of bad relationship between Girdharilal's son, Krishan, and your Radha. Last night they met somewhere secretly in the dark, God knows what they did or did not, but someone saw them and reported to Krishan's father. And you know what he's like, a donkey-headed *halwai* (confectioner) and a man of caste on top; he beat his son badly and Krishan disgorged everything, every detail. It's bad, isn't it? These are the signs of *kalyuga*, the age of the devil. It all scares me to my spine, you know. But don't you say too much to your daughter, she's young and pretty. Just make her understand politely. I hope everything is okay until now but if anything's gone wrong then do tell me, for I've antidotes for all the ills. You know me quite well I'm a God-fearing and quiet person but I can't keep out of your distress...' she hadn't finished her speech yet when Reshma relinquished her, entered her house and slammed the door shut behind her.

'Radha!' Resham roared.

'Yes, Ma,' came Radhika's soft but scared voice from the makeshift kitchen.

'Come here!' Reshma lowered her pitch but the authority was intact.

'What's the matter, Ma?' Radhika stood by her side, shaking.

'Where were you last night?' Reshma asked imperiously. Radhika was alarmed. She got a hunch that something had gone wrong.

'I was here, sleeping upstairs on the roof, Ma,' she replied in broken speech, her intestines twisting with fear.

'So you've learned to tell lies also?' Reshma said with piercing rage, looking sharply into Radhika's eyes. Radhika found herself unable to confront that gaze and dropped her eyes down to stare at the floor.

'Tell me the truth if you want to avoid the wrath of your brothers. Nothing but the truth,' Reshma warned. .

Now Radhika was trapped with no escape route whatever. No lie of any magnitude would suffice to acquit her from the charge; only the truth might help. Radhika fell down on the feet of her mother, sobbing and shedding the tears of confession, penitence and for the absolution of her guilt. Reshma was a woman herself and a mother on top of that, with years of experience behind her grey hair. What youth could do to a person was nothing alien to her. To be the mother of a daughter of marriageable age was no easy task; and on top of all else was the stark poverty, and belonging to the lowest rungs of the society. Had things been in her control she would have married her only daughter off a long time ago. Her helplessness transformed itself into tears and began to stream down her eyes. She began to pat her daughter softly on her back while Radhika continued sobbing, sighing and snivelling, with her face flung into her mother's weak lap.

Reshma, with her limited numerology, began to count the number of years in which her daughter had seen the autumns, for the springs were counted by the rich and well-to-do while the poor and deprived kept account of the autumns, the leaf-falls alone. They counted not the laughter that came once or twice in a lifetime, but the tears that came as regular visitors. Twenty-two autumns, Reshma counted on the tips of her decrepit fingers, and her eyes began to float in salty waters again.

When all the four eyes dried up, sobs halted and snivelling ceased, Radhika, with her face still dumped in the cross-legged squat of her mother, began to tell everything truthfully, from Shakespeare under the Banyan tree, to Krishan's constant teasing and chasing of her. He had shown her the dream of marriage against all odds, and had met her adamant resistance for months and months, until the first meeting on the night of the crescent moon. It had been followed by a few more until, last night someone had seen them.

'You haven't done anything wrong, have you?' Reshma asked seriously and under the quail of a terrible tremor.

'No, Ma, I swear by your head,' Radhika said and touched her mother's head with one hand.

'Right... Now, this is the end of it all. These so-called caste people only defile us. They treat us low-caste women like things and toys to play with. They can't marry us. They only utilise us like a little bit of pickle or chutney with the main dish for the change of taste that's all. Don't ever trust any one of them, understand?'

'Yes, Ma. Worry no more about me now. You'll never hear a thing about me from now on. I'll die before I do anything like that again, I promise,' she assured her mother and herself, too.

And, before anyone else from within the village could tell them anything about the incident, Reshma herself took her sons in close confidence and told them the whole thing. She told it in a manner that was less a blame on the character of their sister than a reminder to them as elder brothers to find a suitable boy for their sister to marry. The only person who held any grudge was Kinner. But he didn't accuse his sister of any sin but his friend Krishan who, he thought, had stabbed him in the back. Kinner talked to no one about it but began to shrink away into the abyss of his own mind.

It was after this incident that Kinner took it as a challenge to educate his sister to the extent of making her an independent woman in her own right. Radhika was already brilliant in reading and writing, all learned from Kinner, but now she faced another challenge if she was to make others respect her. She began to work hard and with a vengeance.

One day, long after this incident, when I went to visit Kinner at his mud-hut, Radhika opened the door for me. To my amazement, she looked quite different to what she used to. She had assumed the character of a very serious girl with well-weighed and chosen words for her speech, a kind of vanity in her eyes, an air of self-confidence and grace in her gait, and a warm but touch-me-not smile reflecting from her countenance.

'Is Kinner home, Radhika?' I asked with a little hesitation owing to the new dimensions her personality had gathered.

'Yes, he is, working on his magnum opus,' she replied with a dim smile and let me in.

Kinner had a small corner in the far end of the courtyard of the hut, covered by corrugated sheets of metal, to do his work. He saw me coming, gave out a busy smile and engaged himself in his work, polishing the finished sculpture.

'Am I interfering with your work?' I asked, only for the sake of it.

'What if I say yes, you are?' he said as usual.

'Does it mean that you want me to go?'

'What does my wanting matter to you? There's no respite from an obstinate soul like you, is there?' He attempted to provoke me.

'Why do you have to insult me all the time, yaar?' I supplicated in mildness.

'Shut up and have a close look at what I've done,' he said to me and began to examine his sculpture from different angles while I stood watching him and his sculpture from the back where it looked like pure and simple stone.

'All that it looks is rough and tough stone, nothing else,' I said with sarcasm and chuckled.

'It would, to a fool, accustomed to seeing things the wrong way round, like the two idiots who tried to hit the nail with its head against the wall,' he responded with an equal attack.

The joke of two idiots was quite famous. They lived together in a house. One day they decided to hang some framed pictures on the walls to give them a better look. They went to the shop, bought some nails and a hammer and came back.

'Right, you hold the nail against the wall and I'll drive it in with a bang of the hammer,' said one idiot to the other.

The second idiot complied with his instruction and held the nail with its head against the wall. The first idiot hit the hammer on the nail but it didn't go in. He hit the hammer again but to no avail. He did it again and then again but the nail didn't move in, even a fraction of an inch.

'Now, you hold the nail and I'll bang it in. I'll see how it doesn't go in,' boasted the second idiot. But despite the swap of operations, the nail didn't go in.

'This nail might belong to the opposite wall,' said the first idiot and took the nail, holding it in between his forefinger and thumb, to the other wall. The second idiot hit it with the hammer and the nail drove in.

'See, I told you. This nail belongs to this wall instead of the other one. But you'll remain a fool all your life,' the first idiot said proudly.

'That means half the nails belong to this wall and half to the other wall,' concluded the second idiot.

'Exactly. But you come to understand things too late. You are an idiot,' reprimanded the first idiot to the second.

'But how shall we know which nail belongs to which wall?' questioned the second idiot without taking the other's insults to mind.

'Let's take all the nails back to the shopkeeper and ask him,' suggested the first idiot. And off they went to ask the shopkeeper.

'Shall we go and ask the shopkeeper who sold you this stone? You might've hewed it the wrong way round?' I tried to drag Kinner on the stones.

'Shut up, you penny-worth of a scribbler!' He scoffed at me. I was happy that his mood had softened.

But jokes apart, when I really looked at the sculpture I was totally mesmerised. The important thing was that he had used black stone for this sculpture, which had helped him create what he had conceived. The sculpture represented a young woman with long tapering face studded with gloomy eyes, thick brows, a singular nose and slightly parted lips. The features drooped to form an image of a terror-ridden character, imbued with a sense of incessant suffering. It was an absolutely superb piece of artwork.

'Have you thought out any caption for it?' I asked, still looking at the sculpture from various angles and distances.

'I don't know exactly but Sufferings of Eve is one idea. Do you have anything to suggest?' Kinner asked, deeply engrossed in meditation.

'How about Eve Over the Ages?' I replied after a few seconds' thought.

'It sounds a little too symbolic, leaving a lot to the imagination of the viewer. The caption should be a little more suggestive,' he explained.

'Then how about Trials of Eve?' I suggested another one.

'Yes, that sounds more appropriate,' he said elatedly.

Then he called Radhika and asked her to choose one from the three captions. She matched each caption with the image and then opted for the last one. So, Trials of Eve got through the ballot box democratically.

And, although I had begun to think that the model for Kinner's sculpture was none other than Radhika, the moment I left their home, this concept took full hold of me. As Radhika had compared the captions with the sculpture, I now began to compare the sculpture with Radhika. No other colour of the stone could do justice to Radhika's portrait except this swarthy one. Kinner must have made this choice quite voluntarily and after good thought. In addition, Radhika must have endured some long sittings for him to produce this magnum opus. It was an extraordinary piece of sculpture. But with regard to its caption, I still wasn't very happy. As I began to think more deeply about it, many more captions began to float on the surface of my mind, and better ones too. Eve and Darkness; Age-old Darkness; World through Her Eyes; A Bird Who Sang Lugubrious Songs; A Voyage Across the Dark Waters; In Adam's World – these and many more captions surrounded me like history encapsulates you regardless of your intention. Yet, I made my mind up to keep all these captions locked to myself and unlock them only if Kinner asked for another suggestion.

New Horizons

For two consecutive years, Noor Mohammed had paid very brief visits to the village. He did contact me when he came but he was, it seemed, always in a hurry to go back to Lahore. The year before last, when he came, he had said nothing about the play we had staged, as though the whole thing had been wiped out of his memory or he had had some painful experience out of playing it, which he wished to recollect no more. He met me very briefly under the Banyan, asked me how I was, and departed with an assurance that he would try to see me again some time. But that time never came. Last year was no different from the one before, except that he told me he was trying to find a place with some law institute in England to do his bar-at-law. It was strange for us to hear him say this because going to England couldn't be an easy task. Except for Kabir's father, no one else from within our village had ever travelled abroad. That was why we treated uncle Premi as someone special and extolled him for showing such courage as early as the second decade of the century. And if all went well with Noor Mohammed, he would be the second person (and that, too, from within our age-group) to pay a visit to a land that bore Shakespeare, Keats, Wordsworth, Shelley, Hardy,

Dickens and so many others. For a while, I had felt as if the personality and status of Noor Mohammed had suddenly risen higher than each one of us. But instead of becoming jealous of him (save for Kabir) we had begun to feel proud that one of our companions (though a small time one) was going to climb higher up the ladder that would bring us and our village fame and respect in the world, just as Shakespeare had brought fame to Stratford-on-Avon.

But after Noor Mohammed had gone back to Lahore, Kabir said, 'So he's thinking of becoming another Qaed-e-Azam.'

Mohammed Ali Jinnah had earned this name, that meant law maestro, from his staunch followers and he was often addressed by this title by the people who were his close companions. Whether or not Noor Mohammed would turn out to be another Qaed-e-Azam was another matter, but Kabir's scorn and jealousy for him was obvious. I wondered why Kabir had grown so disagreeable and contemptuous.

It was on Noor's last visit that Kinner had asked him for some information about the functioning of the Lahore art gallery. Noor had no clue at the time but promised that he would dig out all the information and write to Kinner. True to his promise, Noor had taken every trouble to collect all the necessary information about the art gallery, including its address and the names of its officials and had written a long letter to Kinner. It was after receiving this information that Kinner had begun to work hard, and with a vengeance, to create his magnum opus in black stone with, I'm certain, Radhika posing as his model.

We were half way into the year 1937 when Noor Mohammed broke the news that he had been accepted by the Law Society of England, assigned a place to do his higher studies in law and was leaving in a week's time for the far off land. Sikander Ali was so elated about his grandson's progress that he paid a special visit to the greatest mosque in the city, expressed his heart-felt gratitude to Allah and his prophet and announced a sum of Rs500 as his gratuity towards the Islamic fund of the mosque. Soon after that, the centre of conversation for the whole village was Noor Mohammed and other members of his family.

'Do you see, Parvati? I told you that your son is good for nothing but you wouldn't agree. Now you can see with your own eyes. What's this writing-shitting and all? Sikander's Noor has proved himself the best. He's going to become a great *vakeel, a poora kanoondan* and this boy of ours, is determined to remain an ink-sprinkler all his life.' My father caught the opportunity tightly by the neck and belched out all his venom against me on my mother.

'You've developed a habit of criticising my Gold. Can't do much about you but I know my son is pure gold. Ask uncle Arjun and you'll know it,' my mother, once again, protected me against my father's disparaging remarks.

'You and your uncle Arjun have spoiled him, induced him to become what he is. He wouldn't have been what he is without your hand in it,' spluttered my father, looking furiously at my mother.

Ganesha, the elephant-god, was the son of Shiv and Parvati in our mythology. He was born as a result of the blessings of Vishnu to Parvati, and was so extraordinary that all the gods came to see him. And when all the gods went away with a happy heart, Parvati, too sure of her beautiful creation, invited the god Shani to come and see her child. But Shani, being known for his wickedness, saw the child and made his head disappear with his wicked magic. Parvati began to cry over this and prayed to Vishnu to do something. Vishnu appeared, chopped off the head of a passing elephant and glued it on to the torso of the child, named him Ganesha, and said, 'Worship him at the beginning of all your deeds and you'll win, for he's auspicious.'

This and many other tales were told about Ganesha. And when I was born my mother, Parvati, (and wife of Shiv on top of that) thought of Ganesha the elephant-god, the symbol of auspiciousness, to celebrate the commencement of her motherhood. But my father didn't agree, (he was such a non-believer) for he didn't want a headless child, or one with an animal head. My mother couldn't do much against the perversity of my father but retained the first letter 'G' and after a lot of mind-boggling thought, named me Gold although, she admitted to me in my late childhood, she only meant Ganesha when she pronounced Gold.

'I know you had that headless Ganesha in your head when bore my son, and now see, he's headless despite the head,' my father said to my mother the day I chose to become a scribbler.

In another tale from mythology, Parvati (like an illusionary magic-maestro) shaped out a boy from her body-grime and assigned it the duty of gatekeeper outside her bedroom. When Parvati's husband, Shiv, tried to enter his wife's dreamland, the guard-boy stopped him, quoting the orders of his creator. At that, an angered Shiv decapitated the boy forthwith. But when Parvati began to lament in loud wails, Shiv saw an elephant standing nearby, beheaded him and attached his head on to the body of the boy and named him Ganesha. Now this story is sure testimony to the fact that my father, Shiv, alone and none else is responsible for my animal head. But he blamed everything on my mother, which is not fair.

Yet, I solemnly declare to all those who can see and read that I never stopped my father from going into the bedroom of my mother. Then, why on earth was he always ready to decapitate me? Probably, my father disliked or even despised both Ganesha and me because Ganesha too, was a scribbler. And, if my mother was so impregnated with the personality of Ganesha that she wanted to name me after him, then was it not possible that other of his characteristics had taken re-birth in me? Being an incarnation of the elephant-god, I was, from the very outset, destined to become nothing else but a scribbler. But my father, Shiv, as had the ancient Shiv, failed to understand the simple logic behind the whole thing and took out cudgels to cripple us, both Ganesha and I, or even a sword to behead us. And why was Shiv (both old and new) so illiterate as not to have read the scriptures? It was clearly written in *pauranas,* the oldest work of letters, that Ganesha was a scribbler, who scrawled very fast in shorthand. The book says that it was he who scribbled the first volume of the epic Mahabharta. The real author Rishi Vyasa went on dictating the story while Ganesha kept scribbling it on the paper; he scribbled much faster than the speed with which Rishi Vyasa gave his dictation. All I had done was replace Rishi Vyasa with the history of the time. So, time was the dictator and I was the scribbler. But paradoxically enough, the old Ganesha had an advantage over me. He had waged a war against the demon king, Gajmukh, converted him into a rat by the use of his magical arrow, and kept him for his local rides. A ride on the back of a rat would certainly outweigh a ride on a bicycle, wouldn't it?

But I had an ascendancy over him. He had scribbled the first volume of the epic Mahabharta, a detailed account of war between *Pandvas* and *Kaurvas* that had engulfed the whole of India, whereas I was scribbling a greater epic *Mahavishva*, an intricate war story that encompassed the whole world. He had dealt with Lord Krishna performing as charioteer for Arjuna the eldest of the five Pandvas, reassuring him regularly that he should only do his deeds and forget about the fruit, and that death was only an illusion because the soul never died. But in my Mahavishva, I was dealing with a host of contradictory forces annihilating each other with *time* being the preceptor of all the combatants. Whereas Krishna met his death in the end, time never died, it only altered its form. The players changed but the arena remained the same, and the match continued.

But I should restrain myself, and refrain from scribbling too fast, like my predecessor. He had nothing else to do but I have. I have to see Noor Mohammed go off to England, and I have to welcome Kinner, who has bagged a big victory. So I must now sum up the *Shri Ganesha* riddle and then pick up my other bits and pieces.

Doing *Shri Ganesha* amongst Hindus and Sikhs means 'let us start in the holy name of *Ganesha*'; to do *Bismillah* amongst Muslims means the same thing. So, in that sense, Ganesha and I were meant to begin things, which was thought to be auspicious although my father hated all the new beginnings except for the law. He would call me lawless before he called me worthless. Despite the fact that no Shani came and made my head disappear to be replaced by another head, much less that of an elephant, my father doubted if I had even been born with one.

If anyone had the legitimate right to grow jealous of Noor Mohammed it had to be me, because his selection to go to England and come back as a law maestro had upset the settled waters of all the streams of my life. My father had forgotten all about 'law' and my 'scribbling' for some years now, but Noor Mohammed's selection re-ignited his memory. It was because of Noor that I had been insulted as never before. But I wasn't jealous of him, not even envious, even less did I want to emulate him, because that would've been the last straw. I was rather glad that he would do the work my father had anticipated that I would do. Yet, Kabir's jealousy of Noor was grossly unfounded, for he was the sun of a poet and not of a law graduate. If anything aroused jealousy or even envy in me, then that was the way the people of the village spoke about Noor Mohammed, his father Abdul Khaliq and his grandfather Sikander Ali. I wished they talked about me in that appreciative way and extolled me for what I did, unlike my father who disparaged me for what I did not. But in our land of saints and sadhus, a hack is seldom respected, a scribe still less so and a scribbler none at all. Although scribblers have left mounds of work behind, like Vedas, Pauranas, Ramayana, Mahabharta and chests full of others, people don't read to find the meaning of life but to worship them for the benefit of life after death.

Yet, my wonderments are so many that I don't know where to begin and where to end. Now, for instance, everyone commended Noor's father and grandfather for his placement in the school of law but nobody said a word of praise for his mother, Shaista Begam, who had actually borne the high achiever. That was always the case with us. If the progeny did well in any field, the father, grandfather, great-grandfather and even great-great-grandfather (if he still survived) received all the credit. But none was given to the women-folk. But if the offspring met an ignominious end then the whole discredit went to the mother, grandmother and even far beyond. In accordance with the law of the land (again bloody law) my father, too, would accuse my mother for not being able to extract the milk of his desires out of me. As though I were a cow from whom he had expected a good return for the investment of a sperm. But my mother never made such illegitimate claims on me despite the crystal-clear truth that she had kept me inside her womb for nine full months. She had fostered me inch by inch, by feeding me on her breast and washing my nappies day in and day out and had allowed me the privilege of saying that I was pampered in the best possible manner.

Anyway, the week that preceded Noor Mohammed's departure had seemed long enough but had shot off like a missile into all the yesterdays. I wanted to see him before he left the village to go to the city, then to Bombay and from there on to England in a cruise ship. When finally I saw him in front of his haveli's large gate, guarded by two rampant lions made of cement one on either side, he seemed quite effervescent with new zeal and his feet hardly touched the ground.

'How long will it take you to complete your course and come back?' I asked him with an overt expression of delight but feeling sad inside somewhere.

'I don't know exactly how long but in no case less than five years, I suppose,' he replied, leaning against the iron-gate with one lion looking at me with open jaws.

'It's quite cold in England, they say, and the chill of winter lasts much longer than the warmth of the summer,' I said as I had heard uncle Premi saying so, although I knew he had never been to England.

'They say so, yes. But you get acclimatised soon. If the *angrez* can tolerate our climate over here, then why can't we tolerate theirs?' He said and laughed dimly.

'And when are you going to leave?'

'Day after tomorrow, in the early morning,' he replied.

'Well, Noor, although we have spent very little time together, I can still say with certainty that we all liked you very much. It's really sad to see you leaving us but we love you so much. There was lot to learn from you but you never had enough time. It's our bad luck. I wish you a very happy journey and all that time you'll be spending in England. We'll remember you and miss you,' I said quite emotionally.

'Thanks Arya, you're so nice yourself. I'll miss all of you as well. And I'll drop you a word when I reach there. Will you respond to my letters?' he asked.

'Are you really going to write us a letter?' I asked with a little doubt.

'Well, I like correspondence very much, you know. I've a number of pen friends in various countries, and when they send me letters I love to read them, especially if they contain some new information about their countries. To get to know new things about new and unseen lands is a frolic in itself. I never stop writing letters until I begin to feel the other party has lost interest,' he explained in detail.

'If it is so then take my word that I'll not only reply each of your letters, I'll keep you well posted with regard to all that happens here. I'd love to receive your letters. Do write me about the land and people and whatever you find funny or serious in England,' I said jubilantly, for that was another aspect of Noor I had never known.

'I will, for sure,' he asserted and proffered his hand towards me for a shake. Not only did he shake my hand but he also gave me a hug, a nice warm hug, an unforgettable indication of goodwill.

Later on the day that Noor Mohammed finally left, another piece of great news came to us. It was almost as though it had been held in abeyance in the far horizon somewhere, waiting for the first piece of news to go before the second could arrive. The first news had taken Noor Mohammed away from us; the second piece of news approached us in the form of Kinner having succeeded in selling his sculpture to the Lahore Art Gallery, for a big sum of eleven hundred rupees.

When Kinner broke the news to me, I simply couldn't believe it. Had he said that he had sold the item for one or two hundred rupees I would've believed it without a speck of doubt, but eleven hundred rupees in that day and age was a colossal sum, which one could only dream of but couldn't find, see or touch. Even to dream of such an amount was like seeing something beyond perception. You couldn't dream of things you had never heard of; not when you had craved for *paisas, annas, chuwannies, dhelies* and rupees. But when Kinner showed me the cheque, I was just stunned.

'It's incredible!' I exclaimed with a sudden delightful shock and kept looking at the cheque with dilated eyes, as a person would when brought out from a dark room into the dazzling sunlight.

I knew Kinner had been to Lahore quite a few times to show his mini artworks to the curator, who happened to be a white man. Had he been an Indian, he would have turned everything down and sent Kinner home, desperate and unaccounted for. But Mr X (That was what Kinner named him, maybe to keep his secret, which was quite permissible because pre-emptory leakage could abort the deal) was made of different clay. He had seen all his miniature sculptures and had appreciated them and Kinner in the highest terms, and had even purchased some of them. But the money that accrued from their sales didn't have much weight. I knew the story of sales to that extent but what happened after that was unknown to me.

'Mr X is a gem of a person. He greeted me so affectionately that I was simply stunned,' said Kinner when I asked him to tell me the story of the sale of his magnum opus in detail. And Kinner was a philosopher at heart, a sculptor at his best, but a storyteller at his worst. So, the sketchy story he told me had to be properly stitched, polished and made ready for rendition.

The curator, Mr X, had promised Kinner some months ago that he would come to his village to see and assess his sculpture, but because of the overwhelming pressure of work he could not keep his promise. At that, Kinner went to see him again and fortunately found him at his residence, alongside the gallery. The curator was, at the time, engrossed in painting a landscape of the Kangra Valley, which he had once been to some years ago together with Mrs Nora Richard, an Irish lady and the planter of drama in the soils of Punjab. Her husband, Phillip Richard, was a lecturer in English at Lahore's Dayal Singh College, and she had come to settle there by that dint. Mr X knew Nora from her early days in Lahore when she had staged Shakespeare's A Midsummer Night's Dream, followed by 'Lady Gregory', Shanti Swaroop Bhatnagr's first Punjabi one-act play 'Karamat' and Ishwar Chander Nanda's 'Dulhan'. The painting that Mr X was absorbed in, presented Nora Richard against a dense backdrop of trees and the undulating landscape that would render the portrait a variety of dimensions. Nora hadn't yet appeared properly on the frontage except for a rough outline that camouflaged only a fraction of the vast expanse of the valley. The painting, a full four feet by four feet, was in oil colours, a costly business. When Kinner saw the size of the half finished painting, he was astounded.

'It's a unique piece of artwork, Mr X,' he managed to say, his eyes wide open and his lips parted in amazement.

'Not yet. Not until I've finished it,' replied Mr X, partly accepting the admiration Kinner had showered on him.

'How long have you been working on this?' Kinner asked.

'Almost three years now. Might take another year or so, depending on the time available to me,' responded Mr X and smiled up as though expressing grievance over the shortage of time in the curator's job.

'When finished, it's going to be a gorgeous painting, an amalgamation of both portrait and landscape, which I should call Portscape,' said Kinner in his insufficient English but Mr X understood his words quite clearly.

'Portscape! That's a good thought,' said Mr X, and was deeply impressed by Kinner's vision.

The Volcano

It was after this incident that Mr X felt obliged to pay a visit to Kinner's mud-hut to assess the sculpture. As if Kinner's fate was already knocking on his door, Mr X did not even wait for another day. He made the decision there to accompany Kinner on his journey home, delaying for only two hours, which he needed to take a bath and get ready. Amritsar wasn't far from Lahore, only twenty miles or so. Mr X had an old banger that took them both to Qila Vasudev in less than an hour.

When Mr X finally saw the sculpture, he was enthralled by its charm, its magical outlines, the eyes that contained melancholic shadows of grief, the parted lips that exuded sadness and misery as well as a vestige of sexual appeal. He scrutinised the sculpture from varying angles, from different distances and was enslaved by its gloomy charm.

'Utterly marvellous,' he whispered and made up his mind to have it. He might have assessed it for a little less but when he saw the mud-hut, its thatched roof and the kind of life being led by the artist and his family, he made the scrupulous offer of eleven hundred rupees, which Kinner accepted unequivocally.

Mr X was extremely decisive in his determination and action. He didn't want to wait another day to take the delivery of the sculpture, nor did he go back and send his subordinates to pick it up and transport it. He wrapped the statue in the fold of an old blanket from within his car-boot, tied it meticulously with rope and, helped by Kinner, loaded it onto the back seat of his car. Then he gave Kinner a receipt, with his signature underneath and left. On the fifth day after that, Kinner received his cheque for Rs1100, made out to Kinner Bharat Chand. When the cheque arrived, he had immediately rushed to share his pleasure with me. I could see the buoyancy reflecting from his face – a mark of self-pride and capability and of course assiduity.

Next day, we went to cash the cheque at the National Bank of India, on who's name it was drawn, with Kinner carrying the proofs of his identity, especially the ration card. But to get money out was like putting your hand into the hideout of a snake, particularly if it was a hefty sum. The bank wanted witnesses to ratify the identity offered but we had none. Surinder, Sonia's brother, could be an answer but when we reached his house we found him missing. So after a full day's travail we had to come back empty handed; much ado about nothing to go closer to our Shakespeare. The cheque was cashed next day when we took uncle Arjun with us, who had his own account in this bank. Kinner opened an account too, deposited one thousand rupees for later use and kept one hundred for immediate requirements.

Kinner and some of his cronies from within the city had been planning for quite some time to start a weekly paper in Hindi. They were all under the strong influence of Kinner and were confident that with him in the leading role they could win the battle. They were all from the downtrodden families but none of them was as bright and erudite as Kinner. In fact, Kinner himself had broached the topic one day when he had spoken on the concept of Harijan – an alternative name devised by the Mahatma for the Untouchables – and had rejected it in favour of some other name to be thought of in future. When he put forth the proposal of starting a paper to educate the masses and to combat the whimsical, rotten and decadent answers to the ills of society, all his mates supported him. But none of them had enough funds to transform this dream into tangible reality. Some of them were only daily wage earners while others did odd jobs here and there. Yet, they were ready to contribute as much as they could spare after meeting their daily needs in the humblest possible way. It was only Kinner who was completely impecunious and he didn't like to enter the battlefield without contributing an equal share. But now things had changed. Kinner had enough money to contribute his share and see the struggle taking off the ground. Including Kinner, there were thirteen of them, each contributing three hundred rupees. This initial amount was enough to get their ideas into print, to be read by people of similar backgrounds. They hoped to build a movement that would topple the hegemony of the so-called class people.

An ordinary office on the first floor of a building in the city was hired, some second-hand furniture was installed, an old typewriter was purchased and the work was begun. A press nearby agreed to print their paper on a very small margin of profit.

The first issue of the paper, Harijan Kaun or Who's Harijan, came out in the first week of 1939. (It was that first edition that I had borrowed from Radhika when I had gone to see Kinner at his mud-hut but had been told that he had gone to the city.) A few months later that year when Kinner, having sold some more sculptures to the Lahore Art Gallery and finding it difficult to cope with his team of unmanageable cronies, decided to take over the paper himself. Although the sales had begun to pick up, there was no money in the kitty, so all his cronies left except the ones who were physically involved in the distribution of the paper or whom Kinner himself needed and trusted. Some time later, Kinner engaged all his brothers in the task of distribution and terminated the services of the remaining elements too, because they had begun to fiddle the collection of sales and returns.

The real change in the editorial policy had begun with the first issue of August 1939, when Kinner had changed the name of the paper to *Dalit Samachar* or Dalit News. They had also changed their own names with a suffix of Vasudev and he had expounded the theory of Dalitism, Dalitology and Dalitlectics. He deputed Radhika as an editor and took all other responsibilities himself as the chief editor. His battle had now begun, and I knew at heart that it wouldn't stop short of victory. New horizons waited for him. The lights flashing and he would grasp with his sixth sense in the time to come.

Book Two

Experiment fails gulf widens

Uncle Arjun Singh and Sikander Ali, the two big landlords or *zamindars* of Qila Vasudev, had developed a measure of closeness since the elections of 1937. They both supported the Nationalist Unionist Party, the former because of his close ties with Sir Sunder Singh Majithia and the latter with Sir Sikander Hayat Khan, who was now the Chief Minister of the Punjab.

The National Unionist Party was composed of landowners or zamindars regardless of their religion. The Hindus, Sikhs and Muslims had united together to form this party as a matter of their common political and economic interest. More than 80% of Punjabis supported this party, resulting in a landslide victory in the elections of 1937, which were aimed at transforming India into a federal structure under the 1935 Act. The Unionist Ministry had 119 seats in a house of 175, with 74 Muslims, 13 Sikhs from the Khalsa National board of Sir Majithia, and 11 from the National Progressive Party.

Both of Qila Vasudev's zamindars were often seen together now. They went together to Amritsar to meet Sir Majithia and other members of the party, and to Lahore to meet the Chief Minister and others of his ilk. And, they came back together too, sometimes after a few days, sometimes just the next day. They stayed overnight even when they went to Amritsar. People from the nearby villages often came to see them with their problems, some of which they managed to solve themselves while for many others they had to go and find solutions from others in the hierarchy. I had never seen Uncle Arjun as busy as now; if I wanted to see him, it would be quite difficult, if not entirely impossible.

While the provincial political affairs of the Punjab were going on more or less smoothly, the rest of the country was embroiled in open animosity between Jinnah's Muslim League and Congress. In fact, the acrimony between the two dated back to the days of elections when Congress claimed to be representing both Hindus and Muslims as the national party but Jinnah refuted these claims. Congress promulgated its stand thus: 'The objective of Congress is an independent and united India where no class or group or majority or minority may exploit another to its advantage and where all the elements in the nation may co-operate for the common good and the advancement of the people of India.'

But Mr Jinnah disputed their claim, asserting that the Hindus were already showing that an independent India would be for the Hindus. In 1938, he accused Congress of killing any hope of a communal settlement or even of wanting one, except the one whose terms it could dictate. He also dismissed nationalist Muslims in Congress as misled or moved by the ulterior motives, and thundered, 'The Congress leaders may cry as much as they like that Congress is a national body. But I say it is not true. Congress is nothing but a Hindu body.'

Jinnah and Nehru carried on a vitriolic war in speeches in which Nehru claimed that the only two significant parties in contemporary politics were the Congress and the British Raj, representing nationalism and imperialism respectively. Jinnah argued that Muslim India was a vital and distinct element in the situation, which Congress did not represent. In April 1938, Jinnah wrote menacingly that if Congress would not recognise the Muslim League 'on a footing of complete equality' and negotiate a Hindu-Muslim settlement, the League would have to depend on its 'inherent strength' to convince Congress that it must deal with it.

Then, in September 1939, things changed for the worse. The Second World War broke out and the Viceroy declared war on behalf of India, without consulting Indians or even Congress, the only party hitherto representing Indian aspirations. In protest, Congressional High Command withdrew all the Congressmen from co-operating in the provincial governments, thereby crippling the provincial ministries and leaving them to be run by the governors. The clash between imperialism and nationalism was at the root of these withdrawals. But, to this protest of Congress, Jinnah dealt a severe blow by exhorting Muslims to celebrate a day of deliverance from the tyranny, oppression and injustice of Congressional rule in the Muslim minority areas.

Following these national developments, a fresh issue of Dalit Samachar appeared in the last week of December. In it, Kinner wrote a comprehensive article analysing the current situation. I read the article sprawling over four full pages and was impressed once again by Kinner's understanding and wisdom. I should like to feature some important paragraphs from his long essay to sharpen the view of things.

"The constitutional experiment was meant to serve as a buttress for the collapsing structure of the empire owing to sweeping nationalism transforming into Indian aspiration of self-rule. The 1935 Act provided an alternative to this in the form of self-governments in the provinces with little or no interference by the ruler occupying the centre. It was a step forward to build a federation with a centre, which instead of being controlled by the Indians was to be governed by the British. At the end of the day, defence and foreign affairs were to be kept under the control of the centre. But the major hitch in the development of such a federation were the princely states, who wanted exceptionally high prices for accession and who rejected the offers made to them by their white masters and proved unwilling sellers. But until now the British had treated their princely allies as honoured partners, expressing gratitude for their allegiance in one form or another while Congress displayed an overt antagonism to them by backing the movements of reforms in their areas. The people of the princely states, too, were sick and tired of their myopic kings and princes who, like parasites, had been sucking their blood and munching their bones. People wanted to see the end of princely autocracies, to which effect they had launched various movements and were thankful to Congress for backing them strongly. But the British had no interest in such reforms because the status quo suited them best.

"Yet the British tactic of retreat to the centre, leaving the provinces to run themselves under Indian ministers paid off spectacularly because the move created an insatiable hunger for power among Indians on the provincial level, which sharpened the divide between religions, and factions within religions. It also made the masses more province-oriented than country-oriented. The taste of power not only generated gulfs on cross-communal levels but also on cross-factional levels in the same community, Sind being just one example to cite.

"The rulers had planned the whole strategy with a view to straining the inexperienced provincial masses and leaders, resulting in the drainage of energy and their final surrender to the centre. But the whole experiment backfired, contrary to what had been anticipated. The climax was reached when war was declared on India's behalf without testing Indian opinion, which resulted in resignations from the Congress ministries in the country.

"Mr Jinnah caught the opportunity and bemoaned Congressional rule by celebrating the day of deliverance. Yet he was fearful that if the British left, Congress would emerge as the inheritor of power in the centre, in which case even the Muslim majority provinces would have to conduct their business under the dictates of Congress. Mr Jinnah wanted to be the third voice in the final decisions of the country's fate. So, the need was to show the Muslims a larger dream in front of which the provincial power bases would have melted away. And such a dream, which had emanated from a group of radical Muslim students in London asking for a separate country for a separate nation of Indian Muslims called Pakistan, did already lay in abeyance. So, the concept of Pakistan, although a bluff as Mr Jinnah would later put it, was to provide the cement to fuse Muslims together and erode the concept of federation, which the rulers had introduced to protract the Raj.

"Mr Jinnah, a barrister-turned-politician and an observer of the 1937 elections, was badly shaken to find himself in an alien land where no one bothered a penny about him. He had returned home from a self-imposed exile in London, to take part in the country's post-British fortune. The experiment of federation and provincial autonomies, which had seemed adequate safeguards once, now looked fragile barriers against the popularity and force of Congress.

"Consequently, at the beginning of the year, Mr Jinnah began to fortify the Muslim League with the intent to build its 'inherent strength' to compel Congress to deal with it. But the Muslim minority provinces could not give the League the kind of leverage Jinnah envisaged. So, he began to woo the leaders of the Muslim majority areas such as Punjab and Bengal. But Jinnah's relations with the leaders of these two areas were often acrimonious, and they dismissed him as an outsider."

Kinner went on analysing the political changes thus far and concluded thus:

"Although the Muslim League has not passed any resolution until now for a separate state of Pakistan, the seeds of such a state have already been sown. Although the appeal of the idea of Pakistan and the reorganisation and strengthening of the basis of the League as the focus of Muslim unity is still limited, its emergence signifies the very fact that the development of political identities in the country in the context of rapid political change, defies the idea that India is composed of just one nation.

"Yet my concern is the situation of Dalits in this vicissitude. The downtrodden or the Dalits come from all the three religions and they are all equally pulverised by the dominant classes. Then what part of India can they lay their claim to? If the Hindus, Muslims and Sikhs are three claimants, then where do the Dalits, who come from all the three communities, stand? Or, are they doomed to live like wretched people even when India becomes independent? We want answers to these burning questions."

The outbreak of War, with the added dimension of dragging India into it under unilateral vice-regal decisions, was a breach of trust, confidence and the principle of autonomy to the provinces that plagued not only Congress but also the public at large. They had suffered terribly in the First World War and were yet to recover from its aftermath. Locally, the worst nightmare still haunted Drupti, the wife of Arjun the fugitive, who, although nearly forty but still without a child, began to shake like a leaf when she heard about another war. To her it meant another bout of capturing men in order to shove them into the furnace of battlefield, and another round of extortion by coercion.

Arjun and Drupti had, some years ago, built up their own small house in the village. The house was composed of two small bedrooms, a bare enough lounge with a small manageable kitchen and a makeshift bathroom. But Drupti was happy to call this small structure her very own where she felt a sense of belonging. Although she had never felt alien in Kirti's home a sense of ownership had always been lacking - the very sense that lay embedded in every human.

When the conditions had turned a little better, Arjun went back to his old village, sold the house there and bought a piece of land in Qila Vasudev. It was after the acquisition of this small stretch that Drupti felt an impulse to do something to generate an extra source of income to help realise the building of the house. If it were all left to the Arjun's meagre wage, the building of the house might have taken ages. She knew a skill long learned from her mother, which she found best at the time to pursue. It was the making of *papad* and *wadian*. All you needed was *maahn di dal* or black beans (*Phaseolus roxburghii*), spices, salt and white gourds or *Benineasa hispidia*. But the work involved a lot of hard work. For instance milling the black beans to the state of flour to make wadian was no easy task to begin with. And then she would have to prepare the proper dough mixed with spices, salt and gourd seeds, then cut away round balls to be dried up in the sun. It was all very laborious and time consuming. Yet, the making of papad involved grinding the dal to a finer state; rolling the papad with a rolling pin also needed good amount of strength in the arms, a healthy backbone and sturdy hands. But Drupti did it all, inspired by the dream of having her own house in which she would have the personal space she so badly needed for her personality to develop properly. Arjun helped her in the evenings and weekends and still worked in his regular job.

When the first lot of papad and wadian was ready, Arjun took them to various grocers' shops in the city only to be rejected by them, leaving him disheartened. These were testing times for him and Drupti. The village grocer was happy to have the stuff, but wouldn't pay all the money forthwith. He would pay only a quarter of the amount with a promise to pay another quarter after a month, so on and so forth. But Drupti needed money to buy the raw material to prepare the next lot. And then, after a good deal of deliberations she conceived another idea.

'Why do we have to sell the stuff to the shopkeepers? Can't we sell it direct to the customers on the roadside, and at a cheaper rate?' she suggested to Arjun.

'It can be done, but how about my job?'

'You can sell it on Saturdays and Sundays, can't you?'

'I suppose I can,' replied Arjun.

So, Arjun began to trade on the roadside, not too far away from the shops, which claimed to be specialising in these two items. The gimmick worked for a while, but soon the shopkeepers began to resent the presence of an intruder who, according to them, defiled their trade terms by lowering the prices. For the first few days they only whispered their anger into each others' ears but then, one day, they all flared up.

'Eh, you can't put a stall here. Understand?' snarled one of them as though he were the municipal commissioner of the area.

'Why can't I? It's a public road and belongs as much to me as to you,' said Arjun politely.

'Yes, you can walk on it but can't sell,' warned the leader.

'But look around, there're many other hawkers selling their stuff. '

'Yes, there are, but they aren't selling what you're selling.'

'Does it make any difference?'

'Yes, it does. You can sell whatever else you want to sell but not these two items.'

'Why?'

'Will you stop arguing or...?' The leader of the shopkeepers hurled a fist at him but stopped short of hitting.

The city of Amritsar had a special bazaar called Bazaar Papadaan. Customers went there with the exclusive intention of buying papad and warian, and other allied produce. Had Arjun gone to sell his wares in another bazaar specialising in something else, people might not buy it, just as they wouldn't come to Bazaar Papadaan to purchase bamboo, fake ornaments or textiles. Arjun had been doing quite well until this problem had cropped and he had no idea how to solve it.

Somehow that particular day went past without much trouble but on the following day, a Sunday, Arjun was rounded up by half-a-dozen young men with grim faces, some scoffing at him and others mocking him.

'Oy, take your fucking stuff and disappear from here before we knock you dead!' One of them issued a stern warning, kicking a foot at Arjun's bundle while the others continued scuffing their shoes on the road. All these men were those who had refused to buy from him when Arjun had approached them in the beginning. They all belonged to one clan and they took it as their birthright to rule the roost He could now feel the potential danger spreading its claws to take him by the neck. Although, because it was Sunday, most of the shops in the bazaar were shut, and there were not many people around to buy his goods, even then the monopolists were not ready to brook an outsider trading in what they themselves traded in, and much less to allow him to do so in their territory.

Poor Arjun was no match for half-a-dozen brazen men with their bodies as stout as those of the oxen. He put the bundle back on his head and went off towards the Golden Temple. Arjun heard them laughing behind his back but thought it better to ignore them. Far from wanting any trouble he needed to sell his product, earn money and realise their only dream of having the house built.

Close to the entrance to the Golden Temple where the flowers were being sold for worshippers to buy and offer the scriptures sat a papadwallah, who grilled the papadom on coal-fire and sold to the people to eat there and then. Having found an empty space, Arjun put down his bundle and began to talk to the lean old papadwallah.

'Do you come here everyday to sell your papad?' he asked, sitting hesitantly by his side.

'Almost every day. Why?' The lean man questioned. .

'Nothing particular. We too, make papad and wadian at home,' he managed to say.

'Who do you sell them to?' The lean man quizzed.

'I was selling the stuff on the roadside in the Bazaar Papadaan but they wouldn't let me do it anymore,' Arjun said with a deep sigh.

'They're all bastards, can't see no one eating *roti*. You can sell 'em here, can't you?' said the lean man, first contemptuously and then sympathetically.

'I can, if no one objects to it,' a jittery Arjun replied.

'Why should anyone object to it at Guru's house? Is that your stuff then?' he asked glancing at the bundle.

'It is,' replied Arjun.

'Come on then, open it up and display it. Guru's gracious and benevolent,' he said, bowing his head to the golden tomb distinctly visible from there.

'Thank you.'

'Thank Guru Ramdasji, not me.' The lean man put him right.

Arjun opened up his bundle, spread a white sheet on the floor and began to display his product in a neat way.

'Your papads seem quite attractive. Pass one to me, let me grill and taste it,' the man said.

Arjun opened up a packet and passed two papads to him. While the lean man was busy grilling them, Arjun kept on arranging his stuff, feeling a sense of security.

'The taste is lovely, too,' said the lean man munching the crispy papad. 'I'd rather buy from you to sell 'em here.'

'No problem at all,' replied Arjun gleefully.

The duo went on very well from day one. It was an added advantage to the customers to taste the papad before actually procuring a packet from Arjun. And by the time evening fell Arjun had sold more than half of his stuff. He was happy and grateful to the Guru. When he reached home and told the story of his trouble and struggle to Drupti, she said with gratitude,' Who can harm a person protected by the Guru himself?'

And the next day, when Drupti began to work on her next batch, after Arjun had left to go to his job, she felt herself moving faster and more vigorously than ever before. Now she didn't have time to mourn her maternal losses, her loneliness and her life's purposelessness, for the purpose had begun to glitter like stars in her eyes - the purpose of having her own small house. The plot of land they had bought was not far from Kirti's house where they still lived. She would go out, cast a glance at the plot with her eyes streaming with tears of happiness and come back to do her work with renewed zest.

Once they had a few hundred rupees in their kitty they contracted out the village builder to do the job. But by the time they had bought bricks, cement and sand, more than half the money had evaporated, like steam from an open cauldron. However, the will to have it all done was as firm as ever. Drupti vividly remembered the day when the foundation of the house was laid amidst tears of delight on her part and the distribution of *laddoos* as a day of celebration on the part of Arjun. The whole structure of the house, including doors and windows as the final operation, took one full year instead of three months as was originally visualised, not because the builder was slacking or just biding time but because of the shortage of money.

The builder had to take up other contracts in the surrounding villages to secure his continuous earnings. If he had depended on their solitary contract, he would have been redundant for over eight months. But the couple had worked very hard throughout the whole year with Drupti making papad and wadian and Arjun selling them in other areas of the city in the evenings and weekends, in addition to doing his fixed job and selling the stuff at the entrance to Golden Temple. But once their home was ready for them to move in, their happiness knew no bounds.

Drupti decorated every nook and corner of the house with flowers, covered each wall with *phulkaris* and adorned each room with a personal touch of femininity. Her zeal lingered for over six months during which she made her home look like the mini palace of her dreams, a small fortress where she could feel safe. But then the same grisly vacuum began to haunt her, as had occupied her entity before - a vacuum caused by the lack of an innocent smile in the household. And the only person she had to cry to was Kirti. But Kirti's fate was no better than Drupti's; it was rather worse.

Stepsons of an Era

Born on the 24th of March 1940 were two stepsons of that era: first a resolution for the new state of Pakistan and, second a new entrant to Qila Vasudev, named Suraj. Although born simultaneously, they differed in all other respects.

The conception of Pakistan was laid as early as 1933 but the gestation period took seven full years, before reaching parturition in the form of this resolution. The idea was fathered as much by the famous poet Dr Mohammed Iqbal as by a group of radical Muslim students in London, who had now been joined by a new member from our village - Noor Mohammed. Their photographs had appeared quite recently in various papers. That might be the reason why Noor Mohammed hadn't written me a single word despite the promises he had made. However, the idea had been given its formal identity by Mohammed Ali Jinnah. He used it to attract the Muslim masses to the Muslim League, which claimed to be the only organisation speaking for them. The resolution caused a frantic tumult among the non-Muslims but a sense of fraternity among its adherents, leading to widespread bloodshed throughout the country.

The conception of Suraj was achieved nine months ago in the forlorn womb of Kirti, who was desperate to have a surviving child, for all her previous progeny had died long before they reached the age of five. She had given birth to eight children none of whom survived to grant her the pride of durable motherhood. Nindi, too, the eighth child, had died two years ago, a year before Drupti and Arjun had moved to their new home. Suraj was the ninth child. A few days after Suraj was born, a fortune-teller knocked at Kirti's door as though some divine force had told him about this new birth in Qila Vasudev. The fortune-teller, a lean, middle-aged bespectacled Brahmin, did not seem to belong to this village. At the sight of him, Kirti was slightly surprised and puzzled. She was fumbling for words when the Brahmin said, 'Don't be surprised! I'm from Qila Bhangian in the city. Arjun, who used to live in your house, told me you were blessed with a son. He works near where I live. He asked me to pay you a visit and tell you the future of the child. Won't you ask me to come in?'

'Come in. I'm so sorry. I just didn't ... ' squeaked Kirti in a debilitated voice.

The Brahmin saw the child and said, 'He must be named Suraj because Suraj never dies. It can be temporarily eclipsed, clouded or covered under dark but it can never die. Your son's radiant forehead, wide and open, shines like the sun. He's born to fight the dark forces of the earth. No amount of darkness and no calamity can hinder his trajectory. His journey through life won't be easy but the final victory will be always his. So name him Suraj and nothing else.'

When the Brahmin got up to go, Kirti asked him how she could pay the price of his forecast to which the Brahmin replied, 'To be allowed to see the child's luminous face is my price. But if you're benevolent a bowl of rice will do.' Kirti gave him a bowl of uncooked rice and he went away leaving Kirti bewildered yet delighted. When she told the whole episode to Bhaga in the evening, he too, was stunned. He had never seen a Brahmin who told things for a mere bowl of rice. In fact, they were quite infamous for cheating, extortion and fraud.

But whatever happened, the name Suraj was accepted as the one conferred by some mysterious force, itself born to fight the dark forces of the earth. Rightly or wrongly, Suraj was the stepson of the year 1940. Neither Bhaga nor Kirti could understand the myth hidden behind the phrase 'dark forces of the earth' and probably they didn't even need to. There might have been a thousand and one more children born on that day of whom they would never know. Even the children themselves might never know who else took birth on the day when the resolution of Pakistan was born. It was not important either. What was important was what had created a lot of jubilation on the one hand and deep turmoil on the other. So, the formal resolution of Pakistan was the legitimate son of the Muslim League but an illegitimate son for the Congress and the Hindu-Sikh India, while Suraj belonged to none except Kirti and Bhaga. Yet, the pair would come face-to-face one day, when the former would inflict terrible injuries on the latter.

It was astonishing to see Kirti and Bhaga bloom once more. Giving birth to eight children and then seeing them all die could not have been easy. It must have been like sitting at the feet of eight volcanoes, watching them erupt one by one and drowning everything in the fuming and seething lava, with no hope of surviving the catastrophe. The first child was a miscarriage, the second was prematurely born, the third's flesh was all rotten, the fourth - a handsome boy - had a hole in the heart, the fifth and sixth died at the age of three plus, the seventh died after having lived for four years and the eighth, Nindi, passed away when he was approaching his fifth year.

Bhaga's only dream of seeing his sons grow, turn adolescent and help him in his fields had been shattered a number of times, and he had now reached the age of fifty-five. At the time of irrigating his field, when his turn to have his share of water came at night, he would often look above into the dark sky and make heart-rending complaints to the invisible God. 'Are you deaf, dumb and blind to my situation? Do you exist somewhere or is it just my unfounded illusion? They say, "Beg no man, beg you alone", but you seem to be a pauper yourself. If you were capable of anything, you would've filled my empty hands with all your gifts. But I don't think you are any better than the paupers on the earth. You gave five sons to my elder brother, Jagga - all surviving, all growing to adulthood - but what did you give me? You gave me the life of a single farmer with no help? Do you think my two hands, two arms and two legs are enough to do this work and at this age? You should be ashamed of yourself when you get your worshippers to call you God. God of what? God of big things? God of kings and queens? Of big landlords? Of all the wheelers and dealers? Probably you are because you give them everything. You give them plenty of everything, don't you? All I asked you was to save my progeny, to save my children. I didn't ask for more money, more land or a bloody throne, did I? No. But how would you answer my questions when you don't even exist? I would be the first one to kill you if I ever saw you...'

And, at another time when he was in a less severe mood he would be somewhat apologetic, 'I didn't mean to swear at you *Rabba* (God). All I meant was that there're millions who have other help to turn to whereas us two, Kirti and I, have no one except you. And if you won't care for us who else will? I fully believe in you. I trust you and that's why I come to you. But you're too careless. There're those who have dozens, and you let them all live. But upon us, you've inflicted so many wounds, and one after the other. You give me a son and then take him away long before he's five. Why do you have to do that to us only? Why not to others? Kirti is now forty-five and too weak and old to bear any more children. But you can't understand this simple logic. Had you understood it you wouldn't have done what you've done to us, would you? My Guru says we should yield to your will but how can I, tell me? Had you done justice to me I would have, but you're such a horrible judge, such a stupid arbiter that I feel like reprimanding you. But don't you mind it because I don't mean it. All I say is that don't be too cruel and careless. Pay attention to the woes of those who believe in you. Thank you.'

Unlike Bhaga, Kirti was more of an introvert, a woman of few words. She had cried and sobbed at every death but hadn't engaged in accusations and recriminations to God. Consecutive births and deaths had hollowed her body and she looked like an emaciated thing now. Her once heavy thatch of hair had now thinned incredibly and turned grey. She had begun to wear a white *chunni* or head-cloth instead of a coloured one - a sign of acceptance of old age though she was only forty-five. On the birth of Suraj, she had smiled once again but the smile lacked the lustre it used to possess. Her extraordinarily white teeth, which once adorned her half-open mouth, now fitted oddly with her sucked-in cheeks and enervated, crusty lips. Even her big and beautiful eyes now bulged appallingly from within their sockets so as to frighten the onlooker rather than attract as they had done years ago. Her eight tragedies had left Kirti with unendurable reminiscences resulting in a gloomy face, wheezing breath, an aching body and a lot of loose phlegm in her lungs. But she didn't complain like Bhaga did. And, if she had been able to pick preferences she would have liked to save the lives of her daughters, for she needed a female helper. Chanddi the warmongering goddess was never on speaking terms with Kirti. But even if she were, she would have caused more terror in her life than any comfort. She was arrogant and over proud with all her sons living and the family proliferating. She had five sons now, the youngest being four years old and the eldest twenty. The four elders helped their father, Jagga, in the fields while the youngest, Chainchal, roamed the streets of Qila Vasudev with a snotty nose. And, Chanddi was pregnant once again. She prayed God to give her a girl this time.

Drupti came to see Kirti almost every day, helped her with the kitchen work, washed her clothes, cleaned her house and did a little bit of shopping for things Kirti required most urgently. One day, when Drupti went to the village shop she found Chanddi already there. Drupti had always avoided her from the day she had entered the village because of her stern looks, specially the grimace with which she examined others from head to toe. Her gaze would send shudders in your spine. It seemed capable of breaking asunder all your bastions and penetrating deep into your inner soul. Once Drupti had tasked Kirti quite confidentially, 'Bibi, what will happen when she brings her daughter-in-law home?'

'How do I know what will happen? Can you tell?' Kirti had counter-questioned in a dim laugh.

'The poor girl will run for her life, away from this frowning bellicose woman and will never come back,' she had asserted like some seasoned forecaster.

'But what about when there are five of them together against one?' Kirti had retorted with her smile expanding.

'Yeah, but they won't come all together and she would take every new comer singly. And by the time there are five of them, each will have lost her sting.' Drupti explained the logic of things in the far offing.

'But she won't be as young and belligerent as now, will she?' Kirti unfolded an opposing logic.

'Old habits die hard no matter how aged you are,' concluded Drupti and slashed the air with her right hand.

Drupti thought of returning home and coming back later when Chanddi was gone. But just as she turned to go, Chanddi caught sight of her and called her into the shop. The chance of evasion was now slim and she had to face the ill-fated moment. A morosely frowning and grimacing look cut through Drupti's whole body and soul.

'How's your so-called Bibi?' asked Chanddi.

'Well, she's your sister-in-law as well, isn't she?' Drupti reminded her.

'My foot! I've never accepted her as one. But she's your Bibi because your husband is from the same village as she, and he calls her his sister,' came the sarcasm from Chanddi. Bibi was the word of respect for your husband's older sister. But the sarcasm lay in the taunt.

'There's no backing from that fact,' Drupti said proudly.

'How about the other fact then?'

'Which one?'

'Does she pay you for the services you do for her?'

These remarks were flagrantly insulting and embarrassing, too. For a moment, Drupti could not think of what to say. But as Chanddi looked at her with contempt, words began to form in her mind.

'Would you pay your sons' wives for the services they'd do for you and your husband?' The counter-question shattered Chanddi into shreds. She could not swallow an equal disgrace and that too from a woman she thought of as of low birth and a close link of her archaic enemy on top of everything else.

'Shut your fucking gob, you barren earth, you mean creature, before I pull the tongue out of your mouth and thrust it right into your arse!' Chanddi roared so furiously that all the customers and the shopkeeper were flabbergasted.

Drupti was reduced to nothingness. She found it impossible to prolong her stay in the shop a minute longer. She turned round and fled with the fringe of her head-cloth tucked into her mouth, her eyes streaming with tears and her throat sobbing inordinately. She didn't go to Kirti's house but to her own. She threw herself flat on her bed and began to lament like never before. 'You barren earth' was what had made her feel even more worthless than a stray straw in a street. She cried, sobbed and shed tears until the last drop of water in her swollen eyes had gone. The incident brought all her forgotten memories back and she felt like tearing apart every seam of the society, culture and civilisation. She felt like burning every particle of the earth and its habitation, and watch the flames rise higher and higher until they devoured the sky, too. She wanted to avenge those who had deprived her of her fertility and womanhood, of her virility and power to produce, of the part within her that was as fertile as any before it was made alkalinic and incapable of turning a seed into a crop. She wanted to inflict severe injuries on those who had forced infertility on her. She gritted her teeth and tightened her fists with so much anguish that her nails dug into the palms of her hands and set them bleeding. She had no idea when the sun walked away to the far horizons and disappeared into an abyss to rise in another hemisphere. She was lost in some kind of labyrinth when a knock on the door from Arjun alerted her.

Poor Arjun the fugitive was as hapless and helpless against the tyrannies of the engulfing, encroaching and swallowing world as Drupti herself. Even in the dim light of the kerosene lamp, Arjun could see his wife's reddened eyes and could envision how she might have cried to reach that state, but had no clue what had caused it all. He was a naïve and simple minded person, very kind hearted but unable to see through the tricks of the world. When he asked Drupti what had happened, she dismissed it all by saying, 'Nothing particular. Only some memories of the past kept coming back.'

But on the following day, when she told the whole episode to Kirti with eyes flooded and sobs rending the walls, Kirti too, began to whimper. She put her hand round Drupti's shoulder and said, 'No malice of the malicious can cause damage to the benign. A sagacious person always wins in the long run and the tormentors always suffer the way they ought to.'

Kirti gazed at Suraj, who was now four months old and was lying on the cot in a state of trance, and said again, 'Look at him. He's God's gift to both of us but only if he lives to give meaning to our lives. Let the dogs bark for they've been made to do so. The day will always dawn even if the cocks don't crow. The sun will eventually rise no matter if clouds conceal its face for a day. Cry no more Drupti! Give all your woes and sorrows to me...'

Kirti's words worked like ointment on Drupti's wounds. She inhaled a deep sigh and let the air out, and felt relaxed as though the exhalation had taken all the sorrows out in its wake. Soon she picked up Suraj from his cot and began to babble with him. When Suraj responded with smiles she increased her babbling to sustain that mirthful response.

The resolution of Pakistan was now at the centre of every conversation and discussion throughout the length and breadth of the country. People would read it time and again, underline every word and phrase, interpret its clauses and watch each other's faces in awe. The division of India seemed inevitable. The resolution said: "...no constitution would be workable in this country or acceptable to the Muslims unless it is designed on the following basic principle, viz., that geographically contiguous units are demarcated into regions which should be so constituted with such territorial readjustments as may be necessary that the areas in which the Muslims are numerically in a majority, as in the north-western and eastern zones of India, should be grouped to constitute 'independent states' in which the constituent units shall be autonomous and sovereign..."

I, Arya Gold, twenty-one at the time, wondered whether our old, antiquated Banyan tree would ever survive the convolutions of its leaves. The leaves had become so curled up as to hide their anger against each other in their hearts, and were seeking only to revenge at the appropriate time. And that time seemed to be skulking somewhere in the dark bushes not too far away from the Banyan. Only Noordin the dyer knew how to propitiate the dark forces of the earth but he was too old now to decode the language of colours. Ageing had taken a terrible toll of him resulting in decrepitude, senility and the loss of his eyesight. He was only eighty-two but seemed like hundred and two. And his son, Ferozdin, on whom now rested all our hopes, had joined the Muslim League despite repeated warnings and advice from Sikander Ali, the supporter of the National Unionist Party. This party had turned down (at least for now) all Mr Jinnah's alluring offers to join the League.

Ferozdin no longer talked about the Banyan tree the way he had done before. He no longer bothered about its antiquated history, its leaves, trunk and branches, rather, he now advocated in favour of slashing the Banyan into two halves, naming one half as the Pakistani Banyan tree and the other half as the Indian Banyan tree. It was weird to hear such things from the son of Noordin, a great chemist whose skills of studying the changing colours of the Big Banyan tree had no match. It was also a bizarre thing to note that he was the same Ferozdin who had once said, 'In me doesn't live my father alone but every generation of my clan. All the experience and knowledge that has accumulated in their craft over the years spent on their acquisition is all mine now. I am not what I am but a sum-total of what I have been in the form of my ancestors.' And now the same Ferozdin was asking to slash the Banyan tree into two halves instead of striving to find a solution to the problem of sudden change in the colours of its leaves, like his father had done in the past. The whole situation perplexed me and I did not know what to do.

Having read the resolution myself, I was fully convinced that it was a kind of bargain counter that Mr Jinnah had contrived so he could compel Congress to deal with the League, for the resolution did not imply or mention the name Pakistan anywhere. Yet, politicians all over the country interpreted it as the Pakistan resolution and nothing less. Even the 'August Offer', made by the Viceroy, predicated this interpretation of the all-India, non-Muslim politicians, whereby the minorities were assured that their views would be given due weight in any policy revision, and that power would not be transferred to any system of government whose authority was denied by a large and powerful element in Indian national life.

And, in case of such slashing of the Big Banyan tree, I mean the country, into two halves, the Muslim League wanted the whole of Punjab to be included in what they called Pakistan. And the Sikhs, the erstwhile rulers of the Punjab, were to be under the dominance of Muslims, which they could never brook. Thus, only a week after this resolution came another resolution from the Khalsa National Party of which Sir Sunder Singh Majithia was the leader and also a Minister in the Unionist Government. It prophesied that, "The Muslim League has created a situation which may mean parting of the ways for the Sikhs and the Muslims with whom the Khalsa National Party has been co-operating in the provincial autonomy regime in the best interests of the Province and the Sikh community...

"It would be the height of audacity for anyone to imagine that the Sikhs would tolerate for a single day the undiluted communal Raj of any community in the Punjab which is not only their homeland but also their holy land."

Maybe, being too young and immature in comparison with these veterans and seasoned leaders, I did not know how to read the text between the lines and interpret the unsaid words. So, I too, began to think that the Lahore Resolution necessarily meant the Pakistan Resolution. And one day when I asked Uncle Arjun Singh about this matter he too, interpreted the resolution like Sir Majithia. The interpretation did upset me but then who was I?

Uncle Arjun, although explicitly calm and composed, was not implicitly so. I could tell that from the way he talked. When he talked normally, his words were compact and coherent, and oozing with a kind of lucidity that delighted you. Small incidents seldom affected the normalcy of his speech. But the way he conversed now - broken and incoherent sentences with very little choice of words - convinced me that there was something formidable inside his heart that incensed him and gnawed at him.

'Uncle! Are you feeling all right?' I asked, a little worried.

'What makes you think I'm not?' Uncle counter-questioned me.

'I know you are not because I've always been quite close to you. There's something disturbing you inside. Please tell me, Uncle, what is it that ails you?' I insisted.

Uncle Arjun did not say anything but began to look into the far distance as if trying to find some link to unfold his concerns. I knew Uncle Arjun could hide from anyone except me, for I was his tried and tested audience and I always adored his opinion. To my astonished delight he soon decided to lay bare his inner soul to me.

'I suppose you're very right in assuming that I'm not happy at all. What's perturbing me continuously is the political situation in the Punjab, the increasing rift between the Muslims and Hindu-Sikhs, the defection of Muslims to the League, the communal politics of Mr Jinnah and the constant weakening of the Unionist Party. Sir Sikander Hayat Khan committed the biggest blunder of history in joining the Muslim League and paved the way for others to follow suit. He's badly played into the hands of Jinnah. They rightly say that Mr Jinnah has played the part of rider, and the horse is no other but Sir Sikander,' he said and paused.

The rumours had been there in the air for a long time but the inside story was known only to the few. Uncle Arjun being close to Sir Majithia must have known every bit of the story. So, my curiosity to know things in detail began to increase.

'Uncle, how did it all happen?' I tried to inspire him to say more. Uncle inhaled a deep breath of air and then bowed his head to gaze at the ground as though attempting to read the fate of the soil of the Punjab.

'In fact, this Unionist Party was founded by Sir Fazl-e-Husain, and he firmly believed that any communal approach to the political tangle of the Punjab would most certainly disintegrate the party because it was based on economic programme and mutual co-operation among all the communities, irrespective of their religious inclinations. It is meant to remain devoted to inter-communal harmony while the Muslim League's objectives are to safeguard the political rights and welfare of Indian Muslims with the intention of acquiring Muslim ascendancy and dominance. In 1936, Mr Jinnah tried his level best to wheedle Sir Fazl-e-Husain to join the Muslim League but he curtly refused. Then there was this All-India Muslim League Conference in Lucknow in October 1937, shortly after the elections resulting in the landslide victory of the Unionist Party. Sir Sikander attended this Lucknow session of the League along with many other Unionist Muslims. Mr Jinnah took advantage of the situation and bound him in a pact called Sikander-Jinnah Pact. The Pact said that the Unionist Muslims would support the League on all its national issues but would not allow it to interfere in the governance of the Punjab. Mr Jinnah was quite tactful. He decided to make progress step by step. Sir Sikander's joining the League eventually took all the 74 Muslim Unionists into it thereby increasing the size and stature of the League formidably in the Punjab where it had had no influence whatsoever until yesterday.' Uncle Arjun stopped here and began to contemplate with his eyes shut.

'And, before this resolution, in March,' Uncle resumed, 'Sir Sikander Hayat Khan had formed a scheme for the Indian federation, according to which, India was to be divided into seven zones with each zone to have a regional assembly and the centre to have very limited powers. But Jinnah rejected it, saying that the Muslim League would confine its demands to the Muslim zones only and not to the whole of India. Sir Sikander and Jinnah didn't agree on a number of issues and by joining the League Sir Sikander lost all his non-Muslim sympathisers. In fact, Sir Sikander has a number of fears: one is the Khaksaar Movement of Alama Mashriqui and the second is the leaning of his men towards the League for which he himself is responsible. Although he's steadfast in rejecting the concept of Pakistan that makes no difference now because the damage has already been done.'

Uncle Arjun once again lapsed into thinking and morbid brooding. Perhaps he was too old now to think or work unstoppably like he had before. Physical as well as mental fatigue seemed to have eroded Uncle's health. I began to enumerate the years Uncle Arjun had lived so far. Seventy-four years was my rough calculation. I wondered how many more he would be able to survive. And the thought made me tremble with fear.

A Daydreamer's Paradox

The spring season had just set in. The trees, plants and shrubs had new leaves forming to cover their bodies, which had been laid bare as a consequence of the leaf-fall of the preceding autumn. Perhaps, they had been put to shame by their own conscience or they just could not bear being naked anymore. The buds on the branches of the Banyan tree looked like newly born babies with their mouths pinkish and red, sprouting and speaking the word 'leaf'. The lower branches on which the leaves had already taken shape looked luxuriant and increasingly comfortable to the eye. I had been watching the phenomenon take place over the years, yet each time I observed it, it seemed so new to me that I would be mesmerised by its magical spell. I always congratulated and thanked nature for its miraculous renderings to us mortals. Renewal was the keyword that kept buzzing in my ears as I watched the spring dawn upon the Banyan and other vegetation. I was and am a staunch lover of nature, which is nothing else but God to me. No other God do I put my trust in but nature.

It was here under the Banyan tree that Kinner had promised to meet me last week. But despite my long wait, watching nature bloom, Kinner could not make it. He had said he wanted to consult me on some important issue. But when he failed to arrive, I could understand how overwhelmingly busy he must have been with his work. Had he broken his appointment with me in the city somewhere, I would have cursed him a thousand times. But if I did not mind his non-conformity to his promise, it was chiefly due to the Banyan tree and the sweetness of nature. So, I had no grievances against Kinner. Rather I was thankful that he had provided me with an opportunity for a prolonged rendezvous with myself as an integral part of nature, for it had now been weeks that I had stayed inside, first due to cold and, second due to my scribbling.

And now, last night, Kinner had dropped a note at my place asking that I see him urgently in his office. He had not begged my pardon for letting me down last time, which seemed rather rude and impertinent to me. Although I wouldn't have said a word, I did at least deserve an apology from him. 'Rascal!' I muttered and decided to take my revenge.

It was Saturday, and I set out on my journey to the city at about 11am. The month of March was neither too hot nor too cold. And what a journey! It took me barely half an hour to reach the city and that too, on foot. I reached the Hall Gate from where I turned into the Hall bazaar, which I found packed with a thick crowd of people, apparently partakers in a marriage procession. It was quite an extravagant show. The bridegroom, in a strangely bejewelled outfit with plumed turban and face covered with cascades of flowers dropping from the forehead, was sitting on a horse that was being led by its groom. The horse was flamboyantly adorned and well pampered, too. Leading the procession was a military band composed of musicians playing all kinds of instruments with their leader in the centre. Following the horse was a huge procession of men, women and children - all in newly tailored costumes - laughing, talking and twittering ceaselessly. I wondered how they listened to each other in that tumult where even the nearest voice was inaudible.

It took me well over half hour to get out of the crowd by threading through in a meandering way, avoiding pitfalls like dropping into the gutter. There must be over eight hundred people in that procession, I thought. I visualised the predicament of the girl's parents, who would have to feed the crowd on reception.

The procession had caused severe traffic chaos, with every vehicle stranded and the drivers scolding each other: car owners to rickshaw wallahs and them to *thella wallahs* - hierarchically. It was all amusing and upsetting at the same time. Taking fast strides, I reached Queen Victoria Square, not too far from the Jallianwalla Bagh. Here, I was surprised to note the way the whole bazaar had been decorated with multicoloured, thin, kite-like buntings hanging from above. The decoration went as far as Surinder's street, which was decorated not only with buntings but also balloons, flowers, tube-lights, wall-tents and dozens of speakers. The broader end of Surinder's street was temporarily transformed into a banqueting hall. So, it was here that the procession was supposed to reach.

And then, just by instinct, I had the inkling that it might be the marriage of Sonia, Surinder's sister, whom I liked so much but didn't have the courage or time to ask for her hand from Surinder or his father. And just as I stood there watching the hustle and bustle of the street, I caught sight of Surinder, too. He was busy as a bee ordering uniformed caterers to do different things before the *baraat,* or the marriage party, arrived. I wondered for a while, whether or not I should go in. My first reaction was to dismiss the whole thing and find my way to Kinner's office. I took a few steps forward on that path. But then, suddenly, it crossed my mind, 'why not see Sonia, if only once, in her bridal makeup and outfit.' The thought was captivating and weighed heavily on my mind. But I still stood rooted there, a few feet adrift from the street opposite, thinking. Sonia had not refused me. My love for her was not unrequited. All she had said was to ask her brother or father for her hand. In other words, she did like me and would have been happy to marry with me, but it was not in her powers to make the decision. The decision had to come from her family, especially the male members. 'Why hadn't I approached Surinder and through him his father?' I groused to myself. 'But was I really serious about it?' asked someone from within me. 'Perhaps not,' came the answer. Ambiguity and ambivalence on the one hand and a vague yearning on the other had been my paradox - a daydreamer's paradox.

I endeavoured to extricate myself from wistful thinking and decide what I wanted to do next. There was no point in crying over split milk now or enquiring about the route to a city to which I could no longer go. So, that was that and I immediately made my move to where Kinner would be waiting for me.

I found Kinner sitting behind his desk with his gaze focused on a big bundle of papers. Hearing my footsteps, he raised his head and seeing me coming, stood up and, for the first time ever in all these years, proffered his right hand for me to shake. It was something right out of the blue, for I wasn't accustomed to such behaviour from him. What I had known was a rough and ready man always in pugnacious mood.

'Welcome,' he said with a smile and I was further flabbergasted. For a moment, I thought I had entered the wrong office or else I was still daydreaming. I felt like pinching the flesh of my arm to make sure I was not somnambulating. I wanted to blink in case the figure in front of me was an apparition. But I did neither. Instead, my right hand lifted up like that of a robot, and plummeted into his. Kinner was all smiles while I was embarrassed and confused.

'Since when has the sun begun to rise from the west?' I asked, almost faint with unexpected change in a petrified personality.

'Quite recently,' Kinner replied and burst out laughing.

'Are you sure I'm the one you wanted to see?' I said again, this time with a furrowed brow.

'Of course I wanted to see you, you idiot. Be seated now.' He pointed me to the chair opposite to him and sat down before I did.

'I can't believe it, man... Are you surely the same Kinner I've known for so long?' I said and took the chair.

'You seem to have developed some kind of fatal disease, I think, of causing dissipation to otherwise dynamic moments,' Kinner began to philosophise the sudden change in him.

I had yet to devise an answer for his phrase when Radhika appeared on the scene. She had grown really smart, perhaps sizzling with youth and brilliance. Her sight intoxicated me for a moment.

'Oh, it's Arya here! What a sudden surprise!' she exclaimed.

'Didn't you know the boss had issued his imperial orders for me to present myself to his highness?' I tried to badger Kinner.

'Don't you think, Radhika, he's begun to bark too much?' he pestered me back.

'What else do you expect of a scribbler, my dear brother?' Radhika said satirically.

The delightful attitude of both Kinner and Radhika was enough of a signal to indicate that the paper was progressing well. I had seen its latest issues and was pleased to find that the word 'Dalit' was no more confined to the people of Dravidian origin but was made to extend its meaning to the whole wide world in the sense of the exploited ones. The Indian masses were now construed as 'Dalit'. This change of policy would bring in good dividends, I had anticipated.

Radhika sat down in the chair next to me and said, 'Where've you been all these weeks? Have you found a job or something?'

'No, I haven't found a job thus far but that's what I've come here for. Can you kindly recommend me to your brother to fit me somewhere in this office? I don't mind being a cleaner if nothing else's available,' I begged importunately.

'Listen boy, we've no theatre company here to employ actors. Moreover, it's a highly reputed paper, the staff of which is intensively trained. Yet we'll be happy to give you a chance provided you learn how to cook, for we can no longer work in starvation or half-starvation, like we have been until now. Understand?' Kinner said with a mask of seriousness.

'That's a good way of refusing me a job, isn't it?' I complained rather pensively. At that the three of us laughed.

'I'll go and make some tea for you people,' said Radhika, leaving a handful of papers she was holding, on Kinner's desk and quitting, still laughing.

After she had left, Kinner opened the drawer of his desk and took out a chunk of typed papers, handed the lot to me and said, 'Go through this article and tell me how you feel about it?' I want an honest opinion from you before I publish it.'

I took the article and looked at its heading "Political paradox: a story of vacuums". The subject appeared to be quite interesting, especially now when the political weather was over-saturated with a variety of paradoxes. It took me well over twenty minutes to browse through the article exclusive of the time spent on tea, which was about ten minutes. Radhika had brought two cups of tea together with some salty mixture, and had left the lot on the desk, saying she had some more work to type right then.

The article began by mentioning the declaration of war on behalf of India, resulting in the crippling of ministries in all the central provinces due to the withdrawal of Congressmen by their High Command, engendering political vacuums all around. The crisis of Indian nationhood deepened as the British made clear their intention to leave. And now, Mr Jinnah and the Muslim League were attempting to gather as much momentum as they could to establish their ministries in those vacuums. They hoped to prove themselves mighty enough to compel the Congress to deal with them as their potential rivals in national politics.

Although it was not yet entirely clear what Mr Jinnah and the Muslim League meant by Pakistan and its practical, geographical or constitutional definitions, the resolution had generated many fears among the Sikhs of the Muslim-dominated parts of the Punjab. The British intention of granting dominion status to India had also caused fears amongst other minorities, especially the backward classes as to what their future would be in an India ruled by Congress. A secular concept of nationhood seemed absolutely amiss while the Hindu nationalists wanted independent India to be the home of Hinduism. Nothing was really clear at this stage except the fact that the Muslim League was swiftly strengthening its position and its base amongst the Muslim masses throughout the country. If Pakistan, as had been made clear by many Muslim League politicians, meant the consolidation of existing Muslim territories in the context of a federation with India and not as a separate state, then why had they invented a new 'name' in the first place? And if Pakistan meant a separate state then what would be its geographical entity and would it be solely for the Muslims, or for a mixed population? All these aspects remained mystified and unclear. Yet one thing was becoming increasingly apparent: the Lahore Resolution of the Muslim League had boosted the position of Mr Jinnah and that of the Muslim League to a degree inconceivable in the past.

In the end, Kinner had convicted the Congress High Command of being a daydreamer, who had paradoxically withdrawn his forces from the provincial governments and had offered those vacuums to the Muslim League in a plate.

Having read the article, I handed it back to Kinner. I was still in a state of contemplation when Kinner asked me, 'So, what do you think about it?'

'I quite agree with you that the vacuums have been created but it's too early to say if the Muslim League will be able to exploit them in their favour,' I offered a stricture to his prophecy.

'I haven't said they've done it already. What I've said is that they might. And it's all in the light of the quick progress they're making,' answered Kinner.

'Since when have you assumed the role of a prophet?' I cut a joke.

'Shut up!' He rebuked me and began to flick through another bundle of papers.

Daydreaming, vacuum and paradox - all these words reflected my own position. I was probably the daydreamer, and Sonia's heart the ministry that I had long withdrawn from, thus creating a vacuum for someone else to occupy. An empty throne is always an open invitation to intruders and invaders to come and take over. But an empty heart is probably all the more vulnerable, for an occupant of the throne can be deposed but not that of the heart. Sonia *had* given me a small space in her heart's territory that was enough for me to extend it further. But I had not cared. I had continued scribbling with the result that I lost whatever small stronghold I had. Now her husband, the man on the horse with a sword in his hand, had finally arrived to conquer that territory, that vacuum, which I had generated. I continued thinking of myself as the Congressional High Command; Sonia's deserted heart as the vacuum that could be occupied, her perspective husband as Mr Jinnah and the wedding procession as the Muslim League.

'I shouldn't have done that!' I murmured to myself but the words escaped my mouth unwittingly.

'Done what, man?' the awkwardly astonished voice of Kinner struck my ears.

'Nothing! Did I say something?' I asked, rising from the hypnotic spell.

'Have you gone mad or something? Who were you talking to, walls?' Kinner railed at me.

'I'm sorry. Probably, I had jumped into a sea, sinking down and down into an abyss,' I said and shook my head.

'Shall I get in touch with the mental hospital in Agra to see if they have a place for you?' Kinner laughed.

'Probably you should because there's very little difference between a mentally deranged man and a prophet,' I retorted.

'You are incorrigible, man. I bet you are,' he said nodding his head madly. I did not respond; instead, I grew serious.

'And, how's your Krishan Kanhaiya nowadays?' Kinner changed the subject.

'He has now defected to the Hindu Mahasabha, and he talks about Hindi, Hindu, Hindustan. He calls these Muslims the *malechhas,* or the dirty ones, like his predecessors used to call your ancestors: *asur, chnadaal and satans etc*. He's up on all fours to have revenge on the Muslims for the tyranny perpetrated on them by the Moghul emperors. He clamours about Temur the lame, Mohammed Gauri, Mehmood Ghazni, Nadir Shah, Ahmed Shah Abdali and incites others of his clique to get ready to take revenge...' I harangued on and on until he stopped me.

'What's happened to him?' Kinner wondered.

'Hindu Mahasabha and RSS have happened to him. But he was never a balanced person in the first place.'

'But he was such a coward, wasn't he?'

'Yeah, but cowards never fight alone. They're afraid of being caught, singled out, blamed and punished. They're always looking for a maddened crowd where they can easily hide their personal identity. You can't blame an individual in a crowd because there's no individual in it. A crowd has thousands of faces, hands, legs and mouths. A crowd is utterly faceless and shapeless, an amorphous mass of rioters and a safe haven for malicious cowards…' Kinner had to stop me again, for my tirade knew no end.

'Wait, wait… What did you eat this morning?' he asked me sarcastically.

'Nothing. I wanted to eat with you,' I said glumly.

'I see! So, you're trying to justify your lunch with us by being voluble,' he tried to dislodge me.

'No. I'm trying to earn it like we earn our wages,' I argued. Kinner smiled up.

'Anyway, jokes apart, your analysis of the crowd has a grain of truth in it. In fact, I've never thought on those lines. It's quite a good subject for an article. Morphology of the Crowd, I should name it,' he applauded me.

'Thank you!' I said in acknowledgement.

'And how about Kabir, the revolutionary poet?' Kinner said with a smirk.

'Well, he's joined the Muslim League and is following the path of his preceptor, his deity, his ideal poet Dr Iqbal who's no more, but had he been alive he would've swapped the word Hindustan with Pakistan, in one of his poems. Do you remember his couplet that Kabir used to read out to us?'

'Vaguely but not exactly. How's it?'

'Sare jahan se achha Hindustan hamara, ham bulbulain hain iski yeh gulistan hamara! *Our India is the best in the whole world, this is our orchard and we are its nightingales.* So, the makers of Pakistan might now replace the word Hindustan with Pakistan in his couplet because Iqbal was the chief architect of the idea of Pakistan. And, Kabir's a stanch acolyte of the great poet.'

'And how about his socialist revolution he advocated so fervently?' Kinner asked and laughed.

'People go from one extremity to the other, that's all.'

'I'm really astonished to hear that. That the son of a passionate Ghadarite could take such a turn is beyond my comprehension.'

'But he has. He's now bought a prayer mat and an Islamic cap, too. He says five prayers a day like a good Muslim believer, goes to *madrassa* and learns the holy Koran, observes the fast as advised and scorns every infidel or non-believer. He derides and vilifies non-Muslims, especially the Hindus as *dal* eaters and thus incapable of fighting a war. He now takes pride in calling himself a fervent Muslim, relates himself to his mother's family and regards his father as a misled man.'

'No! You must be joking!' Kinner exclaimed as if bitten by a snake.

'Yes, it is too true to be trusted.'

'You may be right but I haven't seen either of them for ages. I've been so busy with the paper. That's why I couldn't come to meet you under the Banyan last week. In fact, I often sleep here in the office just because the work keeps me imprisoned here until very late in the evening.'

'How's your paper going, anyway?'

'It has picked up quite marvellously now because I've made it much more open. I've removed the straitjacket in which it was previously floundering and suffocating. The word Dalit no more means a group, caste, class or ethnicity but anyone who is exploited, downtrodden and distressed. Dalit is the exploited one and Dalik is the exploiter.' he explained.

'I know that because I've read some of your latest issues.'

'Good for you!' he patronised me.

The time was nearly 1:30pm now. Kinner rang the bell to call Radhika in. When she arrived, Kinner said, 'Do we intend to eat anything today or should we give it a miss?' His second phrase was probably meant for me so Radhika began to giggle.

'I can't believe your paper's doing well, for if it were then why would you make do without a meal?' I reacted with fake fury. Kinner knew it, and he laughed it away.

'Radhika, how about the others? Are they back from their deliveries yet or not?' he asked her.

'Nag, Bhil and Nishad are here, we're waiting only for Ahir,' she informed him.

'Start cooking chapattis then, I don't think he'll be long.'

At that Radhika disappeared into the building and after her departure something suddenly crossed my mind.

'How old is Radhika now, Kinner?' I asked, although it sounded very rude of me.

'Why? Twenty-three, I suppose,' he answered and looked inquiringly into my eyes.

The Volcano

'Nothing really... Your mother always wanted to marry her off as soon as possible,' I gave the whole thing a sudden twist.

'Well, she was quite old and traditional. What more could you expect of the older generation? But things are changing now. Gone are the days when girls were married off as soon as they turned twelve. We are looking for a suitable boy, but I don't think we're in a desperate hurry,' he said with an undertone of dismissal, which I instantly understood and held my tongue.

I took a copy of the paper from the heap beside me and began to shuffle its pages while Kinner busied himself jotting down some notes. A few minutes elapsed and then I heard some noises from down below, from the bazaar. As the noises neared I tried to figure out what they were about.

'Some kind of procession; it's a routine thing here,' said Kinner seeing my curiosity.

I crossed the room and went to stand by the window that opened out into the bazaar. He was right; it was a procession. They were carrying slogans: samraj -murdabad (death to imperialism); Hindustan - zindabad (long live India). By that time, Kinner had also come over to stand beside me and watch the event.

A fresh bout of civil disobedience under the Mahatma had been going on for over a year now. They had boycotted all kinds of co-operation with the government. Although the various central provinces, from where Congressmen had been withdrawn as a protest against India's forcible inclusion in the war, were being managed by the white governors with the help of non-Congress elements, the non-co-operation of the Congress had landed the Raj in an increasingly vulnerable situation. This procession was part of the same protest, which had been organised by the local wing of Congress.

They carried numerous placards and banners, the wording of which expressed their scorn against India's forced entry into the war and British Imperialism. Some banners reprimanded imperialism for warmongering while others condemned capitalism for its inhuman face. Ever since the beginning of the war, there had been successive strikes, protests, rallies, processions, public conferences and mass meetings throughout the length and breadth of the country. But it surprised me enormously to see the same enthusiasm persist till today. The procession consisted of about five hundred people and it took them nearly half an hour to glide past us. No sooner did the procession finish than Radhika shouted that the food was ready.

It was the first time that I had ever seen them all together. I enjoyed both the food and their sweet company. Radhika served everyone before she dished out food for herself. In the past, they had been poorly dressed but now they all wore reasonably good garments, ate decent food and talked with each other affectionately, thanks to Kinner. They cracked jokes and taunted each other, laughed heartily and discussed business matters simultaneously. Radhika was the centre of attention. She conversed sensibly and slightly reservedly – perhaps because of my presence - and blushed crimson when someone appreciated her overall contribution to the family. She was the only female in the family at the moment but more were expected in the near future. I understood all that from their cryptic remarks to each other that afternoon.

Surely, Radhika had grown wiser and more intelligent, and that was all due to the efforts of Kinner. I tried to envision her as my wife and was thrilled. I gave her nine marks out of ten. She had a dusky narrow face with medium but shiny eyes, a somewhat pointed nose, slightly jutting chin, and a long and superb neckline, her hair was knotted at the back. She was about five foot four inches in height and she possessed a slim and trim figure. What else one could ask for? What attracted you most was the way she responded to you in a slanting smile laying bare her even white teeth, more white when seen set against her smooth, dusky face. Life could turn all heaven in her company. I saw her eating elegantly, smiling splendidly but did it all so evasively that nobody caught me watching her.

We spent nearly an hour sitting together and then Kinner made a move, followed by the others. The time was a few minutes past three and I thought of taking my leave, too.

'Listen,' Kinner stopped me on my way down the stairs, 'can you write an article about the character of a crowd?'

'I'll try,' I said and took my leave.

Build Up of Strength

The Muslim League was now determined to take off politically. To do this it had to muster all its potential strength at the grass-roots level to equate with the power of the Congress, if not surpass it.

Amongst the crucial groups tied into the League's support and propaganda structure were students and other articulate young people who acted as communicators. The vital aim was to recruit every Muslim as a member of the League. Under the directions of Mr Jinnah, the League was made to go increasingly involved in creating local organisations at all levels so they could enrol members in large numbers. The League had begun to recruit and train Muslim National Guards, create publicity networks, including trained and paid speakers, produce pamphlets and tracts and to employ professional musicians to perform popular songs on the stage and attract large audiences. The local Leaguers also went to meat *maulvis and imams* and impressed them with their aims and objectives, their demand for Pakistan, the land of the pure. These men then influenced the masses through mosques and Friday prayers.

Kabir had now turned Kabir Hussain and was the leader of a team of seven young men, carrying out their propitious duty. There were many other such groups working in the city and its surrounding area. Each group had been allocated a specific area where they were to enrol members, stage public conferences and take the agenda of the League to the Muslims. The Muslim population was predominantly on the outskirts of Amritsar, on the outside of the ring road that surrounded the walled city. Quite a large population also lived close to the twelve gates, both inside and outside. The walled city itself had some Muslim pockets but their spread was quite sporadic. Kabir's group had been assigned the area of Islamabad situated on the road leading from Lahori Gate to the Khalsa College, on the Chheharta Road. Similarly, the areas of Hussainpura and Maqboolpura and those of the twelve gates were allotted to other groups.

All these groups were first trained by a band of experts specialising in communication skills, organisational adroitness, Islamic appeal and the imminent dangers, stage control, public performance, politics, linguistic appeal and a myriad other things. Once they were sure the groups were ready to be cast in the field only then did they assign them their areas of operation. The training programme, in fact, was going on at the national level under the auspices of the All India Muslim League. Villages, towns, cities and provinces proliferated with such groups and the work was being done on a war footing. They were duly paid to carry out their duties. No one would expect sheer volunteers to do a good job. However, I had better restrain myself to our Kabir Hussain's bandwagon only.

Kabir Hussain had Abdullah, Fareed, Saleem, Jawed, Nadir and Muneer in his band - all of them in the same age group. They dressed in blue salwaar-kameez with Islamic caps on their heads, as though they were going to the mosque to say their prayers. It was crucial that they said their prayers wherever they were at a particular moment, so they kept their prayer-mats with them. To say their prayers in front of or in the presence of the prospective members had an added effect - it would increase the force of appeal. They had commenced their work of mass recruitment in April 1941 and, by the end of September, they had enrolled nearly 500 members - all of them male because it was not necessary to enrol the females. They were better left to the hearth or to generate more manpower because the count of heads would be the ultimate test in grabbing more land if Pakistan was to become reality.

It may not be out of place to understand their *modus operandi* because in the long run this is what counts. What matters is how you do things, rather than what you actually do. Nothing is new in this world but methodology makes it so. It matters not what you say but how you say it.

Kabir Hussain would be at the forefront with strict and solid instructions to his team not to say a word without his prior permission, which he would condescend, if need be, through the blink of an eye. He would order one of them to give a light knock at the door of a house. If someone opened the door that would be fine and if the first knock went unanswered then the second knock would be a little raucous. If still no response came then the third knock would be more raucous. He was absolutely sure the third knock would produce the desired results, that is, the door would be opened and splayed out like open arms in welcome. But if even the third knock failed to awaken the somnolent dwellers from their deep slumber, the inference would be that the house was either unoccupied or inhabited by an old decrepit soul no longer required for the final crusade.

But if the door opened up within the span of three knocks, Kabir Hussain, clad in *Pathani* clothes like the rest of them, would bow his head slightly, and then with the four fingers of his right hand nearly touching his brow would salute and say, 'Ass-slama Laiqum!' If the man in front replied in the right tone, saying, 'Walla-aiqum-ass-lam!' then more than half the work of recruiting of that soul would be assumed completed. But if the answer didn't come as expected, even then the chances of recruitment were bright when they used some extra effort. 'Sir, we're the workers of the Muslim League, the only party of the Muslims all over India. It has been established by the only messiah of the Muslim nation, the greatest Qaed-e-azam Mohammed Ali Jinnah. We the Muslims, were the rulers of this land of the infidels until yesterday but now they, the Hindus, want to rule us - us, the erstwhile rulers of the land, progeny of Babar, Hamayun, Shah Jahan, Jahangir, Aurangzeb and the rest. Would you let that happen? I'm sure you won't. But the only remedy is to get united under one banner, under one party, as Muslims, as brothers of the only one true faith, the faith of Allah. Let the Hindus have half of this country but the other half belongs to us. How can we tolerate being ruled by them, the non-believers, the cow worshippers, the idolaters and the pig eaters? We can't because we're Muslims. Our religion is Islam, which was sent down by Allah Himself through his Angel and through his Prophet for us to rule the whole world. Half the world embraced Islam, just in the lifetime of the prophet himself, and this is no small thing. And, not because they were forced to do so but because they wanted to, because this was the only true faith, the faith of Allah Himself. Islam is not a man-made religion but is made by Allah Himself. He sent this faith and the holy book together from the heavens. We can't let the non-believers and infidels rule the religion of God, can we? No, we mustn't. So let's get united under one flag, the flag of Islam, the flag of the Muslim League, in the name of Allah and start jihad or the holly war.'

'What do you want me to do for that?' The new client might ask.

'Nothing much. Just fill in this form and join the League like a true Muslim that's all.'

'But I can't read or write.'

'Don't worry, we'll do it all for you. All you've to do is to sign your name or print your thumb mark at the end.'

'All right then!'

'Islam - zindabad. Munir, complete the form of our Muslim brother and get it signed or thumb marked, okay?'

'Okay boss,' Munir would say fawningly.

But that was the practice in the beginning when they had just commenced, for at that stage Kabir Hussain would trust no one. He would treat all of them as a bunch if idiots or half-witted fools. But then, after about a month, when they gave their progress report to the headquarters, the leader of the upper ranks was furious. In one full month they had enrolled only five people, while they had envisaged no less than seventy, that is, ten each. Then they ordered an inquiry into their method of working which resulted in serious reprimands to the captain. It was after this incident that the methodology was altered. Now they split themselves into three subgroups with two bravos in each while the captain supervised the whole thing.

Anyway, five hundred more members of the local branch of the Muslim League, was by no means a bad achievement. The appeal of Islam and the Hindu menace were the two main stratagems that prompted the new membership. The appeal of Islam fed their ego as being the descendants of the great Mughals, and the Hindu menace justified the making of Pakistan as the only viable solution to the peril of the extinction of Islam in a united India.

Then, at the end of the year, they proposed to the local headquarters that they would like to organise a public *jalsa*, which was likely to generate more membership. The proposal was granted permission and Kabir Hussain and his chums fixed the date of 25 December to hold the event. It was also the day of Christmas and was deliberately chosen because the *goras* would be merry-making and if anything odd happened, nothing too substantial would follow from the authorities. Yet, the fears were unfounded because the British were quite happy to see the League flourish and pose a threat to the recalcitrant Congress.

Kabir Hussain had now plunged deep into the activities of the Muslim League. Pakistan had taken the place of Socialism, Islam that of Marxism and the holy Koran was his Des Capital. He very rarely came to Qila Vasudev, and if he did it was only for an hour or so, and

310

that too, to see his mother Razia and none other. Back in Qila Vasudev, Sikander Ali and his son, Abdul Khaliq, had also joined the Muslim League, though they would not put the whole blame on Sir Sikander for wheedling them in.

Sir Majithia had died a few months and Uncle Arjun had been badly affected by his demise. He had now confined himself to the village, more precisely to his haweli. The future of the Punjab haunted him and he could vividly foresee its progressive decay. The loss of a good old friend so overwhelmed him that he began to feel sick and fatigued. He would curse Jinnah for what he was doing to Punjab. 'Only a Punjabi can know what Punjab is,' he had moaned one day and had heaved a deep sigh in disgust.

Kabir Hussain and his cronies commenced making solid preparations for the event three days before the due date. They constructed a proper, three feet high, podium with wood planks, in the maidan opposite Islamabad, adjoining the railway track. The marquees had been hired and were to be supplied and fixed the next day. They had also hired dozens of *darian* or thick jute carpets. The whole pageant was planned in such a way that even if it rained or was too cold due to the chill of December, the people on the stage and in the audience would not feel distracted or disturbed. The setting had been well thought out and was managed with good insight so that it would leave a lasting impression, and look dignified too. Billboards and posters were made ready and distributed on a large scale to attract plentiful numbers. The officials at the headquarters had extended a strong backing and were pleased to witness the zest of the team flying high. Kabir Hussain himself was to be the compere while the rest would carry out other duties allocated to them. Members of other teams were also to be there in case their help was required in any form. The meeting was to start at 7pm sharp. On the high day, an hour before the meeting was due to start, half a dozen high voltage speakers were set up to extend the sound to the whole habitation. Indian film music and Punjabi folk songs were put on to indicate the first signs of the fast approaching meeting. And just as the deafening sound waves of music began to pierce the eardrums the young children, urchins, tramps and indolent ruffians began to gather in front of the podium. Young children with ragged clothes and runny noses began to practise somersaulting exercises, the urchins took to friendly fighting, the tramps sat cross-legged discussing with each other whatever they were capable of and the groups of ruffians occupied their respective corners grinning and sniggering at each other in grim challenges.

The programme didn't start until after eight because, as usual, the high-ranking leaders from the district headquarters didn't bother to arrive on time. It was always for the rank and file to arrive first and wait wistfully for the leaders to appear, an hour or two late, for otherwise the public might assume the leaders were a bunch of easily available monsoon frogs. When the leaders were duly received with garlands around their necks and given their due places on the stage, Kabir Hussain, looking like a young Mohammed Ali Jinnah with a Turkish hat on his head, came close to the mike.

'Brothers, sisters and friends, ass-slama-laiqum to you all. Our beloved leaders whom we all hold in high esteem have now arrived, thanks to Allah. We have outlined a really lively, colourful and guiding programme for our nation, our Muslim brothers this evening. If you would like the whole programme to run smoothly then please do lend us your much-needed co-operation and bear with us. However, before anything else we must thank Allah and his prophet for their protective hands on our heads. We must begin by listening to the praises of Allah and his prophet. So I invite *Janaab* Nizam-ud-din the greatest musician to come and perform the song that will fill you with gratitude to Allah and his prophet.'

The singer with long, henna-dyed hair came over the stage equipped with harmonium and accompanied by a young tabla-master or drummer, and sat cross-legged in front of the mike (which had to be lowered for him) and began to sing.

> Musalmano aapka Islam hai din-e-ilahi
>
> Bakhsha paighamber ne isko rutaba, rutaba- e-shahi
>
> Dekha hai dunya ne iska chaand tak jaho jalal
>
> Noor-e-Allah ki, paighamber ki hai yeh kaisi misaal

(O Muslims! Your Islam is the religion of God Himself to which your prophet imparted an unparalleled status. The world has seen its grandeur and glory mounting to the height of stars. There is no other precedence of the light of God and his prophet comparable to this.)

The song of praise to Allah and his prophet lasted for fifteen minutes after which Kabir Hussain invited three poets of Urdu to read their poetry. Their poetry was in praise of the Muslim League, Mr Jinnah, and the Muslims in general as one nation and incited them to get ready for *jihad*, Islamic crusade, for the achievement of Pakistan.

There were five leaders occupying five chairs on the stage, coming from the local and district offices of the Muslim League. Two of them wore white turbans and sounded like religious leaders, one had long hair strewn at the back like a *pir* and two others were in Turkish caps and had long jackets resembling Mr Jinnah from a distance.

By 9pm the whole space surrounded by the tents seemed to be overflowing with people. The programme was certainly a success. Kabir Hussain filled in the gaps between speakers with his own poetry, which was all propaganda material. The first to speak was Pir Allah Bakhsh, who asserted that the cause of the Muslim League was just but challenging and needed the full support of all the Muslims of the world. Probably by world he meant the whole of India. He emphasised the need for funds and membership to strengthen the League and assured the audience that thousands of his followers were already on the way to join the League, owing to the just cause of Pakistan.

Both the turbaned men were some big landlords or zamindars. They, too, guaranteed colossal sums of money and high rates of recruitment because they saw Pakistan as a supreme dream come true, where the flag of the supremacy of Islam would flutter unceasingly. They said all their *muzahras* (bonded labour or farmers) had already joined the League in Sind and they were certain the League would soon form their government there.

The other two were the co-ordinating officers of the League, one at the tehsil level and other at the district level. They both appealed to the audience to respond even more zealously by joining the League and by raising funds so that their sublime dream of an Islamic state could be realised without further delay.

Slogans were repeated several times during the programme, and they were: "Muslim League - Zindabad; Qaed-e-azam - Zindabad; Nara-e-taqbir - Allah-hoo-akbar i.e. God is the greatest." The whole programme continued till 11pm when suddenly some rival groups of ruffians began to squabble, resulting in a physical fight so that the programme had to be stopped.

Leave Me Alone

Kinner, having the facility of all the vernacular dailies being delivered to him at his office, had read the news of Kabir Hussain's public programme in Islamabad and had felt an excruciating pain in his heart to see his age-old friends digress so deplorably. A few days after that he came to see me late in the evening and said, 'Arya, you ought to do something to save these two wayward deviants. They must be brought back to the right path before it's too late. This road of fundamentalism they've chosen to tread will not only destroy them but will adversely affect the whole village one day. It's all very weird and abominable, too.'

His serious concern about both of them forced me to look into his eyes, which were as benign as his words. He had always been very magnanimous and benevolent at his heart although a little blunt and rough at his mouth but that owed much to the circumstances he had faced throughout his tender years of childhood. I really felt proud of his friendship. I had always thought he was a great artist. But as time went by, I came to see through to his inner qualities, too. Artists are, nearly always, exceptionally delicate and tender from within. They often can't bear to see anybody in pain and distress. Notwithstanding the painful history of his ancestors that had reflected on him and had agonised him constantly over the years, he had no malice or ill will against anyone. In his heart and soul he loved humanity and wanted it to progress and flourish to its infinity.

'What can I do, Kinner? You tell me? You know them both as much as I do - six of one and half a dozen of the other. And, on top of all that the secessionist forces Kabir's in league with, are too formidable and cruel to be dealt with. And fundamentalism, as you've said many times before, is fascinating and gripping like no other fantasy but it always leads to devastation. Maybe I can talk to Krishan and caution him but I don't think I can ever talk to Kabir, for even my sincerest advice might be misconstrued as an attack on Islam or even as blasphemous.' My tongue began to stammer as I uttered the last words.

'Probably you're right,' replied Kinner from within an abyss, his eyes narrowing.

'The forces at work have grown too cruel and inexorable, especially now when the Cripps Mission has arrived with its divisive agenda. All they want is to placate the dissident elements to let them have the contiguous areas and Congress to have its dominion status. Politics seems to be the dirtiest game on this earth.' I had grown a little too emotional.

'I quite agree with you but how can we let our friends drown in the lava of mutual hatred which will then be unleashed on the whole village?' Kinner asserted every word with deep anguish wreaked on his face.

'Then tell me how shall we go about this?' I let myself be flexible and receptive.

'Well, forget about Kabir for the moment and just try to tackle Krishan somehow. I've got a secular Muslim friend in the city. He may be able to help us in Kabir's case. And I must go now, Arya,' Kinner said and left immediately.

The month of January in 1942 was on its last legs. The vegetation was still undergoing its period of torpor. Spring wasn't too far away either. The Banyan tree still shivered with cold. If there was any sunshine, it was so debilitated that it hardly imparted any warmth. If you peered out of the window after your night's sleep, you would see that the crop of wheat, although green, seemed badly battered by cold. Mornings and evenings frequently turned foggy and misty. The sugar cane crop with its stinging foliage would seem to have stayed awake all through the night due to chill. I had an archaic obsession of watching the morning crops closely as though I would be talking to them. And, like all other villagers I, too, made a morning trip to the fields. Defecation apart, the trip freshened me and allowed me an intimate rendezvous with the fauna and flora of the village. In addition, there would also be a distanced conversation with the village folks who, just like me, would be on their morning's business. The early risers would be returning from their morning trip and the late risers like myself would be setting out. This would cause face-to-face meetings with those with whom there would be feeble chance to meet otherwise.

On one such morning I happened to meet Krishan, who was perhaps an even later riser than myself. He was coming from the direction of the village towards me while I was about to terminate my trip. I smiled at him and he smiled back with a cheery face. His somewhat jovial mood augmented my courage. And while we were standing face-to-face, about a dozen feet apart, I caught the opportunity.

'Long time no see. Where do you live these days, yaar?'

'Been busy, yaar,' he said, yawning and rubbing his still sleepy eyes with the palm of his hand.

'Not with cows anymore, I'm sure,' I taunted him slightly.

'They were sold long time ago,' he said, sounding a little edgy.

'Doing some kind of business then, are you?' I questioned despite my knowledge of the truth.

'No, yaar. It's the duties of my party,' he said with a grin.

'Which party, man? You never told us?'

'Perhaps not. It's HMS,' he pouted.

'I see... I never knew,' I feigned complete ignorance.

'Never mind that. How are *you* anyway?'

'Not too bad. Still surviving. Listen, can I see you sometime?' I asked, sounding friendly.

'You *are* seeing me now, aren't you?'

'I mean at leisure.'

'That's what I don't get any more,' he said as though he were now the most important person in the country. 'Meet me next Sunday at 2pm in the Hanuman mandir, okay?' Scratching his head he began to step hastily away. Perhaps the morning pressure had begun to inconvenience him.

'All right, I'll see you there then,' I acknowledged and went ahead on my way to the village, much amazed by the change in temperament he had evinced.

In the 'August Offer' of 1940, the minorities were told that their views would be given weight in any policy revision, and that power would not be transferred to any system of government whose authority was denied by large and powerful elements in India's national life. The 1942 Cripps offer of total post-war independence was the climax of that assurance. Mahatma's campaign of civil disobedience begun in 1940 had begun to dissipate by now but the non-co-operation was still as sharp as ever. But, in the light of the new developments of the war (i.e. attack on Pearl Harbour, the American entry into the war and the fall of Singapore and Rangoon) London was convinced that a new attempt must be made to get Congress collaborating with the government, to help them in the war, which had now reached India's borders. It was also crucial to assuage America, who was pressing London hard. The result had been the Cripps Mission. The Mission's offer not only confirmed the 'August Offer' but also stipulated other conditions, that is, to grant full Dominion Status at the end of the war, or the chance to secede from the Commonwealth and go for total independence. But no part of India could be forced to join the new state. However, the ruse failed to work and its complete rejection by the Congress resulted in open confrontation in the 'Quit India Movement'. Ironically, Jinnah raised an alternative slogan against 'Quit India', and that was 'Divide and Quit'.

On the following Sunday at 2pm sharp, I met Krishan at his permanent address - the Hanuman mandir or akhara Hanuman, the son of the wind. He, too, was waiting for me. He seemed quite curious about what I wanted to meet him for. The akhara or mandir was swarming with people who, I knew at heart, would be as cantankerous as fundamentalism itself. I thought of taking Krishan out of this marsh of religious fanatics that had always devoured thousands of innocent souls.

'Now tell me what you want to talk to me about?' he asked, pushing me into a corner.

'It's quite a serious matter, Krishan. We can't talk it here. It's too noisy. Shall we go to the company bagh?' I suggested. The company bagh or garden wasn't too far away.

'All right, let's go then,' he acquiesced and I thanked Hanuman, the monkey god.

It took us nearly fifteen minutes to reach the company bagh. We didn't talk much on our way save about the good old days, the Banyan tree and the play we had staged together under its umbrella. In the bagh, we found a secluded spot and sat cross-legged facing each other. It was now that I was stuck for words. In fact, I wanted to broach the topic in such a way as to grip all his sensible energies. I wished to appeal to his inner soul and his sane instinct, which, I was still sure, was untouched and benign. Krishan, in his white *kurta-pyjama*, looked straight at me and said, 'Come on now, you Shylock!' This sudden reminder of the role I had played in Shakespeare under the Banyan tree made me laugh heartily. Krishan, too, laughed with me. That was enough to break the tension that stretched across me.

'Krishan! Do you know how many centuries we've suffered as slaves under one foreign ruler or the other?' I posed him a straight question.

'We've suffered tragically, at the hands of Mughals first and then these *goras*, that's how much I know,' he replied.

'No, we suffered even before that. We suffered at the hands of frequent invaders from the west. We suffered at the hands of Brahmins and priests, at the hands of ridiculous social laws and norms they made for us, the way they divided us into four *varnas* and exploited us. You can still see the *varna-vivastha* today, in which the Brahmin occupies the top rank, *kshatryas* the second position, *vaishwas* the third, and *sudras* the fourth and the lowest one.' I tried to take him to the heart of the matter.

'Is that what you've called me for? To give me some kind of schooling?' He flared up a bit, his face frowning.

'No schooling, yaar! We're grown up people now and we must've a style of our own to talk things over. I mean, we can't converse like rustics or young urchins, can we?'

'All right, carry on then,' he said and relaxed a little, permitting me to continue.

'Well, what I really mean is, that to divide ourselves in the name of religion, caste, class our belief is to fall an easy prey to those who benefit from such useless divisions. In fact, by doing so we save *them* the labour of doing it themselves whereby they'd be exposed. We should actually resist them and their malicious intent of making inroads through the fabric of our society. Secularism is the only antidote to all our ills.'

'What're you talking about, man? Who's being secular here? Are these Muslims secular? They take pride in slashing India into two halves, take one half themselves and leave the other half for us. They desire to cripple it, mutilate and mangle it, murder it right in front of our eyes. Should we or shouldn't we let it happen like that; that is the moot question right now. There's no sense in discussing history when the whole country's facing the threat of complete ruin. I don't know about you but we won't let it happen, at any cost, understand?'

'I do agree with you, Krishan, but imagine the mayhem, the bloodshed, which might result from this, the ruthless and reckless opposition. Imagine thousands turning orphans, widows, childless and God knows what else.

'Should we, for fear of that, give them the whole of India? They were invaders, intruders, robbers and crusaders who came and enslaved us, and kept us so for six hundred years by coercion. And now, instead of living peacefully together with us, they want to cut this country into pieces. We'll *never* let that happen, come what may. You keep your fucking lectures of secularism to yourself or go and teach them to someone else not me. Leave me alone! Do you understand, you sympathiser of these ingrate Mohammedans!' Krishan's eyes turned fierce, red and volcanic. He at once stood up and began to hurry away.

'Krishan, Krishan, Krishan!' I kept crying to call him back.

'Leave me alone, okay?' he blurted out savagely and accelerated his speed still more till he disappeared from my sight.

I felt completely shattered, dazed and bloodless. He was one of those thousands, who were active members of the Hindu Mahasabha; all of them must have been fed on the same diet. They seemed to have been brainwashed totally. From Krishan's bloodshot eyes I could easily read the text that was going to be written, the story of dread that would be recorded and the denouement of the drama waiting to be staged. I was rendered wordless, speechless, and was unnerved. There was no point talking to him anymore because this was already the third time I had tried, and the worst one. When I met him last time he had bragged copiously about the agenda of his party but I had, as usual, taken the whole thing lightly and casually as one can always expect from a novice. He had boasted garrulously about Hindi, Hindu and Hindustan, Hindu reawakening, Hindu supremacy, Aryan blood, Suryavansh, Aryavansh and all that crap. The time before that he had only just been initiated into the Hindu Mahasabha. Now I no longer recognised the same naïve and gullible Krishan I had known for years; the one who had played with us, had enjoyed all kinds of mischief with us, had gone to the jungle and had staged the drama of Shakespeare with us. The gap in our meetings had widened when his father, terribly sick of him, had sold the cows Krishan had been grazing. Almost a year had passed by without a close conversation between us. He was busy attending his meetings and I was engaged in my own scribbling. If we met in a bazaar or a street, it would only be a chance encounter and the talk would never go beyond asking each other how things were. But one day, when we met by chance and went to sit in a restaurant in the city, he came forth with queer and bizarre ideas about post-British India, as though independence had already been granted.

He said the new India would belong to the Hindus because they were the legitimate inheritors and that they had suffered enough to be asked to suffer more. He said it was going to be the first *Ramraj* (rule of the righteous) in history and that the Hindu Mahasabha was fully equipped to make that dream come true. He had now withdrawn from being the worshipper of Hanuman, the son of the wind, and was no more a *jatsati* or celibate. He had also decided against being a student of philosophy. While he was talking loquaciously, I was thinking a funny thing in my head: 'It would've been better had he continued grazing cows in the field like he did a year before.'

But he had turned out to be too perverse to do that and had revolted against his father, who then had to dispose of the cows, for when Krishan was in the city, not returning for many days, the cows would rumble with hunger all day. I still remembered the words I had said to him one day, 'Go graze your cattle, you archaic soul.' By archaic soul I meant the descendant of the Lord Krishna. The recollection now took the form of an illusion with me. I thought it might be because of this comment that he had turned a rebel. And the very next moment my own thoughts began to ridicule me, for it was erroneous and unfounded.

Kinner and I met again after about a month to feed back to each other on the project. I reported what had happened between Krishan and I. But he wasn't surprised at all, much to my amazement though.

'Kabir, too, is in the same boat. "Leave me alone," he says,' answered Kinner. 'Doesn't it astonish you?'

Kinner went on musing morosely in his chair behind the desk while I sat opposite him, shuffling through an Urdu daily. There was important news in the paper that Jinnah, with the help of a Muslim businessman MAH Ispahani, had converted the weekly Dawn into a daily paper, making it an invaluable Muslim forum and mouthpiece.

'Have you read this news of the Daily Dawn?' I asked abruptly as if electrocuted.

'Yes, I have,' he replied wearily. 'You can't fight a political battle without a paper.'

Radhika came, greeted me and placed two cups of tea for us on the desk. She was as fresh and oozing with energy as ever. When she was about to saunter off, I caught an invigorating glimpse of her face and was mesmerised. After she had left, I began to sip my tea, still thinking about her. Strange but intimate thoughts were running wild in my mind.

'What a strange similarity between the two verdicts!' I heard Kinner say. And suddenly I felt I had sunk deep into some unknown world.

'What d'you mean?' I asked him, knowing not what he had said.

'Yes, I'm going to explain that. The Congress withdrew their men from the ministries owing to the unjust declaration of war on behalf of India. Then there was this new round of civil disobedience and non-co-operation. But now, when the British are faced with the threat of war entering India's doors through the southeast, and are compelled by America to do something to get the co-operation of Congress, they send the Stafford Cripps Mission, offering vague and ludicrous terms to which the reaction is "Quit India", the unsaid of which is "Leave us alone". And on the other hand, Mr Jinnah says, "Divide and quit India and leave us alone to battle with each other". And now our two cronies, Kabir and Krishan, too, say the same, "Leave me alone" individualising the same version. So, what an analogy between the two verdicts!' Kinner said and began to laugh bitterly.

A Preamble to the Crossing of Swords

Amar Singh, the eldest son of Jagga, suddenly became the talk of the whole village. First of all nobody believed he could've done such a thing, for he was so gentle, cool-minded and suave that he would forgive even the worst of his foes. How could he have beaten up Hassan, the grandson of Chiraghdin Arayin and the son of Farid? Yet everyone knew Hassan was outspoken, cunning and wayward. They could believe any allegation about him, but not about Amar. But when people actually saw Hassan's twisted arm and broken leg they felt compelled to acknowledge that Amar might have given him a wild flogging.

When someone told Farid-ud-din that Amar had broken his son's leg and had twisted his arm he was left awe-struck, not because he trusted it, but because he didn't. He knew his only son well enough and he knew Amar, too. They had been dealing with each other for years now. He himself was Jagga's age. They were two brothers and one sister. Waris, his elder brother, had died in the massacre of Jallianwalla Bagh. Mehndi, his sister, was married in Lahore. His father, Chiraghdin, had been dealing with Jagga's father Niranjan Singh for ages and he had been dealing with Jagga himself keeping the business going as usual. And now the business was in the hands of their children, as normal as ever. But...

Jagga and his sons, along with other crops, grew fodder in their fields, which was often bought up by Farid and his son as it stood in the field. They then sold it in the fodder market, taking it to the city cart by cart every day and made some profit to keep their hearth smouldering and their pot boiling. On the other hand, Jagga and his sons would be saved from the consuming labour of reaping the fodder and marketing it. They had reasonable land and had other things to do. But Farid had a very small landholding. They had to practise an intensive mode of farming to be able to feed the family. Two acres of land was not adequate by any measure, and despite their incessant strenuous labour, they had to spare some time to pursue other modes of earning. They had also bought Bhaga's standing crops in the past and had sold them cart by cart in the same open market.

The relations between Farid and Jagga were quite normal, cordial and mutually beneficial. It was always clear to both the parties how much had been paid and how much was still to be paid. There was no reason for any dispute or wrangle. Then why had it all happened? Farid was unable to figure it out. And, Amar would be the last person to be suspected of harming anyone. But the reporter had specifically named Amar as having crippled his only son. Farid ran to the fields on hearing the news of the mishap, and stopped only when he found himself standing bewildered beside his gruesomely groaning and moaning son. Hassan was surrounded by and being tended by half a dozen people, including a bonesetter from an adjacent village. No one knew who had sent for him. Farid was desperately out of breath when he arrived at the scene, panting miserably and shuddering embarrassingly. It took well over ten minutes before he was able to utter, 'What's happened to him?'

'Amar has walloped him cruelly, broken his left leg and twisted his right arm. The arm seems to have broken as well,' said someone from within the tenders.

'Why? What was up between the two?'

'Don't really know. We just came on hearing him wailing under his weight.'

'Where's Amar?'

'Don't know. He was here when we came.'

And the bad news spread all around the village like wild fire, or like a locust attack. Nobody knew what had preceded the brawling, pounding, pummelling and thrashing except Amar and Hassan themselves. But Hassan was whimpering with lacerating pain and Amar was not to be found anywhere. Yet, the villagers had their own way of conjecturing the probabilities, even possibilities, and every conjecture would be badly sullied, tainted and maligned by the religious turmoil already in the air. So, long before the veritable truth came to light a concocted truth had taken hold of the village, which had actually sprung up from the politico-religious tumult already in the air. The incident was portrayed and construed as a serious battle between a Sikh and a Muslim because the former had committed a profanation against Islam and the prophet. The version triggered a livid animosity between Hindu-Sikhs and Muslims.

Sir Sikander Hayat Khan, the Chief Minister of the Unionist Party Coalition Government had died a few days ago. Sikander Ali, a close friend and ally of the deceased, had not yet recovered from the shock when the Amar-Hassan tragedy took place, exacerbating the situation. He had also joined the Muslim League like other followers of the former, his new colleagues added fuel to the fire, too. The whole thing culminated in the build up of religious tension in Qila Vasudev - the Muslims looking at non-Muslims with suspicion and scorn and the latter returning it in an equal measure.

The Draft Declaration issued by the Cripps Mission had given an impetus to the problem of the Punjab, as one of its concrete features was to permit the right of the provinces to secede from the centre if they so wished. And to do so they were required to prove their dissension by obtaining 60% votes in the Assembly for non-accession to India. The Muslims in the Punjab Legislative Assembly could do that without any hindrance because they *were* well over this percentage. That meant the whole of Punjab would now go to the would-be Pakistan. Here were the tangled strands of the skein that needed sorting out as far as the non-Muslims of the Punjab were concerned. Even a plebiscite could not stop Punjab from becoming part of Pakistan because the count of non-Muslims was only 44%. So, the Sikhs and Hindus together opted for the partition of the Punjab, although Jinnah and his Muslim League were averse to it. But the Mission had no powers delegated to it to partition a province, which climaxed in its utter failure.

The Sikhs in particular were arguing that they could not live under the domination of Muslims in a country where they were the erstwhile rulers. Maharaja Ranjit Singh ruled the whole territory, extending as far as Kabul. The Hindus had suffered tremendously at the hands of Mughal emperors in the four hundred years of history prior to the Sikh Raj. So, they were in favour of partition. But the Muslim League did not want Punjab to be partitioned because they wanted to swallow it all. So, the situation was rendered much more complex, tense and rigid.

Congress did not want the division of the country or its provinces in any form whatsoever. But the Cripps Mission had come ready with all such provisions. His Majesty's Government was ready to grant a new constitution to the seceding provinces giving them the same status as the Indian Union, tacitly recognising the demand for Pakistan. As a consequence, there were protests, processions, rallies and public conferences, in short a national crusade against the British that culminated in the clamour of the 'Quit India' movement organised by Congress. On the contrary, the Muslim League continued fortifying its position in Bengal, Sind, Assam and the North West Frontier Province. They were also ingratiating themselves with the British by providing men and material for the ongoing war.

The tension in Qila Vasudev was the reflection of this national strife. Similar tensions were also to be seen in many other villages of the Punjab. Yet, the real cause of fight between Amar and Hassan was totally different, as Jagga and Bhaga discovered when they asked Amar how had it all happened. 'Well, I was chaffing fodder for the cattle while Hassan was hoeing. He had started his day early and was exhausted. I'd begun my work only an hour earlier and was fresh and vigorous. We were talking affectionately as well as working. Then suddenly he said that he was sick of this life of strenuous work and backbreaking diligence. He said that I was lucky to have other brothers so the work got divided amongst us, whereas he had to do it all by himself as his father had been left with little energy to share the work equally. At that, I said lightly and without malice, that his mother should've produced more children because farming always needed more pairs of hands. He said his mother was physically a weak person and couldn't bear more than two, him and his sister, Sara. Then I taunted him by saying that their religion, unlike ours, permitted them four marriages and that his father should've married more women to bear more children. He said how could his father marry more wives when their small stretch of land was inadequate even to feed the existing mouths. And what guarantee was there that another three women would've produced as many children as my mother had produced alone?

Until this point, nothing serious had taken place. Then I said we humans could only try our luck, for if he would talk about guarantee, there was none even about whether we'd survive another day or not. I said there were all kinds of women in society. There were those who couldn't even produce an egg while many others produced dozens of children. At that he said all women weren't like my mother, who was capable of producing offspring like a bitch. Calling my mother a bitch was what stung me and incensed me greatly. I asked him to take his words back and apologise, which he didn't. I then warned him to behave properly and apologise but he dismissed my warning in derision. I then stopped my work and went close to him.

'Do you take your words back or...' I roared at him.

'No, I won't. What will you do to me, kill me?' He flared up, too, but without reason.

'If you don't then I'll break your legs,' I turned ferocious.

'Fuck off,' he abused me.

I could hear it no more. So, I caught him by the arm and twisted it right to his back. Then I threw him on the ground and locked his leg into mine, and asked again, 'Do you apologise?' to which he said no again. His rude obstinacy accentuated my wrath. So I exerted terrible pressure on his leg, enough to make him scream for help. He screamed and hurled horrific dirty names and abuses at me. I exerted more pressure but he didn't back out. Then I heard the sound of a joint breaking at which I relinquished him, squirming on the ground, shouting and screaming for help and still scolding me. But I didn't care and just went away. That was how it all happened,' said Amar coolly and without loss of poise.

But when, few days later, his excruciating pain had lessened, Hassan, as the aggrieved party, was asked by his near and dear ones how it had all taken place, he had a totally different version to offer.

'I was hoeing and he was chopping fodder. He said he had been to the city the other day and was astonished to hear Muslims talking about slashing the country in two and making one part Pakistan. He said someone called Jinnah was doing it all; that he had made a party called the Muslim League, which talked of Islam, Mohammed, Koran and all those idiotic things. That they taught their Muslim followers to hate Sikhs and Hindus so that they got away with having Pakistan made. Once these Sikhs and Hindus refused to live with Muslims, it would be much easier to make it. Then he began to abuse the Muslims and called them sons of a pig. I cautioned him to stop saying things like that, but he didn't care. At that, I said something equally insulting about his Gurus, at which he flared up and began to hit me hard with his legs and arms. He locked my left leg into his and broke it. He twisted my arm at my back and shrivelled it. I kept crying and saying sorry but he wouldn't listen.' Hassan explained the incident and burst out crying in long wails.

A week went past and then a headline appeared in one of the Urdu papers: "Anti-Islamic Crusade Sweeps Punjab". The story told by Hassan had been sprinkled with more spice to make it sound more vulgar and blasphemous, and published with Qila Vasudev's name in bold letters. This resulted in frequent visits from the press anxious to know more about Hassan the victim and Amar the perpetrator. A mountain had been made out of the molehill thereby aggravating the strife and politicising the otherwise naive, ignorant and credulous villagers.

The consequence was that Ghulam Rasul, washerman, son of Jumma, Mirajdin Kharasi, son of Ladha, and all other Muslims began to build up arsenals in their homes. They were scared of being attacked by Sikhs and Hindus, who, in turn, did the same so that a crop of weapons sprang up all around the village. The fears from and doubts about each other began to reach record heights. Kinner was dazed to see it all happen so quickly. He wrote several articles to extinguish the politically stirred fire and straighten things, which were now in stark disarray, but the more powerful press contradicted it all, claiming it was a cover-up effort.

By now the new Chief Minister Sir Khizar Tiwana had taken over following the death of his predecessor, and was in the middle of building his concrete base. The news of an anti-Muslim crusade could cause severe damage to his position as the leader of the Muslim-Sikh-Hindu coalition of the Unionist Party. Perhaps the whole move had been devised surreptitiously to jeopardise him as he, too, had refused to budge to the pressure of Mr Jinnah to declare his Government as the Muslim League Coalition. But a good number of Muslim members of the Legislative Assembly from his Government had already joined the Muslim League.

So it was at this stage that Khizar Hayat Khan summoned forth Sikander Ali and Arjun Singh to talk things over. The duo, on their return from Lahore, convened both the boys, listened to their respective stories (without paying much attention, of course) and made them embrace each other in reconciliation. So Qila Vasudev was saved from being wrecked - at least for the present.

The Banyan tree was extremely sad. He drooped, stupefied by the happenings around him. Nobody cared a penny about him any more. Everyone went past him without even looking at him, as though he no longer existed in the village, in his own vicinity or in the geography of the country. What kind of living was this? A ripe age, seniority, seasoned experience and knowledge of history did not matter any more to anybody. It was a strange land, occupied by strange people, who bothered no more about their own ancestor, their own family tree.

The old and antiquated times had not been all that bad. People had been less busy than they were now. They came and confabulated with him. They sat under his vast umbrella and discussed everything, every contingency that confronted them. They trusted him as much as they trusted themselves. There seemed to be no one left from the old to impart that kind of respect and adoration to him. The ones who were left from the senior lot had either become demented, turned amnesiac or gone in comas. The new generation had learned a different language, the language of the feringhee. They couldn't speak that language under the Banyan tree, because it was meant to be spoken in cities, restaurants, hotels and other well off places, but not in dust and dirt. And even if they spoke it he would not have been able to decipher it, for his language was the language of the ordinary masses. He had always been the friend of the masses, still was, but they wouldn't care.

He could understand the howling dogs, rumbling cows, whinnying horses, braying donkeys, bellowing bulls, squawking crows, grunting pigs, snorting mules, croaking frogs, twittering birds, fizzing snakes, mewing cats, bleating sheep and strumming children to name a few, but he was unable to understand the language of the modern man.

He had been sad once before, many centuries ago, but that was due to the astute Brahmin. He had shown Gautma the light; the light of why people suffered endlessly and died in despair. That light had made him the wise one, so much wiser than the rest of the world so that he had begun to be called Buddha thereafter. It was Buddha from *buddhi*, which meant intellect. But it was also Buddha, from aged and learned, if you pronounced the *double dee* solidly. He, the Banyan tree, found him the light of Asia and made him the wisest one but the cunning Brahmin ostracised his philosophy to other lands such as South East Asia by his craft and treachery.

The Brahmin had composed the four *vedas* under the Banyan, had written the epics like *Ramayana and Mahabharata* under his umbrella, so the Brahmin thought the Banyan mustn't guide anyone else but the Brahmins alone. The Brahmin didn't like Buddha being shown the light and so banished him from his own land. The Banyan tree was as sad, unhappy and traumatised then as now.

Now there were these new Brahmins around, who didn't bother about the Great Banyan tree, about his magical powers and about his most crucial and secular outlook. So, he was extremely gloomy and melancholic. His sadness was further exacerbated that day when he heard Ferozdin, the son of Noordin, say the Banyan tree should be cut into two halves with one to be named the Pakistani Banyan tree and the other to be named the Hindustani Banyan tree. And the chopping or cutting he had proposed was to take place from head to foot, vertically. Was it not a blasphemy? Was it not a profanation? Yet instead of being penitent Ferozdin had walked away with a swagger and the Banyan tree had felt terrible frustration and anguish in his heart. It was as though a son would imprecate his own father, grandfather, great grandfather or great-great grandfather.

And now, when I, Arya Gold, look at the Banyan tree I simply begin to cry. My heart feels terribly pierced, probably just like that of the Banyan tree. My situation is no different from the Banyan tree either because I too, burn my blood to scribble the feelings, aspirations, concerns and worries of the people of the village without bias and discrimination of caste, religion and ethnicity. I've learned to do this from the secular Banyan tree and none other. Sometimes I think the Banyan tree must have been a scribbler in his past life or else I must have been a Banyan tree myself. Would then they, one day, treat me the same way as they now treat the Banyan? Maybe they will, who knows?

Matter of Substitutes

The resonance of Noor Mohammed's return from England after completing his Bar-at-Law began to be heard a week before the due date of his arrival. It was now mid 1943 and the searing heat the sun exuded made our village like a dessert with scorching sand-dunes shimmering and glaring like the fires of hell. There had been no rainfall yet and the dried up, cracked earth looked up into the sky in anticipation of a drop of water, like the rain bird *papeeha* (rhopodytes viridirostris) with open mouth and choking throat. I wondered how Noor Mohammed would adjust to such heat after five full years spent in a land that was diametrically opposite to ours.

And, just like that of the earth, the political climate was also boiling and steaming with frenzied heat to which Noor Mohammed, when he arrived, would add more fuel. I had been hearing for some time that he was now the secretary of the Muslim League's branch in England. So, the legacy was already there and all he needed was a clear field to act in his own homeland.

Had he come to Qila Vasudev I would have most certainly met with him and asked him how he was. But despite my justifiable grievances, I wouldn't have complained about his not having written a single word to me in spite of his promises. That was for feeble minded whereas I had the heart of the Banyan tree in my chest. 'Lend your services to everyone and forget about the remuneration' was my motto. But Noor Mohammed never got the opportunity, for he went straight to Lahore, which was the centre of all activity, and where he actually belonged. Lahore was the home of politics, of the machinery of the government and of everything that mattered.

Noor Mohammed had been our playwright, our director and our Shakespeare, so it was natural that we, or at least I, should want to see him, even briefly. Who wouldn't desire to meet a long-parted friend once again? Both of Noor's maternal grandparents had passed away and had left their whole estate to their grandson. Noor had duly inherited a sprawling bungalow, all the cash and jewellery, and some land - all in Lahore. They had no child save for Noor's mother, Shaista Begam. So it was again natural that Noor, instead of coming to Qila Vasudev, had gone direct to Lahore. I had an earnest desire to see him, meet him closely, observe and assess him from a new angle. I thought of going to Lahore, but then abandoned the idea, not because of waning interest, but because of waxing heat. Maybe, after the monsoon rains, I suggested to myself, and lingered in the village, holding on to the pain of not being able to see him soon enough.

I had absolutely no idea why I had suddenly grown nostalgic for times gone past; times when we had staged that marvellous adaptation of Shakespeare under the Banyan tree. We had all rehearsed for hours on end, had sat and gossiped without being conscious of night falling and the darkness growing thick and eerie. But now, things had changed drastically, everything had gone haywire: the Banyan tree was sad and Krishan and Kabir had been divested of their sanity and innocence. I thought of calling these times The Age of Lunacy but dreaded the wrath of the wiser ones.

Suraj, Bhaga and Kirti's son, was now three years old. I went to see him quite frequently, at least two to three times a week. The heart of innocence, the gift of non-contamination and the paragon of benignity that the age of lunacy had lost could be rediscovered in Suraj, in his uncorrupted laughter and from the way he talked and behaved. The smile in his eyes was so unaffected, so sanctified and so raw that I wished I could invite the whole world of lunatics to come and see it.

Was it political power that corrupted people? Was it money that depraved them? Was it sheer growth that made reprobates of them? I went on questioning myself but could get no tangible answer. There was a saying in Punjabi that the milky teeth were innocent while the non-milky teeth were corrupt. But Suraj had already begun to eat a small chapatti with dal or vegetable. Then why was he so pure even now? I had no answer, so I thought it better to ask the angel himself.

It was early evening and the sun had just set. But the earth was emitting the tremendous heat that it had absorbed during the day. You could hardly wear clothes on your sweat-sodden body but people still wore them because they could not go naked like the cavemen any more. What they did instead was to wear lightweight or thin clothes, wander in briefs and shorts or in loose sheets swaddled round them. The females, however, had the worst luck for they couldn't rove about in briefs or shorts. The beauty they had been endowed with was not without its own peculiar problems. They couldn't lay bare their chests like the men did; they couldn't uncover their legs up to the thighs while men did. What an injustice to the poor creatures! I felt pity for them.

I was happy in shorts with a thin bush-shirt when I went to see my little angel. When I gave a soft knock at the door, it was soon unbolted and opened by Auntie Kirti. She smiled to see me and said, 'What a coincidence! Suraj was remembering you just a minute ago.'

'Was he really?' I exclaimed and smiled back. Then I followed her to the kitchen where Uncle Bhaga was eating his dinner sitting cross-legged on a cot.

'Sasrikaal, Uncle!' I greeted him and he greeted me back.

'Would you like to dine with me?' he asked, stopping his morsel in mid-air.

'No Uncle. I've no appetite just now, thanks anyway. Where's my angel?' I asked and looked around with anxious eyes.

'There he comes,' said Auntie Kirti, nodding in the direction he was emerging from, having heard my voice.

'Hello, little angel!' I smiled and went to pick him up. 'So, were you remembering me then?'

'Yeth, I wanted to play foothball with you,' he replied with a lisp.

'How about Auntie and Uncle? Don't they play with you?' I asked.

'No... No one does.'

'Never mind, I'm here now and all for you,' I said and held him tightly.

'Le'me go and geth the ball from inside,' he said and began to struggle out of my clasp. I put him on the ground there and Suraj ran to get the small ball. He put the ball on the floor and kicked it towards me, but the kick wasn't powerful enough, and the ball rolled to a stop before it got to me. I picked the ball up, went closer to him, put the ball back on the ground and said, 'Right, Suraj, be strong and hit it hard so it reaches uncle this time.' He frowned with concentration, screeched and gave the ball a stronger kick, but it went only half way across the forecourt.

'That was a gorgeous attempt!' I applauded him. 'Don't worry, I'll give you enough practice to make it reach even farther than where Uncle is.'

'Buth when will I do ith?' he asked drearily.

'Wait till you grow up and you'll do it,' said Uncle.

'When will I grow up?' he asked again, jutting his lips.

'Drink a lot of milk if you want to grow rapidly,' assured Uncle.

'But I do drink milk, don't I?'

'Not enough. Double it up to grow swiftly,' Uncle advised him.

'All right then,' Suraj nodded and went across to the ball to pick it up.

Auntie Kirti had commenced washing the dishes while Uncle Bhaga had taken his turban off and put it on a stool nearby before laying down to relax.

'How are your mother and father, Arya?' Uncle asked me, turning his face towards Suraj and me. We were still busy with the ball.

'They're both fine, Uncle,' I replied briefly. He kept musing momentarily and then said, 'What's this Pakistan business we hear about these days? D'you know anything about it?'

'Only just,' I replied. 'The Muslims don't wish to live with us Sikhs and Hindus, so they've decided to live separately in a country called Pakistan.'

'Where's this country?' he quizzed.

'Nowhere, it has got to be made yet,' I told him.

'How? And where?'

'By dividing India into two separate parts.'

'What? That's ridiculous! And which part do they want to take?'

'Towards the west, I mean towards the river Jehlam,' I said vaguely for nothing was certain yet.

'Is it? But my sister, Iso, lives there. Will they throw her out?'

'I don't know, Uncle,' I expressed my ignorance. But I could see him getting jittery and puzzled.

I played with Suraj for over an hour, drank a glass of milk, which Auntie served me against my resistance. When I left after a soft pat on Suraj's innocent face, he asked, 'Will you come tomorrow?' I said I would and stepped out wishing them all goodbye.

Kinner and I arranged to meet at his bank in the Hall Bazaar where he had opened his first account with the help of Uncle Arjun. He had remained with that bank ever since. I had asked him for some money, which he had agreed to lend me. It was just after the monsoons. The weather had now changed for the better and the heat, although not completely vanished, had adequately mitigated. The air was still saturated with vapour and it was sultry, close and humid, but much less than a month ago. On my way to the city, I saw numerous puddles full of muddy water, which splashed on to the passers-by when something fell in them or some buffalo waded recklessly through. The water wouldn't soak or dry up until the end of September because of that very same saturation in the air. It was sticky but not too hot.

I reached the bank at noon, exactly on time. Kinner hadn't arrived yet. I found an unoccupied chair on the verandah of the bank and sat in it. People were entering and exiting from the bank incessantly. I waited for Kinner watching all kinds of people roving around in the precinct of the bank, in Hall Bazaar and in front of the shops opposite the bank. It seemed as though the area was a meeting point for varying cultures. The Pathans, for instance, wore multicoloured turbans with white caps in the middle. They also wore silky multicoloured jackets with open fronts, underneath which they had long loose shirts with matching *salwaars.* They all had moustaches and beards. The beards were mostly shaved at the cheeks, which glared like pinkish red apples. The doorman of the bank was a Pathan too, and was so gentle and affable that he didn't ask me to quit the chair; rather he smiled to me and left me to myself. Pathans had come from the North West Frontier, Kabul and Peshawar and roamed the whole of India, disseminating their culture everywhere. Their mother tongue was *Pashtu,* but the Pathans in the Punjab also spoke a mixture of Pashtu and Urdu mingled with Punjabi that we all easily understood. A Pathan was always known for his word; he could lay down his life but wouldn't back out from his word or promise.

There were Sikhs around too. They also wore turbans, but in a different way. They, too, had moustaches and beards but they kept them uncut and untrimmed. Their clothes were similar to those of the Hindu and Muslim Punjabis, but dissimilar to Pathans. There were Buddhists and Jains around as well. Buddhists shaved their hair and beards completely, and rambled in loose clothes, sometimes just wrapped in a thin sheet. Jains differed from them in that they covered their mouths to eschew killing any life through breathing.

The Muslims of the Punjab differed radically from the Muslims of the frontier, and in a variety of ways. They looked more akin to the

334

rest of the Punjabis than to anyone else. They spoke Punjabi and in the same accent as did other Punjabis. They wore same clothes and ate the same food. They celebrated the same festivals and had the same cultural roots as other Punjabis. This observation led me to the question of nationality. Mr Jinnah had recently expounded the 'two nation theory', saying that all Muslims were a separate and distinct nation in contrast to non-Muslims. I wondered how Gujarati, Bengali, Marathi or other Muslims for that matter, could have the same nationality as Punjabi Muslims. Language, culture, history and geographical proximity were always at the root of the formation of a nationality. But who could argue with and convince the political masters? They had the political might and therefore they were always right, despite being wrong.

I was deeply involved in my musings when Kinner appeared. He watched me lost in thoughts and looking morosely inert, and said, 'People like you must never drive even a bicycle let alone an automobile.'

'Why?' I asked. 'Because habitual thinkers are a menace to public life. They double the chance of causing an accident than ordinary people,' he said, and began to smile mockingly.

We went into the bank. It took us nearly twenty minutes to take the money out. Having finished, we came out, Kinner in the lead. And just then we saw Kabir and Noor Mohammed step out of a car in front of the bank and come towards us. It was a strange concurrence. Just as they stepped up the stairs of the bank and looked ahead, we were looking straight at them.

'Wow, what a pleasant surprise!' I exclaimed.

Noor Mohammed was stunned to see us but only for a jiffy and then regained his composure. I observed a colossal change in him. Even in that sticky and pasty weather, he was wearing three-piece suit with a tie, although the cloth was light and thin and soft coloured. He had grown scraggy, his eyeballs bulged and penetrated into the soul of the onlooker.

But there was no change in Kabir Hussain except that his eyes now saw things more suspiciously than ever before.

'It's an equal surprise to me as well.' Noor said. 'How are *you,* anyway?' He asked and shook hands with both of us, first with

Kinner being a step ahead of me and then with me. Kabir too followed his act, scrupulously polite.

'Welcome back to India! We're meeting after so many years,' I uttered with an expression of delight on my face. 'I'd expected a close hug from you.' At that, he drew himself closer to me and put his arm round my shoulder.

'Old Shylock!' Kinner cried. 'Always looking for extra benefits.'

'Never mind, we're all old chums, aren't we?' Noor said and pressed my shoulder with his hand already there.

'How are you Solerio-Somnath? Have you lost your poetic tongue or...' Kinner asked Kabir with a light laugh and winked at Noor and I. We now stood facing each other like the four angles of a rectangle. Kabir appeared to have sunk into introspection quite suddenly.

'I'm alright, nothing wrong with my poetic tongue either,' he replied with a bizarre edginess that forbade any more questions. Kinner felt offended for a moment but then brushed it all aside and began to talk to Noor Mohammed.

'How was your stay in England anyway? Must've had lot of new experiences.'

'Plenty of them,' Noor said and smiled briefly.

'We'll sit down sometime leisurely and listen to all your wonderful escapades,' said Kinner cheekily. Noor probably knew what he was hinting at.

'Sure, sure, we'll sit down one day. But for the moment if you please...' He left the 'excuse us' phrase unsaid and took a step towards the bank. He had taken his hand off my shoulder long ago.

'Alright, see you again sometime,' said Kinner and then we began to climb down the bank's stairs while they scurried inside.

Kinner and I were now heading towards his office, silent, listening to or recapturing the moments of confrontation.

'Probably they'll make good substitutes for Mr Jinnah and Dr Iqbal,' grumbled Kinner on the way.

'Which is which?' I retorted.

'Obviously, Noor Mohammed bar-at-law can take the place of Jinnah after his death and Kabir the poet that of Iqbal, who's already dead,' Kinner announced and giggled.

'The Muslim League's quite fortunate to have their future leaders already in the offing,' I said with a chuckle.

We were only a few steps short of reaching the office when I saw a young woman. She was carrying a small child slung to her chest. He was maybe a year or so old and was smiling broadly and looking at the passers-by. I was reminded of Suraj the unsullied angel.

'But there shall be no substitute for the innocence of the little angels,' I just whispered to myself.

'Did you say something?' Kinner asked, looking strangely at me.

'No, nothing!' I said and began to follow him up the staircase.

Aggrandisement of Power and Prestige

'Look, what your Mahatma and the Congress have done.' Kinner suddenly spurted out, pulling his eyes away from the paper.

'Why, what've they done?' I asked, raising my head above from the sheet of paper on which I was scribbling some notes.

'They've fucked up everything again. Haven't you seen today's paper?' He looked at me in irritation.

'Why? I've read it all, page by page,' I assured Him.

'My foot! Have you seen this news of Gandhi's political parleys with Jinnah?'

'Of course I have. What are you talking about, man?'

'Oh! I'm sorry then.'

'That's all right!'

It was my sixth month in Kinner's office, working for his paper as editor, news composer, translator and, also manager when Kinner wasn't there. In fact, because of Radhika, I achieved much more than that.

Kinner had been endeavouring ever since our encounter with Noor and Kabir in the bank the previous year, to wheedle me into his paper, saying, he needed me as much as I needed him, and that we should gather our forces together. I had taken it to mean he wanted me as his partner, which I had no desire to be. I had lingered on through prevarication and procrastination until one day he almost rounded on me.

'Look Arya, enough is enough, no more dilly-dallying. I want straight answers, yes or no, all right? You're my tried and tested friend and I've full faith in you. My paper and I need you right now. You just tell me what kind of money you're looking for and I'll have no hesitation in paying you if I can afford it.' Now, there was no way for me to escape. This was in March this year. I hadn't returned his money yet and now I couldn't postpone things any further. It was equally impossible for me to fix my own wage in the face of the fact that he was much more than a mere friend to me and that we both trusted each other to the extent of blindness. Furthermore, I had absolutely no idea of what I was worth, or whether I was worth anything at all; I had always thought I was hopelessly worthless.

'Look my friend, self-evaluation isn't my forte. But no more dilly-dallying for me, that is a promise. You pay me what you may find me worth. I will join you from next month. Is that all right?' I assured him and held his hand tightly and warmly.

I joined Kinner's staff on 1st April 1944. Everyone in his office was pleased. They treated me as one of them and I felt elated. Radhika took special care of me. At the end of the month, Kinner gave me one hundred rupees as my salary and I was exhilarated. It was much more than I had actually dreamt of.

Kinner accommodated me in his own office. My desk, chair and other paraphernalia were set in one corner, which was opposite to that of Kinner. It was now six months later and the paper had picked up more sales. Kinner had more time to spare, which he used to attend various meetings and collect adverts for the paper. While he was out on business and his brothers out on delivery, collection or printing engagements, we, Radhika and I, spent our time together, either in her office or in mine. She was now totally mine and I was all hers but no one knew about it yet. We had decided to disclose our relationship at an appropriate time, which hadn't come yet.

I now regretted not having joined Kinner's paper earlier. And, when I shared my contrition with Radhika, she elegantly said, 'Nature works in its own strange ways. God probably wanted us to mature a bit and then meet so we could value our union more positively. Remember the mistake I made as a young and immature girl, which later haunted me for months and years? Yet I also learnt a lot from that one grave folly.' Having said that she heaved a long deep but comfortable sigh and looked into my eyes. I said nothing but leant forward and kissed her slightly moist eyes.

I just couldn't believe my fate could take such a good turn. I had always yearned for Radhika but she had always seemed far away to me. Years glided past in that wistful yearning but then, one lucky day, the fate landed me right beside her. The day I joined the office, Radhika welcomed me, although with some reservation. But I, with some struggle, read the script written on her wistfully longing face and in her equally pensive eyes, which told me the story of a girl who looked to the horizon, waiting for a chariot driven by gorgeous horses and occupied by the prince of her dreams.

She was slim and trim but not scrawny, delicate but not fragile, vulnerable but not destructible. She was curvaceous and captivating. A few more days slipped by and she began to notice me. She looked at my face furtively during work. She made an attempt to interpret my interior through a glimpse of my exterior. I knew she had had a nightmarish experience with Krishan and was now scared in case a rope turned out to be a snake. And, it wasn't until one fine day in early May (when everybody was out) that I went to her desk, took a chair opposite to her and said, 'Radhika! Do you know how much I like you, love you and want to marry you!' It was then that she found out the real man within me. At my sudden and sincere words, she had been shocked for a moment, but then she gradually managed to recover her lost equanimity.

'But it's all my side of the story,' I said again. 'Please be frank and tell me if you like, and perhaps love me, and whether you'd like to marry me.' After that, I had left her alone to think and decide.

For three consecutive days after this incident, we had no close conversation, except about things related to the paper. But on the fourth day, she handed me an envelope immediately I arrived at the office. Nothing was written on the face of the envelope though I knew it contained a message for me in the form of yes or no. Yet I wondered why was she driven to write me a letter when she could have easily told me what she thought. It would've taken her just a minute or two. Kinner wasn't in yet. He might come an hour or so late as usual, for he now had a long list of things to be done on his way to the office. He knew that Radhika and I would be there to take care of the office work.

I opened the envelope, took out the folded sheet of paper and began to read it, seated in my chair.

"Please excuse me for writing my mind to you instead of speaking. Although I am in possession of some informal education taken from my brother to compete with life, I remain the same simple and shy village girl at heart. The age of stupid emotions is now gone and I've to think twice, even thrice before I take a step. That's what my brothers too expect of me.

However, I've been thinking about your words day and night and have spent two sleepless nights to reach the right conclusion. I'm sorry for not being able to communicate with you in a proper manner for these few days. I'm sure a person of your calibre, intelligence and deep understanding would certainly forgive me for that.

Now I come to the hub of the matter. I still feel shy to name the word, but it's got to be said to make sense. Yes, I like you and adore you as a man, but I don't really know whether I love you or not. Please don't mind my saying so. But if my brothers agree to it, I would certainly like to become your woman. You can call my *liking* for you *love,* but I really don't know what love is. I was told some years ago, when I had just emerged wounded from a murderous situation, that love was nothing but an infatuation, a stupidity. So, I really don't know whether my liking for you can be given the name of love or lust or what.

I've said enough. So please allow me to close the letter by repeating that you ask for my hand from my brothers. And, when they would ask me about it I would immediately say yes.

Radhika."

Having read the letter, I felt exalted. There was no point wasting a single second, so I went straight to Radhika, took her delicate, long-fingered hand in mine and kissed it. Then I kissed her hair, forehead and took her softly into my not-too-tight arms. She too, felt exhilarated and full of blood. Then soon, for fear of anyone coming I seated her back in her chair and took the one opposite for myself.

'That's my first ever love letter.' I kissed the letter in the grip of a delirium.

'I didn't know how to say that in spoken words,' she muttered, her hands trying to clean the spotless desk.

'But you've said it all so wonderfully and without using even one extra word. All precise and to the point as though any excessive word would make the meaning redundant. I like that. You've been well trained by Kinner. He's a genius. I've a high regard for him.' I kept on admiring anything and everything as though the whole world suddenly wore a new face.

'Thank you,' she said shyly, shiny pearls oozing from her eyes - dew drops of happiness.

And now, our love was four months old. Each day it had a new ply on. Life had begun to seem so charming, so splendid and so delectable that we both felt it was running too fast. We both wished everyone would go and leave us alone and together. Although until now we had told nothing to Kinner he, being clever and practical, in addition to being an artist and philosopher, must have realised that we'd developed a mature and durable bond between us, which would end in a marriage and nothing else. That was perhaps why he'd begun to keep away for a longer time than he had used to. Maybe he was waiting for one of us to pick the right moment and speak to him about it.

After apologising to me for his jibe about the article on Ghandi, Kinner had left the office to attend a meeting in the city, which had been organised by the local branch of Congress. When he returned after lunch, the same piece of news was weighing still more heavily on his head.

'That's what the bloody meeting was about,' he said, almost throwing himself into the chair.

'About increasing the power and prestige of Mr Jinnah?' I asked.

'What else could it be? This bloody Congress is a bunch of idiots, and that Mahatma, he seems more of a clown than a leader. First of all, they behaved as fools by leaving their ministries to be taken over by the Muslim League. So much so, that Jinnah succeeded in forming the ministry in the ancient stronghold of Congress, the North West Frontier Province that had never yielded to the pressure tactics of the Muslim League. And now, Bengal, Sind and Assam - all are taken over by the League. What worth was their protest against the war? You can't afford to lose all your potential political bases and then go on to launch a protest quite empty handed, can you?' Kinner seemed to have been terribly upset.

'I quite agree with you, Kinner. It was a wrong political move in the first place. They began to dig their own grave by doing so,' I ratified his arguments and goaded him to say more so he could disgorge all his inner venom for once.

'And now look at that buffoon again. The Cripps Mission had already handed Jinnah the most powerful lever, that no part of India would be forced to join the new state, rather the aspiring provinces would be given a new constitution and status equivalent to that of India. But this buffoon and bloody Congress, instead of thwarting those moves, have been holding political parleys with Jinnah by personally visiting him, like a child running after his parents or a pony after its mother.

'They've been attempting to wean him away from the demands of Pakistan and begging him like mendicants, holding true to their old history of grovelling at the feet of Muslim invaders. And what have they achieved out of it? Jinnah, whom nobody knew until yesterday, has been made larger than life. Now the leaders of Congress and this clown, all look like pygmies in front of him. Jinnah and his League have now gained so much power and prestige that even the British will have to bow before them, while the clown and Congress are wandering in the political wilderness. Begging receives no treasures, only alms. The treasures have to be battled for and won.' Kinner delivered a long lecture and turned breathless.

Kinner was quite correct on these issues because the only ministry not in the hands of the Muslim League was that of the Punjab where Si Khizar, as Chief Minister, ran the Unionist Ministry, which also contained non-Muslim elements. Mr Jinnah desired to see this Ministry named as a Muslim League Coalition Ministry because most of its Muslim members were now members of the Muslim League. On 20th March, Jinnah himself had gone to Lahore to ask Khizar to announce the Ministry as a Muslim League Coalition Ministry, but only Khizar did not agree. He wanted the regime of the Unionist Party to continue as had been agreed under the terms of

Sikander-Jinnah pact in Lucknow. Kinner was closely aware of all these developments.

'Just imagine,' began Kinner again, 'that Khizar had refused to condescend to the whims of Jinnah seven months ago. And now, after seven months, our clown is again fawning at his feet with a begging bowl in his hand asking for the impossible, and from the same cavorting Jinnah. Would you ever find a greater fool?' He finally hit the nail in the head.

'Why don't you write an article about it?' I suggested, for he was the chief editor of the paper.

'I'm thinking of doing that, but what difference will it make to these idiotic people?'

'It doesn't matter, as long as you record your historical verdict for posterity to see and evaluate,' I exhorted him and he began to jot down the points forthwith.

One day, some weeks later, when Kinner was in a relaxed mood after the publication of the paper, I asked him, 'Kinner, you might've forgotten by now that you're a sculptor, a painter and a philosopher at heart.'

Hearing me he grew a little sad, inhaled a deep breath and said, 'No Arya, I've forgotten nothing. I know what I was and still am. You don't have to remind me of my real work but if you have done so, I'm grateful to you. In fact, this idea of running a paper, establishing myself economically and helping my siblings to settle down - all this was an essential part of my plan.

'I've seen my mother suffering the way she did after my father's death. The poor woman lived a tragically wretched life and with no respite until she died in harness. You know all that don't you? And then my brothers - none of them had seen a moment of happiness. I still remember how hard they all had worked when they were still infants, and for paltry money at the shops of mean and salacious *halwais*. They toiled in the fields of farmers and sold their labour in the squares of the city, loading and unloading bricks and mortar, mixing sand and cement at the building sites but were always rebuked and abused when it came to paying their wages.

'In the face of all this, my art as a sculptor and my paintings were nothing. They were my personal pursuits, which could've brought me enough to survive but it wasn't a question of myself alone. I had to think about them also. And do you remember the day when I came to ask you to teach me, to which you gracefully agreed. It was then that my odyssey began. Probably I was and am the Ulysses reborn, or maybe Jarra the Bheel, who killed Krishna, I really don't know,' he said and laughed like the beat of a drum.

'And you must be holding in your memory my precarious moments when I wandered in the wilderness among destruction and ruins. You people, Krishan, Kabir and you, might've had the premonition that I was and would always be a lover of nihilism but that wasn't true. In fact, I was going through the process of understanding my own personality, my own existence and my own capabilities, if any. I was weighing and assessing everything around me, about my family's entity and about what chances there were for me to succeed. There could be no better place for such musings than those secluded and abandoned ruins where nobody in the right frame of mind would go. It was there that I thought things out. It was there that I put my priorities in order. And, it was then that I read all the books I could lay my hands on. I'm my own teacher, as you know for yourself. I still remember *you, and Krishan and Kabir,* coming to me in those desolate ruins and asking me to accompany you to rallies and processions, which I always turned down furiously because my priorities then were different from yours just as my situation was.

'I'm pretty certain you understood my position to an extent if others didn't. And, Arya, do believe me, I haven't got even a speck of the sense of victimisation now in my psyche, as I used to have then. I just treat it as my rich experience now, which none of you could have. A sense of experience is a virtue while the sense of victimisation is an evil. The former leads you to progress and the latter to devastation of your own personality through lifelong grudges against others, always holding others responsible for wronging you - it's paranoia. In the latter case, you never really make any effort to change or improve yourself because you hold yourself responsible for nothing. Rather you blame others, even for your personal weaknesses. It's all self-pity and paranoia that leads to schizophrenia in the end. I'm sorry I'm going on too much, but coming to the point of my arts, I'll certainly start it again when my mundane responsibilities are over. You probably don't know, but we have some more people in the household now. Nishad and Ahir have got married and have brought their respective wives home. There was no pomp and show, and no marital rites except that our families gathered together and the deals were done. People know it only in our part of the village. No one knows on your side. Nag says he's too old to get married now and Bhil has refused, and I've no right to compel anyone. It's all their own free will and pleasure. My only responsibility now is Radhika, that's all.' This was where Kinner finally concluded his tirade.

I'd listened to each word he spoke with rapt attention, without even coughing, for that might cause distraction or even irritation. In fact, I'd never expected such a long story from him.

'Am I a good listener?' I said, trying to be slightly naughty.

'An excellent one?' Kinner said and smiled, his eyes flickering. I knew his final sentence had concerned Radhika.

Pride, Passion and Prejudice

To my utmost delight, a magical change had now begun to appear in Radhika, both in matters of adorning herself and in the build-up of her self-confidence. Previously, she was too reserved, too fragile and vulnerable, fraught within herself and lacking in the confidence to speak out, although she managed to hide it all in the guise of nicety and under the veneer of good manners. There could have been several factors behind that passive behaviour, two of which were most obvious to me. The biggest one could be her coming from the lowest rungs of the society and being looked down upon by the caste people. The second one was probably the mistake of getting carried away by her fascination for Krishan, which was nothing but an imbecility of youth. That relationship was a vile self-delusion. Nobody had blamed Krishan except his father and mother but they too, had accused him of having chosen a low-caste girl in lieu of an upper class one. On the contrary, Radhika had not only fallen in the eyes of her mother and brothers, but also in those of the village. The whole episode had left her irrecoverably humiliated. If it were not for Kinner making her swim out of that murderous whirlpool in time, she might have drowned.

Although the deep sores and wounds had now healed, the blemishes hadn't completely vanished. Kinner probably understood it all and he must have prejudged my attachment and attitude towards her long time ago. He must have seen through me as a person who, like him, was rebellious and scorned the rubbish of rotten values and hollow traditions. I had had absolutely no idea of the working of Kinner's mental machinery when he invited me to join the paper. In reality, I was totally blind to his foresight. Only now did I realise how much he understood me, how much he understood his sister and our mutual need for each other. When he noticed Radhika sprucing herself up again he was simply thrilled. Perhaps that was why he now kept away from the office for as long as he could.

Although Radhika's sobriety and modesty, as innate qualities, were still intact, she began to dress more smartly. I had never seen her in a *saree* before but now she had commenced wearing it with subtle makeup and a more modern hairstyle. Her medium sharp bright eyes now twinkled like two stars on the clear sky of her dusky face. Her eyes would now flicker when she talked - a kind of body language to punctuate the speech. Her worn out, gaping sandals had been replaced by elegant shoes made from soft leather, and her despicable, long laced handbag had given its place to a reasonably modern purse.

'Radhika! You look really gorgeous now; a ravaging beauty.' I'd whispered into her ear the other day, heaving a deep sigh.

'Will you shut your mouth or I should tweak your ears? Do you want me to revert to my old ways?' she threatened me with mock blushes and stiletto-drawn eyes.

'I implore you never do that, for I'll die even then,' I'd said, folding my hands in an unreal apology. It had made her laugh heartily with her cheeks acquiring all the seven colours of the rainbow.

1945 was a year of tremendous political upheavals, unparalleled alignments and re-alignments and indissoluble conflict between the League and Congress. Jinnah's attitude towards Khizar had grown increasingly obdurate and audacious. He was disinclined to do what the former wished him to do - announce the Unionist Ministry as a Muslim League Coalition Ministry. The whole political environment was in deep turmoil. Kinner was often too preoccupied to take

Radhika home in the evening after the closing the office. Ever since he had started the paper, she had taken the back seat on his bicycle. With her legs dangling on either side, Kinner would drive slowly and steadily while making erratic conversation. Since the beginning of May, he had given this most coveted duty to me and I had been over the moon to assume it. My Radhika was floating in the air when she knew she was to be driven home by me. But we never went straight to the village; instead, we tried to extract maximum benefit from this God-given privilege by breaking our journey at various places such as the Company Bagh, Lawrence Road, or the bank of the *Sultanwind* canal.

To begin with, Radhika did have some inherent fears but they all vanished soon after Kinner gave her courage by saying: 'Life doesn't and shouldn't travel from home to work and vice versa. There's more to it than that.'

In fact, he must have known that we'd developed a deep bond between us and he endeavoured to encourage us. Kinner was only a year older than me but behaved as several years my senior: as the father of Radhika. I liked it too, to be so treated. Maybe, I thought, he anticipated that we would approach him soon, seeking permission to marry. But Radhika and I were just biding time until, one rainy day at the end of July, the worst happened.

The monsoon season had taken its firm hold over everything. It had set in a little earlier this year. Normally it began in the first week of August but this year it arrived too soon. The first flurry took place in mid-July and then stopped as though the clouds had run out of water. The parched earth soaked up the first showers of rain without much effort, like a gigantic empty pan placed on a mammoth furnace flaming with huge fires. The earth was too thirsty to quench its thirst with this tiny amount of raindrops. A week or so went past without a drop and the earth turned dry and dusty again. The farmers began to look up into the heavens in desperation, and then in stark astonishment when they found the skies devoid of a single stray cloud. But then suddenly one day, thick, black, bloated clouds came back from their short stint in some foreign land. It was the last week of July. The first few showers fell intermittently but then the whole heaven became so evenly filled with puffy and sombre ambassadors of rain (*meghadutas in Sanskrit*) that the waterfall knew no bounds. It was incessant, persistent and torrential.

It was in this day that Radhika and I had mounted the bicycle to return to the village. The perfidious monsoon turned out to be treacherous and betraying. When we had embarked upon our journey, it was a poor and scanty downpour, but just as we crossed the railway level-crossing, everything altered magically as though transmogrified. Thick and stony drops of rain began to hit us, and I, as the driver of two fates, found it incredibly hard to stand the thrash of the brazen *meghaduta*. We were completely blinded by the shots piercing our eyes. What seemed like trillions of gallons of water left us drenched and dazed. The brimming filthy, muddy puddles all along the road offered us no respite either. One of them proved itself to be a receptacle - into which we slipped and fell. When we emerged out of that turbid pond, the flurry of rain-bullets grew still faster and more forceful.

Fortunately, there was a straw-cottage on the side of the road and we swiftly scurried in, leaving the bicycle in the puddle so it would get a good ablution. Luckily, there was no one else in the cottage. Inside, it sounded as though a hail of stones were falling on its roof. Radhika was shivering with cold. Her lips had turned bluish and the water ran from her hair and clothes like unceasing streams. By coincidence she was wearing *salwaar-kameez* (trousers and shirt) that day. Had it been a sari, it would have turned transparent and her whole curvy physique would have revealed. Even her present clothes were sticking to her body, clinging so tightly and resolutely that the visibility of her taut breasts became more apparent.

Radhika suddenly caught me watching her contours avariciously and hungrily. At once her eyes dilated and she looked at me wrathfully and turned away, so that her back was towards me. But her back too, looked alluring due to its magically receding contours that formed a concave at the waist. I could resist no more and took her into my arms from the back. She jumped up as if electrocuted and released a sharp scream, at which I let loose my grip amid shameless laughter.

But just then, someone badly battered by the rain entered the cottage. When that person entered, I had my back towards him but because Radhika was facing me she caught a glimpse of the newcomer. I saw her growing pale and puzzled with her eyes askew and rolling, now at me and then at the man. Immediately I turned round and saw my father Shiv standing in front of me. It was a weird confrontation in weird weather and in weird circumstances.

'You...?' He screamed like a person who suddenly confronts a snake, and looked sharply at me, slowly retreating to the far corner. I was dazed. It was like a trap.

'Who's she?' my father roared at the pitch of his voice but I couldn't think of what to say.

'Do you hear me? Who is she, I ask?' he thundered again, looking furiously and spitefully at me.

'She's my wife,' I managed to muster my strength to say words that astonished me.

'What?'

'I'm sorry but it's true. We're already married,' I lied, though sounding like speaking nothing but truth. I wondered where I had got the strength from. By now I was starting to recover from the sudden shock.

'So-this-scavenger-is-your-wife,' he uttered his words one by one. 'Now, don't you enter my house or show me your face all your life, understand?' he yelled at me, and rushed out of the cottage like part of the roaring storm. I didn't bother to call him back. There was no point. We had never seen eye to eye with each other all these years; why bother now? I was living in that house because of my mother, Parvati, and not because of him. I was relieved that the worst was over. I was gratified that I had protected Radhika when she needed me most.

When he had gone and I had recuperated, I turned towards Radhika, who was in tears, aghast and terrified. I said nothing but opened my arms for her to fall in. She gazed intently at me, looked towards her left, then right, and then came running like a fallen leaf and threw herself into my embrace.

When the torrential rain turned into downpour and allowed us an ephemeral reprieve, we got out, took the submerged bicycle out of the bubbling puddle and made our way to the village, heading straight to Radhika's house. None of the brothers was home yet but Soma and Sujata were there. I had met them quite a few times over these past weeks and was deeply touched by their simplicity, straightforwardness and sanguinity. They had no qualms about what they were - poor girls from poor families, uneducated, down-to-earth and without the misgivings that my people had. We (Radhika and I) decided to wait for the men folk, especially Kinner, before reaching a tangible decision although it had already been imposed on us. The girls made some tea and handed a glass to me, which I held in my hand and began to take a tour of Kinner's corner while sipping it. There were quite a few half-finished works scattered here, waiting to be completed by the artist.

Kinner had made some improvements to the house. Two more bedrooms had been added and the kitchen had been extended. The outer courtyard was made of mud while the verandah where the kitchen and the other rooms led from, was now laid with brickwork. Kinner had once told me that he would eventually move to the city while his brothers would retain this house. In fact, it was just a little more than a shelter and could not be called a house by any account, but what else could be done in those circumstances? The outer threshold seemed like a fortified embankment against the flooding pond. All the rainwater from up the village accumulated in this pond, on the banks of which these people lived in mud houses with thatched roofs. Kinner had replaced the old roof with a brick-laid one but all other attributes, such as mosquitoes, flies, creepers, diseases and a host of other ills that went with the situation, remained. I wondered why these people were ostracised to the lowest part of the villages and towns. Even in the city, their likes had been thrown to the dirtiest slums. With no way of earning any money except by cleaning the toilets of the caste people for the most paltry remuneration, it was an abject life, known only to the sufferers who had lived it for centuries, and were still living it. Assigning them the new title of *harijans* was meant to protract their endless suffering, nothing more. They needed no sympathy but the means of supporting themselves to a decent standard: land, capital and skills, but no pity or mercy. How painful it would be for my father, to see me living this wretched life.

To live in such a place and in such an abject state of poverty, to be born from the womb of drastic deprivation, to be denied every right as a human being, to be despised from the day one and then to come out of this hellish nether world by one's own initiative, self-induced discipline and aspiration, was by no means an easy task. Yet, Kinner had done it. Millions died in the incipient stages of such life from common ailments, from malnutrition, from the cruelty of the alleged upper classes, and from God-endowed annihilations. There could have been all those would-be Kinners and Ambedkars, but all were finished at the hands of inequality, hostility, malevolence and maltreatment of the Aryans. I began to feel a terrible detestation for myself and for the people I belonged to. Nowhere in the whole world was seen the kind of inhuman discrimination, racism, fascism, Nazism and apartheid as it was apparent in India. Nowhere else in the world existed a society that was divided into *varnas* on the basis of people's birth and occupation, as it was in India. Nowhere in the world did people enjoy killing other human beings as they did in India.

India was the only wretched and depraved land on the globe that was despicable because of what the Brahmin had done. Every piece of land is God-given; it's nature's playground and is good. But the people inhabiting it make it despicable. The land of India was great too, but when the Aryans entered it, they brought their savagery, their barbarism and their brutal bestiality with them. And the Brahmin stood at the top rung of the hierarchy to make such discriminative laws. He was a crude man with a wisp of hair left untrimmed in the centre of his scalp, a ludicrous parasite who gnawed into the souls of these Dravidians, who worshipped cows while, if threatened by death, would eat their flesh also. The Brahmin was the many-faced monster, nay, even more, an evil. A Brahmin could do anything to a *dalit* woman except for kissing her face for fear of being maligned or sullied by the touch of the *achhoot,* or the untouchable, as though the sex-act involved no touching. The Brahmin even kissed the *dalit* woman, drank her piss and ate her excreta too, although he hid it all from others. The Brahmin was the most cunning impostor, a million-faced devil and the wicked liar whose mendacity had no other parallel.

I had once read a story about the cunning and craft of a most inhuman and brazen Brahmin, who did everything he could to kill an innocent dalit. This hapless dalit had a small daughter and a wife. He had only just convalesced from a long sickness, which had left him extremely debilitated and emaciated. His frail face and enfeebled body was a dreadful sight. They lived in a solitary mud-hut on the outskirts of the village. His wife, another frangible figure, barely managed to keep the hearth smouldering by collecting stray tassels of wheat from the fields after harvest. Their small daughter, as happened in those primitive days, was to be engaged and the ceremony could not be accomplished without the Brahmin of the village. The man, in consultation with his wife, decided to go to the Brahmin, who lived in a sprawling house in the upper caste area.

Instead of going empty handed to the *Brahmin-devta* (the small god Brahmin) the man scythed a good bundle of fodder from what he had sown for his own frail cow, put it on his head and walked off.

'You should eat something before you go, for it might take some time,' his wife said from behind him.

'Don't worry, I'll be back soon and eat it,' he replied from under the weight of the bundle.

He took the bundle off from his head and put it on the floor on the threshold of the Brahmin's house, and stood there, for he was not permitted to enter the house because he was from a low caste.

The Brahmin saw him standing there and asked imperiously, 'Oy, what do you want?'

'Forgive me, Panditji, for not being able to come to you earlier because I was sick with typhoid. I've nothing else to offer you except this bundle of fodder for your cow,' the man entreated in apology.

'But what do you want from me?' Panditji demanded rudely.

'I implore you to accomplish the engagement ceremony of my daughter. We've made everything ready at home. If only you would pay a visit, read the *mantras* from the scripture and finalise it, we'll be highly grateful to you. Rest assured that we've made every arrangement to preserve your purity,' the man beseeched the Brahmin with folded hands, reducing himself to nothingness.

The Brahmin, although sitting idle holding a hand-fan and fluttering it at his face owing to the hot summer, reprimanded him, saying, 'What the hell do you think of me? Do I have no other business to do except your ceremony? I'm too busy now and shall see to it some other day, understand?' The man implored him again, falling prostrate on the ground in front of him, trying to make him see the urgency of the ceremony. The cunning Brahmin thought for a second and found the right artifice.

'Listen! Let me think about it. In the mean while, you take the axe from that corner and cut the log of wood laying outside in the open yard into small splinters for the hearth. Okay?' The Brahmin ordered.

The man thought the small god might well deign to go if he did his job. So, he picked up the axe and proceeded to cut the wood. But when he saw a very thick and solid tree trunk lying flat on the ground, of a size that would need half a dozen brawny men to just move it let alone cut it, he was terrified. The axe he was holding was so blunt and small that it wouldn't even cut a small twig.

The Brahmin came out and cried, 'What're you waiting for now? Do you want me to go with you or not? If you do want me to go then finish the work quickly.'

So the man - without a morsel of food down his throat since that morning and still feeling giddy and dizzy with weakness, began to strike the trunk with his full might but without even leaving a scar on the wood.

'Come on, strike hard, use all the force of your arse and cut it. Don't play with it like a child. Are your balls dried up?' came the Brahmin's encouragement. The man, although already out of breath, was enraged by the Brahmin and attacked the hard trunk with continuous strokes until he was totally exhausted and collapsed, never to rise again.

When the Brahmin realised the man was dead he became restive and fidgety. The fear of other people witnessing the scene of death from behind their closed doors set him shuddering and perspiring immensely. But just then it began to rain, holding people inside their homes. The rain continued until evening and then the evening surrendered itself to night. The dead body was still laying on his land, which was a great danger, flagrant proof of his having killed an *achhoot*. Then, in the dead of night, the Brahmin took a torch and a rope and went to the place where the corpse lay drenched in muddy water. With the help of a strong stick, the Brahmin picked one leg of the body (for touching it might have sullied him) and tied it into the already prepared knot in the rope. Then he began to drag the corpse by the trapped leg until he crossed the border of his own land. He then loosened the knot with the help of the same stick, took the leg out of it and threw away both the rope and the stick into the far off bushes. He himself was breathless by now but was relieved that the corpse did not lie in his land anymore.

Next morning, everyone in the village saw the corpse of the untouchable and knew who had killed him but no one said a thing and the Brahmin got away with the murder of an innocent dalit.

The recollection of the story maddened me, infuriated me and saddened me at the same time. And, suddenly my attention was focused on Krishan the upholder of Hindi, the supporter of Hindu and Hindustan, the active worker of the Hindu Mahasabha, one of the new breed of puritans, who, until yesterday, was trying to entice innocent Radhika - a dalit girl - and had succeeded, too. I felt like shooting all those who feigned what they didn't do and did what they didn't believe. But just then, I heard footsteps entering the house. It was Kinner and his two brothers, Nishad and Ahir. The elder two had still not arrived, and the time was 9pm.

As Kinner stepped in and saw Radhika's face - distraught and dismayed – he looked askance at me. I nodded to him silently, meaning not to worry. Then the three of us - Kinner, Radhika and I - went to sit in Kinner's bedroom on his insistence and as a matter of urgency.

'Well, what's up?' he asked me.

'Nothing much, Kinner, nothing to worry about,' I began to say. 'Just one thing. The time has now arrived when Radhika and I should get married. The sooner the better.'

'But tell me what's happened all of a sudden?' He looked inquisitively into my eyes, at which I had to tell him the whole incident of my father having seen us together and what had followed thereafter.

Having listened, Kinner sank into some bottomless chasm, probably a deep hole of uncertainties. Radhika was looking silently, now at Kinner and then at me, knowing not what to say or do. Kinner took well over ten minutes to emerge from his meditation.

'Well, if we want to arrange a reasonable marriage then we'll have to wait for a few months, say at least three. It's not because of anything else but money. And if we don't mind what people might say, then there's no problem, we can do it whenever we wish. The choice is yours,' he concluded, and then looked at both Radhika and I.

'Look Kinner, I'm not a conservative or a traditional person and far less a believer in rites and customs, and nor are you. So why do we bother about squandering money on inanities? And what will come out of it anyway? But I haven't consulted Radhika on that matter yet because it all happened quite suddenly, like a sliding stone from heaven. You'd better ask Radhika yourself of what she thinks,' I said and quietened.

Kinner looked at Radhika's face inquisitively. But she bowed her head down without opening her lips.

'Yes, Radhika! Speak up and tell me, what do you want?' Kinner asked her, still thinking, which reflected on his brow in the form of a furrow.

'What can I say? I'm happy the way you decide,' she hardly managed to say.

'All right! But now tell me in all frankness; do you like Arya? Would you be happy with him? Is it all in accord with your wishes? Do you consent to your marriage with him?' Kinner asked her so much and in such a direct way that I was shaken myself. Radhika might've felt more incensed but she kept quiet with her head down and eyes fixed on the floor.

'Look Kinner, however wise you may be, this is not the way you should ask her these things. Let me go out and then ask what you may,' I said and got up to go.

Out in the yard, I busied myself listening to Nishad and Ahir, seating myself on a cot near them. They were talking about today's torrential rainfall and the way water had flooded the streets and bazaars nullifying every activity, and the way they had reached the village wading through overflowing puddles, seeing the crops submerged and even the highlands completely awash. I listened to their experience, interposing here and there with my approval. In fact, my whole attention was focused on what Kinner and Radhika might be discussing at that precise moment. But I didn't have to wait for long. Kinner came out of the room after about fifteen minutes and wreathed in smiles. It needed no word said. Everything was quite obvious.

On a Sunday in the middle of August, we all went to the Golden Temple and sat in front of the *akaal takht*. We were a dozen or so people in all - none from my side, all from the Radhika's. She put a garland of fresh flowers round my neck and I put one round hers, and so we entered into wedlock. No scriptures were sung, no rounds around the holy book were performed, no incantations made and no flamboyancy displayed. But yet, we were husband and wife, man and woman and Adam and Eve.

And after this self-styled ceremony we all went to a nearby restaurant and enjoyed our festivity with piquant dishes amidst jokes and laughter. By now we had, with the help of Kinner and his brothers, hired out a small shelter in the city, which was only ten minutes away from Kinner's office. After the merry lunch we all went together to our place, our first new home, sat for an hour and then the lot left us alone to consummate our marriage.

The pride and prejudice of the caste people had failed ignominiously and passion came out victorious through all calamities.

Wreckage of Simla Conference

The war had come to an end and Britain had come out victorious though not without substantial losses both in terms of men and economy. Morale too, seemed to have dropped significantly as an aftermath and the British were not in a position to protract the Raj for any longer, especially when their tried and tested template of forming a federation had met a sterile conclusion. They were in fact mentally ready to hand over power to Indian hands but the only question was, to whom? The war of attrition was ubiquitous and overtly observable between the two claimants of power - Congress and the Muslim League - throughout the country but more so in the Punjab and Bengal. Jinnah, by now, had fortified all the power bases bequeathed to him by the Congress via its 'Quit India' movement. It now meant that Jinnah and League had the power of veto to block any attempt made by the British in the devolution of power if it did not suit them. Such were the circumstances when Wavell convened the Simla Conference to form an Indian Executive Council composed of purely Indian elements under the existing constitution.

When the Simla Conference was announced, Kinner invited me to his office (I was now sharing the office with Radhika) and urged me to make a trip to Simla together with Radhika on behalf of the paper and report developments from there. His courteous offer meant killing two birds with one stone, making the trip both official and recreational. Belated though it was, it was our honeymoon.

'Kinner, why don't you go while we take care of the paper? I'm sure your knack for such matters is better and sharper than mine.' I tried to test him, to see if he really meant what he had said.

'Try to understand, Arya, it's an opportunity that has suddenly cropped up, and it'll give you people a chance to have some time together, away from the usual maelstrom. In fact, I wish Radhika to have a change after all these years. She badly deserves one,' he pleaded assertively and I was convinced.

'Eva! We're going to Simla for our honeymoon,' I told her as I returned to my desk. Radhika was a long name to pronounce, so I had given her a new name of love - a personalised modern version of Eve.

'You must be joking, Sona!' she uttered, altogether disbelieving me, and using the name she used for me in moments of love - an Indian version of gold.

'I'm not joking at all, honestly,' I tried to assure her. 'Kinner is organising our trip.'

Now she believed me because she knew Kinner could do it.

'That's very nice of him,' she said admiringly and gleefully.

'Of course it is, but we'll have to do another job over there.'

'What's that?' She looked sharply into my eyes.

'To send him the report of the Simla Conference.'

'And, how long we're going for?' she asked me as though the conference would be last for a month.

'I don't know yet, but maybe for a week or two, and that's about it,' I told her, making my own estimate.

'When are we going?' she asked again with her eyes flickering.

'Next week,' I said, as though she were already thinking about which clothes to take with her and what more to buy, as modern Eves always did in contrast to the antiquated one, who preferred roaming around naked like her Adam.

We spent most of the following week shopping, buying loose cloth in varied colours, prints and materials and getting the tailors to stitch them for Eva. It was quite a job to do her bazaar (Indian version of shopping) because if you managed to find the right cloth for a suit it would be difficult to find a matching chunni, the head cloth. And if you found a chunni of her liking first, then you wouldn't find equally suitable cloth to make the suit. The textile shops were mostly around the Golden Temple and there were none that we left untried. It was a real test of my patience, labour and assiduity to find the right material for seven suits and matching chunnis. Now they were all with the tailor, waiting to be stitched.

Kinner had instructed us to take some warm clothes with us as it might be colder in Simla, and there could well be a sudden snowfall. I was certainly astonished when Kinner had said that although he had never been to Simla or any other hill station himself. He listened to the radio very regularly so he might've heard such an announcement made. Eva was, however, thrilled to imagine the scene of a snowfall. We had seen many hailstorms in Punjab but never a snowfall. So, the next three days were spent diligently purchasing some woollen sweaters, shawls and mufflers, etc.

'Eh, Sona, look there in that shop. What a beautiful shawl's that!' Eva would exclaim and lead me to the shop holding my hand like a mother. The same delectable commentary went at the sight of sweaters and mufflers. So, until the evening preceding the day of departure, we were so busy that we didn't find time for making love even. And, if I complained grumpily, Eva said she would compensate all my losses in Simla.

The next morning we commenced our journey, travelling from Amritsar to Pathankot, then to Kangra hills and then on to Simla. It took us literally a whole day to reach our destination. Everyone we met on the train wished us a long and happy marriage, and I wondered how they had known that we were a newly married couple. It was not until we reached Simla that I realised that Eva's crimson suit with silver embroidery and matching chunni had leaked out all the secrets. During our journey in the small train that ran only across the hilly tracts, I was fascinated by its slow and snaky gait. Eva, drew closer to me in delirium so that I, instead of feeling squashed, felt as though I was being cuddled. It was only when the train finally reached Simla that I emerged from its miraculous magic spell and, fell into another - the spell of Eva's charm.

The Volcano

We had managed to book a reasonably priced hotel-room in the town right below the Mall and began to settle down. It was quite cold in Simla and we thanked Kinner for the timely suggestion of woollens.

'What time of the year do you get snow here?' I asked the waiter when he came to take our first order.

'Anytime, Sir. There's no hard and fast rule. It's was snowing even last week but it's all melted away now.' The boy seemed quite garrulous and sharp of the tongue.

Our first order of tea with biscuits was delivered in fifteen minutes. The service seemed good going by that measure. Eva had changed her clothes and had now emerged from the bathroom with a fresh face and more vivacity than when we had entered the hotel.

'Come here, darling, have a cup of tea before getting on to the work of compensating my drastic losses,' I took to teasing her deliberately.

'Is that what you've been thinking about all the while from Amritsar? ch...ch...ch... A hopeless case, that's what you are,' she commented smiling. 'What would you expect of a famished man?' I cried.

'What? I've been feeding you every day, haven't I?'

'Only once in twenty-four hours. People eat three times a day in India,' I replied cheekily.

'You ravenous...' she cried back and began to hit me with the pillow taken from the bed, in cheerfully grinning retaliation. But I engulfed her in my arms, collapsed her on the sofa where I was seated and began to kiss and cuddle her in a commotion of giggles while she tried in vain to slip out of my hold.

'The tea's getting cold,' she tried to distract me.

'Never mind the tea, we'll order another one,' I warded off her fake warning.

'Listen, someone's coming towards our room,' she tried another trick.

'Let them,' I said and went on playing the cat and mouse game.

We continued wrestling, resisting, laughing and breathing each other's breath until we grew breathless and slumped motionless on the sofa, overcome by fatigue. Eva's face turned all pink, her hair had gone wild and her breasts went up and down like two balls sinking and floating in troubled waters. I put my head lightly on those undulating sculptures and descended deep into some nondescript sea.

As usual, Eva awoke earlier in the morning than I. She drew back the curtains and saw, much to her delight, that everything was covered with a milky sheet of snow. And still there was this persistent plummeting of soft white, cotton-like flakes on to the ground, over the trees, buildings and on the glass of the window where she now stood. She watched for a few minutes and then hurried towards the bed where I lay, still asleep.

'Wake up, Sona, wake up! It's snowing out there. Look, how crispy and wonderful the whole scene is,' she said ebulliently with her hand on my shoulder, stirring me.

'I want to sleep more, darling,' I said sleepily, turning my side.

'Come on, you shouldn't miss this great opportunity. Wake up, wake up,' she kept pulling and pushing me until I opened my eyes, sat up, yawned and got out of the bed. She pulled me by the arm and led me to the window. The whole thing was really mesmerising. It must've been a little windy out there as the snowflakes kept swinging and swerving.

'It's lovely, isn't it!' Eva exclaimed effervescently, her eyes glinting animatedly.

'Fantastic!' I said, as though spellbound. 'You know the message it gives us?'

'What?' she asked.

'It says, "Go to your bed and make love again" understand?' I whispered into her ear, holding and pressing her against me.

'Can't you think of anything else?' Eva asked, showing mild resentment.

'Not when we're on honeymoon,' I replied, making a face.

'Not-when-we-are-on-honeymoon,' she repeated my words by contorting her mouth and distorting the words one by one.

It made me laugh openly. 'Do it again. I like watching you do that.' I commended her act.

But she didn't do it again. Rather she kept watching the snowfall with a renewed zest and euphoria, and with the innocence of a child who had suddenly found something extremely extraordinary to play with. The only difference was that she was playing it with her eyes instead of her hands. I left her to her newly found amusement and slipped off into the bathroom to give myself a good wash.

The conference commenced the very next day. We had press passes as correspondents of Dalit Samachar, so we found no difficulty in seeking entry to the place. The place abounded with people, especially the leaders from Congress, the Muslim League, The Akali Dal and many other parties. Eva was amused to see various faces closely, that she had only seen in photographs until now, such as Gandhi, Nehru, Patel, Jinnah, Balder Singh and many more. There were quite a few white faces too, who seemed to be ruling the whole thing quite imperiously. Save for seeing these faces from close quarters, everything else was boring and tedious. There was a crowd of press reporters jotting down quick notes in their books just as I was doing. The place echoed with uproar, tumult, accusations and counter accusations, recriminations and hooting, which made one realise how uncivilised and uncouth all the people were. There was an acute expression of extreme dislike and rigidity on the faces of rival groups. Congressmen and Leaguers looked at each other with critical and accusing eyes. They were fuming, steaming and boiling with rage against each other. It seemed more of a fish market than a civil and cultured place for one to be in. I prognosticated that the whole conference would fail fruitlessly. All my fears and malaise were finally proved correct. The whole business ended in a fiasco. Consequently, the overall report that I wrote and sent to Kinner for publication was something like this.

Simla Conference Ends in Fiasco

The Simla Conference aimed at forming an Indian Executive Council composed of the Indian elements through juxtaposing the representatives of all the national political parties of the country, failed ignominiously. The deadlock came when Mr Jinnah insisted that the League must nominate all the Muslim members. He said that it suited the Congress to come into the scheme, for they stood for a united India, and once they came into power they would strangulate Pakistan. In the circumstances, it would not be in the interests of the

Muslim League to accept the offer. In a way, Mr Jinnah used his power of veto, which he had acquired by consolidating all the Muslim forces behind the League, to block all negotiations.

The tension escalated to new heights when Mr Jinnah proclaimed that only the Muslim League spoke for all the Muslims in India while the Congress spoke for the non-Muslims only, thereby rejecting the claims of Congress that it was the national political party with nationalist Muslims as its members. Mr Jinnah dismissed the nationalist Muslims as opportunists. Consequently, the conference got swaddled in argument, contradictory accusations and bitter recriminations, which lead to stalemate and virtual wrecking of the conference.

We spent one week and two days in Simla and then decided to return for two reasons: one was that we were rapidly running out of money, the second was the chill that had begun to intensify. Our woollens were now too feeble to protect us from the mounting cold. Eva was pretty happy and satisfied with all the new gifts I had bought her. She had absolutely no complains, nor had I, because she gave me plenty of what I wanted.

But when we reached Amritsar, we received the most terrible news. My mother, Parvati, had died. She had died only two days ago but Kinner told me that she had already been cremated, so I could not behold a last glimpse of her face. It was a harrowing experience for me to be denied the opportunity of seeing my mother's face for the last time. She was the one who had given me birth; she raised me up, trained me to stand, walk and then run. She was the one who cared for me and always said I was her gold. She taught me to talk and think, to compose tales and fill them with colour so they appeared lively and full of fascination. But now that mentor of mine was gone, gone forever. It was certainly an irreparable loss. No amount of sympathy and consolation could make up for my losses and lessen my suffering.

Eva suggested that I had a duty towards my father as the death of my mother was his loss too, and that I must go to Qila Vasudev and spend a couple of days, if not more, with him. In fact, I had had no opportunity until now to tell Eva how my father had deliberately disparaged me, condemned and belittled me over the years. He would have forced me into becoming a man of law, a profession I most hated. And just because I didn't do what he obstinately desired me to do, he had become angry retaliatory and vituperative. He was as headstrong and obdurate as Shiva, the god after whom he had been named. The mythical Parvati had always suffered at his hands, and so had my mother at my father's. You couldn't tell your wife such things immediately after the marriage and during the merrymaking of the honeymoon, could you? Everything must take its ordained course and time, for otherwise the whole world would run into chaos, just as the Simla conference had. As a matter of fact, this conference should have been held ages ago, before things had been aggravated to this extent. The only plea the feringhee could now give was the war, but then, who was responsible for jumping into it? India didn't want any war with anyone. Then why was it shoved into this seething cauldron? In reality, most people were like my father, Shiv, who did wrong things at the wrong time; they never righted the wrongs, rather they wronged the rights.

Despite Eva's cajoling attempts to persuade me to go and visit my father, I resisted by saying, 'Have you forgotten what he called you - a scavenger girl?' But she said she didn't mind it, which deeply astonished me. I was amazed at the extent of tolerance God had given these Eves. I didn't want to see my father's face. I knew he would blame me for my mother's death because I had married a scavenger girl. I don't say that my mother would have approved of what I did, rather I believe that she would have been equally perturbed. What I actually mean is that my father might have bombarded my mother with venomous words about me and about my mother's *devil-producing womb*. He had done so many times before, resulting in her chronic sickness - the real cause of her decrepitude. He might have done it again in my absence, which caused her death. I didn't want to face the man who vilified my mother's womb. And, even if I went to see him to share his grief, how would I be able to stand and see the weeping Banyan tree, the moaning and groaning of the village earth, tears in the eyes of crops, and the wailing walls of the house, and all those things that retained the imprint of my mother's touch? Would it be possible for me to offer consolation when I was relentlessly disconsolate myself?

And if a conference could fail why couldn't I? Of course I could. It was no more a question of my mother's death but also a question of *Bharat Mata* or Mother India, who seemed to be on the verge of death because brazen, intransigent and uncompromising leaders were bent upon cutting it into fragments. When I compared them with my father, I was disgusted. Shiva didn't like Ganesha, his elephant son, and Shiv, my father, didn't like me, a scribbler. So how could I like him? And, these allegedly politically correct leaders, did they like or care a penny about mother India's millions of children? No, they didn't. Then why would the children care about them?

Having thought through all the pros and cons of the matter, I reached a conclusion and announced it to Eva, my scavenger girl. I had absolutely no intention or even inclination to go to Qila Vasudev, at least not yet. I might go at some other time in the days to come.

'Do as you please, Sona,' Eva said. 'I can't compel you anymore.'

Disruption and Frustration

The general elections, which had been shelved for many years owing to the war, were now announced. The announcement caused an enormous stir throughout the country, especially in the Punjab where there were four major contenders for power, namely: the Muslim League, Congress, the Unionists and the Akalis. Soon the soil of Punjab began to rage with frenzied activity. Workers and volunteers of all the parties jumped into the arena, preparing and checking voters' lists, undertaking canvassing campaigns, organising rallies and processions and causing unprecedented tumult and turbulence. Tongas, rickshaws and trucks mounted with loudspeakers suddenly sprang up and began to throng the roads, streets and by-lanes of all the cities and villages. All the parties treated these elections as a question of life or death. It was now or never.

The clamour continued for over a month until the day of the elections. Kinner and I were eagerly awaiting the results. It had been a neck-to-neck fight throughout. When the results were finally declared the Muslim League had won a landslide victory with 73 seats. Congress had 51 seats, the Unionist Party 19, Akalis 21 and the independent candidates had 11 seats. Despite the League's emergence as the largest party in the Punjab Legislative Assembly, Sir Khizar Hayat Khan formed his coalition Ministry with the support of the Congress and the Akalis, much to the dismay of Mr Jinnah and the Muslim League. It was a matter of political expediency and Khizar had to do a lot of manoeuvring to form his Ministry. The results of the elections clearly indicated that the Muslims of the Punjab were solidly behind the Muslim League and were aspiring to see Pakistan made a reality, with whole of Punjab as one of its provinces.

'I'm not surprised at all to see Khizar having formed his Ministry,' said Kinner, 'because even if the League had tried their best to do it, non-Muslims would never have backed them. But *now*, it is very unlikely that this Ministry will work smoothly, for the League will never let it.'

'I quite agree with you on that,' I corroborated Kinner's vision.

Soon enough, his prophecy began to come true. Far from running smoothly, the Assembly became an arena of mutual recriminations and disruptions and, at times, even physical wrangling. As the dream of Pakistan began to transform into reality, the Sikhs and Hindus of the Punjab, afraid that the League might take the whole of Punjab into Pakistan, in which case they would have to live under the mercy of the Muslims forever, put forward 'A Case for A New Sikh Hindu Province'.

The Labour Party of England, having had the agenda of independence of India as one of their crucial issues on their manifesto, had won the elections of 1946. So, the question of granting freedom to India was now their top priority. The new Prime Minister, Mr Attlee, took keen interest in the formation of plans for the transfer of power to Indian hands. The result was the Cabinet Mission Plan. The plan made a serious attempt to meet the Muslim League's point of view halfway and yet preserve the unity of India. The plan provided limited powers for the centre. The Constituent Assembly to be set up was to have three-tier compulsory grouping. Section A was to consist of Madras, Bombay, UP, Bihar, the Central Provinces and Orissa. Section B was to consist of Punjab, Northwest Frontier

Province, Sind and Baluchistan; and Section C was to consist of Bengal and Assam.

The phrase 'compulsory grouping' triggered uproar and controversy because the Sikhs and Hindus of the Punjab did not want to remain in the Muslim dominated section. As a result, the Shiromani Akali Dal submitted a memorandum to the Cabinet Mission, stating, "As an alternative to the existing province of the Punjab, a new province may be carved out as an additional provincial unit in the united India of the future, and in such a way that all the Sikh shrines be included in it as also a substantial majority of the Sikh population of the existing province of the Punjab."

Congress, too, was against this compulsory grouping and suggested the splitting of the Punjab. The papers carried the official statement of the Indian National Congress: "...there must be no compulsion to any province or a part of a province by another province. The Congress cannot be a party to any such compulsion or imposition against the will of the people ... the rights of the Sikhs in the Punjab should not be jeopardised. In the event of any compulsion, a province or a part of a province has the right to take such action as may be deemed necessary."

This resolution immensely irritated the Muslim League, who condemned it by saying: "... these qualifying clauses confer the right of veto within a section on a province and, what is more absurd, on a part of a province and on the Sikhs in the Punjab."

The whole scenario generated volumes of anger and hostility between the Sikhs and Muslims of the Punjab.

It was on one of these unsettled days that Kabir Hussain came to see us in our office. He was seething with anger.

'I've been watching and reading your paper for sometime now, and what I find is you are against the Muslims. Why?' He challenged Kinner soon after throwing himself into a chair opposite to him.

'It's absolute nonsense and a wrong allegation against us. We're not against Muslims at all. Why should we be? The policy of our paper is a united India and anti-secessionism, that's all. If the Muslim League - as a political Party - is in favour of secession then we're against it,' Kinner clarified calmly.

'Well, in that case, don't you think the Sikhs are secessionist too, as they want to divide the Punjab?' Kabir Hussain quizzed.

'They'd do it only if, and mind you I say *only if*, the League forces the whole of Punjab to go into Pakistan, which now seems inevitable,' Kinner was still mild and composed.

'May I intervene if you people don't mind,' I said and found their gazes focused on me. 'Kabir, my brother, tell me one thing. What made you suddenly lose your marbles and turn a Leaguer from a Marxist?'

'It's my *personal* life and business, and you've no right to encroach upon that,' Kabir belched venomously.

'I'm very sorry,' I apologised to him and quietened.

I could see and feel that Kinner wanted him to take his leave. To expedite the process he asked Kabir if he would like a cup of tea. Kabir refused and got up to go - gravely grim and exasperated. Behind his back, Kinner winked to me and then smiled, hinting that I should ignore him.

My association with Kinner's paper had a great benefit for me. I was now closely involved in all kinds of political developments and knew what was happening everywhere. But there was also a demerit in that that life had become so preoccupied with all this that we seemed to have ceased being humans anymore. All our emotions and sentiments seemed to have been drained by the brazen political vicissitudes. Yet, another question that haunted me was how could you remain untouched by the political upheaval that was affecting you in every possible way. Anything that was influencing millions of lives could by no means be wished away. It had to be faced and dealt with.

However, coming to the point again, Congress had felt that when it came to forming the zonal governments, a province or a part of a province could opt out of the zone. It didn't accept the three-tier Government and much less the limitation on the power of the centre or the Constituent Assembly. Yet, when the Constituent Assembly was elected, its functioning was never smooth because the Muslim League boycotted it and proclaimed it to be void, invalid and illegal.

When the Governor-General invited Mr Nehru to form the Interim Government, the Muslim League joined it too, but only to disrupt its functioning. Congress did want it to function smoothly and without interference by the Viceroy so that later on it could be replaced by the National Government. But League members had entered the Government with the avowed object of causing disturbance so the Viceroy was compelled to interrupt all the time. It was the League's stratagem to undermine the Congress all along and provoke the interference of the Viceroy. As a consequence, the Cabinet Mission failed utterly and so did Viceroy Mr Wavell.

Eva had been sick from flu over the last few days and was still feeling low and listless - very much like the Cabinet Mission, Wavell and the Congress. The year 1946 was moving fast towards its end and the cold waves of December exasperated Eva's condition even more. She had been homebound all the week while I had been going to work, though only half-heartedly. On Sunday I decided to stay home all day. After a light breakfast, which I had prepared for the two of us, I sat by her side on the bed to give her a little massage as she had been complaining of severe congestion since this morning. She had developed breathing problems due to phlegm. Her chest made strange wheezing noises, like the working of a greaseless wheel. I took a small lump of balm and began to massage her back. She said her shoulders and neck were very stiff, so I also brought those areas under my operation.

When Eva felt some relief, she said, 'What if I died?'

That was a weird question to ask, most bizarre in my opinion. 'How can you, darling? You're only a baby yet. You shouldn't talk such things, should you?' I said affectionately.

'A baby! You must be joking. I'm twenty-nine,' she protested in a feeble voice.

'Yes, but people don't die at this age, do they? You've to live a long life, if only for my sake.'

'I just said it because of the way I feel, hopelessly drained of my strength.'

'Not to worry, your strength will soon return. Wait till the flu dies and you'll feel energetic again. Are you sure you haven't missed any dose of your medicine?'

'No. I've been taking it regularly.'

'That's like a good girl. And how do you feel now, after my masculine touch to your body?'

'Don't be difficult, thinking of evil things all the while,' she groused faintly with her mouth partly muffled under the pillow.

'I'm really sorry, darling. I just don't know why I begin to feel sexually active just at the sight of you, let alone a touch,' I whispered into her ear, bending over her body, making sure I had not strained her.

'It is all you men can think of,' she scolded me and shut her eyes.

When she felt sufficiently relieved, I gently turned her onto her back. She gave me a gloomy look and I could see that the deep dark lines under her eyes were becoming increasingly prominent. She had lost lot of weight and vitality in just a week. A terrible dread ran through my spine and tightened my heart, and I began to pat her subdued face and uncombed hair with all the love I could muster.

I decided there and then to take one week's leave from work and look after my Eva before it was too late. Kinner appreciated my decision. And in that week not only did Eva's health improve magically but also her way of thinking. And I had the opportunity to discovering numerous deep layers within her, which had lain mysteriously hidden, not only from me but also from her family, particularly Kinner.

As I dug deeper into her inner being that was veiled under her outer poise, I was shocked to find the depraved and sinister face of the Indian society, which had made her what she was - a badly dented and mangled human being. The caste-ridden society's longstanding tyranny over the non-Aryans had inflicted innumerable inner wounds on them which, over the years, had penetrated deeper and deeper, finding an unconscious acceptance in their souls. They believed that they were born inferior and were meant to stay in the servile service of the upper castes. The final result was that the sordid complex of inferiority no longer needed to be re-injected; it kept reappearing spontaneously in every new generation. The psychological acceptance of degradation as one's final fate is the acceptance of slavery - a kind of institutionalised debasement or mortification. Once this process of humiliation has been completed and innately accepted as God-given fate there's no sting left to bite back or to challenge the perpetrator with.

When Eva told me what her mother had admonished her a few days after the incident of the night of the crescent moon, I was really flabbergasted. She had told Eva that upper caste people were born to rule them, enslave them, torture them and even rape them when they wished. She herself had been forcibly raped by these people a number of times, especially after the death of her husband. She said that they were born in low caste because of their low deeds in the previous life, and that they had to be treated the way they were. She also said that Radhika should avoid any contact or closeness with upper caste Hindus, and even Sikhs, for although the Sikhs looked different, they, too, had the same blood in their veins.

When I asked Eva how then she had come to accept me as her husband, she told me that Kinner had convinced her that *all men were not alike*. Kinner himself had suffered miserably at the hands of these so-called upper castes, as had his brothers. The dreadful, grisly and sinister face of the Indian society as a whole could not be washed clean with one or two examples. It needed a revolutionary change from the grass-root level.

The whole issue had agglomerated in Eva's soul in such a way that she felt a kind of fear for me, too. Under her outer veneer there lurked a highly sensitive and vulnerable person that cried in heart-rending sobs and yearned for hope and help.

I still remembered that Uncle Arjun had not paid much attention to or shown much concern about Kinner. Although, in answer to a question I had posed one day, he had said he did not believe in any caste system because the Gurus had forbidden them from doing so. That was why Kinner had developed his habit of sneaking away and roaming alone in derelict places and wastelands. Had he been given the same love and affection that we experienced, he might not have whisked away like that.

If it was a distressingly painful experience for me to listen to what Eva had told me, then I could guess what kind of abject pain and misery she must have gone through, having lived that wretched life for so long. I made up my mind to exterminate every trace of that inferiority complex from within her.

'Just imagine,' Eva said, 'living in a mud hut at the bank of a pond filled with the dirty water that dropped down from the village. Water that stank of shit and cow-dung, and served as sanctuary for flies, mosquitoes and dead animals, and the mud hut that soaked up that water, in danger of being washed away by the first deluge of monsoon rain. Imagine all this... and then tell... Just imagine yourself being treated like shit by the people of the village, being looked down upon as something lowly, subservient and redundant, useable and disposable, and then tell... Imagine yourself in the garb of a girl on top of all that and then tell. Imagine that you hardly get one insufficient meal a day, and that too, bequeathed by those who treated your mother like a slave and sex object all her life, and then tell. Imagine stealing a turnip from a field because of your terrible hunger and getting a horrific thrashing from the owner, in addition to the groping of your private parts, and then tell what it's all like. Just imagine tolerating it all without having the capacity to express your anger and scorn to anyone, and then tell.

'Imagine your brothers being treated in a terrible way, being insulted, reproved and abused when being paid almost nothing for their hard labour, and then tell. Imagine them crying their eyes out, or shedding blood rather than tears right in front of you and your mother. Imagine yourself half-naked or in tatters trying in vain to hide yourself from the piercing eyes with the cover of your hands. Imagine yourself, hungry and with no money, watching wistfully as the caste children bought and ate things we never had. Just imagine this hellish predicament and then tell me what it all means?'

This was the climax of the reality Eva had actually lived. The lash of every whip had left deep dark rankling scars on her body and soul. I felt as though the sky were falling apart over my head. I didn't have the courage to say a word more. All I did was to press her to myself, kiss her silky smooth hair, her dimly beaming brow and begin to feel her woes as mine. She had continued crying and sobbing, first loudly, as though dense clouds had collided to generate terrifying thunder and then slowing down to match the friction of two millstones grinding, until, finally, the sobs became sighing whispers, resulting in exhausted sleep. She had her head on my shoulder and I continued stroking her lightly like a mother. My mind was full of inexplicable sorrows.

A Compromise with Destiny

The fateful year of 1947 had given its sinister knock at India's door. And the door had to be answered, regardless of what the new year had in store for it. Time waits for no one. 'Absolute, true and mathematical time, in and of itself, and of its own nature, without reference to anything external, flows uniformly.' The great Newton said so, and it will hold true forever.

Events can be checkmated but not the flow of time. The clock of nature never stops ticking while the human clock can and does. Millions of people in the whole world must have welcomed that New Year. They must have wished each other very many happy returns of the day, save for the Indians, for they had lost count of time. Time stood still for India as it had for many centuries. No dawn had dawned normally and no dusk had dropped ceremonially. And the nights had been as melancholy as ever.

Lately, Kinner had instructed me to follow events in the Punjab as closely as possible, write detailed stories for the paper but without a speck of communal prejudice, while he himself would deal with other areas. Yet we both knew the stories would overlap and mingle with each other, for the whole phenomenon was one.

Eva's health had now convalesced remarkably and she was perfectly ready to turn out page after page of typed work, ready for the press to get on with the rest of the operation until the paper was ready for distribution. It was strange to see Kinner, Eva and myself working tirelessly, day and night, with only brief intermissions in between. The important news (which often was bad news) always had to be covered, even if it meant staying awake all night. Even the most crucial news was never deemed complete until a wide public reaction for or against came over to us. I would often think how ignorant I would have remained about the life of a journalist had I not joined Kinner's paper. Even in highly troubled situations we had to follow events, analyse the ins and outs, piece together all the available evidence and envisage the after-effects. Yet, you couldn't flinch from exposing the wrong elements, even if it meant death threats to you. Anyway, to cut the matter short, I took up the issue of the Punjab as advised by my superior and employer, Kinner Vasudev. I was not to reason why, I was but to do and die.

So, in that year I wrote a series of stories regarding what, why and how things had happened in the Punjab. The stories continued appearing every week in the paper until it had to be temporarily stopped, owing to the riots in the city. However, I shall reiterate only those events, which are relevant to our ongoing tale.

On the grave of all the previous attempts to find ways to devolve power to Indian hands, the British Parliament led by Prime Minister Attlee appointed Lord Mountbatten as the new Viceroy of India to replace Wavell. Mountbatten had been conferred with all the plenipotentiary powers to deal with the problem of transfer of power to Indian hands just as he found necessary, without referring back to HM Government in Britain. His departure to India was preceded by a very significant speech of Mr Attlee in the Parliament. He said, "His Majesty's Government wish to make it clear that it is their definite intention to take the necessary steps to affect the transference of power into responsible Indian hands by a date not later than June 1948. His Majesty's Government will have to consider to whom the power of the Central Government in British India should be handed over on the due date; whether as a whole to some form of Central Government for British India, or some areas to the existing Provincial Governments or in such a way as may seem most reasonable and in the best interest of the Indian people."

The echoes of this momentous announcement began to reverberate throughout the subcontinent. It was now felt for the first time that the British were definitely leaving. But also inherent in the announcement was the partition of India, bearing indirect reference to the League's demand for Pakistan that shook the country by its very foundation.

"This may lead to Pakistan for those provinces or portions of provinces, which may want," the Mahatma proclaimed.

So, what was to be done now? The Muslim League's policy of obstruction in the working of the Constitutional Assembly, instigating the interference of the Viceroy innumerably had been seen already. And now this stalemate from London, apparently allowed the right of secession to those who wished it.

The Muslim League wanted the whole of Punjab to be annexed into the new state of Pakistan - a Punjab that extended nearly up to Delhi. So the Punjab had to be saved, if not all of it then part of it, that part at least where non-Muslims dominated or outnumbered the

373

Muslims. And Mountbatten would be arriving soon with all the powers vested in him to transfer power on behalf of the Crown and His Government to Indian hands. The negotiators were to be bound once and for all by the decision reached. There would be no further appeal, dissent or dithering to be seen.

Soon after Attlee's statement Mr Khizar Hayat Khan, Chief Minister of the Unionist Coalition Government surrendered to the pressure tactics of the Muslim League and resigned. He justified his resignation in a press statement, saying: "If I were now to continue to lead a coalition in which the Muslim League is not represented, this might put in serious jeopardy such chances as might otherwise exist of a settlement being arrived at between communities in the province." So, the Punjab was now literally without a government except for the Governor, EM Jenkins. The Muslim League and its rank and file began to see Sikhs as the only hindrance to incorporating of the whole of Punjab into their Islamic State of Pakistan. Passions ran high; tension escalated in the Punjab, leading to the outbreak of riots in Rawalpindi, Attock and Multan on 18th March. A large number of Sikhs and Hindus were left dead, wounded and crippled.

Only a week earlier, The Times, London, had described the situation in Punjab as most critical. It had stated that, "the Sikhs complain with justice that the Muslim League seeks to deny to them in the Punjab the position which it claims in the rest of India." This meant that the League wanted to take the whole of Punjab, Bengal and Assam into Pakistan without letting the non-Muslim portions to opt out of these provinces. And then on the day of the terrible massacres in Rawalpindi, Attock and Multan, the Times again observed in its editorial: "Prolonged agitation directed by the Muslim League against the Unionist Coalition Government of the Province paved the way for the present outbreak of communal violence."

Pandit Nehru issued a statement at the press conference in Lahore after visiting the riot-affected areas: "Obviously all that has happened is intimately connected with the political affairs. I propose to say nothing about that aspect, except this that if politics is to be conducted in this way, then it ceases to be politics and becomes some kind of jungle warfare, which reduces human habitation to a state of desert."

When Lord Mountbatten took over from Lord Wavell on 24th March, he had to face the most critical problem of the Punjab. Soon after that, on 8th April, the Congress passed a critical resolution: "These tragic events have demonstrated that there can be no settlement of the problem of the Punjab by violence and coercion, and no arrangement based on coercion can last. Therefore, it is necessary to find a way out which involves the least amounts of compulsion. This would necessitate the division of the Punjab into two provinces so that the predominantly Muslim parts may be separated from the predominantly non-Muslim parts."

It was apparent that the Muslim League couldn't have it both ways: it couldn't claim to take Muslim majority areas out of India and insist on keeping the non-Muslim majority portions of the provinces in Pakistan. The areas with non-Muslim majorities must be allowed to opt out and join the Indian Union. But the division of the Punjab could only be conceded if the Congress had first conceded to the creation of Pakistan. It was at this juncture that Mountbatten discussed his conjectural plans with the Congress and the Muslim League's Mr Jinnah. Both contenders for power accepted this tentative plan for the partition of India with the provision of letting the non-Muslim majorities opt out to join India. Thus, the foundation of the partition of India was laid down.

The tryst with destiny was harrowing, painful and deeply agonising. But there was no way out except to compromise, to grin and grind. Following the path paved by the big contenders, the Hindus and Sikhs of the Central Legislature, who belonged to the Punjab, wrote a letter to Jawaharlal Nehru for his endorsement and its further submission to the Viceroy and HM Government in Britain. The letter said: "The Muslims and non-Muslims are equally balanced and no Government can carry on without the support of the three communities. Fortunately, the population of the Province is so divided that there are districts and contiguous areas where Muslims and non-Muslims predominate. We have given anxious and deep thought to this problem. After considering all its pros and cons, we have come to the conclusion that the only way out of the present deadlock lay in the partition of the Punjab into two provinces."

The Sikh and Hindu leaders together and separately, now insisted on the division of the Punjab. The Shiromani Akali Dal also asserted that the partition of the Punjab was the only remedy to end the communal strife.

Immediately after this, Mountbatten, after discussing Indian constitutional problems with different leaders, put forth a simple two-point partition plan. On the assumption that Mr Jinnah's power and purpose were sustained, partition would have to be provided for, and partitioning of the Centre involved similar treatment for the provinces where the two communities were evenly balanced.

But when this two-point plan involving the basic principle of partition was put to Mr Jinnah, he said he was against the performance of a surgical operation on the provinces, which had ancient history of unity (as though the country had not). He did want the partition of India but not of provinces so he could swallow whole of Punjab and Bengal. But eventually Mr Jinnah gave in, on the guarantee that the same would apply to the province of Assam, to which Mountbatten agreed.

After this preliminary base on which the actual plan would finally rest, came the Partition Plan, which was circulated to the Governors of various provinces.

1. The provinces, generally speaking, to have the right of self-determination.
2. The Punjab and Bengal to be notionally divided for voting purposes.
3. The prominently Sylhet district in Assam to be given the option of joining the Muslim Province created by partitioned Bengal through referendum.
4. A referendum to be held in the Northwest Frontier Province on the issue of whether it was to join one group or the other.

The Governor of the Punjab, Mr Jenkins, expressed his dissatisfaction with the plan, arguing that it would satisfy neither Jinnah nor Sikhs because it would leave a truncated Pakistan for Jinnah and cut the Sikhs in almost two equal parts. But Mountbatten was optimistic about it. He said that in the last analysis, Jinnah would acquiesce and the only way the Sikhs could improve their position was through negotiation.

When the meetings between Jinnah and Liaqat Ali Khan on the one side and Maharaja Bhupinder Singh and Baldev Singh on the other, were held, the discussion took another turn. It swung in favour of the Sikh demand for the Sikh State in Pakistan with its own separate military establishment, provided they now desisted from supporting the partition of the Punjab and joined Pakistan. But when the Sikhs demanded the right to opt out of Pakistan if they so wished in future, the Muslim leaders did not agree. So the Akali-League negotiations were nullified, which immediately generated unfathomable anger and hatred between the two communities because the Muslims (as fed by their leaders) held the Sikhs responsible for 'deliberately cutting the Punjab into two parts'.

Lord Mountbatten announced the Provisions of the Partition of the Punjab and Bengal on 3rd June, generally known as the Third of June Plan. On the very day of the announcement, Mountbatten told Jinnah that Nehru, Patel and Kriplani had made it an absolute point that they would reject the plan unless the Muslim League accepted it as the final settlement. The Muslim League, therefore, accepted the plan and passed a resolution to that effect on 9th June. "The Council resolves to give full authority to the President of the All India Muslim League to accept the fundamental principles of the plan as a compromise, although it cannot agree to the partition of Bengal and Punjab or give its consent to such partition, it had to consider H.M.G's plan for transfer of power as a whole."

Simultaneously, the All India Congress Committee passed its resolution on 15th June, saying: "In view, however, of the refusal of the Muslim League to participate in the Constituent Assembly and further in view of the policy of the Congress that it cannot think in terms of compelling the people in any territorial unit to remain in the Indian union against their declared and established will, the All India Congress Committee accepts the proposal embodied in the announcement of June 3rd, which laid down a procedure for ascertaining the will of the people concerned."

Likewise, the Shiromani Akali Dal and the Panthik Pritinidhi Board jointly passed a resolution on 14th June emphasising that: "In the absence of the provision of the transfer of population and property, the very purpose of the partition will be defeated."

Giani Kartar Singh, the President of the Shiromani Akali Dal said on the next day, "The Sikhs will not rest contented till the boundary line is demarcated in such a way that it leaves at least 85%

of Sikhs in India, and both the states of Pakistan and India are committed to facilitate the transfer of the remaining 15% from Pakistan to India."

Baldev Singh accepted the plan on the basis of contiguous majority areas and later said, "If the verdict of the Boundary Commission went against the Sikhs, they should be prepared to make all sacrifices to vindicate the honour of the Panth."

On the day of the announcement of the Partition Plan, Mountbatten said in his Radio Broadcast, "The whole plan may not be perfect, but like all plans, its success will depend on the goodwill with which it is carried out."

The Partition Plan of 3rd June or the Mountbatten Plan was in no way near adequacy let alone a comprehensive plan. It was hurriedly made and announced. Yet, the reasons were obvious. The communal passions following the riots of Rawalpindi, Attock and Multan soared so high and the tension between the two communities escalated to such peaks that any protraction in reaching a tangible solution might have exasperated the situation and aggravated tempers. If the leaders, who were actually responsible for igniting fires on either side, could wait until June 1948, then a comprehensive plan could be churned out keeping in view the transfer of population and property so that very few lives would be lost. But, perhaps, even that was not possible in the face mounting tensions, extreme hatred, anger, anarchy and lawlessness.

In the end, it was a compromise with destiny - a destiny that had been long drawn out on the hand of India, owing to its history of slavery from the 8th century onward. It was a destiny that was the natural result of its philosophy of non-violence, renunciation and its inclination towards religion and its caste system. This destiny had to culminate in such a partition, if not today then some years later.

Soon after that, the Central Partition Committee was set up, which was to work on larger issues such as partitioning of India into two sovereign states. The Punjab Partition Committee and the Bengal Partition Committee were established in the same way, followed by the Boundary Commissions. The work of partition began to take place with maximum rapidity.

The date for the transfer of power was fixed as 14th August for Pakistan and 15th August for India because Mr Jinnah and the Muslim League would trust no one. They wanted their Pakistan a day earlier than India. Such was the situation of mistrust between the two communities. Perhaps, mistrust is a lesser word. It was, in fact, hatred, a terrible detestation and animosity towards each other that began to flow down to the masses at large, resulting in a type of jungle warfare.

Rivers of Lava
(A Sea of Blood)

While the Punjab Boundary Commission and the Punjab Boundary Force were engaged in the assigned task of dividing the soil of the Punjab into two, putting fences across new laid borders and leaving the Boundary Forces behind to look after the new divides, the heart of the Punjab was thumping and throbbing vehemently.

A land that was once the land of five rivers - all providing cool, clear and quenching waters - was now transmuted into a formidable livid volcano with red-hot lava churning, raging, fuming and circling in it. The vast volcano of unprecedented mutual detestation and hostility stood at red alert with its gigantic mouth roaring and snorting to engulf anything that came its way. All that it contained in its deep depths was the lava of extreme abhorrence, anger and wrath, looking for an exit, an epicentre to break asunder and gush out with immeasurable acceleration and velocity.

The curled up leaves of the big Banyan tree in Qila Vasudev and a million others in the rest of the Punjab began to unfold themselves, displaying the discoloration of green into yellow and orange - the pigment evincing the yellow blight of hatred and anger and hidden malice. There was no one to study and decode those colours because all the Noordins were now dead and all the Ferozdins had turned Muslim. The Sikhs had become staunch Sikhs and the Hindus had morphed into loyal Hindus. The land was now overflowing with religious and communal fervour with no trace of humanity anywhere.

The first eruption from this stupendous volcano had taken place in March at Rawalpindi, Attock and Multan, and the red hot frothing lava that had gushed out had left 300 dead and many more injured and mangled. That was the inception and there was no stoppage afterwards. The seething and fuming lava had found many more outlets and began to flow from the height of the volcano rushing down into the fields, villages, towns and cities, razing every sign of life to the ground. But these were, as yet, small tributaries. The real eruption was yet to take place, though it wasn't too far away.

It was weird of me to begin to find philosophy by comparing the political situation to a volcano and the lava it belched out, but curiously enough, I did. Who would care to stand and stare at the lava running and flowing wildly and undertake to study its philosophy and its temperament except a lunatic? I just imagined a mammoth volcano rampaging in front of my eyes with its vast stomach full of lava - frothing, foaming and storming to break the walls of the stomach and erupt out. I imagined the wall being hit ferociously by the most ravaging whirl. Soon it succumbed to the momentous thrust and the lava erupted like a jet. It leapt, jumped, sprinted and incinerated everything in its course. Even the biggest stones were melted away, trees were uprooted and fell flat, engulfed by the bubbling, steaming liquid, running with the speed of a supersonic jet, inundating everything, smashing all obstacles, like tiny pebbles, on its way.

The flight of my imagination didn't just stop there. It soared further making me think of the nature and temperament of lava, of its faith and credibility. I felt it had nothing constructive in its character; it was destructive and disastrous by its very nature, calamitous and catastrophic. It was comparable to a huge unfathomable glacier which, when melted, swept everything away, causing a Noachian cataclysm.

The Punjab had only just seen the tip of the iceberg while the real cataclysm was on its way. As yet, we had heard only weak tremors while the thunders of the real quake were in abeyance. The lava was whirling and tumbling inside the stomach of the volcano, charging and gathering momentum. You could see the lava boiling and bubbling in millions of eyes, in those reddened eyes full of hate and rage. Every single eye was a river in its own right that displayed wrath and contempt for those who belonged to the rival religion. Every man had two rivers, each equally flooding with steaming lava. It felt as though all those volcanoes had suddenly turned transparent so you could see the lava fulminating violently and circling inside by dint of some centrifugal force, waiting to break asunder and flow out.

And the Big Bang came when the announcement of the date of transfer of power was made as 14th and 15th August. The volcanoes had already begun to erupt at the beginning of August, letting the lava out to flow into the roads and streets, lanes and by-lanes, villages and towns of Punjab. As the Punjab Boundary Commission led by Radcliff announced the award of tehsil Shakargarh going to Pakistan, and Batala and Gurdaspur to Hindustan followed by Ferozpur, Zira and Fazilka, the eruptions followed one after the other in quick succession. Law and order disappeared leaving the province in the hands of mobs of gangsters who ruled the roost and conducted their business the way they would.

The Punjab Boundary Award was bitterly resented in both East Punjab and West Punjab. The West Punjab resented it for the loss of Gurdaspur district and the Ferozpur canal headworks; East Punjab resented it for the loss of Lahore and the canal colonies of Sheikhupura (including Nankana Sahib, the place of birth of the Sikhs' first Guru), Lyallpur and Montgomery districts. The award allocated thirteen districts to East Punjab and sixteen districts to West Punjab making the area given to each 38% and 62% respectively. Yet, no party was happy. The Sikhs began to lament the loss of their sacred shrines, now left in Pakistan and the Muslims lamented the division of the Punjab to which they had laid their claim as a whole.

The communal riots had started in the Muslim majority areas of West Punjab in March, followed by a chain of rioting until the beginning of August. The Hindu and Sikh victims of those riots then migrated to East Punjab, where they told their stories of tribulation and roused sentiments of revenge and reprisal. The Punjabis of East Punjab then began to work in a spirit of vengeance. Retired Sikh army men along with Sikh soldiers of the Indian National Army organised small squads to kill the Muslims in their part of the Punjab. The Muslims retaliated in the west followed by counter-retaliation in the east. Reprisal followed retaliation and vice versa, till both sides were engulfed in a seething cauldron of bestial passions. The contagion affected the educated and the non-educated alike and the venom spread vehemently to kill every sign of contrasting life. The blight spread to the officials, police and army, too. The Muslims and non-Muslims combated each other, degrading themselves to the lowest level of barbarity. The grim sport of murder, abduction and rape flourished on both sides of the Punjab with unparalleled ferocity. Although the Punjab Boundary Force endeavoured to quell the fast increasing lawlessness, it had little or no success; some of the most gruesome tragedies were enacted in the areas entrusted to it. The Baluch Regiment, a Muslim force, worked havoc in the town of Sheikhupura in West Punjab where hundreds of Hindus and Sikhs were brutally massacred. The scenes were no different in East Punjab. In the district of Gurdaspur, the troops of PBF murdered hundreds of Sikhs in the name of alleviating the disturbances.

Mutual anger and hatred, the very foundation of the partition, enforced the migration of Punjabis on a scale absolutely unmatched in the history of the world. More than twelve million people were stranded on either side of the border with no guarantee of protection from bands of armoured ruffians. There was insufficient food and water for survival and no means of evacuation. The exchange of population had never been considered as part of the partition plan, as though only land would be the important ingredient, but the people themselves were struggling to cross the border in their thousands, on foot, in bullock driven carts and in whatever way they could manage.

The worst, however, happened after the transfer of power on 14th and 15th of August. The Sikhs and Hindus who were now left in Pakistan, were in a stark minority and the Muslims (who were themselves a minority in British India, and were worried about their identity in a Hindu India after the British were gone) had a different opinion of the minorities. Chaudhury Rehmat Ali, the editor of 'Millat and Mission' had written, "Minority-ism means the problem created by those religious, social and political minorities which possess an active consciousness of their own nationality and consequently oppose their inclusion in or assimilation by another nation or state. It is a notorious fact that since the rise of 'Nationalism' such minorities have done greater harm to the nations concerned than ever before, and, therefore most of the nations for their own safety are trying to get rid of them by exchange, expulsion or segregation. And these nations see to it that, whatever the situation, the minorities live rather as 'fifth columnists than a loyal citizens." He wrote again, "We must not have our minorities in Hindu lands. Nor must we keep Hindu and/or Sikh minorities in our own land, even if they themselves were willing to remain with or without any special safeguards. For they will retard our national construction and, in times of crisis, they will betray us and will bring about our destruction."

Even Mr Jinnah had expressed on several occasions his view that the exchange of population was essential for the successful partition of India. He proclaimed on 15th December 1945, "There will have to be an exchange of population if it can be done purely on voluntary basis." Then, in November 1946, he said, "The exchange of population will have to be considered seriously" The result was the subsequent riots in Muslim majority areas in March 1947. Without a word of remorse about what happened and without asking his Muslim brothers to calm down, he further said, "Sooner or later the exchange of population will have to take place."

His proclamations provided the Muslims with more ammunition and also an argument in favour of their actions.

So the Hindus and Sikhs living in West Punjab, which was now Pakistan, were fully convinced that there was no place for them in that Muslim state. Consequently, there was a mass exodus of non-Muslims who were obliged to leave behind their houses, businesses, land and money, and headed towards the border empty handed. Although the Sikhs of Lyallpur were loath to go, the Pakistan Government was determined to drive them out. Mr Jinnah instructed the Governor of West Punjab to expel all the Sikhs from Pakistan. He reiterated his orders in a letter to Francis Mudie. "I am telling everyone that I do not care how the Sikhs get across the border; the great thing is to get rid of them as soon as possible. There are signs of 300,000 Sikhs still in Lyallpur, but in the end they, too, will have to go."

All these statements were adding fuel to the fire, igniting every volcanic heart, letting the ferocious lava out to perish and burn human lives. Arson and murder were the order of the day; the abduction and rape of girls and young women was now a virtue. And as the tattered refugees went eastwards, the communal scorn and sense of reprisal also spread, causing the migration of Muslims from East Punjab. Trains overflowing with the dead soon began to be exchanged. The first such train was sent to India in August and then the counter-crusade began, repeating itself time and again, now from one side and then from the other.

A vast assembly of Muslims in Naushehra Virkan, in the Gujaranwala district, some armed with swords, clubs and spears and brandishing pistols and muskets, was addressed by a police officer, Mehdi Khan.

'Muslim brothers! The Sikhs and Hindus in East Punjab have massacred thousands of our brothers. They pillaged their houses and set them alight. They kidnapped thousands of Muslim girls. Not only that but they stripped them naked and defiled them in public. They forcibly took them home and made them their concubines. But I'm astonished to see these *kafirs* still roaming freely and safely in your village. Shame on you! Go and put them to the sword, rob them of everything they have, take possession of their daughters and sisters and let no one escape your wrath. I guarantee you the protection of the police force. Go! Pakistan - Zindabad!'

So the devastation began. Sikhs and Hindus ran for their lives and the Muslims followed with savagery in their hearts. It took scarcely two hours to plunder their houses and set them ablaze, slaughter dozens of men and pluck away their female folks under cover of blood-smeared weapons. All the young girls were gathered together in an isolated barn and were locked in. They lost their chunnis (the head-cloth the sign of their honour, innocence and humility) in the process of escape, had their clothes torn apart, received horrible bruises, and were attempting to hide their private parts by the spread of their hands. Their eyes were full of dread like those of sacrificial lambs. They had no idea of what might be done to them. Their were terrified, their lips quivering, bodies shaking and numbness gripping their hearts by the minute.

Some Sikhs, who, for fear of death and other eternal losses, agreed to embrace Islam, were herded up in another big yard. The barbers were summoned instantly and, with their razors and scissors glittering and dazzling, they came running to avail themselves of their chance of an abode in heaven by converting infidels into Muslims. They began to fleece the infidels like sheep so that in no time a rich crop of hair and beards was heaped up like bundles of hay stacked in a field. The rite of conversion was then followed by a barbarous dance by the conquerors. But the task wasn't complete, for they were only half Muslims yet. Then they were circumcised violently, the victim being held forcefully down while the barber slashed the flesh off the penis. The blood that oozed dyed the earth crimson. That was followed by a second bout of dancing, which grew more fierce and savage than the preceding one with dozens of pairs of feet preparing a fine mixture of blood and mud to make the land marshy.

Mehdi Khan was a low ranking police officer who had just been relieved from his duty in Amritsar. As a result of many Muslim constables and low ranking officers having fled from East Punjab together with the weapons and ammunition, the Government had now transferred others to Pakistan for fear of danger and threat from them to the non-Muslims. These constables and officers had now resumed their duties in Pakistan. Mehdi Khan was one of many who might be busy doing similar jobs in the towns and villages of their new country.

An army officer, Mr Singh, had just come home to his village in the Jalandhar district on a brief holiday. But what a holiday! There was not a moment of peace, either during the day or at night - no relaxation whatsoever. All the adjoining villages were burning, the flames rising higher and higher, the smoke engulfing the whole surrounding area. Loud human screams and laments sounded out over the entire environment. People were clamouring, bawling and yelling for help as they were savagely butchered and thrown into fields, pathways and yards, or channels which otherwise carried water to the fields. And the worst was the screams of girls and young women. They floundered and struggled to get out of the brutal and vicious male grips, their hair gone wild and their eyes distending with fear. They were being whipped and slapped to make them obey the orders of their new masters. Frayed clothes, broken glass-bangles, torn hair and odd, shrivelled shoes were seen scattered on the dusty paths, roadsides, in the fields, and in the gutters.

Here the victims were Muslims and the perpetrators Sikhs and Hindus. Many Muslim villages were wiped clean of any sign of life as a matter of vengeance. The Muslim migrants to Pakistan were attacked in the dead of night and butchered. The village of Dasuha, in the Hoshiarpur district, was transformed into a sea of blood. All the men folk were put to the sword and all the young females kidnapped by gangs of Sikh ruffians and hooligans. Here the Muslims were a minority and the non-Muslims a majority. And the retaliation was exactly equal and opposite. But the soldier from the Indian Army, Mr Singh, was dazzled to see it all in front of his eyes. He had seen dozens of battles, but never the one like this. He decided to go back to his barracks in the army camp so he could sleep, at least during the night.

A convoy of 25 trucks, the drivers of which were all Muslims, was sent from the refugee camp in Sialkot Cantonment to Amritsar. When the convoy reached the bridge of river Ravi, near Shahdra, the trucks were halted.

'Why have you stopped?' one of the refugees asked. All 25 trucks were packed with Hindus and Sikhs, including men, women and children.

'We're going to the town for a cup of tea,' answered one of the drivers carelessly. The drivers had now assembled under a Banyan tree, a little distance from the main road. They looked triumphantly at the long queue of trucks and started off, leaving the innocent refugees unprotected. Half an hour later a mob of Muslims, numbering hundreds, all armed with a variety of weapons, invaded the trucks. It was carnage. The passengers were frightened and stampeded, jumping out of the trucks and running wildly hither and thither, desperately trying to save their lives. The mob chased them, massacred them and got hold of the young girls for the post-operational carousal. Scores of girls and women, screaming in alarm, plunged into the river Ravi. And so the water of one of the five rivers of the Punjab was dyed red. Having killed the kafirs, the mob took to ransacking the trucks for money, gold or whatever they could lay their hands on. Bodies lay scattered on the road, the fields and the bank of the river for the dogs. Vultures, who had already begun to hover in the sky, looked earnestly at the fresh red human flesh.

The Deputy High Commissioner of India in Lahore wrote: "Some 3000 to 4000 Muslims surrounded a non-Muslim train which had arrived from the village of Dadar Khan. This wretched train was attacked soon after it left Dadar Khan, leaving quite a few dead, and some women abducted. It was attacked again this morning at Mughalpura, with about 80 dead. The train could not proceed to Amritsar as the Muslim driver ran away. All the passengers in this train were non-Muslims."

The Commanding Officer of the 2/1 Gurkha Regiment wrote: "The Battalion arrived at Ambala Cantonment Station at 12:30pm. The Adjutant reported to the Commanding Officer that a train containing dead bodies was stationary on the line next to ours. Holes caused by Bran-guns bursts were visible in all the coaches. The driver of the train, evidently intending to let the massacre continue, had driven the train into open country and disconnected his engine. All the passengers of this train were Muslims."

S.D.O. Shahbaz Khan had recently been transferred from Gurdaspur in East Punjab and taken charge of Bhakhar, in Mianwali district, in Pakistan. All the big Muslim landlords of the area knew Mr Shahbaz Khan had taken the reins of police power in his hands. They all gathered together in the hour after lunch to greet him and extend their warm welcome. Elite Hindus, too, were with them. "Khan Sahib, it's our good luck that you've taken charge of our area. We assure you of our full support and co-operation in whatever form you want it," one landlord said on behalf of all others, putting a garland of fresh flowers round Khan Sahib's neck. Others repeated the gesture.

"Thank you for the goodwill gesture and greetings," Shahbaz Khan began. "But I'm very much surprised to see nothing at all has happened here. Bhakhar is living absolutely peacefully while Gurdaspur, from where I've come, has been totally exterminated. Muslims were slaughtered there like cats and dogs; Muslim girls were abducted, raped, murdered. But here... I'm really amazed."

And that was all. On that same evening, 3000 Muslims assembled up at the beat of the drum and began to kill non-Muslims. They burnt their houses, raped their women and depredated their life savings. A vast stream of lava flowed unhindered through the town of Bhakhar and devoured every non-Muslim life. The morning saw all the roads and streets scattered with corpses.

A band of 250 Pathans from the Northwest Frontier Province entered the city of Lahore, armed with rifles, pistols and muskets. They waited for nothing. Forthwith they pounced on the Hindus and Sikhs and began to fire at them in every bazaar and street. They broke open their doors and looted their houses, and then set them ablaze. They shot down every non-Muslim indiscriminately except for the young girls whom they took to one side. Soon, the Muslim mobs of Lahore also jumped into this crusade, this act of ethnic cleansing. It was their chance to acquire and occupy the kafirs' houses, lands, cash and other belongings. Thousands of men busied themselves in ransacking the non-Muslim houses, shops and offices, and took away whatever they could. Some of them were loaded with more stuff than they could carry, while others had fewer items, for they had entered the feast late. No one paid any attention to the dead or those who were tragically wounded and were groaning for help, a drop of water or for another brutal stab so that they could breath their last, for oscillating between life and death was more tortuous.

Lahore's population was 41% Hindus and Sikhs. They had had no idea of the fate they would confront when their Lahore belonged to Pakistan. Not only were they freed from the yoke of a foreign ruler, but were also relieved of their lives. Their erstwhile best neighbours had awarded them with *mukti* - a great redemption from life's intolerable atrocities, thanks to Allah.

A train loaded with 4000 non-Muslim refugees was deliberately misdirected to Kamoke station in the district Gujaranwala, where an equal mob of Muslims was waiting for its arrival. All the men in the train were decapitated and all the girls were kidnapped. The District Officer of Kamoke later distributed these girls amongst his police officers, friends and relatives.

A train crowded with non-Muslim refugees started from Wah, in the district of Attock and was deliberately stopped in Wazirabad, in the district of Gujaranwala, and was kept captive for two days. It was attacked three times. Thousands were killed and the girls were abducted; no survivor was ever reported.

Counter Revenge

A spate of revenge attacks had already begun in East Punjab as early as the beginning of August. But now those counter attacks had taken a more serious turn.

The inspiration for this didn't emanate only from a simple sense of vengeance, but from a host of other factors, too. The long repressed and unfulfilled desires of having young and beautiful girls for sex could have been one factor. Social restraints and taboos, which exerted themselves in peaceful times, disappeared in the time of war of hostility and especially in the withered circumstances of collapsed law and order. Anything could be done with the girls of the enemy because it could be easily camouflaged under the façade of revenge. Even the social norms, which normally formed the basis of legislature, were relaxed in the face of tyrannies perpetrated against co-religionists. So, riots, revenge and counter-revenge made it possible for terrible atrocities to be perpetrated against the enemy.

Let us go to tehsil Nawan Shahar, in Jalandhar, and then to a village called Mahalon. I am picking up one village from hundreds of others for no specific reason, except that all of them offer the same picture. In fact, I should like to substitute Mahalon's name with a simpler one - Graveyard, for you get a graveyard in almost every village. The name suits this village and many others, which have now been reduced to ashes. This generalised name presents all colours of the painting with equal lucidity and yet preserves its integrity.

The time is late evening. A large stable in the village throngs with females. Some of them belong to this village while many others have escaped from other villages, which have now been turned into morbid graveyards where ghosts and vampires now dance with gusto. One of those villages was once known as Bheen and the other one as Jabbowal. All these villages belonged to the Muslims Rajputs who were horse traders, cattle raisers, oil producers, weavers and farmers, etc. Now many of them are dead and the rest have come to assemble here in this village, so they can go to the nearest camp and be safely transported to Pakistan.

There is another village nearby called Sahibpur, but for our purpose let us name it Jalaadpur, or Executioners' village. A large troop of executioners, perched on horses, is coming this way, raging furiously, looking savage and snorting as their horses are. 'Akalis have come! Akalis have come!' The whole graveyard begins to resonate with dread. The rabble arrives and the leader of the gang, with long beard and moustache and a blue turban, has a rifle in his hand. Others, too, have pistols, rifles, swords and spears. Some seem retired army men while others are ordinary village folk. But they are all Sikhs and middle aged.

The stable door is locked from outside and it is being policed by some young men armed with similar weapons. Some of them are camouflaging themselves in trees while others are hiding behind the walls; a few are lying like snipers on the roof of the stable. The executioners open fire just to test the response. The response comes and the cross firing begins, killing a few people on either side. The firing mixed with the screams of the victims causes panic inside the stable. The executioners fortify their positions and continue firing with equal and opposite reaction to the protectors of the stable. But just then, a shot on the stable lock alters the whole situation. One of the invaders rushes to the factory-size door and drags it open. More than a dozen horsemen storm in. It is difficult to identify faces in the dim light of the oil lamps. Many girls sprint towards the well and jump into it. But the predators know the aged and middle-aged females can't commit suicide, only the young ones can to save their honour. But despite a hard chase, half a dozen girls plunge into the well with water bouncing up in six wild explosions. It feels as though six heavy stones have been thrown into the water from a good height. The tragic jumps make the panic much more profound.

The mob of Sikh ruffians begins the massacre. They kill the incarcerated ladies at random and amid terrible melee of wails and bawls, and stampeding creatures. No one knows who is dead and who is alive. Then the executioners pick up seven young girls in quick succession, for there is no time to waste. They pull, push, elbow, jerking and yank them out. The voices of those girls are choked with terror, their mouths dry with fear, eyes stunned and noses running.

Fifteen ruffians and seven girls - half of the men are in front of the herd and half behind. And it has grown dark now. The girls are being driven like cattle by those who are armed with swords dyed in red, and rifles and pistols.

"Keep moving quietly, you Muslim bitches! If anyone of you tries to run away, I'll shoot all these bullets into your teats, understand?" The leader with the rifle commands and the girls obey his orders without resistance. They take them all to their village, the executioner's village. The seven girls were divided among those who had not already had their share of the booty.

Some reports of rumours

A sizeable group of Muslim refugees reached Sheikhupura, and, soon after that, the Additional District Magistrate received a telegram that the Sikhs had attacked Joyowala Canal Colony and the Muslims living there - the telegram had been sent by the Sub-divisional Officer of Canals. A curfew order was soon promulgated on the town for the hours between 6pm and 6am, during which time the houses of non-Muslims were set on fire. On the following day, the Baluch Regiment of the Punjab Boundary Force fired indiscriminately on the Hindus and Sikhs with the result that hundreds of men, women and children lay dead everywhere. The story of attack by Sikhs was a rumour.

On the 18th August at 3pm, a rumour was set afloat that a batch of Sikhs had attacked Muslim women who had gone to celebrate Id-ul-fitter in the Partap Garden. Muslim National Guard volunteers ran to the spot with naked swords, shouting provocative slogans inciting Muslims to rise and slaughter the Sikhs. The rumour resulted in a large loss of Sikh lives."

On 11th August, false and wild rumours were floated that Sikhs were going to attack Muslims, whereupon Muslims rogues, with the help of gangsters from the neighbouring villages, made a concerted attack on the non-Muslims of the Gujarat near the river Chenab.

Evacuations on foot - a report

Of all the modes of evacuation of refugees on both sides of the border, the organisation of foot convoys seem to be the most effective mode for the peasants of the Punjab, who are tough and hard by nature. One foot-convoy enabled ten thousand refugees to be collectively moved out, along with their bullocks, carts, household goods and cattle. A strong foot convoy could defend itself with the help of the military against hostile mobs. About one million non-Muslims have crossed into Indian territory on foot within a month, and about the same number of Muslims crossed into the soil of Pakistan in the same duration. Later, a big caravan consisting of 300,000 people came into India as a foot convoy from Lyallpur and Montgomery districts.

Forcible conversions - a report

More than 200,000 people are reported to have become converts in order to save their skins from the Muslims, protect their property and save their girls from being abducted and maligned. The District Liaison Officer of Gujaranwala said, 'The non-Muslims embraced Islam as a matter of expediency in the hope that some day the Hindus and Sikhs would come back to Pakistan and the old order would be restored.' In Multan, thousands of non-Muslims converted to Islam in order to save their lives and the honour of their families. The total estimate is 5000 men. In the district of Mianwali, about 600 men were converted forcibly. In Dera Ghazikhan, the converted men have very sad stories to tell. Even men as old as forty had to undergo the pain of the conversion ceremony, resulting in profuse bleeding owing to circumcision.

Abducted women - a report

In the recovery of abducted women, the Government of India achieved greater success than the Pakistan Government. Statements exchanged between the two governments indicate that 25,856 and 9,366 abducted women have been recovered in India and Pakistan respectively. No less than 4415 out of 30,335 abducted non-Muslim women are declared as non-abducted by the Pakistan Government. About 4191 abducted women, 13.8% of the list furnished by India, have been declared dead by Pakistan whereas in India only 3.3% were found to be dead.

The Volcano

Refugee camps - a report

The refugees in Pakistan are mostly concentrated in fourteen camps located between Kasur and Attock, the main camps being at Lahore, Lyallpur and Montgomery. In India, one big camp with a capacity of 500,000 is situated at Kurukshetra with a second line of camps at Amritsar, Gurdaspur, Jalandhar, Ludhiana and Ambala. The transit camps in border districts serve as feeders to the second line camps, and they in turn serve the central camp of Kurukshetra.

Post-script - a brief

The year of 1947 as a whole but from August onwards in particular was the year of riots, arson, murder, depredation and large-scale abduction of women. The rivers of lava of hate and anger flowed torrentially and unhindered resulting in a sea of human blood spilling in all directions.

The Walled City and Beyond

Ever since the first train full of dead bodies of Hindus and Sikhs had arrived at the Amritsar station in mid-August, the city had lost its sanity. The frenzied activity of retaliation - attacks on the Muslim areas and counter-attacks by them - had gripped the whole city. Muslim mobs took control of most of the twelve main gates while non-Muslims occupied the centre of the city surrounding the Golden Temple, hoisting all kinds of weapons in their hands. Some outer areas that adjoined those gates, but were actually in the jurisdiction of the city, were also controlled by the Muslim mobs. Any non-Muslim who happened to be in the Muslim areas - either entering the city or trying to get out through those gates - never came or went home alive. Nor did their bodies arrive. All the Muslim homes in the city centre were pillaged and set ablaze and their inhabitants put to the sword by the Sikhs and Hindus. Non-Muslims in the Muslim majority areas met the same fate.

We - Kinner, his four brothers and two sisters-in-law, Radhika and I - were lucky to be inside the city centre, in Dalit Samachar's building, not far from the Golden Temple. The paper was no longer in production. The press where we got the paper printed had been locked up and the workers had gone to find their ways to their villages to be with their families. It would have been incongruous to publish the paper at this time of extreme chaos when it could not be distributed. Even the shops that sold our paper were now shut. For who would think of earning money when their very survival was at peril? Anything could have happened to anybody at anytime.

None of us had gone to Qila Vasudev for over two weeks now, and we didn't know what might have happened there. However, we were highly apprehensive for it because most of the surrounding area was a stronghold of Muslims. I experienced a strange kind of fear and nausea, assuming that my father was there in the village, all by himself in the house. All my scorn for him and my attitude of revolt against him seemed to have suddenly melted away. My sense of detachment from him had now evaporated altogether and I prayed to God that he should be alive and unscathed. It was a year since I had seen him last and I felt a sense of remorse, a sharp pricking in my conscience for not having gone to see him, even after the death of my mother. Why was I so hardened and callous in my behaviour towards him? The very thought began to torture me and made me feel despondent.

'Sona! You shouldn't feel so low, guilty and self-mortifying. I hope your father is safe and sound along with other people in the village.' Eva attempted to encourage me and inspire my dwindling courage. 'But Eva, how shall we get to know how they actually are? Shall I go myself to the village and find out?' I said, and began to shed tears. 'Please don't, Sona, don't cry, unless you want me to cry as well.' Eva put her arms round my neck, patted me warmly on my back and then, plunged herself into a convulsion of sobs and tears. But soon she took the reins of the galloping emotions in her hands and pulled the horses back.

'Remember Sona, the disaster hasn't befallen us alone but the whole country. Think of those who've already died for no reason, or been rendered homeless, made orphans and widowed. Your own reports of the last few weeks show it all. Then, why do you cry?

Please be strong and keep your courage high before I lose my grip over myself,' Eva said, brushing my hair with her hand. Her words comforted me unusually and, I wiped my tears away with the palms of my hands.

A recent rumour had it that a train overflowing with the bodies of Muslims had been recently sent to Lahore, as an act of retaliation and that not even a child had been spared. The Muslims of Lahore, Lyallpur and Sheikhupura had now begun to reap a bigger harvest of non-Muslims, which they would soon load and consign to India.

Kinner and I heard it all said in the bazaar of Guru Ramdas Inn, right opposite the Golden Temple. Having heard a group of people discuss it, we exchanged dazed glances and felt disgusted, fearful and completely unnerved.

'Remember that jungle we once went to?' Kinner whispered to me.

'Yes, I do,' I whispered back.

'That might've been a little more civilised that the one we're now in; at least it let us out unharmed, but this is really and truly a barbarous one. Human beings are, perhaps, the most ruthless and brutal animals. Withdraw the law and order and billions are killed and raped in no time.' Kinner inhaled a heavy puff of air and then exhaled it, filling the space between us with acrid vapour.

The whole area of the Golden Temple was overflowing with people. The marbled *parkarma* - the passage running on all the four sides of the *sarovar* (holy pool of nectar) - the front space of the *akal takhat*, the *darshani deodi*, the Guru Ramdas Inn and the road in between, where we presently stood, as well as the precincts of *Baba Atall,* a little distance to the west were all crowded with people. There wasn't an inch of space left unoccupied. And those people! May God save us!

There must have been over 100,000 of them in the vicinity, all in pain of one form or the other. There were as many stories there as people. Each one had a tragic tale to tell because more than 95 per cent of them were refugees, who had entered India either on trucks and trains, or on foot. They were groaning with their pain, their hearts broken with the loss of their loved ones, their eyes streaming like flooded rivers and their wails and laments saturating the whole environment with dread. It was all very horrific and harrowing.

Some of them were half mutilated and some totally crippled, while many others had gaping wounds in one part of the body or the other - all wrapped up in squalid bandages with blood seeping through. It was heart-rending to hear them crying for help, importunately begging and accosting others to find some treatment for them. There was no shortage of food there because of the Sikh tradition of *langar* or free food from the donations made by the *sangat* or worshippers to the house of the Guru. And, the Guru Ramdas Hospital next to the inn was doing all it could to treat the wounded, free of cost, again as a tradition. But what could half a dozen doctors and a dozen or so workers do when the number of patients ran up to one tenth of a million with still more arriving and constantly increasing the total? People sat or lay here or there, in small groups of close relatives, friends and acquaintances, talking of their woes and the test of destiny they had had to pass through and the tyrannies of bands of ruffians they had had to confront. Each family or group had lost someone in this wholesale holocaust. Someone's daughters or sisters had been kidnapped while others' husbands and or sons had been gruesomely butchered in front of their eyes. Many of them had lost their small children and didn't know whether they were alive or dead. And if they were alive, in what condition they would be?

Some were telling their stories of survival in pathetic tones. Having left their homes with little but the clothes they were wearing, they had come across vicious and wild bands of Pathan Muslims, with naked blood-sodden swords and rifles in their hands, sniffing at non-Muslims like hunting-dogs. At the sight of them, the victims hid themselves in crops and remained there until night fell. They would cover a few miles each night on foot and then conceal themselves again during the day. It had taken them over a month to reach here, in tatters, starved and thirsty.

The people who came in convoys of trucks and trains had mind-boggling and horrendous sagas of their survival to tell. They had witnessed death standing an inch away from them with its wide mouth awesomely open to swallow them in one bite. There were those, whose daughters had to plunge into rivers and wells to keep themselves from being abducted, raped and defiled. When these people wept it felt as though the skies would soon fall apart. Some impoverished and severely battered mothers had given birth to new children on the way, and had been hobbling on to cross the borders. Many had seen their worn out and emaciated parents dying on the roadsides, in crops or on the banks of muddy ponds for want of a drop of water, or for the simple reason that they could no longer walk a step further. They had to be left where they had fallen, for human predators were hunting them down. They could swoop down at any time and from anywhere.

There were hundreds of children between five and ten in the precinct, who had somehow survived the carnage but had lost their parents, brothers and sisters, and were looking around with vacant eyes for a familiar face. Their world had been ruined in just one month with no hope left in it. They were now deprived of parental love and affection, and perhaps, would continue to feel the extreme pain and misery all their wretched lives. And the wounds, even if healed temporarily, would never completely be effaced, but would become open again at the slightest stir of events.

Terribly frightening were the wails of bereavement from women who had lost their husbands and children in this ordeal. It was appalling to see them crying and whimpering to themselves and then suddenly quietening and looking blankly into the skies as though maddened. The future was absolutely bleak for them and, probably they could foresee that with their empty eyes. Everyone was grieving for his or her own losses and injuries, so there was no one who could come to the rescue of any other.

The whole precinct was teeming with shattered and shrivelled, battered and bruised, and broken and dented people. They were perhaps the erstwhile proud owners of happy homes, content and vivacious in their own way, but now they had been reduced to nothingness. The humiliation they had suffered at the hands of fate had divested them of their pride, made them feel low and abject.

Kinner and I made a full round of the *parkarma* and were terrified by the sight of each spectacle, each person and by each story we heard. The whole thing could be epitomised in one phrase - Infinite Human Tragedy.

We heard local people saying that the whole of the outer city was on fire. Muslim mobs had plundered the non-Muslim houses and set them alight. We got out of the Golden Temple and turned right by the hospital to head towards *Baba Atall* so we could climb up its enormous height and watch the fires from there, if only to ascertain the truth of the rumour. But it was so full of people that we had to think of some other means. The people confirmed that they were there because something horrible was happening on the outskirts of the city.

We knew we were safe as long as we remained well within the walled city while beyond that wall death was dancing its ferocious dance. We made our way back towards the Golden Temple again, sidled past the crowds on the main road and headed to the clock tower, a part of the temple itself on the eastern side. We began to climb up its stairs. Soon we were at the top of the tower where numerous other people stood watching the flames in awe.

Hundreds of houses, shops and other buildings were burning in the outer city, in almost all the directions, but more so in the north, west and south. Towards the Gate Hakiman, Gate Lahori, Gate Bhagatan, Gate Gilwali and Gate Khazana, huge fires could be seen, and thick blue-black smoke whirled up towards the heavens in prodigious curls. The gruesome red tongues of conflagration rose higher and higher, letting the smoke rise from below, surpass the flames and spread all around, hiding the skies from the eyes. It was no ordinary fire; it was like the fire of jungle, sweeping across swiftly and devouring the surrounding areas in bulks. We were situated at such a height and place that if there were no smoke we could have had a glimpse of Qila Vasudev on the other side of Gate Hakiman. But nothing was visible now across these fires, the density of the smoke, which went up in huge whirls There must have been hundreds dead if that was the extent of the fires. The sight sent me reeling. Despite a weak downpour the fires weren't undermined, rather the flames grew larger and higher and the smoke spread on the horizon, like innumerable blue-black monsters eating into the spirit of civilisation, culture and all that people had achieved over the centuries. 'It's terrible ... disgusting ... abominable!' Kinner exclaimed painfully.

'It's just incredible but utterly true!' I exclaimed back.

'Shall we go to the Salt Market Square and find more about it?' Kinner asked.

'It's so dangerous, Kinner!' I flinched.

'Yes, it is. But we'll go only as far as safety carries us,' he said. Already he had taken the lead, leaving me to follow him without a word.

And soon, we found ourselves climbing down the stairs of the clock tower, and striding through the Golden Temple towards the exit that would carry us to the Salt Market Square. The bazaars and streets were crowded with astounded and curious people - all Hindus and Sikhs - talking to each other in droves. There were smouldering shops and houses in the Bamboo Bazaar, which had been set ablaze by the non-Muslims after annihilating their owners two weeks ago. Apparently, they were Muslims. But most of the inner city or the walled city was owned by the Non-Muslims and it was safe for us. Kinner was walking quite swiftly, threading his way through the crowds very sharply. I was lagging behind, progressively distancing myself from him until I decided to run after him to catch up. Inside the central bazaars, everything seemed deadly silent except for the panic and hysteria that had now pervaded for so long that it had ceased to surprise. It felt as though we had grown accustomed to it or had learned to live with it. But such large fires did seem abnormal, something strangely extraordinary. The glimpses of the wild fires kept dancing before my eyes, even when I was walking fast after Kinner. The outskirts seemed to be incinerating, perhaps dying forever.

And now, we were in the Salt Market Square with the Hindus and Sikhs assembled there in hundreds, not just in the square but in the gullies and bazaars adjoining it and in the wide road we had just crossed to enter the square. Beyond this point was the Timber Bazaar that led to Chowk Chirra and then to Gate Hakiman, and the road to Qila Vasudev. The Timber Bazaar looked like a no man's land, for it was completely deserted. Not a soul seemed to inhabit it. Far away, at the end of the Timber Bazaar, the square was again full of people, a large throng but, because of the distance, they looked like smudges scurrying around. 'Bastard Muslims! Pigs! Swine! Malechh Qaum!' exclaimed a person from beside us - by *malechh Qaum* he meant a disgusting people.

Most of the men in the crowd had weapons in their hands varying from swords and clubs to anything. Some stout men were in the front lines. I identified a couple of them, who seemed to be from the Hanuman Mandir. I had seen them fighting a dual in the *akhara* or the arena, along with Krishan. He knew them more closely.

The sky above the din was mysterious, obscure with stray clouds bumping into each other, mingling together and then segregating. The sun seemed to be playing the game of hide and seek with the clouds and with the shadows of clouds walking on the earth. Sunshine and shadows followed each other in the Timber Bazaar, which was scarcely wet even after the scanty showers that had fallen intermittently in the morning. The time now was just before noon but the monsoon seemed to have run out of water. Probably the land needed no water now. All it needed was more blood. The land was perhaps bloodthirsty, as were its people.

I was standing high up on the pedestal in the centre of the square, which was fixed with four wooden poles for electrical wiring, and was looking along the Timber Bazaar in a hazy daze. I could see as far as the next occupied square only to note the smudgy and blurred small figures, but no farther. Kinner, being taller, was able to see things from where he was, alongside other men behind the four sturdy rows.

My nostrils could feel the acrid smell of the smoky air but not to the extent it might have been if the direction of the wind were towards us. People in this vast assembly knew hundreds of houses and shops had been set ablaze after looting, for the people who had managed to escape this morning long before dawn, must have told them their stories of destruction and woe. The people around me were furious and were gritting their teeth in mounting anger.

The din was maddening and it was impossible to call someone from a distance of five yards. Other men on the pedestal next to me were saying that some police constables had gone to assess the situation, and that they were actually waiting for their return to find out more about how it had all started.

'Who sent those police men there?' I asked one of them.

'A *sardarji* with a broken arm and leg came in a tonga. He said his family was stranded in a Muslim house right opposite to his. He had to bribe the two Sikh constables to escort his family safely here,' the man told me, his throat almost choked after speaking loudly.

'When did they go?' I asked him in a loud pitch, which was hardly audible to any other.

'About an hour ago,' he replied in a similar falsetto.

And soon we observed some shadows trembling in the far distance - smudges, creeping towards us. I felt myself in the grip of some malaise, thinking the crowd on the other end of the no man's land might be advancing towards us. It was a strange premonition that almost tore me apart and exhorted me to climb down from the pedestal and disappear. But then I concentrated on the crowd around me and said to myself, 'You aren't alone, man. Keep your courage. It's not manly to do so.' And then, somehow, my own reproach to myself propped me up. The shadows were getting nearer by the minute - six shadows in front and one-and-a-half at the back. And soon the shadows began to transform into human figures, although it was still impossible to say who was who, or who was male and who was female. By now they had covered half the distance of the Timber Bazaar, which now appeared to be not completely abandoned.

The whole crowd was looking at the approaching people quite anxiously. When they were at a distance of a hundred yards, someone from within the throng began to run towards them. He was a young, turbaned man of short height - about five feet. When he approached them, they all clung to him and he to them. They began to cry out while the two policemen with rifles on their shoulders continued walking towards us, following a woman and a young child. As they came closer I was astounded to see that the woman and the boy were no other but Auntie Kirti and her son Suraj, with dishevelled hair, bleak faces, torn clothes, and barefooted. Kinner turned round and looked at me in awe, and then, as though driven by some magical force, I jumped off the pedestal and we both began to run towards them. When Auntie Kirti and Suraj saw me, they both burst out crying with their arms wide open, running towards us like the broken branches of a tree to the earth. They clung to me and I to them, as though we were meeting after years of separation. After greeting me, Auntie Kirti moved to Kinner and clasped him amidst long lamentations. Suraj stayed glued to me. He was crying bitterly with his lips quivering and tears streaming down his cheeks in torrents. I too, was crying and shedding tears with the sudden shock of the unexpected. What kind of times had befallen us? Times of lava, of hatred and anger, of deep detestation and profound hostility.

'I never thought I would see anyone alive again from my village,' cried Auntie Kirti, groaning bitterly and clasping me tightly once again.

'Why?' I asked, haunted suddenly by my earlier malaise and presentiment.

'Because it's all over! Not a soul is alive in the village!' Her wails pierced the sky.

'Oh my God!' I was staggered.

'Let's move from here,' said Kinner, who always had excellent control over his nerves, even at the worst of times.

We escorted them towards the Salt Market Square, Suraj in my arms and Auntie Kirti being supported by Kinner who had his arm around her. The crowd made a way for us to get through and we trudged on until we reached a slightly vacant place at the far end of the bazaar.

The next thing was to go home somehow. But we knew Auntie Kirti was so exhausted, and in such a shattered state, that she would not be able to walk that far. I felt, at her plight, as though she had travailed through thousands of miles of woods and rivers abounding in ferocious animals, snakes and serpents and blood-sucking monsters. She might have been able to trudge a little more in search of life at the other end of the tunnel if we hadn't met her suddenly. But now her mind and body, and her inner strength were abandoning her.

'Arya! You pick up Suraj and I'll carry Auntie on my back. Let's move and go home first, for there's no other way out,' Kinner commanded me.

He was perfectly right. There was no other way out. There were no rickshaws around and no other means. So, we did what was plausible in the circumstances and reached home in about fifty minutes, breaking our journey in between for Kinner to balance his breath. Suraj was seven and he soon took control of his nerves and strength.

A Journey through Blood

The Volcano

It took Auntie Kirti some weeks before she was able to tell us the story of her woes, the story of devastation that had taken place in Qila Vasudev, the overt genocide that had followed, until she and Suraj had reached the Salt Market Square where we had met them, purely through serendipity. She hadn't fully recovered from the shock and had become languid and gloomy so that she spoke for a little while and then turned overwhelmingly melancholic. A terrible grief seemed to have subdued her, grief at the loss of her husband, Bhaga, and she was unable to cope with it.

She had grown too weak to speak for long. Pouring out too many words at once made her breathless, resulting in deep sharp cough. I knew very well that she had never been very stout person from the very beginning; rather she had been an enervated, lean and scrawny figure. The birth of eight children, prior to Suraj, with none surviving, had made her a destitute of fate. And if there was any deficiency left in her adversities, it was compensated for by her elder sister-in-law Chanddi. And now, fate had numbed her completely by claiming her husband.

India was now independent, of course. They were celebrating the arrival of this new freedom in Delhi as also in Karachi. But what had befallen millions seemed to be nobody's business among the leaders. The story of death and destruction told by Auntie Kirti was horrifying but desultory, incoherent and many times incongruous also. It lacked order, specificity and continuity. She would start one episode and, leaving it halfway, would embark upon another one, and then another and so on. Then we would get her to resume from where she had left the story and get it completed. Later, I would piece together the whole thing and accomplish one episode, then another, and so on until the whole saga stood immaculately explicit and clear without hollow recesses in between.

Everything in Qila Vasudev had been calm and quiet until the end of June. People had long forgotten the scuffle and tension that had taken place between Amar and Farid, and had engulfed the whole village. People did hear bad news coming from the west now and then, but took no real notice of it. But as time glided past, the bitterness and sharpness of the news increased. And then, one day, a telegram from the district of Jehlam came to Jagga, saying, his sister

Ishar Kaur, her husband Piara Singh and their son Balwant had been killed. This macabre news caused a terrible stifling, stir and friction amongst the communal groups of the village. Relationships became fraught and partial. Each group began to look at the other with suspicion.

On the other hand, Kabir had now assumed leadership of the local branch of the Muslim National Guards. He had begun to frequent the village in order to make sure the Muslims of the village were safe. His overt interference in everything exacerbated the already tense relations.

Then, Krishan, somehow, got to know what was happening in the village. He too, had improved his position in the Hindu Mahasabha and was also closely involved in the activities of *Rashtrya Swamsewak Sangh*. He was no more under the influence of his father or mother and did what he liked to do. As a sharp reaction to Kabir's swaggering activities, Krishan began to march through the whole village with his RSS scouts all in uniforms, just as the Muslim National Guards did in the city. The tension began to soar until the day that it escalated to the highest degree and resulted in a physical battle between the two rival groups. The fight with cudgels and clubs continued for over fifteen minutes with Krishan and his party shouting, 'Pakistan - Murdabad' and the party of Kabir vociferating, 'Hindustan - Murdabad'. Soon after that, Uncle Arjun Singh and Sikander Ali together interfered and separated the two groups with the former taking away Krishan and the latter, Kabir. Except for inflicting ordinary injuries to each other, nothing serious happened. No death took place that day. But the confrontation was enough to trigger new troubles and awaken the sleeping volcano.

At the end of July, Noor Mohammed came to the village with two big trucks under the protection of the police and evacuated their home. He took his grandfather, father and mother to Lahore. His sisters had already gone. People of the village watched them leave wistfully but said nothing. Nor did anyone of them say anything to the villagers. Even Uncle Arjun only came to know about it later on from my father. The village seemed no more the same village as it used to be, as it had been for years.

Uncle Arjun *akhbarwalla* or newspaperwallah was now disappointed. He grew utterly dismayed and dispassionate about everything. He issued a telegram to one of his sons to come and take him and his wife away with him. And soon, his youngest son, Gurbir, came and took them both away. This had happened in the first week of August.

Departure of Uncle Arjun changed the whole scenario. The Sikhs and Hindus of the village began to feel insecure and unsafe because of the predominance of Muslims in the adjoining villages.

Then one day, Kabir too, brought a truck under the protection of his Muslim National Guards and vacated the house, and took his mother Razia away, perhaps to Lahore. Two or three days after this, the corpse of Krishan came to the village. He had been stabbed in his stomach with a dagger and had died on his way to hospital. The rumour had it that a Muslim National Guard had killed him while he was caught in a crowd. The killer had managed to escape.

Having heard about this incident from Auntie Kirti, I instantly thought of the words of the fortune-teller, learned from Krishan ages ago. "All the stars at the time of his birth were travelling in the right direction and showed maximum illumination, indicating all the gods were rejoicing at his birth... The demons are scared of such light, the brilliance of comets, and the one who is protected by such resplendence fears no one, but is feared by the dark forces, both of heavens and of earth. The ultimate victory is awarded to the illustrious one such as Lord Krishna - I should bow my head to his powers. Your son's face shines like the moon and, his eyes glitter like stars - the very indication that he'll be an earnest devotee to you, a devotee like *Shrawna*. Yes, he's like *Shrawna,* the one who sacrificed his life in the service of his blind parents, carrying them on his shoulders in the two pans of the scale. The moon and the stars are devotees of the sun and the earth. Your son shall win every battle, and who-so-ever tries to block his trajectory shall be destroyed. And when I say his name must start with the letter K, I mean he has Lord Krishna's hand on his head. A part of the Lord himself lives in him. He's a fraction of the Lord himself - an atma, a fraction, broken from paramatma, the totality. Even the name Krishna would suit him splendidly, but the choice is yours."

But our Krishan - a fraction of the Lord Krishna himself - wasn't killed by *Jarra the Bheel* this time but by some fanatic Muslim, who hated him and his fanaticism but loved his own.

Auntie Kirti was telling us about the way Krishan's mother Rukmani and his father, Girdharilal had burst out wailing and lamenting on the body of their son. Rukmani had torn her clothes apart, plucked her hair out and beaten her chest so ferociously that the mourners were scared in case she died too. None of Krishan's sisters came to the funeral due to the threatening uncertainties. Ever after the death of Krishan, both Rukmani and Girdharilal were as good as dead. Girdharilal spent all his days in the *Mandir* opposite, sitting cross-legged like an ascetic who had taken a vow of silence, and Rukmani stayed home in seclusion as a recluse, gazing vacantly into the air.

The day when the first train, overflowing with corpses of Hindus and Sikhs, came to halt at the station of Amritsar, everything changed for the worst. The good thing was that Kinner's brother and his two sisters-in-law, Soma and Sujata, had already shifted to the city, in the building of Dalit Samachar on the insistence of Kinner.

The first attack on Qila Vasudev, a truly savage one, came from a *jatha* or a clique of Sikhs, armed with swords and spears. There were about thirty of them, all on horseback, all ferocious and brawny with turbans on and tied with a strip of cloth round the bearded chin to the top of the head so the turban didn't fall off. It was late evening and the downpour was on. It had been raining all day but only lightly. Yet, the puddles were full with turbid waters from the previous heavy rains. The village ponds were also brimming to their full capacity. People were preparing to get to their beds when suddenly they heard the dull thuds of galloping horses approaching the village, and then entering it like a ferocious storm shaking the trees and whistling though the trees, generating a heart-rending terror.

It seemed as though they already knew where the Muslim houses in the village were. First of all, they went to Sikander Ali's haweli, guarded by two rampant lions of concrete. One of the men roared: 'Come out, you rascals!' But getting no reply and finding no lights on, they broke open the iron-gate, stormed in and smashed the main door. Discovering the house completely deserted they were infuriated and set it ablaze. Soon the flames swelled up illuminating the whole surrounding area.

First of all Bhaga and Kirti felt the attackers were Muslims and thought they should run for their lives. But when they saw Sikander's haweli burning, they concluded the ruffians must be Hindus or Sikhs. They had been hearing the news and rumours of attacks, murders, arson and loot for a long while now and knew the same might happen to their own village one day. But they had nowhere to go.

'Bring all the Musalmans out here right now!' bellowed the head of the gang.

The horsemen began to hit the doors of the Muslim houses with their feet and weapons. The weak, worn out and weathered wooden doors were unable to resist for long. Many fell apart.

In the meanwhile, Jagga and Bhaga came out of their houses, dumbfounded and bewildered, knowing not what to do.

'It's a Sikh *jatha*, I think,' said Bhaga, shuddering like a leaf in heavy winds at the sight of rising flames.

'I know they are, but what shall we do?' Jagga asked, his teeth clattering. Soon Jagga's sons, Chanddi and Kirti, came out, too. Then they all saw Arjun the fugitive running towards them, followed by Drupti.

'Let's go and request them to forgive these poor people,' suggested Amar, rolling up his sleeves. He was about to go when Jagga rebuked him and caught him by the arm.

They were pulling them out - men, women and children - by force. And in a matter of minutes, all the Muslims of the village were standing out there surrounded by the horsemen, the Singhs, or lions, of Guru Gobind Singh, the tenth Guru. The girls - Hassan's sister Saira, Ghulam Rasul's wife Kali, Imamdin Lohar's or blacksmith's daughters Feroza and Sharifa - had lost their *chunnis* in the process of being driven out forcibly, their clothes had torn apart and their hair was loose. They were standing with their heads down like sacrificial goats. The men, old Ladha Kharasi, or miller, and his son Mirajdin, old Maula Bux and his grandson Khairu, old Chiraghdin arayin and his son Farid and grandson Hassan, old Jumma dhobi or washerman and his son Ghulan Rasul, had all been rounded up and stood there imploring importunately, hands folded and head down, for their lives.

'Forgive you? Why? Did your *mazhabwalla* (co-religionists) forgive our brothers and sisters? No, they slaughtered them all and sent us trains full of their corpses as gifts! We'll do the same with you now. Right! Bravo, put the young *sulliyan* (Muslim girls) on one side and kill all the rest!' The order was given by the *jathedar*, the head of the gang.

Soon the girls were relegated to one side, pushing and pulling them like dead things, and, all others including old women were ferociously forced into a line. Then the five selected ones (as a tradition - Guru's five loved ones)) were assigned the *holy task* of beheading them as their pittance to the Guru, who had always forbidden his Sikhs from harming the women, children and the weak. The victims were already more than dead inside. All that was needed was to put their breathing bodies at rest, and that was no big task.

'Kill!' Came the command. In seconds, they were all beheaded. Their heads dropped into the puddles like balls taking a plunge into a pond of muddy water, and their bodies fell like planks of wood, splashing the mud on all sides. The torsos made momentary stir and became motionless - as still as their breath.

'Now burn their houses!' the leader commanded again. And soon, the valiant men picked up burning faggots from Sikander Ali's incinerating haveli and set the houses of the dead on fire.

Then they turned towards the bitterly sobbing and wailing girls, four of them - too small a booty for the lot - slung them on their horses amidst their loud and piercing wails for help, spurred the horses and disappeared into the distance with the cry, '*Bole so nihal, sat siri akal*' - happy shall be those who say God is truth. It was the slogan with which they had initiated their *holy* task on arrival.

After the noise of the galloping horses had completely died down, the Sikhs of the village ran to the place of the carnage. Chanddi too, went to see the scene but Kirti and Drupti didn't. They both went home and collapsed as if they themselves had been decapitated. All through the night they kept moaning and groaning and shedding tears. The skies, too, shared their grief and burst out into calamitous thunders climaxing with heavy showers of unceasing rain. By the day the village earth was awash with blood, which kept flowing (mixed with rainwater, of course) through the streets, rippling over stones and draining into the two ponds with the mud-huts of the poor on their banks - the houses of the so-called untouchables.

By now the news of the gruesome massacre must have spread to all the surrounding villages and even beyond because the very next day a batch of six people, armed with guns, came to see the relics of the butchery. They knocked no door, nor did they trouble anyone. They just looked at the bodies smeared in mud and blood, their half-burnt houses, which were still smouldering, and then looked around at the village with grim faces and bloodshot eyes. They began to whisper things to each other. They must have seen the ragged head-cloths of the abducted girls begrimed in mire because one of them cried aloud, 'You bastards!' After that they left the village, staring intently at the unscathed houses of the non-Muslims. Their gazes were ferocious and shattering. Their visit left just one question in every eye: what to do now?

Prior to the visit of those strangers, all of them, including Jagga's five sons, were thinking about digging graves for the dead but now they had to repudiate that idea. Instead, they began to collect weapons to protect themselves and their homes in case a counter attack came. In fact, it was expected anytime. In the evening, when those same people came again, they watched cautiously while the ladies began to reel with fear. However, the people had now come with three carts, into which they loaded the bodies, and their heads, and quietly drove away. The total time taken was no more than an hour but that hour was a testing time for the men of the village, as also for the women. Even now, the grip of fear and impending danger was holding.

Jagga and Bhaga began to think of leaving their homes and living somewhere else until the troubles had cooled down. But where to go was the question. And they had no clue. Was the city safer than the village? Even if it were, they had no blood relation there to find refuge with except for a distant acquaintance. And who knew whether they themselves were alive or dead.

Although the five brothers had now fortified their home from every side, the fortification was no match for guns and rifles. Their clubs, swords and spears were too fragile against those kinds of weapons. They knew that many Muslims had automatic weapons at their disposal – as did the Sikhs. The dread of the unknown kept increasing every hour, every night and every day, until a week later when they finally decided to vacate the village and take shelter at the Guru Ramdas inn. When Chanddi raised her concern about the household belongings, the eldest, Amar, said, 'The major thing is to survive this holocaust. If we live we'll make more, even double what we've got now. Let's save our lives first.'

The final decision was reached that they would leave the village next day, all together. To get out of the dilemma was comforting. So tonight was the last night they were staying in this forlorn and desolate village while tomorrow they would be abandoning it. But only God knew for how long.

The ladies began to cook for tonight. All of them had their evening meal together including Bhaga, Kirti and Suraj. Arjun the fugitive and Drupti had left after the decision was made, saying they would meet them in the morning. After eating, all of them went to their respective beds. The aftermath of food mixed with the comfort of decision began to show their effects, making the men folk snore immediately. Even Bhaga was snoring in the partitioned part of his house while Kirti was scrubbing the pans. She had prepared all the food this evening except for the chapattis, which were cooked by Chanddi. Kirti wanted to put everything in order before leaving. At last, Kirti herself was dosing, Suraj was lying on the cot right beside her while Bhaga was in the verandah.

Just then, Kirti heard the thunderous scream of a hurtling train and knew it was half past eleven. She knew the goods train came daily at that precise hour. The scream of the train was soon followed by the sound of galloping hooves, coming towards the village. Terribly frightened and confused, she got up at once, ran to the outer door, opened it and looked out. A huge mob of horsemen with incendiary wooden torches in their hands, stormed into the village.

'They've come! They've come!' She raised an alarm in a fit of fury, frenzy and bewilderment. At once she ran to Bhaga's bed and shrieked, 'They're here, they're here.' Only half awake, Bhaga was too stunned to comprehend everything properly. But soon he rose to his feet and the first thing that came to his head was Suraj.

'You take Suraj and run to the crops. Quick! I'll meet you there,' Bhaga said and fumbled for his shirt and shoes.

Kirti picked up the sleeping Suraj, ran to the door and then to the fields. She disappeared into the darkness with the speed of a typhoon.

Bhaga climbed up the partition wall and jumped to the other side. The others too were up by now and were extracting their

410

weapons from their hiding places. But alas! It was too late. The mob of Muslim crusaders was already there. They were countless, but even if they had had a fixed number, no one could have counted them at that hour of calamity. They at once set the whole building on fire by throwing incendiary wooden devices through the windows and doors. The clothes and bedding, and wooden furniture caught fire quickly and soon the flames began to rise. They could no longer remain inside; to face the enemy was the only way forward. But when they stormed out with swords and spears in their hands, their figures got illuminated with the rising flames, and the horsemen opened fire at them. The same was happening at Drupti's house, that of Girdharilal, Shiv Singh and other non-Muslim houses. But nobody went to the settlement of untouchables towards the ponds. The Muslims had already been wiped out, and now it was the turn of non-Muslims. In much less than half an hour the avengers finished their holy work of jihad and went away like the reflux of a tidal wave.

Auntie Kirti and Suraj, hidden behind the thickets of trees, bushes and shrubs, saw the whole village burning like a momentous volcano, erupting and gushing out millions of ton of lava - red, hot, seething and scalding lava readily transforming into gigantic flames of fire. Although the firebrands had now left, she was unable to pluck up the courage to return to where she and Suraj had come from. All she had heard were the last screams of the dying ones. She knew it was all over. She shuddered in stupefaction.

The flames were rising higher and higher despite a mild downpour and the houses were burning like her heart. Nausea and dread possessed her completely. She was incapable of emitting even a shrill cry. But she was sobbing bitterly with Suraj held tight in her arms. She had no idea what she was required to do. Drained as she was she could do nothing to save any half-held life, if there was any. Yet she thought she should leave Suraj lurking behind the thickets and run to the rescue of her husband. She couldn't take Suraj along, no way. But the spooky dread of flames, the dread of the dead and of the formidable horsemen possessed her again. What if someone was still there?

The whole village was reduced to a virtual graveyard, and tonight seemed to be the night of killing and cremation simultaneously. Suraj was sobbing bitterly. His innocence had already abandoned him. Insanity knows no innocence and the latter cannot survive in the reign of terror. Mother and the son spent the whole night moaning and looking at the clouded sky that had no condolence to offer. They felt the sky watched them derisively and smirked by sending dazzling flashes of lightning followed by the thunder of clashing clouds. The whole night kept burning in their terrorised eyes until the first light appeared.

When they reached the smouldering house, they found everyone lying dead in front of it. Bhaga had fallen prostrate with his face turned to one side and his mouth half-open. Chanddi and her small daughter, the only one she had born four months ago, were also dead. The small girl had perhaps died under her weight when she had tried to protect her from the bullets but had collapsed on her when she was badly shot. Jagga and his five sons, too, lay lifeless in the puddles in the foreground of the house. Suraj ran to his father's dead body and tried to shake him up, like he had done many times before while he was asleep. But he was no more to respond to his son's incitement. Kirti pulled him away from the corpse and kept dragging him until they reached Drupti's place. Suraj had been looking back at his dead father all along. Drupti and Arjun, too, were lying dead in front of their house, which was burning like the others. Kirti felt stranded in the village of ghosts and was rendered deaf and dumb. Suddenly she shuddered like a weak rock under the pressure of a heavy landslide and collapsed on the bog with her head held in her hands. She burst out into hysterical bawls at the loss of her only faithful and loving friend, Drupti. They had always stood by each other, even in the hardest times. Kirti's loss was irredeemable. Her eyes were flooding and streaming unstoppably.

'What happened, Ma?' asked Suraj, holding her frail shoulder with his small hand.

'Nothing. Let's go,' she said and stood up with the deepest sigh of her life, took Suraj's hand in hers and gazed once again at her smouldering house. Then they walked towards the exit of tne village.

When she and Suraj took the first turn of the street to the right, she was again flabbergasted. The house of Shiv, my father, was also burning and he was lying dead in a pool of blood and water. Further away, near the mandir, the house of Girdharilal and Rukmani Devi was also smouldering, but she had no strength to go and see if they were dead. It was all too frightening to keep looking at. Suraj was totally bewildered and dazed. He had seen too much in just one night, and at an age that was too vulnerable. Dread had gripped his soul tightly. Auntie Kirti could tell that from the way he was trembling, unable to let out a scream. She held his arm securely and went ahead. Her glance suddenly shifted to another whirl of smoke on the left. Uncle Arjun's house was reeking. This was his usual family home where he had lived since his marriage. The other house where he spent his time alone, and met those who came to see him was on the other side right beside his land. Auntie had no idea what might have happened to it.

Auntie Kirti felt as if she had been caught in a hell of fires all around and the dead with shrivelled and contorted faces slept in pools of blood and mud everywhere. She was running out of patience and strength, and could collapse again if she lingered there. So, hurrying Suraj along, she picked up her pace and bypassed the whole devastation, shunning all the horrible images in her mind, and reached the outer ring road of the village.

The dim light of the day-break had now been replaced by a white light in which they could see things much more clearly. Having reached the exit, they stopped to think where to go. And then last night's discussion and final decision flashed up in her mind. Guru Ramdas inn, opposite the Golden Temple was the only answer. They took the road leading to the city.

The roadsides had corpses scattered here and there, with dogs taking care of them. She was alarmed to think the same might happen soon with the dead she had left behind in the village. Suraj was absolutely dumb, and watched the half-consumed skeletons with awe and nausea. Dragging him along, Auntie Kirti walked as swiftly as she could, no more looking at anything, just covering her mouth and nose with the fringe of her head-cloth.

Packs of more dogs appeared, growling at each other, claiming the corpses. As the daylight turned clearer, the annihilation became more conspicuous. Despite her conscious effort to avoid her eyes falling on the remnants of life - puddles and streams of blood with dog-eaten human limbs floating about in them - but she could not succeed. Suraj was too young, scarcely seven, to assess the losses but the impression of the most grisly reality confronting him was being registered in his mind and would be indelible for the rest of his life. The dogs with blood-smeared jutting mouths and the scrambled dead with lost limbs reigned on both sides of the road. It was like passing through a succession of graveyards the borders of which intermingled with each other. The bog and blood had blended into each other to form brownish marshes.

They now approached the railway level crossing. It was a few feet higher than the rest of the earth. And, as they went over it, the scene on the other side was even more horrendous. Station Bhagatanwalla was on their right hand side, about quarter of a mile away. The huge square of wasteland stretching from the outer wall of the city to the station and from the Gate Bhagatan to the Gate Hakiman, was no less than fifty acres in size. That huge square was overflowing with dead bodies. The malodorous stench that came and irritated their noses made them feel like vomiting. There must be thousands dead in that stony and thorny wasteland. At the sight of those innumerable corpses and herds of rummaging dogs, Kirti felt her blood coagulating, and her heart pouring out, as if to fall on the marshy path. Apparently, the massacre outside the wall of the city must have been going on for some time. But they had known nothing about it, and had thought everything would be fine if they could only get to the city. The sight of pools of blood and mire on both sides of the muddy road with dead floating in them sucked the life out of her. It all made Suraj shudder in terrible panic.

The distance they were required to cover to reach the Gate Hakiman and enter the city was well over two furlongs yet.

With her mouth and nose wrapped more strongly in her chunni, but those of Suraj absolutely exposed, they plodded on and on. It was an odyssey and Auntie Kirti would remember it for the rest of her life. She had been to the Golden Temple scores of times before, but today it was like going through a hell with scalding cauldrons of oil waiting to be thrown in.

Until now they hadn't met a single living soul, and, that was perhaps why they had been moving on. But now she had grown suddenly afraid of the living, for the dead could do no harm. They could only frighten them. But living men could turn them into corpses. It was like losing faith in life and in living creatures. There were some stray dogs groping with the corpses on the roadsides but the wasteland had hundreds of them, who were eating their fill and revelling savagely. But no dead denied them the right of munching whatever part of their body they liked. They might have been harmful when they were alive, but not anymore.

Mother and son entered the Gate Hakiman and cast a cursory glance at the open sewerage that ran all around the city. That too, was full of half-consumed bodies and was being guarded by truculent dogs, their mouths stuffed with bones. They hurried in and lumbered on. They wanted to reach the inn before the living ones pounced upon them, killed them and threw their corpses on to the sewerage to take their place on top as late arrivals. They were barefooted, just as they were when they had stormed out of the house to take shelter in the groves. Although their feet were smeared badly with the mixture of mud and blood, yet, being bare footed was less deleterious to their lives if they were not to arouse the attention of the lurking death. And death could be lurking anywhere. It could be hiding in alleyways, behind the doors and windows, above the rooftops, in the dark corners and on the deserted roads. It could swoop upon them at anytime.

And just as they reached the square before the *Chowk Chirra* there it was: death in waiting, with its gigantic mouth wide open to swallow them. A mob of Muslim ruffians with metal helmets on their heads and armed with all kinds of weapons began to run towards them. Kirti was about to crumble and collapse when she caught sight of a lady peering down on the road from her house, from behind the half open window, all in dread.

'Please save us!' Kirti implored earnestly, folding her hands, her mind and body yielding to utter hopelessness. Suraj began to tremble relentlessly at the approaching crowd of savages. Only a minute more and they would be lying dead on the road. But just then the small iron-gate, a step above the road, opened. She got them both hurriedly in and locked it shut. Kirti was out of breath, gasping endlessly and Suraj was still crying and sobbing. The mob arrived and began to beat the iron-gate with their feet and clubs.

'Master!' the leader of the gang exploded. 'Send these kafirs out and let *us* deal with them. You've six kafirs locked in there. What kind of a Muslim are you? Shame on you... *thooo*.' The leader vociferated and spat at the door with utmost scorn. They kept banging at the door but elicited no reply.

'We'll set the house on fire if you don't open the door,' one of them issued a warning to the dwellers but they kept quiet. And then, the gang commenced looking around for kerosene, for matches alone wouldn't do the job.

By now Kirti and Suraj were up the stairs, sitting awe-struck, confused and petrified with the rest of them. Kirti met the man of the house, his wife and their two young daughters, and four other people belonging to the house right opposite theirs. The middle-aged lady was the mother and she had two young daughters and a boy of fifteen sitting by her side - all bewildered and distraught. The lady's husband, a doctor, had managed to escape an earlier gang that had attacked them an hour or so ago. Dr Singh ran his surgery from within his house. But this morning when they were ready to quit in their own *tonga* to go to the Salt Market Square where they owned a house, the gang of Muslims had attacked them. Dr Singh came out first and got his leg fractured when one of the ruffians hit him hard with his stout club. Dr Singh began to run lamely after the tonga, which the frightened horse was still pulling. The mob ran after Dr Singh in order to catch and kill him. In the meanwhile, this same door had opened up to let the four of them in. Dr Singh had managed to jump into the tonga and had taken possession of the reins. He whipped the horse to make it run fast, and forced it to a full gallop. The mob chased the tonga up to the next square but couldn't catch it. Then they rushed back to find Dr Singh's family. They stormed through the big open gate of the house (the size of a citadel) and began to loot and rampage through it, but couldn't find a soul. The mob had no idea whether the family was there or had taken refuge in the home of Professor Faiz, a lecturer in English literature at a college in the city.

The professor and his wife, Sakina, had come to live in the house, which they rented from Dr Singh, some fifteen years ago when the Professor first acquired the job. Originally, he belonged to Lahore and so did his wife. Professor Faiz and his wife were superb human beings; everyone in the neighbourhood loved and adored them. Their two daughters had been born in this house. Dr Singh and his wife, Saraswati, in the house opposite had two boys and two girls. The elder son was already in the Salt Market Square, living with his newly wedded wife.

An hour later the mob returned with gallons of kerosene, spearheaded by their leader, who shouted again from below: 'Will you hand over these infidels to us or you want your house burnt?' But Faiz returned no answer. He knew they couldn't set the house on fire because of the solid iron-gate with equally strong iron-frame and no other exit or entrance to the house. The mob, probably, was only threatening and intimidating them just in case the Professor succumbed to their threats. But when Faiz didn't budge, the mob began to loot and put other abandoned houses on fire. They ransacked Dr Singh's house, which had already been pillaged by the previous mob, and set it ablaze. More threats came from the mob at intervals but the Professor didn't surrender to any of it.

Some more time passed by and then they observed from within the slits of the closed windows that opened out into the bazaar, two policemen armed with guns marching towards them. Apparently, Dr Singh had sent them to escort his family to the Salt Market Square. Or maybe his son, having received the shocking news of the situation, had made these arrangements for their evacuation. Dr Singh must have known that they had found refuge in Professor Faiz's house or perhaps he had seen them entering there when the mob was chasing his tonga. The policemen, at the sight of the rampant hooligans, shot some rounds into the air and they all fled with their tails between their legs.

When the policemen reached the house, Professor Faiz waved to them from above, inquired about the person who had sent them, and then brought the six of them downstairs to see them off. The holy couple hugged each one of them with their eyes streaming and sobbing emotionally. Even in the face of inexplicable communal hatred and anger, their sanity had remained intact.

'It was only by the twist of luck that we were saved. Maybe just for the sake of Suraj, my mascot. Had we been away from the eye of those benevolent saviours we would have been killed. A Muslim family saved us from the wrath of Muslim fanatics. May God keep them safe and happy and give them a long, long life,' said Auntie Kirti in the end, sobbing bitterly again, but now under a heavy burden of gratitude to the godly couple.

417

Burial of the Dead

Some four months passed by before the tornado of loot, arson and butchery came to some abatement, though didn't stop altogether. Some pockets of Muslims still existed in the Indian Punjab, just as there were non-Muslims in Pakistan's Punjab, especially near the newly drawn borders. They still carried on their acts of revenge and counter revenge while the freshly formed governments seemed unable to stem the tide, owing to unrelenting pressure of work and completely dismantled infrastructures.

The refugee camps still overflowed with battered and homeless people, deprived of even the basic necessities of life such as food, water and clothing. And yet more people were crossing the borders. The abducted women were being exchanged and housed in the camps. According to recent reports, Pakistan had declared a large number of abducted non-Muslim women as un-abducted and, another large number to be dead. However, many non-Muslim women were refusing to come to India, due to the rigidity of social norms, for they knew they would never be accepted by their parents, siblings and husbands. That was precisely why hundreds of evacuated Hindu and Sikh women were still rotting in the Indian camps, causing a new breed of pimps to mushroom up and do their usual wicked business. The sale and purchase of these women was to continue even for ten years.

Auntie Kirti had been pressing me hard to go to Qila Vasudev for some weeks. 'The dead never find salvation until their bodies are cremated,' she said. 'Their souls keep roaming about their bodies because they can't relinquish them until they're cremated. The soul is scared in case the dead body is claimed by the devil's soul, and so, doesn't leave it, even for a split-second. You must go and collect whatever's left of those bodies and cremate them so the souls are salvaged and are free to find another shelter in another body.'

'How do you know all this, Auntie?' I asked, seemingly serious and curious but chuckling inside. The elapse of time had lessened our initial pain.

'*Bete* (son), I know it because our holy books tell us. An unredeemed soul goes straight to hell but the salvaged one to heaven. It's the body that perishes while the soul lives for eternity. You must go as soon as possible and redeem those souls still bonded to their bodies.'

I didn't want to prolong the discussion any further and disturb her somewhat settled mind and thoughts. So I said, 'Don't worry, Auntie, we'll go as soon as the disturbances are over.'

But she still pestered me at least once a week and would hear some kind of pretext from me for not going. In fact, I wanted to go and do something about the remains of my father, but I was deterred because of the continuing unrest. If I ran into difficulties, I might not turn out to be as lucky as she and Suraj had been.

But now, because the state of affairs had somewhat improved, I had begun to run out of the ammunition of prevarication and procrastination. I discussed the whole matter with Kinner, who, instantly voted in favour of Auntie Kirti. A week later we started off to Qila Vasudev.

Kinner had made all the necessary arrangements. He had hired two rifled policemen, two horse-driven tongas and had prepared all his brothers to accompany us with at least a dozen sacks.

The curfew was still imposed from 6pm to 6am, and during day and night, armed police patrolled the city. The orders were that anyone found roaming out there would be shot dead on sight and without warning. These stern orders had kept the criminals at bay and had brought some peace to the city.

When our tonga entered the Gate Hakiman we were stunned to see so many skeletons of the dead in the open sewerage system, in the fields, and in that vast square behind the Bhagatanwalla station, of which Auntie Kirti had told us. The stench was so offensive and nauseating that I felt like vomiting. There was no flesh left on those skeletons now. The skeletons were badly split and disfigured. Stray bones broken by dogs, vultures and other carnivorous predators were scattered as far as the eye could see.

'How about their souls? Are they still wandering about them?' I asked Kinner, reminding him of Auntie Kirti's beliefs.

'Ask your Lord Krishna, not me,' said Kinner smartly and smirked.

419

The road was terribly broken in places with deep wide holes, which not only impeded the running of the horses but also made the tonga jump up and down, jarring our bodies. The torrential rains of the end of August seemed to have undermined it completely with all the asphalt swept to the sides and into the adjoining fields. The condition of the road after the railway level crossing was even more pathetic with holes as wide and deep as the Persian wells. But the drivers somehow managed to take us safely across by meandering around these obstacles.

When we were a little distance away from Qila Vasudev, I began to prepare myself for the worst scenario of the disaster of the village, as Auntie Kirti had narrated it. I felt the journey like a voyage through that part of the North Atlantic Ocean where the Titanic had crashed against the iceberg. It was heart rending.

We stopped the tongas at the entrance to the village and took to walking on the unpaved passage. When I cast a scrutinising glance around the village, my eyes saw nothing but wholesale devastation. Some houses seemed half-burnt while others were absolutely reduced to ashes and rubble. The half-burnt houses had only their blackened walls standing while the rooftops, having the support of timber, had caught fire rapidly and had crumbled to detritus. Doors and windows had been reduced to charcoal. Dozens of stray dogs now owned the place, sharing it with vultures, rats and jackals. There were no cattle left in the village; God knew where they had gone.

When we reached our street, I became nervous with fear of the unknown, which I might have to confront, and it sent a shudder down my spine. I felt reluctant to go ahead and stopped, but Kinner goaded me on. Our house was completely reduced to rubble; even the walls had collapsed. In front of it lay a skeleton with its limbs broken away and scattered in the open forecourt where it was being sucked by ants and worms. This was what was left of my father. But I couldn't see his soul around even if it was there. I had last seen him alive a year or so ago, in the last monsoon, when he had caught Radhika and I in the thatched hut. And now, I was seeing his bones, hollow and dog eaten. What a tragedy it was!

We went further ahead. On our right stood Uncle Arjun's house; a ruined and demolished museum where every book and the other items he had been collecting for years had been reduced to a pinch of ash. He had done the wisest thing in going to stay with his son.

Uncle Girdharilal's house too, was a heap of charcoal, its partly standing walls smeared in some sombre substance; the rubble was being guarded by two skeletons and a pack of howling dogs. The temple opposite to the house was half demolished with no one in attendance.

From there we went to Auntie Drupti's and Arjun the fugitive's house that was situated nearly two hundred yards before Auntie Kirti's. We could see nothing there but debris and a few limbs rolling about in the open, in front of what remained of the house. The main skeletons were either missing or buried under the ruins of the home that it once was.

Uncle Jagga's and Uncle Bhaga's houses - both reduced to skeletons of half-fallen walls with girders sticking lamely on them - were in fragments. There were a number of skeletons there but it was difficult to identify who was who. In fact, all the skeletons were broken apart and scattered. The scene here was most appalling and terrifying. It would have maddened me had I been alone there, even in daylight.

The Muslim houses too, including that of Sikander Ali, were in ruins. Every sign of human life and habitation had been wiped out of existence in Qila Vasudev, the antiquated village whose history went back to the times of Lord Krishna. It had been depleted of its very entity. And there were thousands of such villages in both the Punjabs that had met similar fates. The freedom of the country had cost them their lives. Time had been paid too heavy a price by the history of humans.

'What do we want to do with them now, Kinner?' I asked.

'Well, let's collect whatever's left of the dead, put them in sacks and bury them somewhere. What else can be done?' he replied mournfully.

'Bury them where?' I asked.

'Does it really matter where, why and how you die and get buried? Probably, not,' he reiterated the words I had once said to him in life's context. All he had done now was replaced the word 'birth' with 'death and burial'. 'What does matter is when, and at what point of time in history, you die and get buried. And, whether you die like a human or like a dog, that's what matters.'

'You're right, Kinner. Let's begin.' I yielded to his sanity.

We took one sack each and began to fill them with fragile skeletons, the bones of whatever was left of our near and dear ones. There was no need, no time, and probably no relevance in separating one remnant from the other, for we wouldn't be able to even if we desired. The remains were already jumbled up by the rendering of the predators. As we did our work, the dogs barked and howled at us as though we were trespassers encroaching upon their legal territory. But we didn't care about their threats. They had had their frolicking and we had to scrub clean the plates and kitchens.

It took us over two hours to collect the remains. The work was backbreaking but we accomplished it. Kinner's brothers did most of it and with great regard. Now the question was where to bury those sacks.

'It would be difficult to dig a large grave in the village earth because the ground's gravelly and rocky, hard and unrelenting. So either we bury them in a field or in the cremation ground of the village,' Kinner enumerated the possible options.

'The cremation ground is too far away. To bury them in a field would be a better idea, but which one?' I tried to figure it out.

'The nearer the better,' he suggested.

And the nearest fields were ours. Kinner's brothers found some spades from the rubble of our house and Jagga's. I showed them the field and they began to dig. The work was hard but Nag, Bhil, Nishad and Ahir did it all in just two hours. They took one corner each and commenced excavating the ground with full force of their bodies, slashing and throwing out a solid amount of earth with each stroke. In the end, the central earth was dug by all of them together. Once the grave was ready and deep enough to conceal all the sacks, Kinner and I began to throw those sacks in. Then the four brothers refilled the grave. No rites were performed and no incantations were mouthed. It was enough that the remains of Qila Vasudev were finally buried under its earth. There were millions whose bones and skeletons were still tossing about in the wastelands and the sewerage systems with no one to collect and bury them and salvage their souls or spirits (if there were any) so they could find shelter in another body.

Having finished the work, we went and sat near the Banyan tree. The month of December was quite cold but we were sweating due to arduous manual labour.

Autumn had descended on the Banyan tree and he had lost many leaves as his co-inhabitants. He looked awesomely sad, lonely and isolated. He was a living witness to all that had happened in the past and had now happened in the village. Had he been able to speak he would have described each incident of horror in such detail and with such intensity that even the most eloquent and powerful writer would have felt shattered. I could see him crying with pain, anguish and heartache. He, the tree of light and wisdom and of sublime friendship, was now lamenting the devastation of his own village. All his remaining leaves, his branches, bloated roots, primary, secondary and tertiary trunks, and his long beard were now melancholic, doleful and droopy. They made us so as well. The weak winter sun sifted through its now-scarce leafy network and came to kiss our faces in utter despair. I became extremely sad for the Banyan tree, my oldest friend. I could hear him speaking a thousand and one things to me - all very sad and grim. He would be left all alone in this wasteland when we went away. And it made me feel sad, guilty and uncomfortable.

'Let's go and see what's happening to our mud-huts,' said Kinner and stood up. No one had touched those mud-huts, but no one was living in them either. Everyone seemed to have gone away. Quite suddenly a thought flashed through my mind. Why had nobody had touched these huts? The answer, perhaps, was simple. No one gave a damn about them and their dwellers. What would they get out of them? They counted them neither as Muslims nor as Hindus or Sikhs. This indifference was what lay at the root of their plight. They came in no human grouping and were not even counted as humans. That was what Kinner's warfare was about. While everyone else had turned sectarian they had remained pure humans, as they had been today in the process of burial.

Bhil had the key to the lock of their door with him. He unlocked it and let us all in. The monsoon had caused some damage to the walls and the roof but otherwise nothing too tremendous had happened to it. There was nothing in there except a couple of bare cots because they had taken everything to the Dalit Samachar building.

Kinner's corner was just as he had left it. The policemen began to look curiously, amused by Kinner's sculptures and half-hewn raw stones.

'Who does it all?' asked one of them, holding a piece in his hands.

'He's the artist and he does it all,' I said, pointing at Kinner.

'Marvellous!' The constable appreciated the work.

'Thank you!' Kinner acknowledged the applause with a smile.

The time was now 5pm and we needed to get out of there and reach home before 6pm, the time the curfew started.

'Shall we move?' I asked Kinner with my eyes fixed on my watch.

'Yes, we should,' he said, holding my hand and ascertaining the time.

After we had all come out, Bhil locked the door of the mud-hut behind us. The tonga wallahs saw us coming and began to get ready for the return journey. I took one last look at the Banyan tree and became dreary again just as the Banyan himself had. He seemed to be calling us back to keep him company. But we were deserting him despite his silent appeals, his isolation and his melancholic look. But we had to go, for that was our destiny.

On the way, Kinner, as though from within a deep well, said, 'Today, we have buried the most shameful era of our history, but it will keep surfacing time and again and will haunt us for centuries to come.'

I had nothing to say against Kinner's prophecy. I only looked intently into his eyes but they seemed far away, perhaps juxtaposing centuries gone by and the ones to come and picking up similarities in their common character: blood and blood and more blood.

We were silent. Silence appeared to have taken hold of everything around us. The only noise that broke the silence was when the tonga jerked over a bump, or down into puddle and its wheels and frame jumped and creaked. A good part of me seemed to have been left in Qila Vasudev, which was now a vast stretch of wasteland, the air of which would never again bubble with life. It would be decades before the city would extend itself to reach its expanse and swallow it forever, annihilating its individual identity as once a self-sufficient village.

The surrounding area was now dreary and cold. The winter sun was disappearing fast, probably afraid that it might lose its strength if it continued warming the infinitely cold land.

A fearful shiver ran through my bones and I felt as though I were freezing too. My state stimulated me to think of fire. I wished I were sitting by the side of a smartly burning wood fire like we used to do on the occasion of *lohri* - a yearly festival meant to commemorate Dullah Bhatti, a seventeenth century hero of the Punjab. He depredated the wealthy people and distributed all the booty amongst the poor masses. He was the hero of the people but a criminal in the eyes of the Mughal Law. The Mughal Empire met its tragic end and was forgotten but the heroism of Dullah Bhatti survived and was remembered to this day. I wondered whether history would remember those who died for nothing and, whether their souls would ever part from bodies that were never cremated.

Cremation - Auntie Kirti's word began to buzz in my mind. There could be no cremation without fire amongst Hindus and Sikhs. But we had only buried the bones, surrendered them to the soil. We hadn't cremated them the way Auntie Kirti had wanted us to and that could be an aberration in her eyes. The truth, if told truly, would be torturous for her.

'Auntie Kirti wanted us to cremate the dead,' I said to Kinner, almost abruptly. By now we had entered the city. The crowds of people had subsided but the curfew siren wasn't on yet.

'You only cremate the corpses, not mangled frames and stray bones. And, you don't have to tell her what we've done. Just tell her the way she wants us to tell her.'

'But that would be a stark lie.'

'Yes, but a lie is better than truth if it sustains life.'

There could be no winning with Kinner. He was far too practical in every way.

The army had begun to patrol the city roads, a nocturnal control over a corpse of the city. Whatever remained of life was fleeing to its safe havens. Life seemed such a costly affair. But death was dirt-cheap. Desire it and have it, if not by the sword of a ruffian then with the bullet of an army officer. Rumour had it that over half a dozen night wanderers had been unduly killed over the past two months. And the remaining life had grown more cautious.

The two policemen with us got off the tonga in Chowk Chirra. Kinner thanked them earnestly for the safety they had given us and gave them some more money as *bakhshish,* in addition to what had already been given at the time of contract. At the Salt Market Square, we too, got off and waved goodbye to both the tongawallas after a handsome tip. The tongas could go no further owing to the narrowness of the roads ahead.

The time was quarter to six, and we still had fifteen minutes to reach home. But the road to the Golden Temple was empty, already abandoned. The shops were shut and the shutters fallen. Life appeared to have abandoned the entire city. It seemed like the city of the dead.

I had seen these roads, lanes and alleyways always in full bloom and had taken it for granted that they would remain so forever. I had seen people roaming these roads until past midnight, particularly during the *Dussehra* festival. Then there were long cavalcades of bullock-drawn vehicles decorated in charming colours, carrying actors performing various scenes from the Ramayana. They would call them *jhakian* or glimpses from the great epic. Almost all through the night the bazaars bubbled with ebullience with side shops still open and vending all kinds of delicious sweetmeats. Even the hawkers pushing wooden contraptions on wheels continued selling their goodies. The city would go to sleep only when the first light of the day enlivened the sky. Those were the days! But now, the city lost life at six and regained only a part of it after six in the morning. What a trajectory of the planets!

The Dalit Samachar building came first on our way. Kinner's brothers disappeared into its folds. Kinner wanted to go in, too, but I stopped him. I requested him to come to see Radhika and Auntie Kirti and Suraj. He looked into my eyes mischievously and acceded to my request. He knew I wasn't very good at twisting and turning things the way he did. He was to play my saviour once again. The small streets and alleyways were free from the stringency of the curfew. The army-control or capture of the city remained confined to the high roads, the twelve main gates of the city and the open prominent squares. Or at least we thought it so. Each pocket had its own small alleyways, known only to the locals. So, via these alleyways, we proceeded towards my place. And, no sooner did we step into the house than the siren went, echoing macabre warnings in its alarming sound.

All three, seemed to be waiting for us. And just as we appeared they came running towards us, Suraj clinging to my knees. We had hardly found spaces to settle down when Auntie Kirti, almost breathless, began to rain questions on us. How did you manage? What was the condition of the bodies? Where did you organise the firewood? Where did you cremate them? Were the bodies identifiable? How much had the pyres burnt when you left? When shall we be able to collect the ashes? Did you say the last prayers? If so, did you pray for the redemption of their *atma*? Who did the prayer and how? There were questions and questions and questions. Kinner must have seen why I had asked him to come here with me. I knew the answers to all those questions were beyond me. So, I left it for Kinner to contrive them in his own way.

Eva had left for the kitchen soon after we sat down. Now she was back with two cups of tea. They had probably had theirs already. We didn't bother to ask. Kinner took up a cup from the coffee table, sipped it thoughtfully, looked at me sitting by his side as a protected one, and began to pour words out. I couldn't keep myself from wondering about how he had devised the whole false story, and a convincing one on top of that. Auntie Kirti was soon raptly absorbed in its detail.

'Well, Auntie, we did everything exactly the way you wanted us to do...' he began. He explained in a magical language the way we had gathered the remains of the deceased, put them in a long row, and, how we had rummaged for firewood through the fields, the half-burnt houses and the woods across the canal. He told her how we then built up the pyres of cremation before setting them alight, and how we prayed to God for the redemption of their souls. He assured her that every member of the family had his or her own pyre built independently, the smallest being that of Auntie Chanddi's small daughter. He said that there were ten of us. Had we been less than that all these things would have been extremely difficult for us to do. But thank God, he said, heaving a long sigh, everything had gone well with the cremation. He told Auntie Kirti that the last prayer had been read out by a proper priest, whom we had hired from the city and, who had joined us late due to some pre-planned engagements. The prayer was long and collective and made keen supplications to God to grant the dead a place in heaven. Kinner had gone on and on until Auntie Kirti interrupted him, saying, 'When shall we collect their ashes to dedicate them to the Ganges?'

'You don't have to worry about that Auntie. We'll take care of all that with the help of the priest, who will then carry the ashes to *Haridwaar* to offer them to the holy Ganges. Every rite would be carefully performed. You just bless us and take rest.'

Kinner had said everything so seriously and promisingly that Auntie felt a profound satisfaction in the depths of her heart, which was apparent from her pacified face. At that precise moment, she rose to her feet, came closer to us and gave us her blessings with one hand on Kinner's head and the other on mine.

'Live long my children! May God be with you all the time!' She announced with glittering pearls oozing from her eyes. She left the sitting room and went out, maybe to her room to say her own prayers in privacy.

Kinner looked at me and I at him, and then we both looked at Eva whose eyes had begun to water too.

'When shall we go back to our village?' asked Suraj from beside me.

'Very soon,' answered Kinner, propping up a hope however false. But Suraj was satisfied. A glimmer of happiness showed in his eyes.

'I had better go now,' said Kinner, and got up.

'Sleep here tonight, brother,' invited Radhika.

'No. They'll be waiting for me and it's been already a long day. I must go now. It's only round the corner,' he said and stroked her back with lots of love and warmth.

I slipped on my shoes to accompany him for half the way as we had always done for each other.

In the alleyway, we strode quietly. I was full of adulation for him. When we reached the point of parting, he stopped as usual. I didn't expect him to say anything more than, 'See you tomorrow, goodnight.' Instead he said, 'Life is like a wall that needs bolsters to keep it from falling. These bolsters could be made of anything: religion, faith, philosophy or even false convictions. Make sure your bolsters don't harm anyone. Man never invented anything that was of no use to him. Fact and fiction together make life worth living. None alone lasts long.'

It was all very astonishing for me: a new side of Kinner opening up right in front of me. 'What's your next move in life?' The words slipped out of my mouth without much thought, as though voluntarily prompted by his small speech.

'Don't know exactly. But maybe to extinguish the appalling fires of all hues that threaten to devour our small planet day and night. Or perhaps to save the remaining innocence... See you again, and goodnight!'

His pace quickened as he made his small homeward journey. My eyes stayed glued to his solid back until he vanished at the turning of the alley - an old turning, but a new way.

Acknowledgements

My heart-felt thanks are due to the followings:

To Devinder for supporting me all the while, for she always wants to see me successful.

To Alka for encouraging me to achieve my goal as she was fully convinced I could do it as I've always done.

To M.R. Bhardwaj, a good friend, for being the most crucial trouble-shooter for my computer problems.

To Chris Sawyer, my editor, without whose sharp eye this book wouldn't have been this book.